AND INTO THE *REAL* WORLD

The president was introducing the commencement speaker, and Kate forced herself to concentrate. A plump woman in her fifties took the podium. Her plain, stern-lipped face was hazily familiar as that which, in photographs of feminist rallies, usually appeared just behind that of Friedan or Steinem.

"I envy you women," she was saying. "The path is so clearly marked for you. There will be no need for you to repeat the mistakes of my generation. You will be free to go out and have anything and everything you want!"

Kate listened attentively. The message was clear: go out and do something and be sure that it is creative and meaningful, that it gives you power and above all makes you a success. But now the speaker was retiring from the podium. Wait! Kate shrieked silently. Don't go yet! You haven't told us what that something is, nor shown us how to get it. The path isn't clear . . . no, not clear at all.

Also by Lindsay Maracotta

Hide and Seek

Angel Dust

The Sad-Eyed Ladies

EVERYTHING WE WANTED

LINDSAY MARACOTTA

PINNACLE BOOKS NEW YORK

EVERYTHING WE WANTED

A Pinnacle Books edition, published by arrangement with
Crown Publishers Inc.

Crown edition published in 1984
Pinnacle edition/August 1985

ISBN: 0-523-42565-1
Can. ISBN: 0-523-43510-X

Printed in the United States of America

PINNACLE BOOKS, INC.
1430 Broadway
New York, New York 10018

9 8 7 6 5 4 3 2 1

To Peter for everything

EVERYTHING WE WANTED

Part 1

*R*ULES FOR BECOMING MORE POPULAR

1. Be enthusiastic. Compliment kids on their hair and clothes and things.
2. Laugh at other kids' jokes.
3. Dress RIGHT. Things to buy:
   a. a bleeding madras blouse
   b. a wraparound skirt in seersucker
   c. Weejuns penny loafers
   d. A toggle coat
   Get more babysitting jobs if your allowance doesn't cover it.
4. Don't be afraid to talk to cute boys.
5. Go out for more sports, even if it makes you feel like a spaz.

Kate Auden rested the tip of her ballpoint pen on her lower lip and clicked the retractable nub in and out while she read the list over carefully. The study hall dimmed to the vacuous gray of the overcast March day; her attention narrowed to the blue-ruled Marble composition book in front of her.

After a moment, she added another item.

6. Don't stare at people!!!

Again she examined her work, and again she found it lacking. Each item in itself was good, but the whole still failed to unlock what had become the crucial mystery of Kate's life—how to achieve that dizzying brand of social superiority some of her classmates seemed to have been graced with. Her list failed to explain *why*. Why was Bob Resnick, who was president of the student council and on half the varsity teams, somehow not as cool as Ricky McHallis who never ran or went out for anything and sometimes seemed hardly part of the school at all? Why was it that Betty Ferraras, who had those popping insect eyes and the kind of laugh that made your neck itch, could go with practically anyone she wanted, while Joan Bosky who was far prettier—practically a dead-ringer for Romy Schneider—had to settle for second stringers?

And why, why was it, Kate wondered with sudden despair, that even if she followed every item to the letter, it still wouldn't change the dismal reality that it was 1964, that she was fifteen years old and near the end of her sophomore year. And that she was still one of the most unpopular girls at East Pine Grove High.

Kate had been seven when her parents fled a slipping neighborhood in Philadelphia for the more wholesome environs of Long Island. The town of East Pine Grove had been spanking new—one of dozens that had sprung up seemingly overnight on the bankrupt potato farms and fallow pumpkin patches of the area. It was a bleak, treeless community of

Colonial split-levels and "Colorado" hi-ranches, each, with its postage-stamp patch of lawn, a bare shoulder shrug away from its neighbor. The town had no center, just a zig-zag of sterile shopping strips and a desolate, bottle-strewn field destined to become an All Weather mall. Its roads led to parking lots and driveways and turnpikes and ultimately, Kate had come to believe, to nowhere.

The baby boom had created these sprawling develop-ments, and from the first, East Pine Grove swarmed with children. During long summer twilights, great mobs of them commandeered the streets for gargantuan games of war and potsy and red rover, red rover, causing cars to brake and cruise gingerly through like boats in shallow waters. As the light faded, the play grew boisterous, sending small bodies careening against warm asphalt, knees skinning on curbs. And then the mothers would begin to call: Laur-a! Rob-ert! Cecil-ia! each name hovering breathlessly for an instant in the downy air before being absorbed forever into the night.

Kate counted these twilight gatherings among her happi-est memories—for they were times when she felt she truly belonged. Most of her life she had been weird Kathy Auden, the too tall, too skinny girl with legs like sticks and drooping hair and great mooning eyes that earned her the nickname Witchy. "Witchy's got cooties," the sixth-grade boys would chant as she sat reading alone along the cyclone fence at recess. "Witchy, where's your witch hat?" "Eeee, Witchy, don't change me into a frog!"

Weird Witchy Auden, the girl who was always alone. And though the hated nickname had gradually fallen away after she entered junior high, precious little else about her situation had changed.

Kate sighed bitterly. The worst of the matter was that not only was she peculiar but her whole family was as well. She thought of her twin sisters, Barb and Ginny, now away at an

upstate teachers' college. Though a remote five years younger, Kate had known intuitively that the flaring wool jump-
ers and white kneesocks they favored through high school
marked them as hopelessly out—as did the way they
squealed and got frantic over drippy things like band practice and the ankle bracelets they wore *outside* their socks,
and their dopey friends who went out for the math team and
the stamp club and Future Homemakers of America.

Then there was her sister Pammy, a year younger and
hardly more of an asset. While growing up, Pammy had
been enormously fat, a waddling egg of a little girl plugged
up at one end with a grape lollipop. But last year she had
suddenly slimmed down to solid but normal proportions—
and then astonishingly had metamorphosed into what was
known at East Pine Grove High as a "hood." She ratted her
hair into a massive, tilting beehive, petrified in place by
about half a can of spray; she raccooned her eyes with
gummy black liner and murdered her lips with a kind of
white chalk. And when she passed Kate in the halls, she
would sidle her armored eyes toward the wall to avoid
claiming the acquaintance.

And then there was her father. Here, at least, Kate felt
some title to normalcy. Her father was a supervisor for the
Long Island Railroad; like all other fathers she had observed, he left for work before eight, returned after five, and
dozed all evening before a succession of westerns: "Bo-
nanza" and "Gunsmoke," "Rawhide," and "Tombstone
Territory." When he spoke to one of his daughters it was
almost always to issue an order or a scolding invariably
couched as a question: *Didn't I tell you kids not to play in
the garage? Can't you take that blasted radio somewhere
else?* But that, too, seemed little different from other fathers, none of whom seemed to have much to do with their
kids.

But it was her mother who was unquestionably the worst offender. Everybody in town knew what a kook Mrs. Auden was. On fine mornings she would amble out to the patio in her green robe, her wiry red-brown hair vaulting straight up on her head, and whoop out, "Good morning, Mr. Sunshine, good morning! Good morning, birds; good morning, butterflies; how are you?" all in a kind of singsong baby talk that would send her daughters into a dither of mortification. "Mom!" one would protest, "everyone can *hear* you." "It's a nice day," she would retort, "so why shouldn't everybody know that I'm glad for it? Good morning, Mr. Clouds." But at last she would come inside and throw on one of her terrible rick-racked dresses and attack her hair so it frizzed out at the sides instead of on top and drive off to her job at the post office annex at the end of Debrett Avenue. And there, to her daughters' further despair, she would sing along with the Muzak from behind her little barred window, and call exuberant greetings to strangers, and burst into cheers ("Yaaay!" she'd go and clap her hands) at the appearance of friends.

It was not that Kate didn't love her mother. It was just that at times she couldn't help wishing for the type of mother who stayed home decorously, mixing up cupcakes, playing mah-jongg, catching up on her ironing . . . or if she *had* to work, giving ballet lessons in the cellar like the Gemettis' mom, or primly teaching second grade like Sue Galloway's. The type of mother who could tell her which top matched a plaid pleated skirt and how to act around boys. A mother, in short, who could show her how to be like everybody else. Because by the time she had finished junior high, that was Kate's primary goal: to fit in with everybody else.

Looking back now, it was easy to see where she went wrong. She had tried too hard. When she attempted to appear interested, she was accused of being nosy, of always butting in, of staring at people. She offered a boy on her block a ride to a pep rally her dad was driving her to, and he boasted all over school that she had asked him for a date. And when she invited a new girl in school to come over, she declared to the more popular crowd that "that Kathy Auden sure is pushy."

Before long she began to suffer the consequences of these mistakes. She set her lunch tray down at a table and was told sharply that the place was saved—although from her retreat in the deserted back of the cafeteria she wretchedly watched it remain empty for the rest of the period. Several days later, a boy assigned to do a science project with her crossed his eyes and made a strangling sound in his throat and the whole class tittered.

Worst of all, when sides were chosen in gym for field hockey and volleyball, she was called last—last after the hoody girls who would sit out the period in the bleachers anyhow; last even after Caroline Hooser who was called "The Blob" and whose gym suit stank of stale onions. The message was clear: she was a loser. Cast with the drips and the uglies, the girls with B.O., the boys who wore white ankle socks and dumb plastic pen clips in their shirt pockets. A total reject.

In high school she tried to correct her former mistakes. If she had been too pushy before, now she presumed on no one's attention. She dressed in drab, unnoticeable colors and crept diffidently down the halls. She began to think of herself as a gawky brown wren of a girl, an insignificant figure who blended into shadows. Her only distinction was that she was smart—a brain—but that was a brown thing too: the brown of numbers and textbooks and chemistry formulas. The drowsy brown of study.

She was a Brown Person. And the more she studied her more luminous classmates, the more convinced she became that they were right to reject her. A Brown Person wasn't worthy of their attention. And all the lists and resolutions in the world weren't going to change that. Not ever.

WITH A STUTTERING finality, the bell marked the end of the period. Kate flipped shut her notebook and rose to join the elbowing crush toward the door. To her surprise, someone fell into step beside her—a junior named Terry Klein whom Kate knew hardly more than by sight.

"These things are such a bloody drag," Terry said. "One more second and I really thought I'd die."

Kate smiled uncertainly. Terry was something of a rarity at East Pine Grove High—someone who couldn't be immediately classified. She wore skirts well above her knees and makeup that made her eyes flower hugely in her face—like Jean Shrimpton's in the Yardley ads, though Terry wasn't nearly as pretty. Her rather mocking, supercilious air set her apart from both the sullen hoods and the peppy, self-confident "collegiates."

"Where do you go next?" Terry asked her.

"I've got trig in the new wing."

"With O'Brien? Jesus, I had her last year. A real pig and a half. I nearly fainted when I found out she passed me. I was positive she knew I despised her guts." Terry stopped in front of the gun-metal gray door to the girls' room. "I'm dying for a ciggie. Why don't you wait a minute?"

Kate hesitated. Smoking in the girls' room was an alarming infringement of the rules—something she associated only with hoods and the doltish girls in secretarial courses who didn't expect to graduate anyway. But an invitation of any sort was a welcome novelty. She followed Terry inside.

Terry fished a pack of Winstons from the ample pouch of her shoulder bag; she lit one, then began attacking her already heavily laden lashes with a wand of mascara. Through the mirror, she scrutinized Kate. "You know," she said, "you could be kind of cute if you tried a little makeup."

Kind of cute! Kate flushed with pleasure. It might not be much of a compliment, but it was more than she was used to. She took the wand Terry held out and dabbed it inexpertly on her lashes. They did look better, she thought. Her hazel eyes lost that mooning, too-big-for-her-face look and became—yes, pretty.

"You've got great eyes," Terry assured her. "But you ought to let your hair grow. Short hair's out now."

"But when it gets longer it just hangs so stringy."

"You're *lucky* it's straight, that's the look. I hate this frizzy mop I've got. But I'm going to try ironing it like all the English girls are doing . . ."

The period bell cut off the rest of her words. Both girls raced into the hall—Kate with a secret thrill that for the first time in her life she would be purposely late for a class.

They began to meet every day: at first in the halls between classes, and then after school as well, often strolling back through the mall construction to Terry's house. The more Kate saw of Terry, the more fascinated she became. Terry had her own dormer room papered with posters of the Beatles and Rolling Stones, huge, blurry faces grinning down from every corner. By some mysterious means (she was always broke) she managed to acquire every new single by every British group to hit the charts and played them ceaselessly on her portable hi-fi. And she bullied her wispy, whining mother with an impunity Kate found amazing.

Terry was tuned into a world far beyond the reaches of East Pine Grove. She spoke intimately, as if from firsthand experience, of the latest and most enthralling developments in London—Pop Art and discotheques and "happenings" and the "gear" new photographers—making it crisply clear that she was just marking time till school was over and she could assume her rightful place in the scene.

But in the meantime it was torture. School was a drag, a grotty awful jail in which she was forced to do time, and she had nothing but contempt for the other inmates. "God, what a load of peasants!" she would declare, moping through the packed halls after lunch. "What a boring bunch of slags. And the laugh is they don't even know it. It's only the weirdos like us, Kate, who'll ever make it out of this asinine town."

She had a precise and vivid vision of her own future, which gradually she expanded to incorporate Kate. Day after day, they huddled in the sanctuary of the dormer room, eating Mallomars, stacking albums on Terry's wobbly turntable, and endlessly refining the details. They were going to share a two-bedroom flat on the King's Road in the Chelsea section of London. Terry would be a society columnist for *English Vogue*; Kate's career was less distinct but certain to be equally glamorous, creative, and exciting. They would dress in the most daring clothes from Mary Quant and Courrèges and mix with all the brilliant denizens of Swinging London: Lennon and Jagger and Twiggy and David Bailey and The Shrimp—all the fab Faces that were almost *too* fabulous to be real. And they would be pursued of course by the most famous, most gorgeous, most eligible men. After a good whirl, Terry would settle upon Brian Jones of the Rolling Stones, while Kate wavered between Paul McCartney and David Warner as he appeared in *Morgan*! At this point, their "careers" conveniently evaporated, and the vision faded into a misty happily-ever-after of glamorous—though decidedly domestic—bliss.

Kate drank it all in. Terry made it sound so real, so intensely possible. There was magic expectation in these afternoons, a feeling that something wonderful was about to happen. Alone at night, Kate began to weave elaborate fantasies. In some, a rather indistinct young man, a composite of all the shimmering faces on Terry's walls, rescued her from danger; in others, they were thrown together unwillingly in exotic surroundings. But each ended the same way: with a first kiss. Lips brushing electrically against hers, and those most thrilling of words murmured in her ear: "I love you."

Love, after all, was everything. To be in love—hearts pounding, eyes meeting searchingly, a feeling of giddy, dancing euphoria—that, Kate knew for certain, was the most marvelous and significant thing in the world.

It must be coming, she told herself. If only she could stand the wait.

And one evening in early summer, while walking the now familiar route home from Terry's, Kate saw her neighborhood as if for the first time. On the stoop of a dingy white Cape Cod, a hefty woman in tight pink Bermudas bellowed abuse at one of her children: *"I catch you at my rhododendron one more time I'll smack you silly."* From the yard next door came the sputtering futility of a lawn mower refusing to start. Beyond that was the Hollomans' house, the only house in the neighborhood with shutters painted red instead of gray or white. And then the Laredos' who once sparked a local furor by planting ivy on their lawn instead of grass.

Narrow, depressing people, in a narrow, depressing town. Kate shuddered. All her life she had thought of this place as the whole world and had wished desperately to fit in . . . suddenly she felt a rush of gratitude that she never would.

Oh, Terry was right. The kids at school *were* peasants. Even the popular ones, the self-assured athletes and organizers. They were stuck in this town or somewhere just like it. They would marry each other and put on weight and push lawn mowers through the sifted rose-dust of summer, while she, Kate, would soar to the highest stars!

Suddenly she began to run.

"I TRIED TO catch you before homeroom," Terry said. "I've been dying to tell you—I met a guy! Wait'll you see him. He's gorgeous, a Brian Jones look-alike."

Kate's heart sank. Lately Terry's faith in their vision of the future seemed to be wavering. The notes she passed to Kate between classes were now filled less with predictions about London, more with complaints of how bored and depressed she was, how her mother was driving her spare, how she was half thinking of quitting this boring dump of a school and getting a job at A & S or Gimbels in the mall. And now this—a boy here and now who could only distract her more from the future.

Kate had another reason to be depressed. In three weeks she would be sixteen. And despite all the promise she had felt in those eager afternoons, the stark fact was that no one had ever asked her out on a date. Sixteen and still available to babysit on Saturday night. Sixteen and home watching "The Man from U.N.C.L.E." while her younger sister sneaked out with boys in Kate's own class. Sixteen and never been kissed.

Over the next few weeks, Terry continued to rave about Lonnie. He was, she burbled, just about brilliant. He had a job in a boatyard right now, but it was just a temporary thing—really, he was a super guitarist and was about to start putting together a group. And God, was he sexy! "We made out for three hours last night," she would confide with a significant drop of her voice. Or: "We were supposed to go to the movies last night, but we never made it." She seemed eager for Kate to press her to reveal more, but Kate never took the hint. She and Terry had often talked about sex, but always as something in the far future—an event of such misty proportions and thunderous magnitude it could scarcely be imagined. The idea that Terry could actually be doing it *now* was too fantastic to even consider. No, it couldn't be true. And yet Terry continued to drop hints— about being "sore," about Lonnie's terrific ass. And Kate, unwillingly, continued to wonder.

A week after Kate's birthday, Terry caught up with her in the hall. "Are you busy Friday night?" she asked. "Lonnie's got this friend he wants to fix up."

"With me?" Kate breathed.

"Sure, with you. Listen, I've seen this guy Mike, and he's really cute. Should I tell him it's okay?"

"All right." Kate was trembling as she made her way to her next class. Her first date—it had finally happened! Okay, it was only a fix-up, but still, that had to count. The name Mike seemed suddenly imbued with infinite possibilities. Mystery. Charm. A shy smile, an easygoing personality. Lacrosse-player good looks. But what . . . oh, God, what if he didn't like her? What if he took one look at her and thought she was a dog? Or suppose she just sat there goggling and tongue-tied instead of carrying her share of the conversation . . . or said something so idiotic he'd know he'd been saddled with a reject?

By Friday night, a hundred possibilities had run through her brain. Half ended in romance. In the other half, she was dumped by Mike in various humiliating ways, always right in front of Lonnie and Terry. By the time the doorbell finally rang, she was hiccuping with fright.

But it was only Terry who stood on the stoop. "Come on," she said, "the guys are waiting in the car." She led Kate to the curb where a red Mustang with a bashed-in right fender stood idling, and Kate ducked into the back seat. "This is Mike, and this is Lonnie," Terry announced, but

Kate scarcely heard her. In all her imagining she had failed to consider the one possibility that confronted her now: Mike was totally repulsive.

Even in the dim light of the back seat it was obvious. He had a sharp furtive face that bloomed with acne and hair that drabbled over his ears in oily commas. He wore a jacket made of sleazy fake leather that cracked like dried-out soap and pointy-tipped, high-sided shoes. "Howaya?" he said sullenly and bared a row of tiny, jagged teeth.

Kate cast a wild glance at Lonnie in the front seat. He wasn't much better. His lank blond hair cut in farmboy's bangs didn't give him the least resemblance to Brian Jones. Nor did the close-set eyes, nor the small, moist mouth pursed around a cigarette. Kate was stunned. How could Terry, who had pictured herself tripping down the King's Road surrounded by the most adorable, exciting men in the world, be attracted to such a . . . such a *creep*?

The worst of her fantasies had come true—Kate discovered herself speechless. But it didn't seem to matter. As they pulled away, Lonnie and Mike launched into an involved and technical discussion of a certain '57 Corvette Stingray that was for sale at the Texaco station at the northbound entrance to the expressway—and from that into the comparative merits of the Corvette and the GTO. This last topic carried them through pizza and root beer in an unsanitary-looking parlor (with Terry beaming mute approval) and continued through the twenty-minute ride back to Lonnie's apartment. Kate frantically tested excuses in her mind: *I forgot, I told my mother I'd be back by ten. . . . I think the pepperoni gave me food poisoning. . . .* They all sounded so patently phony. She had no choice but to trail helplessly behind the others up a rickety outdoor stairway and into Lonnie's tiny, littered set of rooms.

Terry and Lonnie disappeared into the bedroom and shut

the door. Kate shoved aside some motorcycle magazines and sat down stiffly on the ratty Chesterfield couch.

"You wanna beer?" Mike called from the kitchen.

"No, thanks," she said quickly.

He brought her one anyway and sat uncomfortably close to her on the couch. She watched while he popped his beer, chugged, then wiped his mouth with the back of his hand.

"So," he said. "You in Terry's class or what?"

"No, I'm a junior. One behind."

"Yeah?" He belched. "Think you'll graduate?"

"Of course," she said haughtily. He really was a jerk. It ought to be obvious that she was college material and not some sleazo dropout.

Without further preliminaries, Mike pressed his mouth against hers. Startled, she jerked back, but his lips remained mashed against hers as if they had become glued. He began to twist and turn his head in undulating passion; his tongue darted out and squirmed importunately against the barricade of her clenched teeth. Kate was appalled. His pimples were grinding against her chin—she tried to remember if they were catching. And worse, his hand had begun to worm its way beneath her blouse. She tried to inch backward, but the arm of the couch cut her off from behind and his arms pinned her from the side. She had a jolt of fear as she felt him fumble at her bra clasp. At the same time she became aware of a sound from the bedroom—a rhythmic creaking that could only be the rocking of bedsprings. Whatever doubts she had vanished. Now she was sure—Terry and Lonnie were going all the way.

And then another thought struck her with devastating force. This—this!—was her first kiss.

She burst into tears.

"Oh, man!" Mike said. "A friggin' crybaby."

* * *

KATE'S FRIENDSHIP WITH Terry was effectively over after that night. But in April, when Terry announced she was going to marry Lonnie after graduation, Kate still felt a stab of betrayal. She dug out the notes Terry had written her the year before with all their dazzling prophesies. "I know it will happen this way," she had written. "Oh, Kate, it will be so *beautiful*!" But it had all been just talk. Meaningless, useless talk.

She faked a strep throat and stayed home for a couple of days. When she returned to school, she became aware again of what an outsider she really was. For a year she had lived snugly inside a cocoon of dreams. Now everywhere she went she overheard bits of conversation—about who got smashed at John Peck's latest dune party, or the really bitching thing that happened Friday night at the movies—hints of all the things she had always been excluded from.

But something strange had happened. She didn't care anymore. After all, she had only one more year at East Pine Grove High. One more year before she escaped the detested pumpkin-colored halls and was free—off to soar into the greater and far more glittering arena of college. She had brains, and that was her passport out. She began to realize that she had never really needed Terry at all.

And then one day in her senior year, as she was walking through the new mall after school, she noticed some boys watching her. One wore a swimming-team jacket lettered BELLPARK—the name of an affluent town on the north shore. He was sharp-looking, she thought, a surfer blond with hunky shoulders—the kind of guy who in her own school didn't even know she was alive. As she passed him, she saw him nudge his friend and say—quite distinctly—"She's a doll!"

Her face burned; she lowered her head and walked faster. They were laughing at her, she thought. Making fun of her "mod" short skirt and white go-go boots and her droopy long straight hair.

Safely out of their sight, she turned and examined her reflection in a dark shop window. The Brown Person mocked back at her—but only for a second. Then someone else appeared: a tall, pretty girl with big eyes and warm honey-brown hair brushing her shoulders . . . a girl who would naturally attract the attention of the sharpest-looking guys from Bellpark.

As she stared at the reflection, Kate felt again the shiver of expectation that had marked those enchanted afternoons in Terry's room. Wonderful things were in store for her: this seemed promised. The year was 1966, the world was young and full of great changes. . . .

And she was going to be part of it all.

ANDREA HERRY LOOKED UP AS THE BELLS IN THE CLOCK tower struck a sonorous four. She had been at Hadley College for women in Allington, Massachusetts, for—she did a rapid calculation—approximately one day, two hours and twenty minutes; and now the red-and-white taxi making a sharp turn out of the quad carried her mother on the first leg of her journey back to St. Louis. The departure of her mother was like the lifting of a heavy veil. Vanished was the curtain of caveats and unspoken disapproval: how shocking that so many of the girls smoke . . . too many Jewish faces . . . such shabby wallpaper in the dining room. . . . She was gone, and Andrea was finally free to relish her new environment in her own way.

So far everything seemed absolutely right. The Georgian dorms weeping ivy, the quad with its shade trees and straggle of bicycles, the brash modern buildings rubbing shoulders with brooding Victorian halls on the main campus—it

19

was all exactly as she had imagined coming East to school would be.

The other students were so far just a blur of faces and names hazily remembered. The school prided itself on its admissions policy of "geographical distribution," and it excited Andrea to speculate on which exotic territories her classmates represented. In her own dorm—her own *house*, she corrected herself—she had so far met one student from a working ranch in Idaho, another from Honolulu, and a delicate, shy-eyed Asian from Bangkok. Each one had a look of eager inquisitiveness, of "Who are you?" that Andrea knew she had as well: a brightening of the eyes that declared every moment was a discovery.

She was particularly eager to learn more about her roommate—Kathryn Ann Auden, from East Pine Grove, New York, who had only arrived this afternoon. Andrea had dashed back to her fourth-floor room to pick up a sweater before accompanying her mother to yet another parent-freshman orientation affair, and there had been Kathryn and her parents and a tumble of suitcases on the untaken bed. Andrea had registered eye liner, a daringly short skirt, long straight hair like a folksinger's, a cigarette held with sophisticated measure, and was grateful her mother had elected to wait downstairs. She could just picture her censorious look, the lift of her eyebrow, hear her murmur something about "bad influences"—perhaps even haul Andrea to the registrar's and insist she be removed to a single room. *Thank you, dear God, for not letting that happen*, she offered silently—for she had had enough of single rooms to last her a lifetime.

She was the only child of elderly parents: her mother had been forty-two when she was born, her father nine years older; and Andrea had lately come to suspect she had been a "mistake," the product of her parent's naïve assumption that they were too old for "anything to happen." Over the years she had caught her mother staring at her with something like bewilderment—as if wondering who this child was who had so thoroughly disrupted the order of her middle years.

Andrea's father had died of a heart attack when she was almost four. She had shadowy memories of a houseful of strangers: large, soft-bosomed women bending to kiss her in a waft of violets and naphthalene; an ancient uncle who flipped quarters in the air and caught them in the crook of his elbow. "Your daddy's in heaven," they repeated solemnly. And then they had all gone away, leaving the quiet to settle in—a quiet as fixed and impermeable in the old Tudor house as the half-century's must that clung to its baseboards.

That house . . . Andrea had not been sorry to leave it. It had been dank and gloomy even on the sunniest days. Most afternoons when she had returned from school, she had found a light burning in the foyer—a signal her mother was home nursing a headache, a backache, or her worsening arthritis, and that Andrea was to creep noiselessly to her own room without disturbing her rest. On other days, the house would be completely dark: and this would mean her mother had mustered health enough to go down to help out at St. Bartholomew's.

Louisa Herry had, throughout her married life, flirted with any number of Protestant denominations; but upon her husband's death she had settled plumply back into the Lutheran faith of her own German ancestry. At first she had been content to luxuriate in the lavish sympathy extended by the clergy to a pious widow with a small child. But such attentions seduced her: she became "very active," devoting more and more of her time to bake sales and casino nights, to chairing the altar flowers committee and supervising the redecorating of Dr. Kopple's study. She threw herself into the attendant charities with all the energy her illnesses—real and imagined—permitted. And at home she ran her daughter's life as if that, too, were a charitable activity. Andrea was impeccably "provided for": there were piano lessons, dancing school, an Ozarks camp in the summer. But there was a dispassionate quality to her upbringing, and Andrea felt as though her needs were a duty indistinguishable from her mother's many others.

And so from an early age she had learned to look for love elsewhere. She had a family of dolls, over thirty of them. Some were without arms, legs, hair, but she cherished each one equally—the blackened, one-eyed Raggedy Ann as much as Samantha, the expensive walking doll with her "real" auburn hair.

And in church she had God's love. When she was little, she had confused "Our Father Who art in Heaven" with the picture of her own dead father framed on her mother's dresser, and she had never quite relinquished this image—a balding man in a striped polo shirt gazing benignly at her from behind heavy, square black glasses. It gave her a warm, proprietary feeling: God was real; He watched her and cared about what she did. And as long as she did nothing bad, He would continue to love her.

When she was fourteen, she entered St. Elizabeth's, a small Lutheran girls' school; and here she was the happiest she had ever been. She was not one of the leaders—the fearless, self-confident girls who won debates and organized secret sororities—but she was always among their coterie of best friends. She had a malleable, willing nature that they found useful—Andrea could always be counted upon to fill out a committee, serve refreshments, support an opinion. Moreover, she was perfectly content to be a follower. She had no wish to run the show: the only thing she asked for was love.

And everyone in the school *had* loved her, she was certain of that. Even the grumpy, footsore cafeteria ladies; even the slack-mouthed retarded girl who passed out the mimeographed announcements—they all brightened when she was around. And in *The Voyager*, her class yearbook, she had been voted "Most Valuable," with the motto "Ain't She Sweet" written under her picture.

She had soaked up this affection like a plant taking in the rain, storing it for the time when she had to return home—to the gloomy Tudor house and her mother's distant, disapproving eyes.

Andrea sat down now on the steps leading to the quad and stared at the turning where her mother's taxi had disappeared. Funny, she thought: her mother had something to say about almost everything—sloppy housekeepers, unleashed dogs, foreigners, Negroes, welfare recipients, the Kennedys . . . everything except what really mattered. Feelings, love, fears, and wants—anything intimate was absolutely taboo.

Andrea laughed remembering how she had learned about sex. Until the age of eleven she had believed God implanted babies in the tummies of women, and they popped out the navel to be born. But then her friends began to whisper and giggle about ladies and men in bed together, and from what they said, Andrea pieced together a new picture: a mother and father sleep side by side and during the night something comes out of the father and travels, possibly by means of the bedsheet, to the mother. It sounded strange, and for a year she pondered it without further enlightenment. And then one day during assembly, Patty Dreiff filled her in on the facts.

She hadn't believed it. "You made that up just to gross me out," she accused Patty.

"No, I didn't," Patty declared. "Look it up for yourself if you want. It's in the encyclopedia."

At home, Andrea flew to her new World Book and looked up, as Patty had told her to, *Reproduction, human*. She read slowly, with great wonder, as a tingling feeling grew deep down inside her. She looked up *penis* and *vagina*, and then went to the old double-volume Webster's dictionary on its stand for *orgasm* and *ejaculation*. By the end it all came clear to her: sexual intercourse. And suddenly she was swept with revulsion. How disgusting that these avuncular reference books—the very ones she turned to for reports on the War of 1812 and Brazil, Our Friend to the South—could contain such gross things! She was sorry she had started looking it all up—now she wished she didn't know. Of one thing she was certain: none of this would ever, *ever* have anything to do with herself.

But her body had other plans for her. At fifteen, she began to develop: hips formed, elbows and knees became blunted angles. And then her breasts grew full and deep until they were lush enough for a *Playboy* centerfold. "Thirty-two C," pronounced a sweating saleswoman at Barton's as she swung her frayed tape measure like a conductor's baton, and Andrea's face burned with shame. Suddenly her body no longer felt like her own. She thought of her new breasts as "them"—completely separate entities which nature, in a moment of carelessness, had affixed to the wrong chest. Certainly they didn't go with her schoolgirl face, her round, innocent blue eyes, or her windy light hair.

Of course she had always joined in when the other girls did arm-circling exercises and chanted: "We must, we must, we must improve our bust!" But her friends had received small, manageable bumps, A and B cups, while she had received "them." It just wasn't fair.

She began to cherish a ridiculous hope that they would someday disappear—as suddenly and as completely as they had arrived.

In the meantime they caused her nothing but trouble. They jiggled when she walked and bounced up and down when she ran. And she caught her mother gazing at her now not with bewilderment but clear shame. It made Andrea feel so dirty that she wanted to hide beneath layers and layers of clothing.

And boys. Suddenly boys she had known for years—had gone swimming with and studied her Small Catechism with and danced the mashed potatoes with at scads of birthday parties—suddenly they were nervous and weird around her, fidgeting their hands in their pockets and shifting their eyes off to the side. In groups, though, they were just the opposite, staring at her body as if it were public property and making grinning comments to each other. Even in places she thought she'd be safe, like the church rec room during the young people's Koffee Klatch, she overheard them: "Boy, that Herry is some sexy baby. She's sure got a swell pair of boobs."

Sexy. The word had become branded on her like a disfiguring birthmark. And all because of "them."

And it didn't stop there. Her body had further treacheries in store for her. One horrible day—so awful that even now, three years later, she hated to think about it—one of the seniors in her Latin class had whispered to her that there was some jelly on her skirt and she'd better go check herself. Andrea was puzzled: how could she have sat on jelly? But dutifully she went to the girls' room, and there, twisting herself, she discovered it: a ragged, raw-looking spot of red that saturated the beige seat of her uniform. It was no bigger than a quarter, but to her it seemed enormous. Everyone must have seen it—including Mr. Woijeck when she had gone up to the blackboard. It was the most hideous, horrible thing that could possibly have happened, and she wished she could die.

She tied the arms of her cardigan around her waist so that the back of the sweater hid the horror, and went to the nurse for permission to go home. At the corner of Furth Street, she stopped in a drugstore and bought a box of Tampax. This, she knew, was what her friends used—and besides, she had seen it advertised in *Seventeen*.

For once she was glad the house was empty. She locked herself in the upstairs bathroom, shed her spoiled skirt and panties, and opened the package. There was a folded set of instructions on top: as it directed, she sat on the edge of the toilet and spread her knees. Then she unwrapped one of the tampons. It reminded her disconcertingly of a firecracker, the string like a fuse falling limply from the cardboard tube.

But now came the hard part. According to the instructions, she was supposed to gently insert the tampon tip into the vaginal opening. But she had no idea where the opening was. She never touched herself ''down there''—not with her fingers—and she certainly couldn't now when it was all sticky with blood. She consulted the diagram in the instructions. It showed some paisley-shaped organs and connecting tubes, but from a side view, as if seen through a transparent thigh. There was nothing to show where it all came out.

She'd just have to find this opening on her own. She poked herself experimentally with the tampon and met with nothing but solid flesh. She jabbed it harder and cried out in pain as it bent against her pubic bone. She threw the bent tube away and opened another, this time angling it down. But this time the tampon slipped out of its inserter and fell, with a smug plop, into the toilet.

''Darn!'' she cried.

Grimly, she tried again, one after another, until she had gone through the entire box of ten. Nothing went inside her. Maybe she had no vagina, she thought wildly. Maybe she was a freak, a mutant. Except that the blood must be coming from somewhere.

She put on a fresh pair of panties, stuffing them with toilet paper to catch the flow. Then she gathered the pile of broken, bloodied-up firecrackers and stuffed it deep inside the trash bin where her mother would never find it. And then she returned to the drugstore and purchased a box of Kotex sanitary pads, writhing with embarrassment as the male clerk gave her change.

But the pads at least proved easy to use. Except that the next day, as she dressed in a clean uniform for school, it seemed to her she sort of . . . bulged in back. She took a few steps, patting herself behind. Yes, she was certain there was a noticeable protuberance. Panic welled up in her: How could she go out of the house trumpeting her shameful secret?

After some experimentation she discovered that if she walked with her pelvis thrust forward and her thighs sort of brushing together, the bulge disappeared—which was what she had done ever since on days she had the curse. Still, she never felt totally secure during those times—especially around boys. There seemed nothing she could keep private from them and their prying eyes.

She wondered now if Barry had been able to tell when she had had her period. Barry . . . why had he popped into her mind? She would never know why he had singled her out: Barry Kissel, the basketball star of Immanuel, St. Elizabeth's brother school. He had an open, snub-nosed face, crisp brown hair, and the bouncing candor of someone who expects to be liked—and he could have picked almost any girl in her class. But he had picked her, and by the middle of her junior year they were going steady. Suddenly other boys could talk to her again without stammering and sidling. There were no more wolf whistles or grubby remarks when she went by. The ring she wore around her neck marked her as exclusive property, off-limits to trespassers. She made sure she wore it in conspicuous view wherever she went.

Barry treated her as if she were something rare and fragile. With him, she could almost believe that the mirror lied—that she really was as floating and ethereal as sunlight. Of course, not everything about going steady was wonderful. French kissing, for one thing—there was something gross about Barry's tongue in her mouth; and she could never stop thinking about swallowing each other's gum, or worse, snot balls when one or the other had a cold. But she loved the hugging and cuddling and "straight" kissing. And when his hands made tentative advances on her breasts or thighs, it had been easy to stop him. He *expected* to be stopped. He respected her.

Barry graduated and went off to Stanford. Andrea began her last year at St. Elizabeth's, marking the day of his return for the Christmas holidays on her Peanuts calendar with the huge gold star. She missed him; since he had been gone, the quiet at home had seemed more lugubrious than ever. But at last the gold-starred day arrived, and his familiar knock rapped jauntily at her door.

"Barry!" she squealed and threw her arms around his neck.

It took her a moment to realize he had changed. His hair was longer and there was the ghost of a mustache above his upper lip. Gone were the neat button-downs and chinos; now he wore a workshirt over bell-bottom jeans. Even the way he talked was different, faster, and kind of slurred with a lot of slang like "man" and "really wild." She listened to him with growing uneasiness. What had happened to her Barry—the combed, gentlemanly boy who had left only three months ago?

It was almost a relief when he began to kiss her. But almost immediately his hands wandered to her breasts—and when she pushed them away, they traveled insistently back. "Barry, please," she murmured.

"Don't be so hung up," he said in his strange new voice. "You're a big girl now, it's okay."

"Don't forget my mother is sleeping right down the hall."

"I'll be really quiet," he said with a laugh.

He drew her back to him. Any minute now he'll stop, she told herself, it's just the excitement of seeing me again after so long. But he didn't stop. He slowly pushed her down until he was lying almost completely on top of her, and her plaid skirt had ridden up above her knees. She felt him fumble at himself. And then he grabbed her hand and placed it at his groin. Her fingers closed over something warm and fat and slippery, and a wet stickiness flowed onto them, while Barry made a noise deep in his throat. She let out a horrified cry and tumbled away from him.

"How could you?" she gasped. He had done "it" right here in her mother's living room, with her mother lying just down the hall. There was a sticky drop of "it" drying on the brown cushion of her mother's divan. She ran into the kitchen, washed her hands thoroughly, then returned with a wet towel and began to scrub the cushion.

"Don't make such a big deal of it," Barry said. "It's a completely natural thing, you know."

"Not with me it's not," she declared.

"Oh, man, are you hung up. Let me tell you, Andrea, there's a lot of women around who don't have your inhibitions."

"Well, I'm not that kind of girl. Maybe you know a lot of tramps at college, but I'm not one of them."

"Jesus, Andrea, that stuff went out with the Dark Ages. And anyway, if it's just your reputation you're so worried about, you can forget it. All the kids thought we were making it all last year anyway."

"They did not!" she flashed out.

"Sure they did. Ask your friend Susan. Or Buddy, or Clark, or any of them."

She paled. "Did you tell them that?"

"I didn't have to." He smirked. "With a bod like yours, who'd of believed anything else?"

She thought about it for a long time after he had gone. It couldn't be true, she decided. How could her friends act so fond of her if they believed she was a tramp?

But just in case, she continued to wear Barry's ring—for if anyone *did* think she was no longer a virgin, it would be far worse to have them think she was an unattached one as well.

BUT THAT WAS behind her now. She was a thousand miles away from St. Elizabeth's! No one here would even suspect her of having a reputation. She could start completely fresh.

A figure on a bicycle rode through the arched brick entrance to the quad and waved to her. Andrea waved back. It was Jean Ferguson, her "Big Sister"—the sophomore assigned to help her adjust to school more easily. Andrea had met her yesterday and been instantly entranced. Jean had sleek, short dark hair and a lithe, athletic body, and her far-spaced gray eyes held Andrea's confidently. Even Mrs. Herry had been charmed; and Andrea had thought, here is someone wonderful.

And now, watching Jean on her bicycle, *clean* was the word that came to Andrea's mind. Trim and attractive and inestimably clean. Nothing filthy could ever touch Jean Ferguson—of that much she was sure. From now on Andrea was determined to model herself on Jean.

*T*HE VARIOUS HOUSES IN WHICH JEAN FERGUSON GREW up had one thing in common: each was filled with beautiful objects, silvers and pastels and soft, mirrored wood that shone in the skillful disposition of light. Each house was a perfect environment wrought with exquisite care by Jean's mother who was herself—as people constantly remarked—the perfect woman. Dorothy Hassan Ferguson had been raised in Athens, Georgia. Transplanted to the Yankee reaches of Maryland, she brought with her all the chivalric ideals of southern femininity as well as a certain rigidity which her own mother had referred to as "backbone." She was a devoted wife and mother, an inspired cook and ingenious hostess, an exemplar of superb taste in all matters of fashion, arts, and décor.

She had fluttered, this beautiful, poised, and well-spoken belle, through the daily ministrations of Jean's life, dressing her, correcting her manners, in all ways doing her best to raise the perfect daughter. And then watched with bewilder-

31

ment as this, of all her efforts, failed. Jean, from an early age, rejected her lessons entirely and turned instead to her father for a model.

Ray Ferguson was an energetic, strong-willed man, a former U. Maryland football star who had built a thriving stepstool- and ladder-manufacturing company from "nothing but spit and a rag to shine my shoes." He was a man who respected winning above all else. He voiced vigorous contempt for bench-warmers, second-stringers, fumblers, runners-up. And Jean realized early in life that her mother deferred to him on all matters of significance. The family vacationed at a northern Michigan lake, where her mother shivered the entire time inside a heavy sweater, because that was where the hunting was good, and Ray Ferguson liked to hunt. He chose the family cars, the new houses, and the topics of conversation at the dinner table. When he traveled on business—as he frequently did—his absence was marked at home by a tranquility that to Jean seemed dull and stupid. When he returned, there was a tension in the house, as if the air itself were being stretched like a rubber band. Jean intuitively recognized this as power. Power that came from being in the world—from achieving and winning. And intuitively she sensed she could get this power for herself by aligning herself with a man's world: by playing their games, and doing their work, and despising everything her mother stood for.

She was a tomboy. At Christmas, she left the bride dolls and cunning pink china tea sets under the tree to appropriate her brother Denny's fire trucks, soldiers, and Erector Sets. She built forts and climbed trees and double-dared boys to follow her across a ford of slippery stones. She especially loved being the only girl among a pack of boys: then it seemed she really had become one of *them*.

At first Denny, who was sixteen months younger, was her accomplice. He let her sneak pairs of his overalls and polo shirts to wear in place of the embroidered white sweater sets her mother chose for her. And when she came home covered with mud and scratches he backed her in her story that she had been pushed by a gang of older boys, knowing full well she had actually instigated the roughhousing.

But when Jean was about eight and Denny seven things began to change. Instead of accomplices, they were becoming rivals, pitted against each other in an endless contest set by their father. On a warm May day, he would hand them each a trowel with the challenge: "Let's see now, gang, who can dig up the most weeds." In February there would be a race to build the biggest, fattest, most lifelike snowman. At the lake in July there were swimming races and diving contests, and not even a campfire could be built without first measuring each child's stack of kindling. During the school year, their report cards were compared and the better one praised and glorified, the all-A scorer honored with an extra heaping of love and attention.

Jean threw herself into the competition with all her might. But as they grew older, it seemed the harder she strove to win, the more her brother backed down. In the water she could sense him relaxing his stroke, letting her push on ahead. His grades slipped; he brought home fretful notes from his teachers complaining that he often wasn't working up to his I.Q. The competition was becoming lopsided: Jean found herself sweeping the field.

And yet she was losing out to Denny in the most crucial contest of all. Her father's attention began to slip steadily away from her and focus ever more firmly upon her brother. It didn't make sense. *She* was the winner, the one who pushed herself harder and harder to excel at school, in athletics, as a leader of every sort. With each new trophy and A+, each team captainship and student council office, she ran to her father and placed it at his feet. And still he insisted upon turning to Denny.

At dinner she would look eagerly at her father. "Guess what, Dad? I won the freestyle and butterfly today against Baylor. And our team won the meet, which means we're in the all-county finals."

Her father would reach out and rumple her hair. "That's my champ!"

"Jean, please don't slump like that in your chair. And I do wish you'd clip your hair back before coming to the table. You know how it falls in your face when you eat." This from her mother at the foot of the table, dressed in cool, crisp linen, her hair freshly washed and scalloped becomingly around her heart-shaped face.

Jean would automatically push back the offending lock and continue: "Miss Jolis thinks I could be Olympic material with more training. There's this coach in Illinois that takes kids for the summer, he's supposed to be the best."

But her father's eyes would already have shifted to her brother, eating quietly, still lost, no doubt, in the reverie of whatever book he had been currently absorbing.

"You get that math quiz back yet, Denny?"

Denny's eyes would lift dreamily toward him. "I got a ninety-eight."

"Let's go for a hundred next time, okay. There's no stopping short if you want to get anywhere in this goddamned world. You don't score till you're one hundred percent over the goal line, just remember that, kiddo." He would put a forkful of rare beef in his mouth and chew with the same vigor with which he consumed the minutes of his life. "Who was that kid you had around here Sunday? Bobby, Billy something . . ."

"Bobby Sullivan," Denny would say warily.

"Friend of yours?"

"We hang out sometimes."

"He looked like a real loser to me. That skinny build and weasely kind of face. When I offered to shake his hand, he wouldn't even look me in the eye. What kind of kid is that who can't even look his friend's father in the goddamned eye? Just remember, kiddo, you hang around losers long enough and people are gonna start thinking of you as a loser."

Denny would bend closer to his food without replying. It sometimes seemed to Jean that beneath his dreamy façade Denny possessed a will as clear and obdurate as her father's. But he puzzled her. He was on the winning side—why did he seem so eager to abdicate? And she was beginning to realize that her father would never take her own accomplishments seriously. The way he saw it, she was a girl, competing only in a girl's sphere. There would be no special Olympic training for her. No special anything—not now or ever. The way he saw it, it wasn't worth it.

SHE WAS NO longer the only girl running with a pack of boys. Gradually her former playmates had come to regard her as an Other, a being apart. She marked the change from the fifth grade, the day Ben Gilbert ran up to her in the playground and slid his hands down her chest even though it was still every bit as flat as his own. The year after, Sammy Holmes leaned over the back of his school bus seat and kissed her firmly on the lips. By the time she entered junior high, boys were calling her on the phone, nervous and polite, straining to govern their suddenly unruly voices as they invited her to a party or a gym hop.

She was, she discovered, pretty. She had inherited her mother's regular features without their too-showy opulence. Her hair was good, and her body was small, slender, and fluid. She recognized from the flurry her looks sometimes caused that she had acquired yet another trophy.

By high school, the boys her age seemed silly and immature, particularly compared to the seniors—glamorous older men who owned their own cars, football captains and basketball stars already looking ahead to college. And of these, one stood out from the rest: Karl Shapiro, a popular rugby player with hulking shoulders and the vivid, ice-blue eyes of a Paul Newman. Every girl in the school harbored a secret crush on Karl. Jean made hers public. She told everyone that she was madly in love with him, shadowed him in the halls between periods, hovered by his locker until he appeared. When at last he capitulated and asked her to come with him for a ride, she was not in the least surprised. She had thrown herself into the pursuit of Karl as she had into every other competition—with the full expectation of winning.

They meandered through the back streets of town in his famous green Mustang with its silver racing stripe. The sycamores were hazy with buds, and there was the sweet smell of spring in the air. It was, Jean decided, the most wonderful afternoon of her life. She gloried in the envious looks of other girls as they sailed past. What dopes, always talking about how Karl Shapiro made them tongue-tied. Jean found him perfectly easy to talk to: in fact, she could hardly keep quiet. She told him all about a wonderful book she had discovered, *Thus Spake Zarathustra*, how Nietzsche sometimes seemed to know exactly what she was thinking. She impressed him with how much she knew about rugby, and she made him promise to teach her how to drive a stick shift.

At dusk, he drove her home. She raised her face expectantly, an invitation for a passionate kiss. Instead, he pecked the side of her temple like a daddy.

She opened her eyes. "Don't you want to really kiss me?" she asked.

Karl made a mugging face, then shook his head.

"You think I'm too young, don't you?"

He gave a laugh. "I've made out with lots younger than you, baby."

"Then why not me?"

"You really want to know?"

She nodded.

"Well, don't take offense, but it's the way you act. Guys like to be made to feel masculine. Like they're on top. They want a girl to make them feel stronger and smarter. Protective, kind of. But with you, it's like you can take perfectly good care of yourself."

"But I *can*."

"That's not the point. Christ!" Karl hunched a shoulder against the steering wheel. "Look. Don't you know how to flirt?"

"I guess maybe I don't," Jean said stiffly.

"Then watch Missy Carson sometime."

"That idiot!"

Karl grinned. "Missy's no dope. She knows exactly what she's doing. Hey, she's got a way of looking up at you with her eyes sort of half closed that makes you want to ravage her on the spot."

"Not me, she doesn't." Jean opened the car door and walked, shivering with rage, into the house. Missy Carson. That fool! That gabbling, primping, eye-batting *girl*! That was who Karl Shapiro thought she should emulate!

"Jean, is that you?" her mother called from the kitchen. "The Coaines are coming for dinner tonight, so I want you to put on something nice. The royal-blue pleated with the georgette blouse would be fine. And after you've changed, would you please come help Lenore with the hors d'oeuvres?"

Her mother, Jean realized, must once have been a Missy

Carson. All it had won her was the right to be bullied and pushed around by a husband who took little notice of her. The right to rule over the petty and insignificant domain of the house and kitchen.

Never, Jean vowed. She would rather be alone for the rest of her life than give in to such a bargain.

Upstairs on her bedside table lay a book that Denny of all people had given her for her sixteenth birthday. It was called *The Feminine Mystique*. Jean had read it three times in as many months; and though it seemed addressed to women her mother's age, she had drawn from it the startling and thrilling confirmation that she was right. And if the Karl Shapiros of the world refused to accept it . . .

Well, then she'd make it so they'd have no choice.

WHY DID YOU PICK HADLEY?" KATE ASKED.

"I don't know," Andrea said. She stood at her dresser carefully unrolling fat barrel-shaped curlers from her delicate hair. Through the mirror, she glanced at Kate sprawled on her bed. It had been only five weeks since orientation, but the sight of her there, her ale-colored hair splayed out from under her and her slender legs intertwined, was already intensely familiar. As was their cramped little room with the maple-red drapes from Woolworth's and the Indian madras bedspreads and the Paul Klee poster thumbtacked illegally onto the wall. It already seemed more like home to Andrea than the house on Furth Street ever had.

She pursed her lips as she considered Kate's question. "I guess it was my mother's choice. She thought it had the best reputation."

"You're kidding! Didn't you have any say in it at all?"

"Sure I did. I mean, ever since I first read Fitzgerald I

wanted to come east to school. But I just didn't care which one.''

"F. Scott Fitzgerald? Is that what he wrote about?''

It was Andrea's turn to be surprised. "Didn't you ever read *This Side of Paradise*?''

"No, but I will if you've got it here.''

It was remarkable, Andrea thought, that of all the freshmen on the floor it was Kate whom she really found the most compatible. At first they had appeared to be grossly mismatched. Andrea was fastidious and regular in her habits. She rose with the breakfast bell whether or not she had an early class, studied in the same section of the library, and each night, before getting into bed, rinsed her feet in the tub so as not to get any grit between the sheets. Kate, on the other hand, habitually slept through her ten o'clocks. Before opening her eyes, she groped for the arm of her portable stereo; then, with Donovan or the Rolling Stones or the Lovin' Spoonful wailing, she pulled some jeans from a heap on the floor and staggered off to begin her day. She read most nights till long after midnight—books which, as far as Andrea could tell, had nothing to do with her courses. When and if Kate studied was a puzzle to Andrea, who wouldn't dare attend a section class unprepared.

But an intimacy had grown quickly between them through the simple fact of coexistence. Casual, getting-ready-for-bed chatter had led to the blurting of confidences, which evolved into long, rapt dialogues encompassing school and the past and a dozen topics of suddenly urgent interest. And now it seemed to Andrea the most normal thing in the world to share her thoughts with Kate.

Kate sat up on the bed and folded her legs Indian fashion. "Do you want to know why I came here?'' she asked. "On my application I wrote it was because of Hadley's high academic standing and its great diversity and all that. But the *real* reason was because it was near a lot of boys' schools.''

Andrea peered at her uncertainly. Kate had a way of declaring the outrageous and then laughing at Andrea's solemn acceptance of it. She decided to be noncommittal. "How come you didn't go someplace coed?'' she asked.

"Because this way you've got the best of both worlds. The men are there when you want them—on weekends or if you feel like a date at night. But during the day, in classes and everything, they're not around to distract you. I mean, can you imagine having to face a guy at breakfast?''

Andrea thought of that meal—drowsy girls in bathrobes and hairpins fumbling through the *New York Times* while they shoveled in a second helping of soft-scrambled eggs. "God, no!'' she shuddered. She undid the last of the curlers and shook the baby-fine wisps back from her face. Everyone was wearing their hair long now. All over campus were girls with great streaming sheets of mermaid hair to hide behind. But hers never grew beyond her shoulders; and no matter what she did, it always ended up looking as if the wind had gotten to it.

"I didn't really care where I went to college," she went on. "I'm not planning to do anything with my education anyway. All I want to do is be a housewife.''

"You've *got* to be kidding.''

"No, I'm serious. I want to marry someone nice and secure with a good job. And I want a house with a huge backyard and scads and scads of kids.''

"Well, not me," said Kate.

"You never want to get married?''

"Oh, sure. But not till really late, like when I'm around twenty-five or -six. I want to work for a while first.''

"Doing what?''

"I don't know. Something exciting where I can meet interesting people and travel and things. And in the meantime I want to date a lot. I want to go out with a lot of different men and be taken to glamorous places and have a terrific time. That way, when I do fall in love, I'll know it's the real thing. And after I'm married, I'll never have to feel I've missed anything.''

"What about . . ." Andrea hesitated.

"What about what?"

"Are you going to try out *ev*erything first?"

"You mean sex?" Kate laughed.

Andrea gave a quick nod.

"I don't know. I suppose if I was much older and really serious about someone it would be okay. I mean, I don't think it's that important to save it for your husband. It might even be better to have some experience." Kate sank back upon her elbows. "What about you? Are you still a virgin?"

"Of course," Andrea said stiffly. She waited, half expecting Kate to challenge her: *With a body like yours who'd believe it*? But Kate merely murmured, and Andrea relaxed.

There was a quick rap on the door. She turned and smiled as Jean Ferguson popped her head in.

"Hi, Andrea," Jean said. "I'm going down to catch the Fellini flick at Wilder Hall. *Juliet of the Spirits*; it's supposed to be terrific. Want to come?"

Andrea felt a surge of disappointment. "I can't. I promised Kate I'd go with her to a mixer at Yale. There's a bus leaving pretty soon."

Jean glanced at the other girl on the bed. "Oh, hi, Kate. I didn't see you there. Well that sounds a lot more exciting than sitting in some old movie. Enjoy."

"Thanks," Andrea said half-heartedly. She had already begun to have second thoughts about the mixer. Now she entirely regretted her decision to go.

"Talk about virgins," Kate said after the door had closed again. "There goes the original ice cube."

Andrea bristled. "What makes you say that?"

"Can you imagine any guy getting to first base with her? She'd flatten him to the floor first."

"For God's sake, Kate, you make her sound like some kind of lesbian."

"Oh, no, she's much too straight for that."

"So why don't you like her?"

Kate shrugged. "I guess because she's so pushy. She's always trying to run everything."

"She's a natural leader," Andrea said loyally. "People always look to her to get things done. They have confidence in her."

"I guess," Kate said. "It's a matter of interpretation."

Andrea didn't reply. She suspected that Kate was jealous of how well she got along with Jean. Kate's own Big Sister was a furtive, goggle-eyed math major from Knoxville: during their obligatory dinner together, they had sat in silence, staring at each other with glum dismay. Whereas Andrea's admiration for Jean had increased steadily. She gloried in the cool efficiency with which Jean read the minutes at house meetings; she practiced Jean's forthright laugh and even considered trying to force her fly-away hair into a sleek helmet like Jean's.

She turned from the mirror and began to get dressed, adroitly maneuvering her robe so that it shielded her body from Kate's sight. It continued to shock her whenever Kate stripped naked in front of her. But then Kate had been raised with sisters. Andrea was certain that she'd never become accustomed to someone else's eyes upon her body.

THE TRIP TO New Haven took a little over an hour. The bus was full, mostly with freshmen in high spirits. Andrea sat with Kate and Marcie Kingman, a flashy, moon-faced girl from Kalamazoo whose frequent use of the words *shit* and *fuck* was strangely contagious. Marcie had obtained a contraband copy of the Yale freshman directory, and she and Kate pored over the pictures.

"Oh, shit! There's that little turkey I met open-house week. . . ."

"The guy next to him looks like a real stud. . . ."

". . . an absolute animal . . ."

Andrea said nothing. She was becoming increasingly nervous about the evening ahead. For Kate, mixers were already old hat: the expedition offered the excitement of the new without the terrors of the unknown. But as the bus rolled through the Gothic stone gates of Yale, Andrea's stomach contracted with dread.

They disembarked in front of Saybrook, the residential "college" that was giving the mixer, and dashed through a thin drizzle inside. The mixer was held in the dining hall, a huge, open room with a soaring peaked ceiling. Other buses had preceded theirs: the room was packed with boys in jackets and jeans, girls in turtleneck sweaters. A four-man rock group, whose careful shagginess marked them as students, pounded "96 Tears" into protesting mikes. At intervals a strobe light made an old-time movie out of the entire hall.

Andrea trailed after Kate, who plunged confidently into the crowd. They pushed their way through to the beer tap. Andrea reached for a sopping paper cup. When she turned back, Kate had disappeared. She glanced about wildly but could see no sight of her, nor Marcie, nor any other familiar face. Panic gripped her. She drifted to the sidelines, clutching her cup, feeling at once ignored and brutally on display. No one, she was sure, would talk to her, no one would ask her to dance.

But someone was approaching her. Dressed in a corduroy jacket and wide tie, the young man had side-parted blond hair and the kind of strong, rounded jaw that seemed made to go with a pipe. "Do you detest these events as much as I do?" he was saying.

"It's pretty awful."

"Then let's leave. Would you care to go for a walk?"

"It's raining," she said.

"We can stay under the colonnades. Come on."

He introduced himself as Douglas Carroll. He was a junior and came from South Bend, Indiana. There was something a little stuffy about him. He spoke in a weary voice that reminded Andrea of certain professors. His syntax was oddly formal, as if each sentence was a fragment of a lecture. But she was grateful to him for singling her out. And she liked the way he steered her through the hushed maze of courtyards, one hand protectively under her elbow. She liked, too, the way he directed the conversation so that she never had to grasp for something to say.

He asked the perfunctory questions: What was her major? Where was she from, and did she know a girl named Sue Cabrini at Mount Holyoke who was also from St. Louis? He then proceeded to tell her—in rather more detail—about himself. He was a comp. lit. major but intended to go into law. His two roommates, both of whom were named David, were "philosophy mavens," and they, too, had their sights on the bar. He had a golden retriever at home named Edmund Wilson and, though "structurally flawed," F. Scott Fitzgerald was his favorite author.

"Mine too!" Andrea exclaimed.

He gazed at her with fond approval, rather as a father would look at a child who had just uttered something clever. She almost expected him to pat her head. Instead he led her to a small arched doorway. "This is where I live," he said. "My humble domicile. Come on up."

Andrea followed him up two flights of a winding stone

stairway. She had never been in a boy's bedroom before and wondered if there would be anything embarrassingly intimate about it. But Douglas's suite had a homey look. There was a largish common room filled with cast-off furniture and books—heaps and piles and shelves full of books. Off this was a room with bunk beds in which, Andrea imagined, the two Davids dreamed in tandem. Douglas slept opposite in a tiny cubicle which was once, he explained rather proudly, the accommodation of a young gentleman's valet.

He poured Hearty Burgundy into thick glasses. Then he sat beside her and described a paper he was writing on Ezra Pound, who Andrea gathered was a poet. Douglas's erudition seemed breathlessly vast. He had obviously read so much, pondered such recondite subjects, that her own puny thoughts paled in comparison.

When he kissed her she felt flattered that he wanted to. She happily kissed him back. But he drew back and frowned.

"You don't kiss the right way," he declared.

"I don't?" she said, astonished. She had never imagined there was a technique to it, like fingering on a piano or skating backward.

"You shouldn't press your mouth against mine," he said. "Suck in with your lips. Like this."

She concentrated on doing as he showed her. But was there more? Should she be moving her head differently or doing something with her tongue? Suddenly she felt terribly deficient. Certainly kissing the right way was one thing that should come naturally. And as she worried about that, she realized something else—his hand was smoothing its way down her back, heading inexorably for her buttocks. If it reached her backside, if he touched her there, he was sure to feel a telltale bulge. Then he would know her most consummate shame—that she was wearing a sanitary napkin.

She sprang, with a cry, to her feet.

"The bus," she said quickly, as he stared at her in alarm. "I mustn't miss the bus."

HE CALLED THE following week and invited her to the Cornell game. Andrea signed out for her first overnight. Early Saturday morning she crammed into an Avis sedan with five other girls and hurtled down Route 90. Douglas met her in front of Woolsey Hall and hustled her off to a party in someone's room. There was a viscous green punch that tasted like melted lollipops but, after half a glass, made her tipsy. Then they joined the river of students that flowed toward the Bowl where they cheered through a Yale victory. The alma mater swelled up from the alumni seats: "For God, for country, and for Yale . . ." as everyone waved white handkerchiefs in slow unison. Andrea shivered happily.

"Like it?" Douglas asked.

"It's wonderful," she said. She looked up at him. He was so smart and kind, so good-looking. At that moment, she thought she loved him.

Dinner in the Saybrook dining hall had a Mexican theme. Then another smoky-room party until curfew when all women had to leave the dorms. Douglas brought her to her room in the New Haven Motor Court. They caught the last half of *Spellbound* on television, cuddling and kissing—Andrea sucking in furiously—during the commercial breaks.

Spellbound came to an end. The credits for the Nightowl Movie began to roll, and still Douglas gave no sign of leaving. Andrea yawned pointedly.

"Tired?" he asked.

She nodded. "I'm exhausted."

"Lie down then." He got up and flicked off the set, and gratefully, Andrea sank back on the pillows. But instead of putting on his coat, Douglas tumbled down beside her. "This is much better," he murmured.

He began kissing her again, this time in earnest, all tongue and hands and knees trying to pry apart her legs. She blocked him as best she could. They wrestled for what seemed hours, neither of them saying a word. Andrea didn't know what to do. She couldn't demand that he leave since he had paid for the room—he had paid for the entire weekend and probably thought she owed him something at least for that. And how could she make a scene if she had to face spending the entire day with him tomorrow? She tried to conjure up the feeling she had had for him at the stadium—the spark of being in love. But all she felt now was an alarmed distaste.

Gradually the attacks grew weaker and at last stopped. Douglas's deep, even breathing told Andrea he had fallen asleep. With a sigh of relief, she huddled as far as possible on her side of the bed. It was cold, but she didn't dare pull up the spread for fear of waking him and provoking a fresh attack. Nor did she dare climb over him to get to the bathroom.

And so she lay shivering, with a bursting bladder, as the night crept endlessly on. From time to time, she drifted off to sleep, only to be jerked awake again by the stirring of the strange body next to her. At last light seeped in from behind the heavy curtains. Another ice age dragged by; then Douglas stretched and opened his eyes.

He smiled at her. "Good morning. Looks like another sunny day, doesn't it? Did you sleep all right?" Not a word about the silent wrestling match of the night before. Nor did he seem to find it the least strange to awaken fully clothed on a still-made bed. He glanced at his watch. "Christ, it's nearly ten-thirty. We'll have to hurry if we want to make brunch. I'll hop back and change and pick you up in, say, forty-five. Okay?''

It was a blessed relief to be alone again. To relieve her aching bladder and shed her stale, itchy clothes and tumble into a steaming hot shower. She wandered through the rest of the day in a fog and fell soundly asleep in the rental car on the way back to Hadley.

She intended to say no the next time he invited her down. But then she received a letter on blue-bordered Yale stationery: *Andrea, I'm entangled in Virgil's net. Which is to say I'm already quite fond of you, and I like the feeling. . . .* And when he called, he was so positive, completely confident about the plans he had made for them, that she couldn't bring herself to contradict him. She would go, she decided, but she would firmly refuse to let him come back to her room.

But being with him, she found herself even less able to make a stand. He so naturally took charge that they were together again in the motel room before she even realized it. Each time she went to see him, they ended up wrestling— always in total silence—on the bed. And each time, through sheer perseverance, he got a little further. First undoing her bra, then his mouth on her nipple, and finally the shock of his touch between her thighs—the private place she never even touched herself.

It made her feel dirty, disgraced. She was certain that Our Father in Heaven—the portly, balding man with the querulous frown—was watching with grim displeasure through his black-rimmed glasses. None of the dirty things she was doing escaped his gaze. Douglas would only scoff at her if she told him this. He constantly put down religion and churchgoers; he thought it hilarious that one of his roommates used a crucifix as a swizzle stick. They were so sure of themselves, Douglas and his friends, and they had such potent ammunition—Hegel, Nietzsche, Jean-Paul Sartre. She didn't dare let him know that on Sundays when she wasn't with him she still slunk meekly into chapel.

SHE RETURNED TO St. Louis for spring break. Her room had a barren, aired-out look, as if she hadn't really been expected. Her scrapbooks, bulging with snapshots and programs, all the memory-laden detritus of her years at St. Elizabeth's, had been boxed and consigned to the basement. And her vast family of dolls had disappeared. "They were just gathering dust," her mother said. "I threw away the broken ones and gave the rest to the foster child fund."

Poor Raggy with her missing button eye, and one-armed little Alice, and Darlene, the baby doll, with her torn legs. . . . Andrea, for the moment, felt as broken-hearted as if they had been real children. She spent the rest of the break running errands for her mother, whose arthritis was much worse, and avoiding her mother's bedroom with its silver-framed picture of her father.

"I HAVE A surprise for you," Douglas said. It was the third week in April; a scent of damp crushed grass rose from the courtyards of Yale. "You don't have to stay in that dreadful motel this weekend. I'm putting you up in my room."

"But that's against the rules," Andrea said. "Won't we get in trouble?"

"Not if we're cagey about it." The social rules at Yale were breaking down, he explained to her. The students were fed up with the school trying to act *in loco parentis*—if they were old enough to be drafted into an illegal and murderous war, they should be old enough to run their own lives.

But until the rules were actually done away with they had to be careful. And so Andrea had to tiptoe like a cat burglar up the winding stairwell, so that the proctor wouldn't hear her. In the room, she had to speak in a muffled voice, and when she laughed too loud, Douglas and his roommates hissed "shhh" at her in a chorus.

Sometime after midnight, Douglas took her hand and led her into his cubbyhole of a room. "Sleep tight, you two," said one of the Davids, and Andrea flushed. Of course, they must have realized by his absence that Douglas had been spending the night with her. But it still felt strange to be so obvious.

She lay down on the lumpy single bed. Without preliminaries, Douglas pulled off her clothes. By now she had grown accustomed to lying naked with him beneath the sheets and to letting his hands roam freely over her body. When he did this, he would rub himself against the mattress, then stiffen and shudder and soon after fall asleep.

But this bed was so narrow that he was sprawled half on top of her. She could feel his erection against her leg. His hand burrowed in her crotch. She wriggled, trying to maneuver herself out from under him. And then she gave a gasp. There was a sharp stab of pain in a place she had never felt before—a place both inside and outside of her. When she moved again, the pain grew deeper. It was his finger, she realized—it had located that secret entrance that she had once tried and failed to find. She felt an overwhelming sense of violation. An invasion of everything that was private. Stop it! she wanted to scream. Leave me alone!

But she couldn't. Not with his roommates scarcely five feet away. Through the thin door she could hear them arguing about structuralism and Claude Lévi-Strauss. She would rather die than let them know what was going on.

Douglas was squarely on top of her now, nearly smothering her with his large body. She bit her lip as the pain grew suddenly stronger. It was as if he were trying to force three fingers at once into her, or even his fist. It was too much, she thought in a panic. He was going to rip her. But then he suddenly pulled away from her and stiffened and shuddered, and she realized with shock that it wasn't his fist, it had been his thing. This was it, everything, going all the way. And it had all happened because she was too embarrassed to make a fuss.

Douglas opened his eyes and smiled. "Congratulations," he said. "I now consider you a real woman."

FROM TIME TO TIME, THE BROWN PERSON STILL STARED out at Kate from the mirror. These were the days when her hair seemed to hang in limp strands, when her eyes disappeared and her complexion took on the sallow pallor of a shut-in. On such days, Kate hid within her baggy red gymsuit and slunk around campus avoiding anyone she knew.

But that happened infrequently now. Most of the time she was the new Kate, pretty and confident, and slightly outrageous. She was known for flouting the creaky traditions of "gracious living" Hadley was steeped in. At Friday afternoon tea, she sprawled on the floor with her demitasse cup, ignoring the urgent signals of distress the genteel, German-born housemother sent her. She crept into Wednesday morning assemblies wearing nothing but a sweater pulled over her nightgown and walked out conspicuously during the faculty "clap-out" to go back to bed. By the end of her first six weeks, most of the freshmen on campus knew her name.

But it was by her new success with men that she measured

her real popularity. Suddenly she found herself in great demand. Boys called who had seen her picture in the freshman directory. Cars full of boys on road trips from Williams or Dartmouth or Yale pursued her through the quad. She was rushed at mixers and fraternity parties. When the phone on Kate's floor rang in long rings, meaning an off-campus call, more often than not it was for her.

She began to date furiously and with a happy pity for the girls left behind. Poor things, left for another evening of bridge, or knitting, or grinding at the library. It was clearly so much better, Kate thought, to be in the company of men. There was a moreness about them. Their rooms, smelling of dirty socks and spilled wine, teemed with treasures: books she had never heard of before by Aldous Huxley and Richard Farina and Hermann Hesse; psychedelic posters that sprang alive under a black light. From her dates she learned about Marvel Comics and Day-Glo paint and Ho Chi Minh. And drugs of course. The vocabulary of drugs rolled off their tongues like the argot of some outlandish civilization: Grass. Dope. Weed. Take a hit. Man, did I get stoned. . . .

To Kate it was all new, all charged with a glancing, brilliant excitement. Each new masculine voice on the phone, each new "caller" who presented himself at the watch desk pushed the Brown Person further back into the invisible recesses of the mirror.

She had a shock when she received her first-semester grades: two D's, one C, and a B−. It was true that she had cut classes like mad and until reading week had rarely even touched a book—but then she had seldom studied in high school either and always had straight A's. Worse, Andrea had made dean's list with a 3.2 average. "You know what a grind I am," Andrea had said apologetically. Which was true—she never even cut a class. But still Kate was shaken.

She began her second semester with the firm resolve to study more. But as the weather softened into spring, her resolve weakened. By the end of March, Kate could hardly concentrate at all; after fifteen minutes in the somber reading hall of the library, she would feel a compulsion to propel herself into the sun and the stirring, fragrant air. There was an ache deep inside her, a yearning that she couldn't satisfy. She began to date again, even more than before.

And then it happened. She fell blindingly, crushingly in love.

His name was Keith Farmer. He went to Minton College, a small men's college six miles from Hadley, which was considered Hadley's brother school. Kate met him at a touch football game on the Minton green. From her first look, she could tell he was cool, someone to be seen with. He was tall and rangy and almost spooky-pale; his soft brown hair hung to his shoulders, and he wore a battered old slouched hat with perfect authority. Halfway through the game, Kate began to regret that he was on her team—she wanted an excuse to touch him.

Afterward, when all the players gathered in the tap room of one of the fraternities, she mustered all her courage to approach him.

"Could I have a cigarette?" she asked.

"Sure." He gave her a Marlboro (Why did all the most attractive men seem to smoke Marlboros? she wondered.) and lit it for her. "You got tackled pretty hard in the last play, didn't you?" she said.

"Yeah." He hunched and kneaded his shoulder. "I think this baby's going to be sore tomorrow."

"If you need a remedy, I give a pretty good massage," she said. Her boldness both astonished and alarmed her.

He grinned. "Old family secret?"

"Yeah, passed down from generations." She was relieved that he had taken it as a joke—that he hadn't been completely turned off by her aggressiveness.

They talked about the game and Dylan ("Positively 4th Street" was playing on the jukebox), and for some reason the poetry of William Blake which neither of them had actually read. Keith seemed amused by the conversation, but also somewhat detached—his manner suggested that being with her was fine but if she went away, that would be all right too. She really didn't believe him when he said he would call.

But he did and invited her to a production of *The Hairy Ape* given by the Minton Maskers. She found him as attractive and as elusive as before. Each time she saw him, she wondered if she ever would again. And each time she fell deeper in love. Everything about him drove her wild—his slouch, the patched knees of his Levi's, the way he held a cigarette between his thumb and forefinger. Playing lacrosse and being from South Dakota and majoring in anthropology took on glamour simply because they were attributes of Keith. She was convinced that he was the most desirable boy around. She was sure every girl who saw him must want him. Keith . . . even his name was perfect. *I love Keith*, she whispered to herself a hundred times a day.

But he continued to have that slight air of detachment. Only when he was kissing her did he seem as completely absorbed as she was in him. Then his entire being centered upon hers. He belonged to her and she wanted it to go on forever. But then curfew would loom and they would race back to her dormitory, with Kate once more uncertain as to whether she would ever hear from him again.

The semester was drawing to a close.

One Saturday night, they sat among a group in Keith's fraternity house gathered around a bubbling hash pipe. As

Keith put the black tube to his lips, Kate leaned toward him. "I signed out for an overnight," she whispered.

"You want to stay over?" His voice was hoarse with the effort of holding in the smoke.

"If you want me to."

"Sure." He grinned, exhaling, and passed the tube to her.

She drew in and the smoke welled large in her lungs, infusing the room with new texture and color. The music seemed to originate in her own brain: *Do you believe in magic*? She did—an entire night with Keith all to herself stretched out before her.

One by one, and in couples, the others drifted away. And then she was following Keith to his room on another floor. It was a room choked with dust and so littered that a dropped sock could be lost for weeks. The sheets on his bed were sour and indelibly creased and he had painted the windows black. To Kate, it shimmered with glamour. If only she could burrow into the rest of his life the way she now burrowed into his musty army-navy blanket.

She fit eagerly into his arms. She was feeding on his mouth, her hands worshiped his thin shoulders and back. But when he began to pull at the button fly of her pants, she shrank away.

"What's wrong?" he asked.

"I'm not sure if I'm ready yet," she said shyly.

"Don't be afraid. Just let yourself go with it."

"I know. But I've never done this before."

"Trust me," he said. "It'll be okay."

Of course she would trust him. He was *Keith*.

The sensation of yielding her nakedness to him was exquisite. The feel of his skin against hers, the welcome weight of his hard body, the sweep of his soft hair against her cheek, were all luxurious beyond compare. But in his urgency to be inside of her he hurt her. The pain was so startling she gasped. And then just when she began to feel another sensation—something faint but distinct and thrilling—he collapsed, damp and limp, on top of her. She held him, wishing she could lie like this forever. He was totally hers. Nothing else seemed to matter.

His strength returned, and he lifted himself. He shook his hair and grinned. "Hey. Are you okay?"

"Wonderful," she said softly. She wanted to blurt out: *I love you. Oh, how I love you!* But somehow she knew this would be a terrible mistake. "There's some blood on the sheets," she said instead. "Maybe we should change them."

"Forget it. I'll chuck them out in the morning." He was already drifting off to sleep.

Kate awoke with the first light. It was wonderful to find herself in Keith's bed, to watch him sleeping gently at her shoulder. She didn't want to waste such precious moments in sleep. But then a terrible thought struck her: she must look repulsive. When Keith awoke he would see her blotchy face and smeared mascara and her hair a ratty bird's nest and be completely grossed out.

Gingerly, she got out of bed, pulled on her pants and shirt, and crept down the hall to the bathroom. When she pushed open the door, she gave a start. She was not alone. Another girl stood at one of the sinks pulling the hood of a hair dryer over her wet head. "Come on in," she said. "Don't worry, none of the guys will be up for hours yet."

"I see you've got the same idea I had," Kate said.

The girl turned on the dryer. "If you think we want them to know what we *really* look like," she said over the roar, "you must be crazy."

KATE SPENT TWO more magical Saturday nights in Keith's bed. Each Wednesday he would call and ask the same question: "Are you busy this Saturday night?" She was bewildered. *He* was the one she was sleeping with. How could he even imagine she would make other plans?

And then she was swept up in the exigencies of reading week, trying to cram a semester's worth of study into the week before exams. She finished the year with more dismal grades, including a glaring F in geology. But this seemed insignificant beside the fact that she now faced an entire summer away from Keith. Fourteen long weeks without him.

She returned home. Through the windows of the train, she saw the familiar spirit-crushing tangle of asphalt and blank boxes. East Pine Grove seemed to have grown shabbier over the past year. The houses cried out for paint, the sidewalks were cracked and scarred with the ghosts of abandoned potsy games. And there was her father, waiting in the car, a copy of the *Daily News* propped against the steering wheel. And her mother stood on the platform, waving and skipping up and down: her hair stood straight up from her head, and her white sweater was buttoned askew over baggy polyester pants.

During the ride home, her mother kept up a running monologue. ". . . Ralph Hicks came into the P.O. the other day. Remember you had him for geometry in the tenth grade? He said you were very bright but never wanted to raise your hand and be called on. Oh, and Mrs. Dellasandro wants to know if you'll be available to babysit. She just had her *seventh*, can you beat that? I told her you had a job lined up, but maybe Saturday nights if you want to earn some extra money. . . ."

Kate sighed. Nothing had changed. Here she would always be the same old Kate—the weird, gawky Brown Person who had nothing to do on Saturday night. She concentrated on Keith. His silky hair on the pillow. That was her reality, not this.

She had a job as a receptionist at a dental clinic, which she hated. There were long hours with nothing to do. She flipped through *Newsweek*, staring at colored spreads of kids her own age in places like Haight-Ashbury and the East Village, painting their bodies, wearing feathers and bells and playing music in the streets. She felt the world was passing her by. Only thinking about Keith made being marooned in East Pine Grove bearable.

She spent the entire Fourth of July weekend composing a letter to him. She labored to make it sound as if she was having an amusing, event-packed summer, but wanted him to know she still thought of him. She hesitated an entire day before signing it "love" and dropping it in the mailbox, then checked every day for a reply. She received a postcard of a Florentine madonna from Andrea who was touring Italy with some sort of youth group and a letter from Marcie Kingman complaining bitterly about being stuck in "this shitty asshole of the universe, Kalamazoo." But nothing arrived from South Dakota. He probably hates writing letters, Kate told herself. All men do. They never got into the habit.

The summer rolled blankly on, tumbling at last into a blustery Labor Day. Kate bid a happy goodbye to the dental clinic. She stopped for the last time at the A&P to pick up some items for one of her mother's haphazard dinners. As she wandered up an aisle looking for pickle relish, she noticed a hugely pregnant woman pushing a cart at the other end. A little boy about a year old sat in the kiddy seat. He reached for a bright pink cereal carton.

"I want," he cried.

"No, Jeffrey," his mother said.

"Want." He reached again and knocked it off the shelf. "I said *no*," his mother snapped and slapped his hand. He began to bawl. "Shut up, Jeffrey," she yelled. "You cut that racket out or I'll smack you good, goddamn it!"

The voice echoed down to Kate from one of the long, wistful afternoons of the past. It was Terry. But, oh, how she had changed. She looked fifteen years older, her hair in a frazzled knot and her swollen body encased in a stained gray tent. But it was her face that was the most altered. It wore a look of bitter congealment, a look that said she was finished. Her life was set as if in an aspic. She would never escape. Not now.

Kate felt a dry chill as she watched Terry lumber away, still muttering threats at her wailing child. At home that evening her mother sprang a surprise: she and Kate's father planned to retire at Christmas. They were busy finalizing plans to resettle in a condominium community in South Carolina. Pammy had been accepted by a nursing college and would leave the following week. One of the twins had married a serviceman and gone to live with him in Oklahoma; the other taught second grade upstate. Kate would have no more reason to return to East Pine Grove.

AS SOPHOMORES, KATE and Andrea were entitled to a larger, airier room on the fourth floor of their house. From the ceiling, Andrea looped the green fish net she had purchased in Boston. Kate covered the walls with posters—Sgt. Pepper, *Avant Garde* magazine, a mind-blowing drawing by M. C. Escher. They completed the décor with the red curtains and madras bedspreads recycled from the year before.

Kate settled in and waited eagerly for Keith to call. Minton College began its term a week later than Hadley; it was another full week before she heard from him. When she saw him, she thought she would choke with love. He had grown a mustache—a dear, sparse little one that looked as if it had been penciled in—and now parted his hair in the middle like an Indian brave. She tried to read his feelings. He seemed happy to see her, but from the animated way he

talked about the raft trip he had been on, it didn't sound as if
he had missed her much. But when at last they were alone
together in his room, he made love to her so intently that all
her doubts disappeared. "Jesus, you're beautiful!" he murmured as his body covered hers. She clasped her arms
around him triumphantly. He belonged to her. How could
she have ever thought otherwise?

Spinning, dizzy love. She floated through the following
days, exulting in the brilliance of the New England autumn
as if it were a projection of her own feelings. Nothing could
lessen her euphoria—not even a message from the dean's office informing her that she had been placed on academic
probation. Who cares? she told herself. Everybody knew
that grades were obsolete. They just fostered useless competition in courses that had no relevance anyway. Tudor kings,
eighteenth-century symbolism . . . what did any of that
matter? The important thing was *now*, to live in the moment.
And her moment was Keith.

Wednesday slipped away without the expected call from
him. By Friday, Kate began to worry. By the following
week, she was frantic. She clung to her room afraid to go out
for fear that she might miss his call. Her ears strained constantly for the phone. When it rang, her heart stopped.
When her name was called she raced to answer it. But it was
always another voice on the line. She was brutally abrupt to
those unfortunate callers who had the presumption not to be
Keith. She hated all other men.

Andrea tried to console her with possible explanations.
"There's a lot of things that might've happened," she said.
"Maybe he's got a bad cold and doesn't want to give it to
you. Or maybe his parents are here, and he's been with them
the whole time."

After two weeks, Kate could stand it no more. She
dressed carefully, brushed her hair until it gleamed, and

tucked a notebook under her arm. She caught the intercampus bus to Minton. As she crossed the green to Keith's fraternity house, several boys glared at her. During the week, a female on the Minton campus was an invader. They resented her bald intrusion into the sanctity of their all-male haven.

Keith was in his room. With him was his friend Reg whom Kate had met several times. The new Cream album was on and the pungent scent of incense didn't quite disguise the odor of marijuana.

Both boys looked startled to see her. "Hi," Kate said tremulously.

"Hi, Kate. How's it going?" Reg said. His eyes sidled nervously toward Keith, and he stood up. "Well, man, I'm starved. Think I'll head down for some eats."

"Catch you later, man," Keith said.

When Reg had gone, Kate went over and kissed Keith's forehead. He remained immobile. "What are you doing here?" he asked.

"I came over to use the library. I've got this paper due on, um, modern dance. . . ."

"And we've got this heavy dance department?" he said caustically.

God, of all things she could've picked, what a dumb thing to say. "I mean the history of it," she said quickly, "and your library's got a couple of books ours doesn't." She was so nervous she thought her knees would give way. If only his face wasn't so completely expressionless. "Anyway, I just thought I'd drop by and say hi." She forced a grin. "How've you been?"

He shrugged. "Pretty busy. I've been booking like shit. Some of these courses I'm taking this semester are a real bitch."

"In anthropology, you mean?"

"Nah, that's a gut. It's some other stuff I need to graduate."

"Oh." In the pause between them, Eric Clapton sang "I'm So Glad." "Well," Kate said finally, "I just thought I'd see how you are."

"I'm cool."

"Good. Well I guess I'd better get back." He didn't contradict her. She began to panic. "Listen, Keith," she blurted out, "if there's anything I can help you with . . . I mean, I've got a really light schedule this semester, so if you need any papers typed or anything, just let me know."

"Yeah. Sure."

"See you, then."

"Yeah, see you."

She turned and fled. She didn't wait for the bus but thumbed a ride with a farmer in a rattling flatbed truck, squeezing back her tears until he had dropped her at the gates of the quad. Then they came bursting out with violence. She ran past the startled freshman at the watch desk and up to her room where she cried in loud, wrenching sobs, not caring who heard her. How could she have done it? Gone chasing after him, made such a fool of herself and then practically groveled at his feet. . . . Over and over, the scene played in her head. *A paper in modern dance. I could do some typing for you.*

She heard the door open and gratefully raised her blurred face from the pillow—she needed some of Andrea's mothering right now.

But to her dismay it was Jean Ferguson standing beside her. She proffered a half-full bottle of Cutty Sark. "I heard you were upset and thought you could use this," she said.

Kate rose above her misery long enough to enjoy a flourish of contempt. Most of the upperclassmen still kept a bottle of whiskey or vodka stashed in their closets, a vestige of the days when sneaking a drink was regarded as a daring act of insubordination. But nobody really drank anymore—at least not the hard stuff. Liquor was the Establishment's balm, for Dow Chemical executives to get blitzed after a hard day napalming babies, for the gray-flannel-suit brigade to endure their alienated days. Smoking grass with its gentle and communal high was the infinitely cooler thing to do.

"Thanks, Jean," she said haughtily, "but I don't do that stuff anymore."

"Make an exception. That's what a man would do, go on a good, stiff bender and get it all out of his system."

"I'm not a man."

"No reason you can't act like one if it'll do you some good."

It was hopeless, Kate thought. She would never understand. "Look, Jean," she said, "I'm really feeling rotten, and I don't think getting drunk is going to do any good."

"Then what will?" Jean pursued.

"Nothing. I'm just going to have to go through it. It's my own fault anyway. I went chasing after somebody, so it serves me right I got hurt."

"Men chase after girls all the time without anyone saying it serves them right."

"That's different."

"*Why* is it different?"

"It just is," Kate insisted.

Jean sighed. "If you're so intent on being miserable I guess there's nothing to be done about it. I'll leave this here anyway." She set the bottle on a dresser. "In case you change your mind."

Kate watched her leave. For a moment indignation edged out all other emotion: Who the hell did Jean think she was?

Didn't she know what it was like? Hadn't she ever been in love?

But then she dropped her face back onto the pillow and forgot Jean, forgot everything but the seamless, crushing weight of her own misery.

*A*NDREA BALANCED A PLATE OF BUTTERED RYE TOAST and a cup of coffee—extra light with one heaping teaspoon of brown sugar—up the three flights of stairs to her room. She set it beside Kate who lay listlessly in bed. This had become a ritual: each morning Andrea brought an offering designed to tempt Kate out of bed in time for her nine o'clock class.

Kate took a sip of coffee.

"How is it?" Andrea asked anxiously.

"It tastes like black," Kate said.

"Not enough milk?"

"No. I mean it tastes like ashes or soot or something. Black. Dead black. Everything does. Everything looks and feels black. I wish I never had to wake up again."

"Don't say that," Andrea begged. "It'll get better. You'll go out and meet someone else . . ."

"Not like Keith," Kate said. "I'll never find anyone as great as Keith. You never really met him so you don't know. But he was so gorgeous and smart and *every*thing. I mean,

67

he was incredible." She sank back and stared up at the ceiling. "I'm tired. I think I'll cut botany lab today."

"Oh, no," Andrea said firmly. "Lab attendance is required, and you've already cut it twice."

"Who cares?"

"You've got to care. If you don't pass your science requirement this year, they're going to . . ." She stopped. She had been about to say "cancel your scholarship" but remembered how Kate hated being reminded that she had financial aid. She said instead, "They might think about kicking you out of school."

"Oh, shit!" Kate attacked the coffee again and took a bite of toast. "I shouldn't have slept with him," she said. "I should've held out. If I had, I don't think he would have dumped me."

Andrea glanced away. The day before, Kate had confided that she had gone to bed with Keith. Andrea still did not know how to respond. "You did what you felt was right," she mumbled.

"It did feel right," Kate admitted. "God, nothing in my life ever felt more right. That's what's so weird. If it was so great, why am I so sorry I did it? Why does it seem like such a mistake?" She picked up the toast again, but set it down untasted. "You've never been to bed with Douglas, have you?"

"No," Andrea said quickly.

"I didn't think so." Kate swung her legs over the side of the bed. "Oh, God!" she said. "How the hell am I ever going to concentrate on a bunch of *plants*?"

Andrea watched her drag out to the bathroom. She felt tainted by her own hypocrisy. Kate had confided in her; why had she felt compelled to lie in return?

But she still couldn't bear to let anyone know she wasn't a virgin. She kept her circlet of dusky pink pills hidden deep in her underwear drawer and swallowed one daily in furtive secrecy. As if she were doing something illegal.

She had dutifully begun on the pill after that first time last April. "I pulled out in time, but just barely," Douglas had said. "You better get a prescription for the pill." It was more an order than a suggestion. She was relieved to discover how easy it was to obtain them. She made an appointment with the most expensive gynecologist in town (he was booked three and a half weeks in advance) and he had scribbled out a prescription right in his office with no third degree at all. She hadn't even needed an examination.

But she was dismayed by the pills' effects, that no one had ever told her about. For one thing, the first day of her period became immensely painful, like a hammer slamming away from inside her lower belly. Worse, her breasts had become larger. In fact, her entire body had acquired a new layer of padding beneath the skin, like the insulating layer in a ski vest, so that she was even more voluptuous than before. And it sometimes seemed that the entire world was responding to her body with a leer. In Italy during the summer she had been pinched and followed wherever she went. In Ravenna, a hoary old man had brushed up against her breasts and croaked: "Lotsa milk, eh?" In Rome, the young men on their Vespas made obscene kissing sounds at her, as if calling their dog or cat, and made the equally obscene gesture of raising a hand and rubbing their thumb against the other fingers. It had made her want to run and hide with shame.

Coming home, she had found little relief. Suddenly it seemed that all anyone talked about was sex. "Let it all hang out"—that's what everyone was saying. Now she was supposed to take it as a compliment when a boy she had never seen told Douglas: "Your girlfriend's got great tits." Or, when dancing with another boy, he leaned toward her and said: "From the way you move your body I can tell you would be great in bed."

The ridiculous part of it all was that she wasn't great in bed. She wasn't anything in bed. She simply lay still while Douglas charged after his own climax. And afterward he'd crow and congratulate himself and she let him believe he had set off all sorts of sensory fireworks in her as well. But all she felt was a dull craving that lingered after he had fallen swiftly to sleep. She had discovered that Douglas wasn't all-knowledgeable about sex. And in other ways her foundation of awe for him had begun to crack. She had begun to catch him in little mistakes and instances of slopping thinking. Like the paper on Wallace Stevens that he had read to her last week. It seemed to her that he had missed a lot of what "The Emperor of Ice Cream" was about—its symbolism of transience, the melting property of the moment. . . . And yet she didn't challenge him. She knew how easily he could twist her opinions to make them seem "jejune" (a favorite word of his) or uninformed. And anyway, a man's ego had to be protected. Wasn't it her duty to preserve him from self-doubt?

Someone in the hall yelled, "Man on the floor!" Andrea gave a start. She still wasn't used to the fact that men were now allowed upstairs during the day: she lived in fear that she might go barging into the hall one day in her bra and panties and run smack into someone's date. Things were changing so fast. Almost every week another rule was swept away, another century-old tradition abolished. It was strange not to have to wear a skirt to dinner anymore or go to assembly on Wednesday morning. Suddenly there were no more curfews, no more limits on the number of overnights they were allowed—which meant she no longer had an excuse not to visit Douglas every weekend.

The thought caught her cold. Why should she want to

avoid seeing Douglas? He was the man she was going to marry. Whose children she was going to bear. She would be seeing him for the rest of her life. . . .

Her thoughts were interrupted by Kate stomping back into the room. "That jerk Laurie Cole, bringing a guy up at the crack of dawn! You can't even have any *priv*acy anymore." Still muttering, she pulled on a pair of jeans that hadn't been washed in weeks and a ratty black sweater and left, late but better than never, for the lab.

Andrea collected her books. She had no class till eleven, but she could use the time in the library. She remembered she had borrowed Jean Ferguson's notes from the gov lecture she had missed with that sore throat last week. She would drop them off on the way.

Jean's writing had been a surprise, she recalled, as she picked up the red spiral notebook. A back-slanted left-handed scrawl that had been almost illegible. Who would ever connect it with Jean who was so ordered and breathtakingly legible in everything else she did?

She found Jean typing at her desk. "I brought your notes back," she said and handed her the notebook.

"Thanks. Did you have any trouble with them?"

"Not much," Andrea fudged.

Jean suddenly handed the book back. "Why don't you keep them? I won't be needing them anymore."

"Are you dropping the course?"

"Not just the course." Jean gave a grin. "You're the first to know. I've decided to quit school."

Andrea stared at her.

"Don't look so shocked," Jean said, laughing. "It's something I've been thinking about for a long time."

"But you can't," Andrea gasped.

"Why not?"

"Because . . . well, because you're president of rec

council and house treasurer, and you're taking honors.
There's too much for you here.''

"It's not enough.'' Jean reached out and touched her arm.
"Andrea, believe me. I know what I'm doing. And I hope
you'll have enough faith in me to think so too.''

Andrea felt chastised. She was being selfish, thinking not
of Jean but of herself, because for one moment she had
drifted back to an empty dancing school, where she waited
long after the other children had been taken home the day
her mother had simply forgotten she was there. Stupid. No
one was abandoning her now. She looked at Jean with her
grave, heart-shaped face and black slash of bangs. Jean was
her loyal and affectionate friend: nothing was going to
change.

"I think whatever you do will be terrific,'' she said.

JEAN HAD COME TO HADLEY WITH THE HIGHEST EXPECTA-
tions. She imagined it would be full of girls like herself,
girls eager to discover the mechanisms that made the world
run. Without boys around to hog all the glory, she would for
the first time have a real chance to excel.

But she was quickly disillusioned. Her classmates exasper-
ated her. Too many of them earned high grades because they
had been taught that good girls study hard—not because they
had any driving desire to learn or excel. They were well-
mannered girls brought up not to make waves. Jean found it almost laughably easy to take charge. "We'll do it this way,"
she would say firmly, and seldom was she challenged.

And even here, men seemed to rule by proxy. She
watched with disgust the way engaged seniors flaunted their
diamond rings, as if they were decorations from some
bloody-fought battle. And those that were about to graduate
with naked ring fingers had an air of frantic desperation. "I
wasted four whole years!" one lamented at breakfast one

morning, and, though it was intended as a joke, her laugh did not quite ring true.

Jean resented too the way Hadley revolved around the weekend trip. She saw little reason to interrupt her life, to pack and travel God knows how long, just to see some boy she hardly knew. Besides, she had been dating college men since her junior year in high school, and by now found them only minimally interesting. Too many of them were becoming less like her father and more like her brother Denny, eager to toss away the very privileges of their sex that Jean most admired. Love and flowers and rock-and-roll: all that only bored her. And when they fumbled for her skirt zipper or the clasp of her bra, her impulse was to push them away. Not that she was worried about what her mother delicately termed "giving in." After all, Nietzsche had said there was a morality of masters and a morality of slaves. But when she did have sex, she wanted it to be with a man—not a fumbling, tentative boy.

By the beginning of her junior year she had become restless. She was elected president of the recreation council and threw herself into a new project: a week-long arts festival intended to surpass anything the college had ever done before. She worked in a fury, contacting printmakers and madrigal singers, mime troops, jazz trumpeters, Off-Broadway playwrights, cajoling them into taking part for free. She courted the dean's office for more expense money, recruited volunteers, plastered the campus with posters. It was a resounding success: the local paper awarded front-page coverage, and the campus buzzed with talk of it for a month afterward.

But when it was over, she felt flat, more bored than before. It had been, after all, just a collegiate event; what had truly excited her was the brush with the *real* world—artists and agents, people making real things happen. She had become more curious than ever about the way the world was run: how lights went on and paper found its way into note-books and riotously colored pictures came to decorate the cartons of breakfast foods—not the physical process of such things, but the systems that made them happen. As she sat in her austere little room finishing a paper on Toynbee, re-viewing her notes for a "written" on Chaucer, her frustra-tion grew immeasurably. These people are dead! she wanted to scream. This is the past, and I'm alive here, right now, in the present! And more than ever she was eager to become one of those who set the world's wheels in motion.

She flew home for Thanksgiving. While she was growing up, this had been a torpid holiday, one to suffer through stoi-cally. But the tension between her father and Denny had fi-nally exploded into warfare; now dinner was the scene of long, bitter shouting matches over Vietnam and the draft, the length of Denny's hair, and his refusal to go to Prince-ton, which he had pronounced elitist and decadent.

On Sunday night, after Denny had flown back to Antioch, she approached her father in his study. "Dad?" she said. "I've been thinking of dropping out of school."

"What the sweet Christ are you talking about?" he bel-lowed.

"I feel like I'm just treading water there. I want to be out *do*ing something."

Her father hitched up the sleeve of his shirt as if preparing to make a fist. But instead he pointed the remote control at the television, and the picture swirled off. "What kind of crap is that? I've been shelling out thirty-five hundred bucks plus a year to send you to that goddamned school."

"That's just the point," she said quickly. "I don't think you're getting your money's worth. I feel I've gotten all I can out of the school."

"What you're *supposed* to get out of it is a goddamned diploma.'' A vein bulged on his temple, a ridge of mottled, pulsing skin. Jean stared at it intently.

"What do I need a diploma for?" she said. "Even if I graduate magna, or even summa, it won't do me much good. I don't want to be an academic, molding away the next ten years in grad school."

"Then what the devil's hell *do* you plan to do? I don't see a ring on your finger, kiddo."

Jean's eyes flashed dark with anger. "That's not fair! You're always telling Denny not to get married too soon. 'You'll just be saddled, saddled, saddled,' that's what you're always telling him."

"It's different for a man, for Pete's sake."

"Why are people always saying it's different for a man?"

"Because it is, that's why," her father said. "A man's got a career to establish first."

"But I do too. I want to go into business."

"Jesus Christ! What the hell do you know about business?"

"Nothing," she said. It was true. It had always been Denny who had been taken to the factory, allowed to work the machines and ride with the men in the forklifts. "I was hoping you'd teach me about it."

"This is ridiculous," he said.

"Why? I thought you wanted me to be a success."

"You're absolutely right. I want you to be like your mother, the most successful woman I know."

"The hell she is," Jean cried. "She's petty and pathetic, and just because she lets you push her around, you come to her defense."

"Shut your goddamned mouth before I shut it for you."

There was a look of concentrated fury in her father's eyes that she had seen before—the day five years ago he had slammed Denny against a garage door because Denny had dared to contradict him in front of one of his friends. It struck her coldly that her father was quite capable of hurting her. But she did not need his blessing to do what she wanted to do. Her success would eventually prove to him that she had been right.

She turned and walked out of the room.

SHE RETURNED TO Hadley long enough to notify the stunned dean of her class that she was officially withdrawing and to collect her things. With the remnants of a small trust from a dimly remembered grandmother, she bought a '61 Dodge Dart, and Andrea helped her load it. Before setting off, she took a final look around the quad. There was the house in which she had lived for over two years. There was her old black Schwinn still crouched against its kickstand, left for anyone to claim. She was amazed at how little she felt to be leaving. She gave Andrea a hug, slid into the car, and drove off.

Six hours later, she was in Washington, D.C. It seemed to her the logical destination. While she was growing up, Washington had been The City, a magnet that drew people by its culture and commerce. Though Jean had little interest in politics, she liked the idea of a city that erected monuments to power—a city that summoned winners and expelled losers.

For the first few days, she stayed with a second cousin who taught Eastern religion at Georgetown. Then a classified ad led her to a cheap sublet on Columbia Road. It was a characterless, sparsely furnished apartment in a dingy neighborhood, but this scarcely mattered. What was important was that it was a place of her own.

She registered at an agency called Career Expanders whose ads promised in bold type positions for people with "some college." A bored-looking man with a nervous sniffle skimmed her résumé. He appeared singularly unimpressed with her achievements—the concerts and arts festivals she had produced at college, the lifeguard job at camp, and the gymnastics classes she had taught at home—his eyes brightening only at the bottom of the page. "You type eighty-five words a minute. That's very good. Do you have any shorthand?"

"No."

"How about speed-writing?"

"Well, I had a system of taking notes at lectures. . . ."

"We'll say speed-writing then. I think I can arrange an interview for you right away." He made a call and copied some information onto an index card. "This is something very exciting," he said, emphasizing his enthusiasm with an extra sniffle. "It's a job in the glamorous national headquarters of a big corporation, IMI. A personnel woman will see you right away, but you've got to hurry. This one will be snapped up quick."

"YOU'LL WORK IN what we still call the typing pool," said Mrs. Inover of personnel. "Of course, a lot of our typing needs have been eliminated by the Xerox machine. So more often your job will be as a roving secretary—sort of an in-house 'temp' if you will. You'll fill in for any regular gal who is out sick or on vacation. And you'll be on call to any executive who needs extra assistance. After six months, if your work has been satisfactory, you'll be promoted to Secretary I and permanently assigned to one of the lower-level managers. Is that clear?"

Jean nodded. The job was neither glamorous nor exciting. But she liked the looks of IMI. It occupied an entire building of mirrored granite just over the Key Bridge. Its lobby was a vast, elegant gray cave through which footsteps echoed with solemn dignity, and there was a bustling, purposeful air about the people who passed in the corridors. She felt a momentum, a propulsion of energy through space which she gropingly identified as opportunity.

THE TYPING-POOL AREA was dishearteningly ugly: a midsection of the tenth floor marked off by low, maize-colored partitions. It was lit by broad, flat panels of fluorescent bulbs. Half a dozen young women sat beneath the glare, their fingers poised upon IBM electric typewriters of varying vintage.

As Mrs. Pulin, the supervisor, introduced her, Jean made a cursory survey of her new coworkers. Two were overweight with plain, scrubbed faces; the rest wore high hairdos, heavy makeup, and inexpensive and exaggerated versions of the latest styles—minis, velour tunics, knee-high boots of synthetic leather. They seemed to register Jean as merely a brief diversion from the monotony of their workday.

Mrs. Pulin assigned her one of the identical metal desks and her first task—to retype a letter on which corrections had been scribbled by hand. The corrections were scarcely legible, and Jean worked arduously to decipher them. But when she reread her finished work, she discovered she had typed one sentence twice.

"Damn," she muttered, yanking the page from the roller.

The young woman at the neighboring desk glanced over. "Did you mess up?"

Jean nodded ruefully. "I did a sentence twice. I'm going to have to do the whole thing over."

"No you don't. Just white out what you did wrong."

"I can't. That would leave a hole right in the middle of the page."

"So what? They don't expect it to be perfect. Just so's you can read it."

"I want to get it right," Jean said firmly and rolled in a fresh sheet of paper.

"Suit yourself." Her neighbor shrugged. She was one of the miniskirted ones. She wore stiff false eyelashes that fanned oddly above her narrow eyes and a "fall" that was a shade or two lighter than her own dark blond hair. At precisely twelve o'clock, she removed her Dictaphone earplug and leaned again toward Jean. "Want to come with us to lunch? The cafeteria here is a pretty good deal."

Jean had retyped the letter, this time flawlessly, and had not yet been assigned anything else. "Sure," she said. "I'd like to."

"Your name's Jean, right? I'm Marjorie."

Two other women came over, whom Marjorie introduced as Marie and Cecilia. As they made their way to the third-floor cafeteria, Jean learned that the typing pool was split into two factions, each of which despised and avoided the other. Her companions crowed over snaring Jean for their own camp.

They settled with trays at one of the tables. "Tell me about the company," Jean said.

"It sucks," Marie declared. She was a tiny girl with a sharply pointed nose and hair the unlikely color of cante-loupe. "Wait till Pulin really starts in on you. You're new so she's going easy, but watch out. She's like Gestapo. Once you get on her hit list, she never lets off."

"That's not what I mean," Jean said. "I want to know about the company in general. What does it do?"

The three exchanged puzzled glances. "They make a lot of paper stuff," Cecilia said. "And I guess they own companies that do other stuff too."

"Then how is it run?"

"All the big shots are up on eighteen and nineteen," Marjorie said. "But you hardly ever get to see them. Mostly you'll be working for the accountants and sales creeps."

"What happens on the nineteenth floor?" Jean pursued.

Marjorie shrugged. "Who cares? I don't want to run the lousy company. I'm just waiting till I meet the right guy. And when I do, I'll quit so fast it'll make you laugh."

"Speaking of which . . ." Marie cut in, "Miss Bitch Rhoda's got a new boyfriend. I heard her telling Santini that he works in Senator Proxmire's office."

"He's probably just a clerk," Cecilia said hopefully.

"He's probably married," Marjorie added.

"Every guy in the whole damned world is married," Cecilia wailed.

Marjorie flicked her bristling lashes at Jean. "You going with anyone?"

Jean shook her head.

"Well, are you ever in for a shock. There's like four girls here for every guy. And even the married men are really spoiled because they've got so many chicks after them. They can play around all they want. And believe me, they want to plenty."

"If I were you, I'd get used to being single for a while," Cecilia said.

"That's all right," Jean said. "I'm not really interested in getting married."

Three pairs of eyes narrowed suspiciously. "How come?" Marjorie demanded.

"Because I want to work. I won't have much time for a husband and domesticity if I'm out building a career."

"Oh, God, she wants to be like Grabowski!" Marie giggled.

"Who's that?" Jean asked.

"One of the executive secretaries. She calls herself a career girl because she's been working here for about eighty-nine years. But man, if any guy ever asked her, she'd be gone like a shot. You can tell she's frustrated as hell because she crosses and uncrosses her legs all the time.''

All three girls dissolved in giggles. It was no use, Jean realized. Her companions seemed to view life as a limited series of slots into which everything must fit. A woman with a career equals a career girl which equals a Grabowski. It would be futile to try to convince them that her own aspirations lay vastly beyond this. Though indeed Jean herself hardly knew yet where they lay. She felt like a swimmer inching into a cold lake whose opposite shore lay just beyond the horizon. All she needed to do was paddle out a little way to have a clear vision where she was headed.

She turned down all Marjorie's future lunch invitations and ate alone at the counter of a nearby Chock Full O' Nuts. The rival faction of the typing pool—Sue, Carol, and Rhoda—approached her in a delegation, but she rebuffed their overtures as well. All six reacted first with bewilderment, then hostility. She noted with some amusement that resentment of stuck-up Jean Ferguson had at last succeeded in uniting the typing pool.

Fortunately, Jean had begun to rotate, serving various executives on the different floors. She worked for a pot-bellied salesman who stared at her breasts, a garrulous assistant director of promotion, an accountant with a defective hearing aid who asked her to repeat everything she said.

And gradually she acquired knowledge about the company. IMI stood for International Mills, Incorporated. It had originated with a small paper mill in West Virginia; now it had thirty-two divisions and held vast forest lands throughout the South. Recently it had begun to acquire small companies rapidly, many of which had little or nothing to do with the manufacture of paper: a textbook publisher, an airconditioning manufacturer, a bicycle rental chain. This last fact puzzled Jean. It seemed an eccentric quirk in an otherwise remarkably sober organization.

She began to type the executives into two groups. The first she called "lifers": these were middle-aged men with titles such as "district sales coordinator" who had gone as far as they were going to go and were now just marking time until a pension. Lifers quit the office on the dot of five. They were meek and scraping to their superiors and petty ogres to the people below them. They reminded Jean of house dogs, protecting their little patch of yard with fierce-sounding yips and growls, but cringing, tail wagging furiously, when their masters came around.

The second type was the "gunslinger." He was ten years younger than the lifer and obviously on his way up. The lifers were terrified of the gunslinger and with reason: he would kill if necessary to get where he wanted.

It was this last group that Jean admired. On days when she found herself working for a gunslinger, she felt more alive, more totally absorbed than ever before. But such days were rare. More often she was relegated to the plodding, territorial pace of the lifers.

Her life settled into a routine. She had no social life. She icily dismissed the cocky junior clerks who came sniffing around the "new kid's" desk and instead filled her evenings studying shorthand (her college note-taking skills had proved woefully inadequate), reading, or simply walking about her neighborhood.

She had been working at IMI for nearly three months when Mrs. Pulin approached her desk, her face majestic with news. "You're being sent up to the nineteenth floor today," she informed Jean breathlessly. "The senior vice president's secretary is out with a cold and you're to fill in. You'll be working directly with Mr. Dreiser."

Jean smiled. At last she was to receive a glimpse of the Olympian heights.

Mrs. Pulin bent closer to her and lowered her voice conspiratorially. "You're the only one of my girls I would recommend for this job. Your work has been far above average. There's a possibility—a slight possibility—you could skip Secretary I and go directly to Secretary II."

Go directly. Do not pass Go, Jean thought wryly. Mrs. Pulin, like "her" girls, saw the world in terms of slots.

The nineteenth floor was a vastly different world. The carpets of its reception room were lusher, the lighting softer, the furnishings richer than any in the more plebeian floors below. Everything about it spoke of contemplation rather than brute toil, of the requisition and enjoyment of money rather than the making of it.

A haughty receptionist buzzed Jean inside. Another minion led her through several antechambers into a wide corner office. John Dreiser rose from behind a marble-topped walnut desk. "Miss Ferguson. Thank you for coming," he said.

He was in his early to mid fifties, tall, and if his waist had thickened at all with age, the cut of an expensive suit concealed it handsomely. His gray hair was slightly longer—and therefore more youthful—than that of any of the men on the floors below. His eyes, also gray, were intelligent and alert. This, and a posture of wary aggression—shoulders set forward and slightly hunched—belied the domestic plushness of his office.

He was, Jean decided, a gunslinger. One who had taken enormous risks and had seen them pay off in the highest way.

"It's going to be a bit hectic," he said, "so shall we start right away?"

"I'm ready," she said.

"Good. I've a series of meetings beginning at ten, so let's get some letters out of the way first. Do you have your pad?"

This proved the last quiet moment Jean was to have on the job. John Dreiser's office was a maelstrom of activity. Phones rang, visitors arrived and departed, memos snowed upon her desk. She placed calls to the chairman's office, to Tokyo, New Orleans, and Lisbon. She addressed letters to senators and bank presidents, slit open embossed invitations from the Smithsonian, the National Gallery, the Republican National Committee. The pace was exhilarating. Never had she been so eager to get out of bed in the morning nor more reluctant to return to it at night.

And her ambition took a giant step forward. She had revered her father's place in the world. She had imagined that he revolved within a vast sphere of contacts and activity. But now she saw that there were spheres far greater than that, with dimensions the measure of which she was only beginning to realize. John Dreiser had opened her eyes.

Much of the correspondence that passed over her desk had to do with a company called The Homesteader. There were a lot of technical documents that she didn't understand. But she was able to gather that this was a Texas fast-food chain that specialized in fried chicken and ribs. And that Dreiser was keenly interested in having IMI take it over.

On Friday, Dreiser asked her to take a memo to the board of directors. "This will be an outline of the proposed acquisition of The Homesteader, Inc.," he began.

"But why?" Jean blurted out. "I mean, why should a paper company like IMI be interested in a string of fried-chicken stands? It doesn't make sense."

He paused and looked at her. For a moment she felt pinned by the enormous concentration of his stare. She dropped her eyes. "I'm sorry. I didn't mean to interrupt."

"No," he said. "That's a very good question. And I believe I have a good answer."

She glanced up in surprise.

"There's a very fashionable term in business right now. It's called 'synergy.' It means different parts working together to create a bigger whole. What that adds up to is that everybody's scrambling to diversify. Companies are looking to branch out, no longer hitching their wagons to just one star. It's such a strong trend that I believe IMI can't afford to be left out. Are you with me so far?"

Jean nodded eagerly.

"All right, then, why Homesteader? As you say, a bunch of fried-chicken stands? Well, the fastest growing user of our packaging products is the fast-food industry, and my feeling is that it's going to continue to take off. This is a young country, thanks to the baby boom. And these are the foods that young people like to eat." He drew a cigarette from the pack of Camels that was never far from his fingertips. "For the past year I've been looking to tap into this market. Homesteader has good management and a good product. They doubled the number of their Texas franchises in two years. All they're lacking is cash to go national. And cash is what IMI can supply. I think it's a good match.

"So then. Does this reasoning seem sound?"

"Yes," Jean breathed. "Perfectly."

He smiled wryly. "If I can get the board to agree with you, I can start sleeping again at night."

Jean raised her pencil, ready to return to work. But he was still looking at her. "Is this your first job?" he asked.

"Does it show as much as that?" she said, chagrined.

"Only in a refreshing way." He leaned back, inhaling. "You went to college?"

"Yes, to Hadley. For two and a half years."

"That's an excellent school. My daughter is thinking of applying there."

It startled Jean to hear him mention a daughter. Of all the men she had worked for, he was the only one who had never received a call from a wife. Yet of course a man of his age and position would have a family. Still, she couldn't help feeling a twinge of something . . . disappointment?

"Louise will be back on Monday," Dreiser said. Jean's heart sank. Back to the plodding pace of the lifers. How was she going to stand it? But he continued: "I'm going to have my hands full with this deal for the next few weeks. I could use some extra help. Would you mind staying on?"

"I'd be glad to," she said without hesitation.

LOUISE, DREISER'S REGULAR secretary, was tall, tiny-headed, and pretty, with a thin mouth canceled out completely with white lipstick. She wore pants suits in shades of pastel. And she had a jumpy, fidgety manner as if she were constantly waiting for an important phone call. "It's madness!" was her favorite expression. "It's complete madness what He expects me to get done! I won't be out of here till *eight* at the least." She referred to Dreiser always as "He" or "Him" with an implied capital *H*. And she worked in a state of perpetual crisis, as if only her own superhuman efforts prevented IMI's entire operation from tumbling down.

From the beginning, she made it clear that she considered Jean an interloper and that Jean was to make no further headway into her territory. She guarded the intercom with passionate zeal and snatched the phone from Jean's hands. "*I* know which people to put through," she stated. "I wouldn't want you bothering Him with cranks." She delegated to Jean the most menial tasks: Xeroxing and coffee fetching, the routine typing and filing.

As the days slipped by, Jean's frustration mounted. She

could sense a growing tension in the air. Men with brief-cases hurried in and out, and Dreiser wore a distracted, inwardly focused look. He greeted her vaguely in the rare instances he noticed her. Jean felt as if she were in a theater in which the drama was being played behind the curtain. And Louise was making quite sure she didn't slip backstage.

In the middle of her third week, there was a lull. The phones rang less frequently, and for the first time since Jean had worked for him Dreiser left the building for lunch.

"What's happened?" she asked Louise.

"They're waiting," Louise said.

"For what?"

"Oh, it's much too complicated to explain."

Jean didn't press her. She had already discovered that Louise's air of being privy to inner secrets was largely a fraud. In fact, Louise understood little of the work she was given to do.

By five o'clock, things were still quiet. Dreiser was sequestered in his office with an elderly woman from the Arthritis Fund. "Nothing important," pronounced Louise. She was clearly restless. She began to pack things into her pocketbook. "Nothing more's going to happen today, so I might as well leave," she said. "I've done overtime every night so far. You don't mind sticking around, do you?"

"No. You go ahead," Jean said.

"I mean, as long as there's *one* of us here . . ." Louise slung her bag over her shoulder. "See you tomorrow."

Shortly afterward the phone rang. Jean saw the Arthritis woman leave, and then Dreiser came out. His face was tense and agitated. "Where's Louise?"

"She went home," Jean said. "She thought you wouldn't need her anymore."

"Damn! Look, something's come up. I need to get a lot of work out right away. Can you stay?"

"Of course."

"Good. Come into the office." She followed him in, sat at the leather chair facing his desk. "There's another firm putting a deal together on The Homesteader," he said. "If I don't move right away, I'm going to get caught in a bidding war. I need to get a complete deal memo out by morning."

"I can stay all night if you want."

"We just might have to work all night. Can you use an adding machine? As I throw out numbers, I want you to start adding them up."

They began to work, soon joined by the company's head counsel, a short, moon-faced man bearing a carton of documents. There was no talk other than what was necessary for the job. At eleven, Jean dialed out to an all-night deli for sandwiches and coffee that they ate as they continued to work. The lawyer left at one. Three hours later, Jean pulled the last of twenty-three pages from her typewriter and handed them to Dreiser who nodded with a weary smile.

"We've got it," he said. There were arcs of sweat under his arms and his hair clung damply to his forehead. He stubbed out one cigarette and lit another. "You don't smoke," he said.

Jean shook her head. "I've always been pretty athletic. I never would do anything that might cut down my time."

"I figured you for a jock. What are your sports?"

"In high school it was swimming and gymnastics. In college I played a lot of tennis."

"Are you any good?"

"*Very* good," she said decisively.

Dreiser relaxed into the back of his chair. "Tell me, Jean, where do you see yourself going? Marriage and babies? A house in Chevy Chase with a two-car garage?"

She gave an involuntary shudder. "I don't think so. That's where I *came* from."

"Then what? Do you want to work your way up here to executive secretary, maybe take over Mrs. Pulin's position someday?"

"God, no!" she exclaimed.

"So?"

"I guess," she said, "I'm after *your* job."

There was another of those unsettling pauses in which she couldn't discern what he was thinking. Had she overstepped her bounds? But then suddenly he smiled. "You *are* a competitor," he said. He glanced at his watch. "You must be beat. Call yourself a taxi and go home. And take as much time off tomorrow as you need."

"I won't need any," she said. She felt charged with energy. She doubted if she could even sleep at all.

She was in the office by nine the next morning, still high. And it was a moment of triumph when Louise turned to her with a look of bewilderment. "He says he needs *you*. You're to go in with your pad."

In the days that followed, Jean seldom left the office before midnight and arrived in the mornings at seven, which was when Dreiser arrived as well. He relegated to her all work having to do with The Homesteader. She had never worked so hard in her life, and she thrived on it. The greater the demands, the more energy she was able to summon. She whirled through each day in high spirits, oblivious to the black looks hurled at her by Louise, who had become her bitter enemy.

And then suddenly it was over. John Dreiser was on a plane to Dallas, and Jean learned that the acquisition had been a success only through a memo circulated to all employees. Louise once more presided over an office that was now eerily still. She quickly dispatched Jean back to the typing pool.

Jean returned to her gray metal desk, hating John Dreiser.

He had picked her up, shown her what she could do, and then dropped her, summarily, when she could be of no further use. He had never even thanked her, she realized. The bastard.

And then Mrs. Pulin was hurrying toward her clutching a green assignment sheet. Where to now? Jean wondered. To some dusty district manager obscured in the bowels of the building?

But Mrs. Pulin was agitated, fluttering the green sheet in her hand like a hankie. "It's unheard of!" she gasped. "Jumping straight from typing pool to Secretary III . . . it's against any kind of precedent. A lot of my girls have seniority—what in heaven am I going to tell them?"

It was several moments before Jean realized that John Dreiser had made another acquisition.

*I*T WAS NOW JEAN WHO OCCUPIED THE DESK IN THE BEIGE-carpeted antechamber outside Dreiser's office. Louise had been transferred, with a mollifying raise in pay, to the major packaging division. Jean's first act was to strip the desk of all her personal touches—the spindly dracaena with the "Flower Power" button pinned to the pot, the cute plaster gnome, the pencil holder shaped like a snail. She now had a work surface that was clean and functional, holding only a typewriter, neat stacks of pads and paper, gleaming stainless-steel correspondence files.

On her first day, Dreiser welcomed her with a simple "Good morning." Jean was hurt. No mention of the close, grueling hours they had spent on the Homesteader deal, not even a thanks for her performance. But as days went by she began to understand that for Dreiser a completed deal was no longer of interest—he immediately looked ahead to the next challenge, the next risk. And Jean herself had received a tangible reward—that was worth more than any effusive praise.

These were the first lessons in Jean's extensive tutelage. John Dreiser demanded her top efficiency as a secretary. But at the same time he began to instruct her in the workings of business, obviously grooming her to become much more.

His first step was to make her read everything she could about the company—letters, memos, the company newsletters and press releases. He would often later refer to them to make sure she had digested what she had read.

He then had her sit in on meetings under the pretext of taking notes, afterward drilling her on what she had observed. "Bob Whiting kept glancing at his watch. Do you think he was nervous or just bored?. . . Did you notice Hal Levine's hesitation when I asked for his latest numbers? Do you think that was deliberate?. . . Who there would you say was the best prepared to make projections?" Learn to read people, was his direction. Watch for the unwitting gesture— the tic, the blink or roll of an eye—that might give them away. "Several years ago I cut back on smoking," he told her. "Then I realized that every time I took a cigarette it was telling someone something—that I was anxious, or under tension, or that I considered a certain detail crucial. Now I make sure I have a cigarette in my hand at all times."

In order to give her exposure to other of the company's officers, he had her hand-deliver memos. To Jean this was a humbling experience. "So you're John Dreiser's new gal," said one man. "Why does he always get the pretty ones?" Another kiddingly pointed out that wearing her skirts almost to her knees was going to give secretaries at IMI a bad name. "Why so serious?" asked a third. "Let's see a little smile."

"They treat me like a silly doll," Jean complained to Dreiser.

"Of course they do," he replied. "They're used to secretaries either flirting with them or else cowering before them as if they were God Almighty. It's up to you to make them realize you're different.''

"But how? They only see me for twenty seconds."

"But they *see* you, don't they? The way you're dressed can tell them a lot."

Jean glanced down at herself. Since she had been at IMI she had worn variations of the same basic outfit: a white man-tailored blouse paired with a dark straight or A-line skirt. "I don't dress like the other secretaries," she protested.

"No, which is good. And your instinct to develop a sort of uniform was good too. But you want it to be the uniform of a professional. You look like an orphan attending a charity school." She blushed, and he softened his tone. "You say you're after my job. Then why not dress like you already have it? Buy some good-quality suits and have them well fitted. And get rid of that pocketbook that looks like a schoolbag. You ought to be carrying a briefcase."

"I can't afford all that," Jean said.

"You can't afford not to," he said bluntly.

She spent the following week's lunch hours at Bonwit's and Saks cringing at the price tags on wool and gabardine suits. But once she had tried them on and seen what transformation they effected, she no longer regretted draining her meager savings account. John Dreiser had, as usual, been right.

She was learning quickly. At night she took courses in economics, accounting, business management; by day she was absorbed in John Dreiser's instruction. And at last it was beginning to fit together. The way the world worked— just how the tree in the forest became the lurid pink-and-orange cereal box on the breakfast table. Each step involved someone making it happen, a hand upon a lever. And Jean was beginning to see how that hand could be her own.

A year after she had become his secretary, Dreiser promoted her to the title of executive assistant and awarded her a tiny beige office at the end of the executive corridor.

To celebrate, he took her to dinner. It was a French restaurant at which Jean had frequently booked tables for him over the past year: the captain greeted him with deference; other diners nodded in recognition as they crossed the room; and they were settled into their table by the owner himself— a smiling Breton who pressed Jean's fingers thoughtfully to his lips as if testing for succulence. Jean felt a rising excitement. She was well accustomed to the effects of Dreiser's power within the office; but that its influence should extend so far beyond was a thrilling consideration. Once again her ambition expanded to accept this new and more vivid dimension.

She opened the menu, masking her surprise that it contained no prices.

"Do you have any preference in a wine?" Dreiser asked her.

"How about a rosé?" she ventured.

"I think we can do somewhat better," he replied with a hint of amusement. Jean knew she had blundered. But in high school, Lancer's and Mateus had been "sophisticated," and in college no one had drunk anything but cheap jug reds. And her parents rarely drank wine at all—they plied their guests with cocktails, daiquiris and whiskey sours whirled in a blender, or her mother's famous peach juleps.

The wine that Dreiser ordered was dark and old and tasted of horded riches, of old gold buried deep below the earth. There was still so much for her to learn. All the finer things of life . . . she wondered if John Dreiser would teach her these as well.

But as she gazed at him over her glass, it struck her how

little she actually knew about him. He gave out little about his private life. She knew that he was separated from his wife who lived in Hilton Head and bred Borzoi hounds and that he had a fifteen-year-old daughter who attended the Madeira School. She knew, too, that he was a staunch Republican who detested the counterculture for its ''lazy thinking and childish excesses''—the only time Jean had ever really seen him lose his temper had been while reading about the riots at Columbia, his alma mater. And yet he was manifestly generous with both his money and time. There were lists of charities that he contributed to. And Jean had admitted into his office a steady procession of acquaintances and distant relatives who came for job referrals, financial advice, or similar favors.

Beyond that she knew nothing. Except that he loved his work—that it absorbed and sustained him in a way that she intrinsically understood.

He spoke to her now about her new position and the greater responsibility she was to assume. ''You've taken a big step,'' he said. ''Your parents must be very proud of you.''

Jean dug a fork into a pale crescent of melon. ''I haven't told them yet,'' she said.

''Why not?''

''I don't know. Maybe because I already know how they'll react. My father will tell me I'm being paid 'peanuts.' And my mother will hint that I should be latching on to some bright young man on his way up.''

''And is that not even a possibility?'' he asked.

''No,'' she said firmly. ''I've got no intention of standing on the sidelines cheering on some man in *his* career. Anyway, I don't even like young men. They can't tell me anything because they don't know anything. It's boring to watch them flounder around trying to figure out where they're going.''

Dreiser smiled. ''Did you always have so much confidence in yourself?''

She thought a moment. ''Pretty much. I remember when I was fifteen. I had just taken up gymnastics in addition to my swimming, and there was one stunt that I was really scared to do. It was a back flip onto my hands—just the thought of it scared me to death. And then one day I psyched myself into it. I felt my mind and body working in total unison as I went over, and it was fabulous! From then on I knew I could do just about anything.''

She paused, and he was silent as well, staring at her with the direct gray gaze which even now had the power to unnerve her.

''You're very lovely, Jean,'' he said at last.

She flushed, startled, then looked down, not knowing how to respond.

''I haven't wanted to rush things,'' he went on. ''I wanted to make sure you were secure in your role, that you wouldn't feel threatened by my approach. But I'm sure it's obvious that I've always been very attracted to you.''

Jean's mind raced, remembering times he had looked at her, spoken to her in a way she had neglected to understand until now. She nodded mutely.

''I would very much like to have an affair with you,'' he said simply.

Her fingers tightened around the stem of her wine glass. ''I would like that too,'' she said.

He smiled. ''Are you certain? I want you to understand that I'm not proposing a casting couch. Your promotion doesn't depend upon sleeping with me. No matter what you decide, I still intend to help you.'' His eyes met hers. ''I want you to become a success, Jean. No matter what does, or doesn't, happen between us."

She returned his grave smile. "I'm still certain," she said.

"Then I'm glad." He lit a cigarette and began to talk about his recent trip to Tokyo. Their conversation remained impersonal through dinner. Only after Dreiser had called for the check and suggested they return to his place for cognac was Jean sure she hadn't imagined his previous avowals.

DREISER LIVED in a large old house on Commonwealth Avenue. Jean had expected it to resemble his office—all stripped steel and plush, redoubtable leather. But here were rather cluttered rooms, furniture a trifle shabby, well-worn Oriental carpets. . . . The house reminded her of the wine he had chosen for dinner—that same quality of enduring value.

He poured Courvoisier, then led her on a brief tour of the downstairs, remarking on several recent renovations. When at last he brought her to the bedroom, she was brittle with anticipation.

He parted her dark bangs and kissed her on the forehead. "How long have you worn your hair like that?" he murmured.

"Since I was about nine." She touched a strand. "Do you think I should change it?"

"There are some things about you, Jean, that should never be changed," he said firmly. Then he drew her into his arms and kissed her mouth—not with the importunate, gobbling kisses of the boys she had dated, but a man's kisses, strong and generous and sure.

"Are you protected?" he asked her.

"No," she said with a flush of embarrassment.

He drew back slightly. "I thought all girls these days were on the pill."

"I should be, I guess," she said. "It's just that I never had any need to be before."

"You're a virgin?"

She nodded. It was a foolish admission, she realized. She could hear her mother warning her about "giving in." What a prig he must think her.

But his expression was far from scornful. "You *are* a remarkable girl!" he said. "All right then. Tomorrow I'm sending you to a friend of mine—Carl Franken, one of the best ob-gyns in the city. But tonight, it will be my responsibility."

He kissed her again and began to undress her, tenderly and fluidly, with no hesitations, no fumbling for clasps or buttons. Nor was there any self-consciousness in the way he removed his own clothing and slipped down beside her on the bed. Jean again felt his control and was swept with a shiver of excitement.

He began to stroke her, long thoughtful caresses that drew out the incipient shiver to a pleasing intensity. His skill lay in his patience: he lingered on her breasts, traced soft, smooth circles on her inner thighs. "Do you like this?" he asked again and again. "And here, is this good?" His lips followed the tender excursion of his fingers, always lingering to make sure her pleasure was complete. When at last he entered her she felt herself being opened, unsealed, dipping down past a taut gash of pain, until she heard the sound of her own sudden and startled cry of pleasure.

She slept long and deeply. When she awoke, the sun was sluicing brightly through half-pulled blinds. A white rose lay on the pillow beside her and the scent of warming bread drifted in on soft gusts from the kitchen. She lay for a moment collecting the memory of the night before. She felt somehow free, as if a task she had long put off had finally been completed.

Her eye was caught by a photograph of Dreiser, one of several on the opposite wall. It had been taken about twenty years before: he wore an unflattering crewcut and seemed ill at ease in his loose, boxy clothes. He seemed to have grown more attractive, even younger, with age. It struck her that she no longer knew what to call him. John? Darling? She giggled: what a loony problem. One thing was certain though—in the office she would continue to address him as "Mr. Dreiser." He had spoken briefly to her last night about discretion, their need to be cautious. This, of course, was largely for her own protection. Anyone who found out about their affair would immediately accuse her of sleeping her way to the top.

And could it be true? The thought was startling. No, she told herself. She had come to his bed of her own volition— because she was attracted to him, liked him, admired him.

But, continued the nagging voice, would she have been attracted to him if he had no power? If he were in no position at all to help her?

She dismissed the question. After all, what was the use of speculating about what didn't exist?

She slipped on the woolen robe he had laid out for her at the foot of the bed and went to join him for breakfast.

KATE, IN HER SENIOR YEAR, HURRIED THROUGH THE twilight of a November day, shivering as a fresh wind blew up the chill of deepening winter. Her only protection was a blue-jean jacket embroidered with mandalas. Her legs were bare beneath a miniskirt that was (as Marcie Kingman so crudely put it) scarcely long enough to cover her Tampax string; and though her light brown hair hung straight as glass to her waist, it provided little more warmth than did the thin jacket.

She cut across a lawn and plowed ankle-deep through dead leaves. A whiff of marijuana smoke floated to her nostrils. As it did, she remembered how she had sat on this very same lawn in her freshman year and watched a hoop-rolling contest between the senior girls who were engaged and those who weren't. The memory had a frozen, fossilized quality, as if it had survived from some long-gone Paleolithic age.

The times had certainly a-changed; and Kate, perhaps more than anyone else at Hadley, had participated in the spirit of change. She had hitchhiked alone to New Haven and Boston, ridden on the back of a Hell's Angel's "hog," danced with transvestites and rock stars, and slept on a semen-stained, bedbug-infested mattress in a crash pad in the East Village. She had taken up (in brief succession) the acoustic guitar. Tarot reading, candlemaking, and meditation, and had decorated her room with third-eye symbols.

Yet here on campus, steeped as it was in tradition, the transitions that had taken place were sometimes bewildering. Back when she was little and all the kids had played those swarming, made-up-as-you-go-along games in the street, there would always be some kid whose side was getting the worst of it who would suddenly stop and yell out: "Okay, new rules!" And that was exactly the way it seemed to Kate now—as if someone had suddenly called out "New rules!" and everyone was scrambling to follow them.

New rules. This morning when she staggered into the john, there had been a guy in Jockey shorts brushing his teeth at one of the sinks. Somebody's date who had spent the night. No big deal. Since parietals had been thrown out, there were always men in the dorms; and anyway, modesty was an irrelevant virtue. Still, none of the girls had used the toilet until he was gone—no one wanted to let a boy hear her tinkle.

New rules, new courses. The Black Experience in the Nineteenth Century. Women and the American Political System. Zen Buddhism I and II.

And new problems. Yeast infections with their disgusting cottage-cheesy discharges and itching to drive you crazy. Franny Radner drinking two quarts of quinine water because she had missed a day of the pill, and someone told her quinine would bring on her period. Staying up till dawn in Suzy Peck's room talking her down from a bad acid trip.

And there were new rules in dating, too. Now, when you went on a weekend, chances were your date would simply lead you to his own room and deposit your bag on his narrow single bed. And later, after the good dope and the bad dinner, after the Sly and the Family Stone concert in the gym or cafeteria, and more dope and wine and Procol Harum on a stereo in a black-lighted room . . . then there would be that narrow bed to contend with. Kate had learned that it required the most delicate juggling act of words and defensive gestures. You couldn't just shoot your date down cold. You couldn't resist on the grounds that his nose looked bigger than it did when you first met him, or that his friends were kind of wimpy, and his laugh had a braying edge that got on your nerves—not when you still had to be together for another thirty-six hours. Better to put it on yourself. "It's me," she had learned to say. "I'm going through a weird thing right now, trying to get my head together . . ." and on and on, sometimes until dawn. Once the sun came up, you were free—that seemed to be the rule. No one was into seduction in the light.

Not that she'd been completely celibate, of course. There were times she said yes. There had been Jeremy the end of her sophomore year, an elegant Williams man who had dazzled her with his rich kid's air of privilege. But right after they had slept together, he suddenly turned moody and silent, refusing to tell her what—if anything—was the matter, in fact barely speaking to her at all the rest of the weekend. To this day, she still didn't know what it was she had done wrong.

Then that summer, while working as a waitress in Cambridge, she had fallen head over heels for Marko. He was a poet who supported himself by dealing drugs. Like any salesman, he carried a sample case; and his wares boasted the most tempting Good Humor names: strawberry swirl, purple haze, jamake, orange sunshine. But Marko was into "circuses"—sex in threesomes, foursomes, god-knew-how-many-somes. When she refused to join in, he accused her of being "hung up in bourgeois bullshit morality," and dropped her for a seventeen-year-old dropout who worked in a topless bar.

And then last spring there had been Bobby who went to the University of Vermont. He had black hair as long as hers that mingled with her own when they made love. And he had given her the clap. Even now she hated to think about that time. The scalding pain when she tried to urinate, the white fluid oozing down her leg . . . And the nurse in the infirmary who, despite the broad-minded pamphlets she kept on her desk, clucked censoriously and intimated that it was Kate's own fault. With the nurse standing over her, Kate had called Bobby at his fraternity to tell him to get himself checked. "Will it hurt?" was all he had said. And she had never heard from him again.

Those had been the important ones. The ones she had thought she was in love with and when they had gone had made her cry. But there had been several others. Mostly boys from nearby Minton whom she had gone to bed with because they had seemed momentarily attractive or because she had gotten too stoned, or simply because it had become too awkward or too tiring to fight them off. These were the mistakes. The ones that made her cringe to remember.

Maybe it was because of such mistakes that this year she hadn't felt like dating too much. Of course there was no more stigma attached to hanging around campus on Saturday night—not since women's lib had swept in so strong. New rules again. There was a feeling, unspoken but nevertheless clear, that men were the enemy. Suddenly it was more desirable to be on a strike committee here at Hadley than to go up to Dartmouth for Green Key weekend. Suddenly Gail Kreiger, who was fat-assed and frumpy and had spent her whole time at Hadley buried in a lab, was almost a celebrity simply because she was pre-med. Suddenly Kristin Forth, a sullen, unapproachable deb whom Kate had always vaguely envied, had emerged as leader of a Lesbian Lib demonstration outside Backley Hall.

But if men were the enemy, why then, Kate wondered, did she still ache for someone special? Why did she scan every man's face for potential dearness? And why did the cold air still seem to tingle with the promise that romance and adventure were on the way?

She shrugged away these thoughts as she bounded up the steps of her house. The dinner bell had already rung and women were streaming toward the dining hall. They wore jeans and T-shirts and scuffed loafers; they were braless and their faces were scrubbed, and their long hair frizzed or curled or hung limply in whatever way was natural.

The dining hall was candlelit. It was funny, Kate thought. Though the campus had been beset by strikes and rallies and a free-for-all demonstration outside the faculty center, by free speech and free love and freedom from rules of almost any kind, this one most frivolous of traditions had somehow survived. The soft light now flattered figures that were, for the most part, far from slender. Dorm food was starchy and plentiful; and Kate, who consumed her ample share of potatoes and rice and gingerbread, knew that only through the grace of a peculiar metabolism was she one of the few seniors who hadn't put on weight.

Andrea, on the other hand, hadn't been so lucky. Kate, picking her out at a back table, realized she must have put on twenty pounds since freshman year. Not that she was fat. Full-blown would be a better description. A sort of earth-mother look that a lot of men seemed to really go for.

As if in corroboration, she had a man with her now—Douglas, no doubt, up from Columbia where he was doing postgrad work in English lit. Kate felt a twinge of irritation.

She so seldom had Andrea to herself anymore. As seniors, they had succeeded to spacious single rooms in the clock tower; and though the privacy was a luxury, Kate missed the mothering support and sympathy Andrea had given her in their rambling late-night discussions. And during the day, Andrea seemed perpetually tied up with antiwar committees and petitioning and feminist meetings. These days she even spoke less about Douglas and marriage than about doing some sort of work after she was married—though probably because everyone else was suddenly talking about careers. Andrea was a born follower, Kate decided with slightly bitter exasperation. She could be recruited for damned near anything; and once roped in, she toiled diligently and with sincere concern, while the self-promoting organizers reaped all the credit.

But Andrea was beckoning to her now. And as Kate drew closer, she saw that her companion was not Douglas after all. His shaggy hair was dark, not fair, with full muttonchop sideburns. And he was wearing very un-Douglas-like clothes: a fatigue jacket over a T-shirt with the Black Panthers' logo stenciled in blood red upon it.

"Guess who this is?" Andrea said excitedly. "It's Denny Furguson, Jean's brother!"

Kate looked at him. There was indeed a resemblance to Jean in his wide-set dark eyes and short straight nose. But beyond that, he seemed familiar. "Haven't I met you before?" she asked.

"You've seen me, I think," he grinned. "Medieval Architecture. Halburton's lecture. I usually sit in front near the fire door."

"Oh, right. You sometimes wear that green hat with the feather." Of course, she knew him now. He was a Hadley student—one of about two dozen men who had transferred in from other schools this year in an experiment with coeducation. Kate had paid them little attention. She couldn't help thinking there was something peculiar—maybe *second-rate* was the word for it—about a man who chose to come to a women's college.

But Denny was good-looking, she had to admit. And as with every attractive man she encountered, she geared herself toward making him a conquest.

"We met just now out in the quad," Andrea was saying. "He helped me put the chain back on my bike, and when I told him I was in Edmond House he asked if I knew Jean. . . . I can't believe he's been here almost two months without my knowing it."

Kate fixed her large eyes on him. "How *is* Jean?" she asked brightly.

"Lousy," he said, wrinkling his nose. "I think she's sold out completely."

"What do you mean?" Andrea cut in. "She's got a great job, doesn't she?"

"Sure, in a fascist company. Do you know how much money IMI gave to CREEP last year? And what shit wages they pay workers at their pulp mills? And do you know that they own a factory in Georgia that's the single biggest polluter in its county?"

"But that's got nothing to do with Jean," Andrea insisted.

"Sure it does. It's her company, isn't it? But Jean's got her head stuck in the sand. I saw her last month when I went down to Washington for the mobilization march. A quarter million people, the biggest antiwar demonstration the city's ever had, going on right outside her door, and she hardly even noticed. She was more concerned with some bullshit thing at work than the fact that kids were being tear-gassed right there at Dupont Circle."

Kate was becoming impatient. She had no desire to spend

all of dinner discussing Jean Ferguson. "I was down at the Washington march, too," she cut in.

Denny's eyes swung back to her. "Yeah?"

"Uh-huh. I hitched down with a couple of guys from Minton. We got picked up by a VW van driven by these U. Mass guys who were stoned out of their minds. They kept wanting to turn west and head for the Frisco rally instead. And they kept picking up more and more hitchhikers until there were about twenty of us jammed in back. It was completely insane."

"Far out. Where did you stay?"

"In somebody's grandmother's house in Georgetown. All these kids in sleeping bags on the living-room floor—the old lady nearly freaked out."

"What did you think of the march?" he asked eagerly.

"Fantastic, wasn't it? Did you hear that that asshole Volpe labeled us all red commies?"

Kate had only the dimmest notion of who Volpe might be. Politics bored her—the comings and goings of the Agnews and Kleindiensts and Haldemans were so unpoetic and seemingly far removed from her own life. Nevertheless, she laughed conspiratorially. "Are you in SDS?" she asked.

"Shit no, I'm a hippie not a revolutionary." Denny gave a playful smile. "Peace and love, *sí*. Violence, *no*."

Kate was disappointed. She was attracted to the glamour and celebrity of the radical fringe: the summer before she had met Mark Rudd and had thought him romantic. And in fact she had gone to Washington more in search of romantic adventure than through any real political convictions— though of course she was against the war and Tricky Dick and all that. There had been a sexual undercurrent running beneath it all that she was vividly attuned to. Between chanting "One, two, three, four, we don't want your fucking war" and crooning "Give peace a chance," the marchers were making eye contact, asking each other "What's your major?" jotting down phone numbers. . . . In her more cynical moments, Kate had described the march as the greatest mixer the world had ever known.

But now Denny was leaning toward her with clear interest. This was the moment Kate loved best—the moment she first knew a man was attracted to her. When his eyes and attitude told her that she was desirable, that she had successfully concealed the Brown Person, perhaps forever. Through the rest of dinner she was animated and arch, drenching Denny with attention and basking in the triumph of his eager response.

He left, promising to come by the following afternoon and take her for a motorbike ride in the mountains. Kate, still glowing with the triumph of another conquest, caught up with Andrea as she was going upstairs. "Denny seems like a great guy," she said. "It's amazing how different he is from his sister."

Andrea made a shrugging sound. Then suddenly she turned to face Kate. "Why do you always change as soon as there's a guy around?" she demanded.

Kate stared at her, startled. "What do you mean, change?"

"I mean all of a sudden you start acting like the queen of the prom and cutting everybody else out as if we didn't even exist."

"But I don't . . . I was just trying to be nice to him."

"Oh, come off it, Kate," Andrea flashed out and stomped angrily ahead upstairs.

Kate was stunned. She had never heard Andrea speak harshly to anyone. And to make such an unfair accusation . . . Was she jealous? Could she have been interested in Denny herself? But Andrea was practically engaged to Douglas and was solidly faithful to him. Kate troubled over it as she made her way back to her room. But an hour later

Andrea knocked on her door, a bit abashed, and Kate gave it no more thought.

Denny came the following day to take her for the promised ride up Mount Sven. It was freezing but exhilarating; and when they returned to campus, he let her drive the bike in first gear. She began to see a lot of him. They sat through *Midnight Cowboy* three times, "liberated" a roach clip from an Allington head shop, dropped mescaline and lay on the floor of Denny's room for six straight hours while the Grateful Dead spun ribbons of satin-colored sound in the air. Kate was cutting as many classes now as she had freshman year, but she had learned to select "gut" courses—where instructors were notoriously easy graders or where you could easily bluff your way through. And since the last student strike had brought in pass/fail, it didn't even matter anymore whether she did well or barely squeaked by. More important was living *now*, experiencing the moment. And in this, Denny proved a willing accomplice.

The strange thing was that though they often held hands, they went no further. Denny never even tried to kiss her. She knew that he wanted to. But he was leaving it entirely up to her—waiting for her to signal that she wanted him to make an advance.

Then why didn't she? Denny, in his vagabond fashion, was as good-looking and appealing as almost any man she had ever met. He had a coterie of what Kate mockingly called his groupies—women who clustered around him at lectures and scampered devotedly by his side as he crossed to another class. And he was serious in his efforts not to be a male chauvinist pig. Even the most fanatic feminists on campus, women like Melinda Gaus who wore buttons saying "A woman without a man is like a fish without a bicycle" and advocated castration as a viable means of birth control, grudgingly conceded that Denny Ferguson was an enlightened member of his species.

But that was just the problem. All this being sensitive to her moods and wants, his always letting her take the lead . . . It seemed weak, somehow.

"Doesn't it ever get to you, being around so many women?" she asked him.

"No, I like women," he said happily. "I think on the whole they're far superior to men. Women have had such a shitty deal for so long they've learned how to cope with a certain amount of strength and grace. Which is a lot more than you can say for most of the men in this country. Christ, half the problems in the world are because of men. They treat everything like it's a schoolyard fight, nobody's allowed to back down. Just look at Johnson's policies in Vietnam."

Kate sighed. Denny was concerned and committed. According to the new rules, wasn't he exactly the kind of man she should be attracted to? Then why did it always seem to be the opposite type that turned her on—Mick Jagger mocking "Who wants yesterday's girl?" the Marlboro man riding hard and long across the plains?. . . It was all totally confusing, this gulf between the way she *should* feel and the way she actually did.

And in the spring she fell in love again. It was with a photographer named Paul who had recently set up a studio in Allington. He had an angel face and a body that was slouched and wire-skinny in the desirable fashion of lead guitarists. A part of Kate was aware that he was the stupidest man she had ever been involved with. He called women "chicks" and breathed "Oh, wow!" to anything that pierced the shallow film of his attention. "Oh, wow!" he said, looking at a maple in bud; "Oh, wow!" when he heard a friend had died of an o.d. Yet Kate couldn't get enough of him. Every day found her at his door.

Then one day, after about a month, he opened the door to her stark naked. He let her in; then he padded back to bed where a girl with a snarled cavewoman mane lay also naked. Neither seemed the least disturbed by Kate's arrival. Paul proceeded to roll a joint, while the girl nuzzled his neck, her small breasts squashing against his back. Kate crouched on the floor, trying to look serene, telling herself It's just the new rules, we're all free now, no need to get uptight. But she felt foolish and humiliated, and at last, babbling a few incoherent words of excuse, made her escape.

She wandered back to campus to find a sort of festival atmosphere there. People were stretched on the grass beside the pond, flying kites over the greenhouses, blowing soap bubbles. She was bewildered for a moment. Then she remembered—a moratorium on classes had been declared in protest of the Cambodian bombings. She had been so detached from the school lately that she had completely forgotten about it.

She made her way to Denny's room. She had neglected him shamefully in the past month and half expected him to be cold to her. But he gave her the same delighted grin as always.

"How about some Frisbee?" he suggested. "I've been sitting on my ass all day. I could use some exercise."

She followed him out to the lawn. He had known about Paul—he had seen them together several times at The Stop, the coffeehouse in Stoppard Hall. But it was she who finally brought up the subject as they crossed the lawn.

"I broke off with that guy Paul today," she said.

"Yeah?" Denny looked carefully away. "How do you feel about it? Are you really bummed out?"

"I guess so," she admitted. "But it's my own damned

fault for getting all emotionally involved." She took a tone of mock despair. "Why can't I ever make it with somebody without thinking it's the Grand Passion?"

"What's wrong with that?" Denny asked.

"Because we'll never be really liberated until we liberate our bodies too," she declared. "Men can enjoy sex without getting love in the way. Why shouldn't women too?"

Denny stared at the inverted orange underside of the Frisbee. "Is that all women want?" he said with a sudden and bitter edge. "To get to the same fucked-up place as men in the same fucked-up way? If it is, then maybe I've been giving them way too much credit."

Kate looked at him. For the moment he was defiant, in the brink of walking away. And for that moment, she felt the familiar tug in her stomach that signaled desire.

But then he yelled, "Here, catch!" and flipped the Frisbee toward her. And as she watched him frisk after the wobbling arc of her own inexpert toss, stumbling a little in the clumpy engineer's boots he always wore, the feeling passed. It was just Denny after all. Faithful and completely unenigmatic Denny.

*A*NDREA YAWNED AND SCRUBBED HER EYES WITH THE heels of her palms. The meeting of the steering committee for the May Day moratorium had lasted till nearly 4:00 A.M. the night before. This morning she had had to be up at nine for an honors seminar; and then the speaker for the Bobby Seale Fund had run overtime causing her to miss lunch. And now as she sat on the living-room floor of Camden House, she seemed to float in soft focus, engulfed by a gentle hum of fatigue.

But she was happy. Never before had she felt so useful, so involved. It was as if she was a member of a wide and thriving family to which she could pour out all her love and devotion.

She yawned again, luxuriously, and looked around her. Some twenty or so seniors were assembled in a semicircle on the floor. This was her T-group—T standing for transactional. They met every Wednesday afternoon to talk about being women—to help each other raise their consciousnesses and support their collective efforts at liberation.

The first half of each meeting was dedicated to the discussion of general topics. Andrea had thrilled with pure anger at the compendia of degradations women had been forced to endure through the ages: of bound feet and bound breasts; of living wives sacrificed on the funeral pyres of dead husbands; of concubinage and purdah and Japanese women humbled to ten paces behind; of whale-bone corsets and Latex girdles and stiletto heels. She had thrilled even more to witness the obdurate faces around her, to hear them proclaim: "We're not going to take it anymore!"

In the second half of each meeting, the group focused on one member. She was called upon to talk about her life: the group then questioned her motivations, criticized what they viewed as unliberated patterns of behavior, offered advice and suggestions for change. Andrea felt somewhat ambivalent about this part. She knew the critiques were meant solely for each member's good, but sometimes the sessions became needlessly rough. Last week, for instance, Sunny Jensen had been the focus. Sunny was a bubbly, oblivious preppy, one of a number of women on campus for whom the sixties had rolled right past leaving not a mark. She wore penny loafers and kneesocks and a silver circle pin on her crewneck sweaters, and a two-carat engagement ring coruscated grandly on her ring finger. Undoubtedly she had joined the group because everyone was joining *something*. But last week when she was up, the group had pounced upon her engagement, had grilled her mercilessly on her fiancé Ritchie, a West Point cadet. Sunny had seemed insensible to the growing malevolence of the comments until, inevitably, someone asked if Ritchie was a good lover.

"Oh, I've never been to bed with him," she had proclaimed piously. "He respects me too much to do anything before we're married. But I know that every so often he's slept with other girls to satisfy his needs, and I can understand that.''

There had been a moment of silence. Then suddenly a dozen voices broke out at once. Sunny was a hypocrite, a perpetuator of the double standard. What did she think was so special about *her* precious virginity? And what about those ''other girls''—did she think they didn't count at all? Were they just objects, tissue for Ritchie to blow his fucking nose on?

Sunny had paled and her pointed chin had quivered. She made a feeble attempt to defend herself, but attacks were raining in from all sides; with a little flutter of hands, she burst into tears and ran from the meeting.

''That's right, go live your little bug life!'' someone had called out after her.

They had been too harsh, Andrea thought. Sunny was selfish and silly, but not mean. She hadn't deserved to be so ripped apart.

And now today it was her turn. She would be summoned forth to confess the details of her own engagement. No, *confess* wasn't the right word. It wasn't after all a sin to be engaged. And she didn't espouse the double standard. Moreover she definitely planned to work after she was married in order to maintain her own identity. At least until they had children. . . .

Yet what if the group still turned against her, like they had Sunny? She was so exhausted she couldn't bear it. She told herself the session would be constructive and well intended no matter brutal it might become. But still she felt her palms growing damp.

The discussion today was about sexism in advertising— how Madison Avenue exploited the stereotype of women as either household drudge or sex object. There was a movement to boycott Gillette because of the blatant innuendo in their "Take it all off" razor ads. And then the leader, a woman from Andrea's house named Aileen Rourke, glanced at her watch.

"Andrea, you're in the hot seat today," she said, smiling.

Andrea nodded nervously. She remembered Aileen back in freshman year, a gawking, oddball girl who seemed to be forever peering over your shoulder. Once Kate, with delicious, if wicked, accuracy, had characterized Aileen as an asparagus—tall, thin, and unbending with a waving pyramid of no-color hair—and ever since then Andrea had had trouble looking at her without summoning an image of that vegetable. But that was unliberated thinking. Cattiness, bitchiness, competing with each other on the artificial basis of looks—sisterhood had done away with all that. Aileen was beautiful, as every woman was, in her own way.

Andrea gathered her knees to her chest and took a breath. Twenty pairs of eyes regarded her intently.

"Well," she began, "I guess I should tell you that I'm majoring in sociology, and I've been going with the same guy since freshman year, and that we're planning to get married after graduation. I mean, we've been talking about it. His name is Douglas, and right now he's working on a Ph.D. dissertation at Columbia. Then he's going to teach English. On the college level, I mean. So I guess where I end up will depend on wherever's he's offered a position." She regretted this last sentence as soon as she had said it. It sounded so slavish. Shades of that old song by Little Peggy March: "I will follow him, wherever he may go . . ."

"Are you positive you want to marry him?" The question came from Cammy Loos, a serious, dark-haired girl on her right.

"Oh, yes," Andrea said quickly.

"Why?"

"Because I love him."

"And why do you love him?" Cammy pursued.

Andrea hesitated. "Well . . . because he's very smart and has a good personality, and I think he's pretty handsome. And because he loves me."

"Does that mean he gives you lots of support?" Aileen asked.

"Support? I suppose so. Though we don't talk about me all that much, so I guess I really don't know."

"Why don't you talk about you?" asked Carly Freeburg, whose voice always maintained an edge of indignation.

"Well, he has a way . . . I don't know, sometimes he sort of puts me down." The words were out before Andrea had even thought about them. "Not that he *means* to or anything," she added quickly. "It's just sort of automatic. Like he always calls me 'Little Thing' or 'Funny Face' or some name like that. And he treats my majoring in sociology as a joke—he calls it 'the science of stating the obvious in an obscure way' and doesn't even think I have to *study* for it. And sometimes when we're with his friends, he'll make fun of me in little ways, telling them I'm such a klutznik or the world's champion worst speller, and then laughing as if it was all just too very cute."

She paused for another deep breath, feeling her anger mount just at the naming of these wrongs. And then suddenly she couldn't stop herself. A stream of words poured from her mouth, resentments long hoarded she could no longer contain. How in the john of his old Yale suite he had hung a sign: WHEN BETTER WOMEN ARE MADE, YALE MEN WILL MAKE THEM, and how he and his roommates used to classify women as "dogs," "pigs," or "a real piece of ass." How he thought everything he wrote was brilliant and would tolerate nothing but unqualified praise; and if *he* needed to study, the whole world had to go on tiptoe, but if *she* were the one trying to work, he thought nothing of barging in every two minutes to ask if she'd seen his Petrarch or one of his precious *Alexandria Quartet*, or what did she feel like for dinner, or why wasn't his new Miles Davis put back in its jacket. . . .

"What about in bed?" someone interjected. "Is he a good lover?"

"No!" she flashed out. "He's just as selfish there as everywhere else."

As she said it, she realized that for the first time she was avowing publicly that she was no longer a virgin. She hesitated, but the eyes fastened upon her were sympathetic, frankly encouraging. So many times she had patiently listened to others pour out their problems and unhappiness. To talk about herself and be avidly attended to was, she discovered, a luxury; and it spurred her to speak even more recklessly. "He's never made me satisfied, not even once," she declared. "It's all for his own pleasure. At first I didn't care, I just wanted it to be over. But it's different now. I want more and I don't dare tell him. And sometimes the only way I can sleep afterward is to . . . to do it myself. I always wait till I'm absolutely sure he's asleep so he won't catch me at it. But you know what? I don't even think he knows what it is—you know, the clitoris and everything. For all he thinks he's so brilliant and knows so much, I don't even think he knows where it is!"

This time when she stopped to catch her breath she discovered she was quaking. She was shocked at her own daring. Had she gone too far? Were the other women shocked and disgusted by her admissions?

But then Joyce Kelsey, who was sitting next to her, threw her arms around her. And immediately the rest of the group clustered around her, murmuring that she was so beautiful, so strong, that her courage was marvelous. Andrea returned their hugs fervently, basking in their approval. They really were her sisters. She loved them all.

"Are you still sure you want to get married?" someone asked.

"I guess not," Andrea admitted with a little laugh. "The thing is, I don't really know what else to do."

"What did you see yourself doing if you did get married?" Aileen's question had a didactic tone, befitting her role as moderator.

Andrea thought a moment. "I guess the traditional role," she said. "You know. Having babies and keeping house and maybe some volunteer work."

There were groans and snorts from the group. "Breeding and slave labor," sneered Carly Freeburg. "Is that all you think you're good for? What about realizing your own potential? Isn't there some career you could really get into?"

"I suppose I'd like to do something to help people," Andrea said hesitantly. "Something *mean*ingful."

"How about law school?" Cammy Loos proposed. "You could become a public defender."

"Yes, law school!" Several women echoed the cry.

Andrea shook her head. "I'm not smart enough for that."

"Who says?" Carly demanded. "That sounds like Douglas talking, to me. What's your grade point average?"

"About a three-four."

"Then what are you saying, you're not smart enough? You're a fucking brain! There's no reason in the world you can't go to law school."

"Law school!" The entire group took up the clamor, until Andrea was laughing and nodding and hugging her neighbors again and feeling as if she could leap to the moon.

HER HIGH SPIRITS carried her through the next few days. She registered for the law boards and dashed off a letter to

Douglas telling him that it might perhaps be better to break it off. She remembered the first letters she had written him—how she had labored, composing three or four drafts, poring through books for erudite references, agonizing over each word, just so he wouldn't think her a dimwit. The tyranny of it! She sealed the envelope, quivering with indignation.

But after she had mailed the letter, she began to waver. She thought of how sweet Douglas could be. Of his little surprises: the copy of *Now We Are Six* on her pillow; the Tibetan wind chimes he hung in her window the last time he came to visit. She was struck with guilt for the way she had so baldly condemned him before total strangers. When he called, she would suggest that they talk it over, that perhaps they could work it all out.

But coming back from a morning psych seminar, she found a message in her box to call Warren Nater, her mother's lawyer in St. Louis. Mr. Nater's voice was solemn: "I'm sorry to have to tell you this, Andrea. Your mother died early this morning. You'd better come home."

By evening she was on a plane to St. Louis. Kind Mr. Nater had seen to all the funeral arrangements; she had only to go through the motions. In the chapel, she gazed at her mother's face, waxed, but wearing the expression of quizzical preoccupation that Andrea knew so well.

"This woman was a veritable saint," someone was saying in a low voice that nevertheless carried across the hushed room. "The cancer was diagnosed inoperable a year ago, but she kept it all to herself. Didn't let a soul know she was dying, not even her daughter. That's the kind of courage you don't find much of nowadays."

Andrea, listening, felt cheated and angry. How could you, Mother? she railed at the coffin. How could you deny even this one last intimacy to me?

She sat numbly through the service. The words, the music

had lost all resonance, all depth of meaning. Douglas's mocking of religion and her classmates' indifference to it had successfully taken their toll: she no longer felt cradled by a comfortingly familiar God. And when she went home and saw the picture of her father, still in place on the walnut secretary, she no longer saw the image of Our Father Who Art in Heaven; now it was just a balding, somewhat humorless, middle-aged man whom she had never known, but whose forehead and delicate chin she had inherited.

The old house that had seemed entombed in silence when her mother was alive now seemed haunted by sounds: stairs creaked, drapes rustled, a distant radiator hummed and hissed and groaned. She slept little, and in the morning told Mr. Nater she wanted it sold. No, she wasn't sure yet what her plans would be, but she didn't think she'd be coming back to St. Louis to live.

There was a letter from Douglas waiting for her when she got back to school. She pounced upon it eagerly. Dear Douglas—she needed him more than ever now. She hoped she hadn't upset him too badly with her foolish letter.

But she was not prepared for what she read. "Frankly I was relieved when I read your letter," he had written. "For some time now I've had some fear that we were acting too precipitously . . . both still so young . . . owe it to ourselves to explore other options. . . ."

Andrea read it three times before his meaning finally sank in. Douglas was calling it off himself. There would be no talking it over, no changing her mind. It was final.

It was almost funny, she thought—here she was, struggling so nobly to become a liberated woman, and now suddenly she had no choice. For the first time in her life she was completely alone.

*T*HE CLASS OF 1970 OF HADLEY COLLEGE GRADUATED ON a hot and breezeless day in early June. Six seniors boycotted the ceremony to protest the invalidity of the Hadley educational experience. Several dozen others objected to the conformity and totalitarian symbolism of caps and gowns and accepted their diplomas dressed in jeans, Mother Hubbard dresses, or robes improvised from tie-dyed sheets. Honorary degrees were awarded to Ti-Grace Atkinson, Daniel Berrigan, and Janis Joplin ("for expressing the pain and exultation commingled in a woman's soul through the universality of song"). And roughly half the graduating body had to fake their way through the Alma Mater, having only hastily memorized the words the night before to the tune of "Darling Clementine."

Kate sat through the ceremonies sweltering beneath the heavy black gown, but otherwise numb. She knew that somewhere among the throngs of folding chairs, her mother would be pointing her out to a total stranger or leaping into the aisle to take a blurry snapshot, and her father would be nodding drowsily in his chair. Kate brooded upon her future, which was as undetermined as a roll of the dice.

So many of her classmates were bolting fast from the gate with acceptances at medical or architecture schools or with firm vocations in photography, politics, theater. Even Andrea—Andrea who had never planned to do anything with her education—was, remarkably, now about to enter Chicago Law. While she, Kate, had nothing firmer than a sense of expectation, of being marked for something brilliant and better.

It was strange, she reflected, that most of the men she knew had only the vaguest ambitions. Many of them were still draft dodging and so were planning to teach second grade or attend grad school in such ephemeral fields as anthro, or classics, or comp. religion. Or, if they had already copped a 4F, they were talking about a pilgrimage to India, shipping out to Scandinavia on a tanker, making an underground movie: turn on, tune in, drop out. Denny was leaving for Ecuador in a month for a two-year stint in the Peace Corps.

The president was introducing the commencement speaker, and Kate forced herself to concentrate. A plump woman in her fifties took the podium. Her plain, stern-lipped face was hazily familiar as that which, in photographs of feminist rallies, usually appeared just behind that of Friedan or Steinem.

"I envy you women," she was saying. "The path is so clearly marked for you. There will be no need for you to repeat the mistakes of my generation. The obstacles that blocked us now exist only for you to hurdle. You will be free to go out and have anything and everything you want!"

Kate listened attentively. The message was clear: go out and do something and be sure that it is creative and meaningful, that it gives you power and above all makes you a success. But now the speaker was retiring from the podium. Wait! Kate shrieked silently. Don't go yet! You haven't told us what that something is, nor shown us how to get it. The path isn't clear . . . no, not clear at all.

Part 2

IT HAD BEEN OVER TWO YEARS SINCE JEAN HAD BEGUN working at IMI, but each morning, as she entered the building, she felt a fresh burst of expectation. Each day provided a new challenge. As John Dreiser's direct representative, she had a taste of power that was truly heady. All the teams and school organizations she had captained in college and high school had accustomed her to giving directives. But now, when she relayed an order, it might have consequences reaching far across the country or even throughout the world. She sometimes felt she could hardly contain her excitement; she had to force herself to walk calmly down the halls rather than fly with great leaps and bounds.

Today she was even more eager than usual to reach her office because Dreiser was returning from a two-week trip to Toronto. When he was away there was always a noticeable decline of momentum. His presence sparked not just Jean but everyone around him. When he was there, everyone, from the messengers and secretaries to the other execu-

tives of the acquisitions committee, seemed to respond with
more energy and involvement.

Jean had also missed seeing him outside the office. Their
relationship had developed a comfortable pattern of Saturday nights and Sunday afternoons. She was learning to
appreciate his passions: elegant wines and simple foods exquisitely prepared, bel canto opera, and the glowingly
translucent pieces of Chinese porcelain he collected. And
she looked forward to sleeping with him. Her pleasure in sex
had expanded and deepened under his patient instruction.
She was beginning to trust her own body's responses as well
as her ability to give pleasure to him in return.

But what she missed most of all was simply talking to
him. She could tell him anything, it seemed—from her most
high-flown theories on the meaning of life to the doubts that
sometimes pricked at her self-confidence. At times he made
her see that her thoughts were naïve or undeveloped. But
never did he make her feel they were insignificant. Nor did
he ever—like her father—brush off her true achievements
with a few patronizing and hollow words of praise.

But as time passed, she compared him less and less to her
father. He had eclipsed him in every way. And now it was
no longer her father's approval she struggled for, but John
Dreiser's alone.

These were her thoughts as the elevator opened onto the
nineteenth floor. As she did every morning when he was in
town, she reported directly to Dreiser's office without even
stopping at her own. But Rachel, his secretary, shook her
head. "Not in yet," she said.

"Did he phone?" Jean asked.

"Nope. Weird, isn't it?"

It was peculiar. Though it was only eight-thirty, it was
Dreiser's custom to be in as early as seven on his first day
back from a trip. If he was delayed he never failed to call.

Jean made her way to her office with some uneasiness. By ten o'clock, when he had still neither appeared nor phoned in, she began to worry. She dialed his apartment, let it ring twelve times. When she hung up, her own secretary buzzed her: the treasurer wanted to see Jean in his office.

Harvey Kalb was a bull-faced man with an overbite that pushed his lips into a perpetual snarl. He was John Dreiser's chief adversary within the company: inevitably, there was resistance from the treasurer's office to any proposal that originated from Dreiser's. Jean had spoken to him several times before. His manner had been hostile, tinged with sarcastic condescension that made her certain that he suspected she was having an affair with Dreiser. They had, of course, been as cautious as possible, spending most of their time together in his house and small garden. The rare times they had ventured to dine out had been after working late, when it would not seem unusual for an executive and his assistant to be having dinner together. And in the office they had remained formal to the point of coldness toward each other. Yet Jean knew that her rapid advancement was bound to make people suspicious—Harvey Kalb, who would welcome any way to discredit Dreiser, not the least so.

He did not get up when she entered his office and ignored her respectful: "Good morning, sir."

"We've some bad news," he said curtly. "John Dreiser has had a stroke. Apparently he's been taken to a hospital in downtown Toronto."

Jean felt the blood drain from her face. "Oh, God! Is it really bad?"

"We don't know yet. They're doing tests and so forth, so we'll get some news pretty soon. But in the meantime I'll have to ask you to keep the matter discreet. For both Dreiser's protection and the company's."

"Yes, of course," Jean said weakly. "But what hospital is he in? Can he talk? Can I call him?"

"His wife is with him," Kalb said.

Jean tried to disguise the chill of alarm that ran through her. But Kalb knew he had delivered a putative slap—he was looking at her with a foxy satisfaction. She suddenly felt dizzy. "What should I do?" she asked.

"Nothing. Just carry on as usual. You'll be notified when we know something more definite."

Jean returned to her office and tried to allay her fright with hard work. Time crept by with agonizing slowness. Three days passed with no news, though rumors were rampant. Dreiser was near death. He was dead already. He was mentally alert, but completely paralyzed. He wasn't sick at all but coordinating an elaborate power-play from abroad.

And then at last there was an official announcement: *John Dreiser, senior vice president in charge of acquisitions, has suffered a serious illness. This will necessitate his absence from his duties for an indefinite period of time.*

Jean could hardly believe it. For two years she had worked with this man, confided in him, shared his bed. She had come to regard his continuing advice and support as an integral part of her life. And now suddenly he was beyond her reach. She could do no more than formally express her wishes for his recovery.

With the announcement, her projects had ground to an abrupt halt. People gazed at her with confusion—even alarm—not knowing where she stood. Her phone calls were no longer returned, her mail began trickling away, her memos returned to her, uninitialed, unread.

Once again the treasurer summoned her to his office. "Mr. Dreiser's functions are being temporarily assumed by Carl Laffler in strategic planning," he informed her. "Therefore, it's been necessary to reassign you. Beginning tomorrow, you'll report to Frank O'Donnell, assistant director of purchasing. The department's down on seven."

Purchasing! It was almost a joke within the company, such a slow track it was known as "the pony trot."

"But shouldn't I go to Laffler?" Jean asked quickly. "After all, I'm so familiar with the projects Mr. Dreiser had going. I know what he intended to accomplish . . ."

"Mr. Laffler will have his own ideas on what directions he'll want to pursue," Kalb cut in.

"Yes, of course, but still, with everything I've learned, I could help him . . ."

"Mr. Laffler feels his staff is already complete," Kalb said abruptly.

Jean saw in his expression that she would have no further appeal. She was to be sent to purchasing. She would descend from buying new companies to buying new pencils and erasers and gross lots of manila envelopes, from reporting to a senior vice president to reporting to an assistant department head. It was not a slap in the face this time, it was a blow from a clenched fist.

Kalb was watching her closely. He wanted her to quit, she realized. He wanted a clean sweep. She was suddenly utterly exposed: John Dreiser had protected her more than she had realized. She felt a sudden flush of anger at him. He had taught her to wage lofty campaigns from the sequestered camp of a commander, but left her unprepared to defend herself from the direct fire of a skirmish.

But she would defend herself somehow. She nodded curtly to Harvey Kalb and went to prepare herself for her new assignment.

FRANK O'DONNELL PROVED to be a self-important young man with thick thighs and thick, moist palms, which gave his handshake an unseemly carnal effect. Jean sat across from him taking disdainful inventory. He wore a short-sleeved, drip-dry shirt with soiled collar points; his too-narrow tie was the color of algae; his haircut shouted that it cost four bucks. And he had the indelectable habit of scraping the rim of his ear with a fingernail while he rattled on to her about her future "responsibilities." A born lifer. In ten years he would become head of the department and that was the end of the line, Charlie.

In the following days she sat in her ugly green cubicle feeling a panic, as if the walls were creeping in on her. She had to get out. But how? The department head was a lumbering old fool named Hoag who remarked at the beginning of each staff meeting, "You look very pretty today, Jean," then stared blankly whenever she offered a comment, as if she had spoken in Urdu or Cantonese. O'Donnell's main concern seemed to be keeping her in her place. Almost every day he would buzz her to say his secretary was "in the ladies" or off at the water cooler, "so do me a big favor, hon, and take a memo for me. . . ." Or "type up this fig-ures list. . . ." Or "pop down to the supply closet and get us some binders. . . ." Knowing damn well that such tasks were beneath her, and also knowing damn well that she couldn't refuse.

The other men in the department began to follow O'Don-nell's lead. A meeting time was changed and someone "for-got" to inform Jean of it. A crucial memo somehow failed to make its way to her desk. And when she approached a knot of her coworkers standing in the interminable rush-hour wait for an elevator, their eyes would suddenly crease over with resentment and their talk would veer to the locker room.

"Did you see Jurgensen pass for half a mile and the pissing Redskins *still* lost!"

"You've gotta catch the tits on that new chick in reception. Enough to make a saint come! What's the bet she spreads?''

Jean understood. Get off our turf! they were saying to her. But it's mine too! she wanted to cry. I've always been the only girl in the pack of boys. I've always played on the team. Look! You wear dark gray two-piece suits and so do I. You carry a black leather attaché case that's just like mine. I belong among you.

But she was losing ground. As her confidence ebbed away, she began to make silly mistakes: transferring the wrong sum from one column of figures to another, sending a purchasing order for one ball-point manufacturer in an envelope addressed to its competitor. At last O'Donnell called her to his office and issued a warning in tones of dismal satisfaction: ''I'm afraid, Jean, that unless your work shows substantial improvement in the next few weeks, we will be compelled to let you go.'' She returned to her cubicle, her face burning. The urge to walk out was stronger than ever.

And then she made her greatest mistake of all.

She had been aware for some time that Glenn Alison was attracted to her. He was in promotion—a strange department which, though it had little real power itself, was known as a breeding ground for gunslingers. At first Jean had been repelled by his sharp, thin face with its eyes that seemed too bright, too audaciously knowing. But as she felt herself become more and more an outcast, she began to welcome his friendliness and attentions. She found herself looking for him in the halls and cafeteria, making excuses to go up to the promo department on eight. And when one evening he asked her to dinner she accepted with gratitude.

He took her to a noisy Belgian restaurant near Capitol Hill. The food was bland, the décor nondescript, but Jean didn't care—it was such a relief to be able to relax: to laugh, and talk, and trade notes again with a man who was neither afraid nor resentful of her. She liked Glenn Alison's face now: if before it had seemed insolent, now she saw the kind of bold self-determination she had always admired.

She made no objection when he invited himself back to her apartment, and after several drinks, they tumbled into bed. Jean was starved for sex. It had been over four months since John Dreiser's stroke. Alone at night, her body sometimes seemed like a separate entity, so importunate was its desire, and the touch of the sheets made her ache for a more substantial caress. Now she reached out hungrily for this man, sighing as his body pressed itself against hers. But he entered her almost immediately—there was none of the long and tender foreplay that, with John Dreiser, had been one of her greatest pleasures. And within minutes it was over. He had withdrawn, was catching his breath, mumbling that he'd like to stay, but he could never get to sleep in any bed but his own. . . . And he was gone. Jean glanced at the clock: it was only ten forty-five.

She saw him the following day in the lobby of the building. He was pleasant, he commented on the weather, relayed a tidbit of company gossip, but made no mention of the night before. A week went by, then two, and still he had said nothing, nor had he asked her out again. Jean began to worry. Had she done something wrong, said something to offend him? Or had he found her body distasteful? She imagined now that she saw a smug look in his eyes—a look that said he knew all her secrets. And once, when she passed him in the hall, standing with two other men from his department, she saw him turn and say something, and then all three broke into sharp laughter.

She was totally shaken now and began to make even greater slip-ups at work. There were more warnings from Frank O'Donnell, and then one morning he edged nervously into her cubicle. She knew what he was about to say and cut him off quickly. "I've realized, Mr. O'Donnell, that I've not been fully utilizing my talents here," she declared. "So I've decided to resign and look for something else."

Relief spread into his innocuous face. "I'm sorry to hear that, Jean," he said happily. "But I'm sure, that is, I know you've made the right decision. We'll give you two weeks severance of course, but if you feel you must leave sooner, I won't stand in your way."

She watched him back hastily out. And so she had done it—for the first time in her life she had become a quitter. And quitters were losers, that's what her father had always said.

She had a sudden memory of a day in August when she was thirteen and Denny was twelve. Her father had just whipped Denny in tennis and was climbing into the maroon Eldorado where she sat waiting. "Winners ride and losers walk," he called to his son. "That's the way the real world is, buddy." And they had zoomed off, leaving Denny to trudge the hot three miles back home.

And now she, too, was plodding back to the point at which she'd begun. But this was only a temporary setback: this she promised herself. At all costs, she was determined to be a winner.

AT FIRST KATE LOVED NEW YORK. THE CITY SEEMED ready to grant her endless favors. Its doors had no locks, its streets were crowded with adventure, its towers loomed with the promise that she would quickly scale their heights.

She had landed a "creative job" on only her third day of hunting. She had walked into the theatrical publicity agency of Haber and Switt on West 51st Street—one of a list of places she had culled from the Yellow Pages—on a day they happened to be interviewing for a new assistant. She was brought in to see Harold Switt, who was fortyish, wore a black turtleneck, jeans and sneakers, and chewed gum with his front teeth. He waggled his eyebrows up and down like Groucho Marx and said, "Yowwee! You're the best-looking thing I've seen since my last hot dinner." It was, of course, a sexist remark, and a part of Kate urged that she hurl back some stinging remark about swinish male chauvinism. But instead, she smiled prettily, gazed up so he could see just how large her eyes were, and shook back her long bright veil of hair. What did it matter if she landed the job on her looks? She would prove herself soon enough by her brains and ability.

She was hired at one hundred twenty-five dollars a week. Not a fortune, she knew, but for a while the reflected glamour more than compensated for the pay. It was a thrill to hear the voice of a star on the phone or catch a glimpse of a famous face sailing through the office. And she reveled in the way people looked impressed and became eagerly curious when she told them what she did for a living.

The money didn't seem all that deficient. She shared a decrepit but huge West End Avenue apartment with two other women from Hadley and a recent Minton graduate named Chuck. They had a communal record collection, stole each other's wine, peanut butter, and cottage cheese, and let a slick gray slime collect on the sides of the bathtub for want of cleaning. But Kate's share of the rent was only seventy-two dollars, and she found it an agreeable—even romantic—living situation.

Clothes were no problem—everyone wore jeans and freebie promotional T-shirts. And as for entertainment—there were entire networks of people her own age just starting out, looking for connections and willing to share what spoils they had already acquired. There was always someone who knew someone who could get you into tonight's party at Warhol's Factory, a screening of *El Topo*, free passes to the Bottom Line.

More than anything, New York meant new men.

She was still looking for the special face, the one that would fulfill the promise of all-encompassing love. In the meantime she wove blissful fantasies to put herself to sleep at night. And reveled in being pursued. Her long hair, streaming down to the curve of her buttocks, seemed to draw men to her on the streets, in the subways, across crowded parties.

"Excuse me," a stranger would say, hurrying up beside her as she crossed Lexington Avenue. "I'm a photographer, and I was wondering if by any chance you were a model."

Kate would be all eager attention. *He thinks I'm pretty!*

The chances were that he would invite her for a drink or a cup of coffee, that he would continue to flatter her looks and her independence, hint at glamorous connections that could be used to her benefit, invite her back to his apartment for Polaroid test shots or just to rap a little longer. . . . And chances were, too, that by that evening she would have gone to bed with him.

As she did with almost every man she went out with. Because it was almost impossible to say no anymore. Men just expected it; and if you refused, they made it seem there was something wrong with *you*—that you were frigid, that you weren't *really* liberated. Kate assumed they were right. She prided herself on not being a hypocritical, virginal type. She preened when men told her, "You're a real *woman*. You're so beautifully free."

Her first winter blinked by in a flurry of new faces and experiences. But as the weather turned warmer, she grew less and less content. Her job no longer seemed so wonderful: the touches of glamour no longer disguised the fact that the work was essentially brainless. Phoning the same list of "contacts" day after day, hunting down an obscure brand of tobacco for some imperious British actor, mailing yet another press kit to the reviewer of the *Sparta* (NJ) *Herald* (circulation 16,500) . . . nothing that couldn't be done by any reasonably bright ninth grader. And she was beginning to feel the pinch of money. Her fourth roommate, Chuck, had split for Taos, leaving only three to split the rent. Now every purchase—from a new pair of boots to a taxi ride on a bitterly cold night—had to be weighed carefully for its absolute necessity.

But what had most disillusioned her about the job was the attitude of the other assistants. There were three besides Kate; all were women, all attractive graduates of excellent schools, well read, up on cultural and political events. And all three bitterly resented the fact that they were stuck at Haber and Switt. They complained constantly and did as little work as they could get away with. They lost no opportunity to bad-mouth the partners: Harold Switt was a sexist creep and Bob Haber a slob. They fudged their overtime cards, ripped off stationery and whatever else from the office they could, justifying this petty thievery on the grounds that they deserved much more.

At first Kate felt a superior contempt for their attitude. "If you hate it here so much, why don't you just quit?" she asked.

"Oh, sure, and do what?" one replied. "For every job opening, don't you know there're about two thousand applicants? We're all damned lucky to get this."

"I send out about five or six résumés a week," one of the others added. "All I get is form letters saying it's been put 'on file.' And you know what that means—the circular file."

Kate just shrugged. Maybe that was true for *them*. But she, after all, was prettier, more interesting . . . people stopped her on the street, sought her out in crowds . . . something extraordinary was bound to fall her way. But time passed and nothing changed, and her confidence began to ebb away. If Elise and Karen and Lynne could do no better with all they had going for them, she began to reason, then maybe she couldn't either.

SHE BEGAN TO have days when she felt depressed, seemingly for no reason at all. She would simply wake up in the morning feeling black, the thought of getting out of bed almost too much to bear. And she would drag listlessly through the rest of the day, amazed that she could even function.

It was in one of these slumps that she came to a horrible realization: she could no longer count the number of men she had slept with.

Until the end of college she could. But in the last year had there been a dozen? Twice that? Or even more? She tried to list them and became confused. Should she count the German writer who came before anything really happened? Or the weird, silver-haired guy she ended up with after the Badfinger press party who only wanted a hand job? And that disgusting little man who had brought her up to his video studio and then implied that he wouldn't let her out unless she made it with him on the sofa—that had been practically rape, so maybe that didn't count either. And certainly she must have gone out with someone in February, but she couldn't remember a name, a face at all. . . .

It doesn't matter, she told herself. If it feels good, do it.

Except that a lot of times it really didn't feel good. Sometimes she would be just bored, other times it might hurt or she would actually be repulsed. But still she wriggled and moaned and pretended to relish new positions. And she gasped convincingly when she judged it to be the right time. She faked orgasms, just like any housewife of the fifties. It was all part of being free.

By summer, the black days were beginning to arrive almost every week. And she would go on crying jags that left her face blotched and her eyes puffy and red.

The day of Candy Barris's dinner party, she had been on a jag. Candy was a researcher for "CBS News"; her friends were media people, bright, aggressive, and interesting. Kate had been looking forward to the party all week. But now, staring at her tear-swollen face, all her enthusiasm vanished.

She could not make herself put on the royal-blue hot pants and silver satin T-shirt she usually wore for parties. Instead, she disappeared inside a muddy-brown oversized sweater and baggy brown trousers. And when she arrived at Candy's apartment, she sat hunched in the dimmest corner of the room. She felt invisible, a brown no one blending in with the wall.

There were about a dozen guests eating chicken curry off paper plates and sipping tepid white wine. Kate watched them. They seemed like attractive, successful people. They were happy being with each other; they could have no use for a Brown Person like her. She was glad she had rendered herself invisible.

But strangely, someone was approaching her—one of the men, crouching down beside her, balancing a plastic cup of wine and a laden paper plate.

"I've been intrigued by you," he said. "You look so aloof and independent that I had to come over and see what you're all about."

He had pale blue eyes that seemed to claim attention. "I guess I've been feeling a little antisocial tonight," she said apologetically.

He nodded. "I can dig that. After so many parties, you get sick of the same old bullshit being dished out over and over. It's more entertaining to just sit back and watch the other clowns perform."

Kate was amazed and flattered that he could attribute such snobbish motives to her behavior. She raised her head and swept her hair back and looked fully at him. He was cute, she noted. Rather Slavic looking, with high, broad cheekbones and fine, blond hair swept across his forehead, and those pale eyes.

His name, he told her, was Stephen Luckingbill. He was a graphics designer with a tiny downtown firm that specialized in catalogues. "That sounds like fun," she said. He groaned and described a recent project: a children's ready-to-wear catalogue. All the client could say was he wanted something different. So Stephen designed it as a kid's scrapbook—pictures that looked torn out and Scotch-taped on, that sort of thing. Everyone in his firm hated it—he had to fight to even get it submitted. The client was hesitant, but at the last minute decided to go with it. "And wouldn't you know," Stephen said in a quiet voice, "the crazy thing ended up winning an art directors' award!"

"You must be really good," Kate said.

"I do all right," he replied. But there was no modesty in either his tone or expression. I'm terrific, he seemed to be telling her. And because I've singled you out, you must be terrific as well. We're two singular people in a world full of clowns and hopeless bunglers. Kate felt an infinite gratitude that he had been able to look past her swollen eyes and hideous outfit to see that she belonged on this superior plane with him.

He extended his plate of curry to her, and she discovered that she was suddenly hungry. They nibbled and talked and shared wine until the music stopped and Kate was astounded to discover that they were among the last ones left.

"Look, I'd like to leave with you," Stephen said. Kate felt a shiver. She had assumed they would leave together and return to either his apartment or hers, but hearing him say it so intently was vividly exciting. "But there's something you should know first," he went on. "I'm living with someone right now. Not for much longer, though," he added quickly. "I want to move out as soon as possible. I've been looking for a new pad. It's definitely over. But I just wanted to be up front about it."

Kate nodded with understanding. She wasn't disturbed by his confession—she felt in control, free, and liberated. "It's very important to know when to let something go," she said levelly. "Were you together for very long?"

"About a year. The thing is, she changed. Almost the minute we moved in together she became totally dependent. As if all of a sudden she couldn't do a fucking thing on her own. We had to go every place together, do everything together . . . she became so possessive I could hardly breathe." He shook his head. "It's been a bitch, I'll tell you. Since I told her I wanted out, she's thrown a scene every night. Crying and carrying on. I can hardly stand to go *near* the fucking place anymore."

"I've never understood that kind of behavior," Kate declared. "I think it's emotional blackmail. And it shows so little pride."

His eyes beamed with new approval. "Do you know how rare it is to find a woman who understands that?"

Kate lowered her glance modestly.

"No, really. What it tells me is that you've got a life of your own. *You'd* never have to cling to some guy for an identity."

Kate glowed with a sense of superiority over this leech of a woman he was so rightly casting away.

Later they made love on the narrow mattress on the floor of her room. Stephen was a straightforward lover, if not an imaginative one, and his eyes continued to assert his interest and approval. "We fit pretty well together," he murmured, making it seem as if she had done something splendidly clever.

He called her the following day, and they began to see each other with increasing frequency. Stephen seemed completely happy to be Stephen—he seemed to wake up every day entirely satisfied with who he was and what he did. And why not? After all, he was enormously talented—of that he continued to assure her. His future, whether he chose to continue in the commercial field or explore his potential for "really serious art," he had no doubt would be brilliant. As for the present, he managed to convey the fact that everything he did was in some way the best. His friends were the choice pick of a city fairly teeming with mediocrities. The trattoria in Little Italy he frequented was the *only* one that hadn't lowered the quality of its food to the shabby tourist standard. And let other fools spend lavishly for status cars—his eight-year-old Dodge Dart was the kind of reliable transportation that made by far the best sense.

Each time they were together, Stephen reported to her the progress of his breakup with Melanie. "She's really showing her true colors now," he fumed. She had maliciously thrown out a box of old photos and letters she knew meant a lot to him. She had embarrassed him by criticizing him to a colleague of his. And she had hidden the stereo speakers—*his* fabulous KLH speakers—so he couldn't take them with him. "I was fooled by her for a long time, but now I know what a little bitch she really is," he told Kate. "I just want to get the hell out."

Kate agreed with him completely. Melanie sounded like a pathetic creature: spiteful and selfish, with no pride at all. Kate was different, and she could tell Stephen admired her for it.

At last Stephen found an apartment of his own. It was a small one bedroom in the Yorkville district of the East 80s, with the charm of a broad bay window in the living room. He escorted Kate through the three tiny rooms as proudly as if it were a palace. "The agent tried to sell me on a crappy little studio in the Village for three thirty a month," he said. "When I dug up this place for twenty bucks less, I called her back and said, 'Baby, you'll just have to find someone a bit more gullible!' " He laughed with pure pleasure—

obviously he had scored the best apartment deal in Manhattan.

"It's fabulous!" Kate breathed sincerely. She thought it the most cheerful, charming apartment she had ever seen. She wished she could nestle in below the sweep of the bay window and never leave.

Stephen seemed to read her thoughts. "Listen," he said. "Do you want to share?"

Kate glanced up at him. "You mean it? You'd like me to move in with you?"

"I think it wouldn't be a bad idea. I like living with a woman—the *right* woman. And you could certainly use a better place. I think we've proved over the past month how well we relate to each other."

Kate's mind raced. She would have to hide it from her mother, dig up someone to take her old room. . . . But to be able to stay here, to be with Stephen all the time . . . "It could be fun," she said as calmly as possible.

He kissed her and hugged her hard, and as he did he breathed the words "I love you" in her ear. Her body trembled and a burst of joy ran through her.

"I love you too," she blurted. It was marvelous, wonderful to be able to say it. Not have to keep it bottled up, not to pretend to be cool and casual. . . .

I love you, I love you, I love you. To say it and hear it said back was the sweetest music in the universe.

*A*NDREA, IN LAW SCHOOL, CONSIDERED HERSELF MORE OF a grind than ever. The other first-year students all seemed aggressively self-confident, which Andrea believed could only be underlined by native brilliance. And though Chicago Law had accepted more women this year than ever before, they still totaled fewer than twenty percent of the class. Andrea had never competed with men before and found this sudden preponderance of them intimidating.

But eventually she discovered that the bulk of the work consisted of voluminous reading and learning to think like a lawyer—sheer diligence would ensure at least a modest success. As she began to relax, she found there were actually subjects she enjoyed. Property, for instance, with its quaint, sort of Dickensian, language, and precedents dating, some of them, back to Richard the Lion-Hearted.

Chicago itself frightened her. She had watched the 'sixty-eight Democratic convention and remembered vividly the advancing tactical police cracking the heads of Yippies, kids

148

her own age. And the South Side in which the university was located was particularly threatening, with its dessicated tenements and wary black faces. She never walked through the streets without feeling the haunting presence of potential violence—the same fear that caused many of the female students to wear whistles around their necks and carry slim vials of Mace in their book bags.

But she was happy with where she lived—on the edge of the neighborhood in a run-down house that she shared with three other women. One was an undergraduate, one attended the business school, and one, Barb, was an older woman who worked as a secretary in the law admissions office. They were all feminists. They wore no makeup and let their body hair grow naturally; they wore no bras nor girdles nor pointed-toed, high-heeled shoes, nor any other clothes that would distort their natural woman's shape. And together, they were a sort of community. They shared the cooking, taking care to prepare healthy, natural foods. They hugged each other a lot, ran errands cheerfully for one another, gave each other pep talks and an occasional scolding when needed. And Barb pasted mottoes on the refrigerator door:

> *FOR A WOMAN TO SUCCEED HALF AS MUCH AS A MAN SHE MUST DO EVERYTHING TWICE AS WELL.*
> *FORTUNATELY THIS IS NOT DIFFICULT.*
>
> *TRUST IN GOD; SHE WILL PROVIDE.*

To Andrea, it was a real home. And Barb, with her cropped gray hair, Mexican smocks, and peppy efficiency, was more of a mother than she had ever known.

Between her classwork and little household, Andrea found her life pretty full. She had had a few dates since she had been here, but nothing had clicked, and for the moment she was content without men. The infrequent times she thought of Douglas it was with mild relief, as if a great pressure had been taken off her. She supposed that meant she had really never loved him at all.

But then she wasn't quite sure she understood what love was. What most people—and especially men—meant now when they said love was sex. *Make* love. Of course, it could mean other things too, like giving a flower to a stranger or flashing the peace sign to an uptight-looking cop. But more and more it seemed to her that it meant doing it. Making love.

And the same went for the word *free*. Everybody talked about being free—having no more shame about your body, and being able to take a leak in front of everybody else, and throwing off your clothes like the kids did at Woodstock, and saying "fuck" and "shit" and "piss" the way people used to say "darn it!" And she could hack all that, she supposed. Except that it seemed these days that it all really added up to free love. Do it, do it, do it. And maybe it was good that women no longer had to worry about preserving their virginity at all costs, but sometimes it seemed to Andrea that this pressure to do it, do it, do it was even more of a thrall.

She supposed she was just hopelessly out of step with her generation. But she didn't care—she was happy enough among her little family of women.

In her second year things changed. The subjects she was taking were more difficult: constitutional law with its abstract concepts; the elegant but immense jigsaw puzzle of trusts and estates. With the scramble to make *Law Review*, the competition grew fiercer, the pressure more intense.

Then her family broke up. The business student moved out of the house to go live with a boyfriend; she was replaced by a psych major who kept to her own room where she entertained a changing shift of stoned young men. Shortly afterward Barb left to be with her recently widowed sister in Seattle.

Then Rick Maysell whirled into Andrea's life.

His full name was Heinrich Lane Maysell. He was small and wiry with a cute-ugly face and a bushy red Jewish Afro, and he worked for the local office of the Commodities Exchange Commission. They met at a bluegrass concert on the lakeside steps. Andrea had worn her new orange granny gown. Someone near her had flipped open a warm beer; as she backed off to avoid the spray, she bumped into Rick, who looked at her and said, sort of out of the corner of his mouth, "Rivers of beer flowing over your grandmother's paisley shawl." It was a line that had puzzled her until some weeks later he had hauled her into a revival theater to see *The Bank Dick* and she discovered that W. C. Fields was his idol whom he worshiped second only to Groucho Marx, who was God.

She quickly came to know his other quirks. His habit of calling everyone, including her, by their last names (her own pet name for him was "Koala" because he was short and kind of furry); his obsession, at the age of twenty-seven, with aging. "I don't see why we celebrate birthdays," he would say lugubriously. "It just marks another year closer to death." And when she laughed at him, he would list all the people he knew of who had died before they reached his age: Buddy Holly. Brian Jones. Janis and Jimi. The Big Bopper.

One night, when he came to take her to Due's for deep-dish pizza he looked at her petulantly. "Do you *always* have to wear those dungarees?" he asked.

Andrea glanced down at herself. She had on a pair of Iron Boy overalls and a T-shirt, an outfit she favored because it served as a kind of natural harness for her breasts, keeping them from wobbling too much when she walked. "Don't you like them?" she said.

"I hate them. They're a real turnoff."

"They're not supposed to turn anybody on," Andrea said quickly. "They're supposed to make me feel free and comfortable."

"Why can't you feel free and comfortable in something attractive? I like those peasant blouses a lot of girls are wearing now. You've got great tits, Herry. Why not flaunt what you've got?"

Andrea made a face. "I get too much grief when I wear stuff like that."

"Grief from who?"

"You know, from men. Construction workers and truck drivers. They shout out things like 'Watch 'em bounce!' and then they go bananas."

"So why don't you wear a bra then?" Rick countered.

"Because it's not natural."

"Godfrey Daniels, the woman's not natural!" he exclaimed in his W. C. Fields voice. "Look, Herry," he went on, "on one hand you claim you want to feel free, and on the other you're restricting yourself just to be natural. All you're doing is canceling yourself out."

She didn't actually admit he was right, but one day she simply began to wear a bra again. She even felt secretly relieved not to worry about her breasts sagging to her waist before she was thirty, like tribal women in places like Bechuanaland and New Guinea.

Rick's next campaign was directed against her not shaving her legs and armpits. Once again she protested that it was not natural.

"Neither is brushing your teeth or combing your hair," he told her. "Are you planning to stop doing those things too?"

"That's different. Those are for hygiene and this is only cosmetic. I'd just be conforming to some air-brushed Madison Avenue male fantasy."

"Bullshit!" Rick replied. "It's to give *me* more pleasure, just like I try to be pleasing to you. I wear deodorant and wash my hair every day and change my underwear so I don't turn *you* off, don't I." He gave his hurt-little-boy pout. "Oh, come on, Herry. I see enough hairy pits every day when I shower at the Y."

She shaved. And then she tweezed her eyebrows because he convinced her that "they look too masculine growing all scraggly." And she no longer tied up her hair in little pigtails because it gave her an earth-mother kind of quality that made him feel old. And she began to wear lip gloss because he loved the look of a "just-licked mouth."

But his most ambitious campaign focused on her weight. Once it had become obvious that she was going to sleep with Rick, Andrea had gone back on the pill. After a year's reprieve, she had forgotten how much she hated it—the bruising cramps, the bloated, logy feeling before each period. And in two months she had gained another twelve pounds. Rick began at every meal to lecture her on calorie counts. "Granola's got two fifty a cup, would you believe? And there's over *sixty* in every teaspoon of honey. That brown-rice-and-almond concoction you make is actually more fattening than chocolate cake!"

She tried Atkins and Stillman and simply starving herself to the point that she could hardly concentrate in her classes. But then the urge to eat would prove irresistible, and she would binge, eating her way through an entire pint of Hägen-Dazs, sour cream straight from the container, anything and everything that was in the house, pummeling her hips with one hand while she ate with the other.

"Look, Koala," she said finally. "I could lose weight

right away if I went off the pill. I wouldn't even have to diet.''

He wrinkled his nose questioningly. ''How can you do that?''

''I could get a diaphragm instead.''

''No!'' he said with a squeal. ''I hate diaphragms! They're revolting. They cut out all the spontaneity, and the jelly tastes disgusting, and anyway I can feel it inside. It spoils everything. I mean, it's like going back to the *fif*ties!''

Andrea knew it was useless to argue further. Spontaneous sex was the closest thing to a religion that Rick possessed. If she went to his apartment for dinner, chances were that they would end up naked under his kitchen table. Once at a party, he had coaxed her into an upstairs bathroom and locked the door for a quickie. And more than once when she had spent the night with him, she would awaken at four in the morning to find him pouncing on her.

Do it, do it, do it.

But this was different, she reminded herself. They were in a relationship; they were supposed to be enjoying a healthy sex life. There was no such thing as being ''oversexed'' anymore, the way they used to talk about certain boys back when she was at St. Elizabeth's. Nowadays, everybody wanted to be turned on all the time.

Still . . . Rick would want to do it two or three times a night, four nights in a row. And there were positions— standing up, kneeling with him behind, pretzeled-up positions he copied from a sex manual called *The Closest Thing to Heaven*. And of course oral sex. It was funny, though— putting him in her mouth didn't bother her as much as she thought it would. He had a rather small, chubby penis which, with its broad hood that made her think of a fireman's hat, was sort of cute. And thankfully he didn't mind that she pulled away before he came: she knew she'd gag if he tried to make her swallow it. But what she hated was when he went down on her. In her old T-group at Hadley, there had been much brave talk about learning to love your own genitals—to be as proud of your vagina as a man was of his penis. They had spoken daringly of looking inside themselves with a speculum, even of tasting their own menstrual blood. Yet the first time Rick had edged himself downward, his lips tracing the valley between her breasts to her navel then beyond, spreading her thighs so that he could place himself *there,* she had writhed with embarrassment. It was too slimy. Too rank. How could he not be grossed out by the foulness of its secretions?

And she was right. Because soon afterward he said, just a bit too casually, "Why don't you get that new spray stuff? Whatchacall it, Feminique? The stuff Judith Christ flacks on TV. Just to try it out. . . ." he added quickly.

But to Andrea, it confirmed her worst fears: her odor was so offensive that it required an artificially scented deodorant. She wondered if Douglas had noticed . . . and her gynecologist when she went for her Pap smear . . . noticed and were appalled but were too delicate to mention it. She purchased a can of Feminique and used it faithfully every day after that, whether or not she was planning to see Rick.

Gross, hirsute, and disordered though she might be, Rick continued to stay with her. And she cuddled and mothered him whenever he slipped into a gloom or one of his hurt-little-boy sulks.

One Saturday afternoon, he led her into a toy store on State Street and played for her Jiminy Cricket singing "When You Wish Upon a Star." She listened, enchanted, thinking that she really did love this man. And when the song ended, he said, "What do you think, Herry? Should we get married?"

She turned a beaming face to him. "Yes, let's get married!" she breathed. "Oh, Koala, I love you!"

"I love you, too, and let's go to bed." He pushed her into a taxi though he lived only six blocks away. Within minutes they were falling onto his bed, laughing giddily. He made love to her this time the regular way with him on top. She looked tenderly into his funny, cute-ugly face and thought, so this is the one. This is who I'll spend the rest of my life with. This is who will be the father of my children. And he would make such a good father, the way he always liked to show her things, teach her what he knew about jazz and old movies and his dumb magic tricks. . . . Yes, he would be great with kids, and she was grateful that he wanted to marry her . . . great, grateful, great. . . . The words overwhelmed her and suddenly spilled into a feeling so deep and rich that she curled her toes and threw open her arms and gave herself entirely up to it.

Afterward, as she cuddled against Rick's damp body, she murmured, "I had an orgasm that time."

His body stiffened slightly. "I thought you always came," he said.

She wondered why when they had never talked about it before. And why was there such a peevish tone to his voice? "It was always a little hard for me," she said evasively. "But I don't think it will be anymore. I think it's knowing that we're getting married—it makes it a lot easier for me to let go. I think from now on it's going to be really terrific."

She expected him to be delighted. But strangely, he just grunted. With a sigh, she saw that he was about to go into one of his sulks—and that it was going to take at least an hour of cooing and petting and promising him special treats to bring him out of it.

> *Coordinator Needed For Women's*
> *Informational Cooperative*
> *Little money, much responsibility,*
> *Sisterhood, sharing, and mutual support*

*T*HE AD IN THE CLASSIFIED SECTION OF THE *Village Voice*
immediately caught Jean's eye. It had been two months
since she had fled IMI, a little over a week since she had
moved to Manhattan. Her bruises were still fresh: the words
women, support, cooperative sounded soothing as a balm.

She found the cooperative working out of a decaying
storefront in the East Village. The several dozen women
who were there were all dressed in sturdy, work-a-day
jeans, chukka boots, cut-off men's shirts. They stared with
frank hostility at Jean's business suit and sleek dark hair.
You're not one of us, their eyes told her, if you don't look
like us too. But as Jean described her experiences at IMI—
matter-of-factly, with no indulgence in self-pity—their hostility melted into approval. She had been victimized by men
and that seemed to be the single greatest reference she could
produce. Her interrogators went into a huddle and returned
with the news: "We'd like to have you join us."

Jean was exhilarated. Here was the opportunity she had

been waiting for: a chance to build something with people who were behind her all the way.

The purpose of the cooperative was to dispense information on such topics as birth control, daycare, and impending women's-rights legislation. Jean quickly discovered that there were already ample volunteers capable of collecting and dispensing information. She, as a paid coordinator, would therefore be needed for the more aggressive and skilled tasks of raising funds and securing publicity. She spent several days reading, watching, asking questions. Then she presented her ideas to the other members of the co-ordinating committee.

She sat numbly while her proposals were torn apart by uninformed or simply trivial objections. The meeting dragged through the entire morning and well into the afternoon with frequent eruptions into silly bickering. At last, through sheer exhaustion, a watered-down and impotent version of Jean's original proposal was grudgingly adopted by the group.

Jean now understood what "cooperative" meant. It meant her every action would first have to be approved by every other member of the group—by women who, for the most part, had no managerial experience, who until recently had been waitresses, housewives, potters, sales clerks, or free-lance writers. It was as if she, as secretary to John Dreiser, had had the power to criticize and veto his decisions! Jean left the meeting burning with frustration.

After that she came prepared to fight for her ideas. Yet the stronger and more purposeful she became, the more the other women seemed to regard her with suspicion and resentment. There were exceptions—in particular a young black Radcliffe graduate named Doreen. "I was totally into black power at school," she told Jean. "Had only black friends and would spit in the eye of any white guy who so much as dared give me a look. But like it always is in this country for us, there weren't enough black men to go around. So at one meeting, this brother gets up and starts proposing that we get into polygamy. I mean, this fucker was serious! He was going to take himself a harem and pretend he was making some sort of great political sacrifice.'' She let out her infectious, looping laugh. ''That, child, was the day I switched my allegiance to sisterhood.''

Jean could always count on Doreen to back her up or at least offer an intelligent compromise that would prove acceptable to the group.

On the other hand there was Delia, a whining, self-righteous, and stupid woman of about forty. Delia's husband had run off with an ex-Braniff stewardess. Delia had worked briefly as a hostess in a Queens cocktail lounge and had been fired for chronic absenteeism, but she insisted her dismissal was due to her age. ''Nobody wants a middle-aged woman,'' was her constant refrain. ''We got no more value than a lousy stray dog.'' Jean thought her pathetic, but the rest of the group exalted her.

ONE EVENING WHILE she was staying late to finish a grant proposal, Jean was startled to hear footsteps behind her. She turned to find Patsy Ingersoll, a dainty, snub-featured woman who was one of the founding members of the co-op.

''Did I scare you?'' Patsy asked.

''A bit. I thought I was alone.''

''Sorry. I've been holed up in reception weeding out the Rolodex.'' Patsy hunched beside Jean and peered down at the proposal form. ''How's this mumbo-jumbo coming?''

''It's getting there.''

''Need any help?''

''No. Or wait, there's a file with all the mailing-list stats buried in that stack out front. Think you could dig it out for me?''

"Um," Patsy murmured. But she made no move to go. Instead she continued leaning beside Jean, watching her intently. "God, you're lovely," she spoke suddenly.

Jean glanced up warily. "Thanks, Patsy," she said.

Patsy stared at her a moment longer. Then she reached out and with unambiguous intent caressed the slender line of Jean's shoulder.

Jean stiffened. "I'm sorry, Patsy, but you've got me wrong. I don't go that way."

"How do you know? Have you ever tried it?"

"I don't have to. I know my own inclinations." She held herself rigidly under the pressure of Patsy's lingering hand. "Please, Patsy," she repeated, "I'm honestly not that way."

Patsy relented. She folded her arms, pushing up the sleeves of her faded Levi jacket in a businesslike manner. "Let me ask you a question," she said. "Do you or don't you call yourself a feminist?"

"Of course I do. But that doesn't mean I have to be a . . .." Jean balked at the word *lesbian*. "That I have to be gay."

"That's exactly where you're wrong. If you're a true feminist, there's no other politically acceptable option." Patsy tilted her speckled moss-colored eyes up at Jean. "Look. In this society, any male-female relationship has got to end up with the woman in some way oppressed. You know that as well as I do."

Jean hesitated. "Even if that's true, what difference does it make? I can't just choose to be attracted to other women."

"Oh, yes you can. We're all basically bisexual. It's just our fucked-up culture that imposes its repressive Victorian mores on you and makes you afraid to explore the other side of your sexuality. They've built up like this stone wall inside of you. You've just got to find the courage to rip it down.''

"It's not a question of being afraid," Jean bristled. "It's the way I *feel.*"

"Is it? Then think about it. Are you really that crazy about playing up to men's fantasies? Don't you think it would be nice to drop the role-playing for just once in your life and really be yourself?" Patsy's voice dropped a tone, became conspiratorial. "Can you ever sleep with a pig again after how you said they treated you in that fascist corporation?"

Jean gazed at the desktop, the litter of forms in front of her. It was true she had been avoiding men lately—the memory of her recent humiliation was still agonizingly fresh in her mind. But beyond that there was a certain logic to Patsy's words, something that undeniably meshed. She *had* always felt herself to be playing a role with men. Even with John Dreiser she had always played the grateful recipient to his omnipotent benefactor. . . .

And what if Patsy was right? What if her aversion to making love to another woman was really nothing more than a fastidiousness imposed by a repressive society? Wouldn't she be cheating herself not to find out?

Patsy, sensing her confusion, bent a little closer. "Come on home with me," she urged softly. "We don't have to do anything you don't want to, I promise. We'll take it very slow.''

Beneath the reassurance was a challenge: I dare you. And Jean, delving into herself, discovered that she really was afraid. Perhaps it was for this reason more than any other that she raised her chin and stared levelly into Patsy's watchful eyes. "Where do you live?" she said. "When I'm done with this report, maybe I will drop by."

* * *

PATSY'S RAILROAD FLAT on Avenue B was the sort of hippie "pad" that had been by now well documented in the popular press. No furniture, just water-stained cushions scattered over a splintering floor. A mattress covered in an Indian weave served as a bed. Clumps of peacock feathers in lumpy hand-thrown pots completed the décor. Patsy was no housekeeper. Stacks of tabloids—*Rat, Majority Report, The East Village Other*—toppled in neglected yellowing heaps. A smoldering stick of jasmine incense couldn't disguise the choke of dust and mildew in the fusty air.

Jean, who loved order and cleanliness, perched awkwardly on the edge of a cushion, crossing and uncrossing her feet at the ankles. She watched Patsy light candles, setting a mood as if for a seduction. It *was* a seduction, she realized with a shock and recoiled with the sudden, strange notion. How preposterous to think she could force something as basic as desire. And yet from all she had heard and read, other women had done just that. A question of reconditioning, Patsy had said. A matter of will.

And now Patsy was squatting on an opposite cushion, her "I dare you" smile broadened over her snubbed features. No backing down now. . . . Jean smiled resolutely in return.

Patsy licked and lit a long, narrow joint, inhaled deeply. She proffered it to Jean who shook her head.

"Jesus, you *are* straight," Patsy marveled. "Well, okay. We've got to have something to loosen you up." She retreated through an arch and returned with a water glass of red wine. "Rioja. 'Fraid it's been open a while. . . ."

Jean sipped. The wine was cold and vinegary, making her think with quick longing of the velvety Margaux, the buttery Montrachets John Dreiser had taught her to adore. But he had *taught* her, that was the point—just another manifestation of his power over her. Why hadn't she seen that before? She took a long sip of the sour wine.

"Sorry about that rot-gut," Patsy said. "Sure you don't want a toke of grass?"

"No, I'm fine," Jean said. And waited. But Patsy merely folded her legs, continued to pull on the joint, and launched into an account of the various internecine quarrels that raged behind the scenes at the center. Jean began to enjoy herself. The wine, the candlelight, Patsy's pungent smoke and peppery shop gossip combined in a pleasant haze. How lonely she had been! Jean realized suddenly. Her work had kept her well occupied, but it wasn't enough. And she did like this woman. . . .

Patsy seemed to guess her thoughts. She was silent a moment, then breathed, "God, I'm so glad you're here! But I knew you'd come. I've watched you. So brave . . ." And reaching out she traced an index finger along the contour of Jean's chin.

Reflexively, Jean stiffened. "Just relax," Patsy murmured. "Trust me. Let me make a *real* woman out of you."

Jean held herself still as Patsy stroked her cheek and hair, murmuring words of praise, leaning ever closer, until delicately she brought her lips to Jean's. A shiver ran through Jean. She closed her eyes and tried to experience the kiss as pure sensation. Soft. *Too* soft, and the scent of Patsy's near skin was too sweet, lacking a man's astringency. It was wrong, terribly wrong. . . . No not wrong, just different. Wait, let go, give it time. . . .

Encouraged, Patsy let her lips wander upward, nuzzled Jean's eyelids and forehead, then returned to her mouth with a more insistent pressure. Jean could hear the deep sigh of her breathing, could feel the quick, moist dab of her tongue. She shuddered again.

"Now you see, don't you?" Patsy whispered. "Now

touch me. Don't be afraid.'' She took Jean's hand and placed it firmly upon her own breast. Through thin gauze, Jean felt the shallow rise of flesh like her own, the rigid extension of a long nipple. Something pricked her—excitement, or more accurately a deep curiosity, and experimentally she let her hand close over the swell. And then instantly she was subsumed by a tide of revulsion. She heard her father spit the word *lezzies*, saw his eyes gloat with disgust, and with a gasp she pulled away from the other woman.

"Patsy, I can't,'' she cried.

"Easy,'' Patsy soothed. "Just take it easy. I'll get you some more wine.''

"No, that won't help.''

"Hey, you've come this far, don't cop out now.'' Patsy reached for her wrist, but Jean was already lifting herself to her feet.

"I can't help it,'' she said. "I can't change the way I feel.''

Patsy rose with her. "Is it me?'' she pleaded. "Aren't I pretty enough? Are you still hung up on that cosmetic thing?''

"No, honestly, it's me. I should never have come. I'm sorry.''

The moss eyes hardened to malachite. "I'm sorry too. I thought I recognized something in you, something stronger and maybe willing to take a few risks. But I guess I was wrong. You're just another spoiled middle-class princess scared shitless of losing respectability. I pity you, Jean. You'll always be a slave to men.'' Patsy turned her stare to the wall. "Get out. And don't come back unless you ever have the guts to break out.''

Jean made her way to the street in a turmoil. The last fifteen minutes played again and again in her mind, leaving her with a sickening sense of shame. But why? Because she had allowed herself to touch another woman's breast? Or because she had acted cowardly, had backed down when she should have seen it through?

She didn't know, didn't know. And there was no one she could turn to to find out.

The incident continued to trouble her for several days, aggravated by Patsy's pointed coolness to her whenever they met at the co-op. But at last it was overshadowed by her excitement in winning several small victories in her work. The first was the pledge of modest funds from a foundation she had been assiduously courting. The second was that a local newscast ran a story on the cooperative, interviewing Jean as a spokeswoman. The response was overwhelming—the phone rang continually for days afterward—and Jean was elated: it was the breakthrough they had desperately needed.

She was not surprised that no one in the co-op congratulated her for her successes. All accomplishments were supposed to be the result of "group effort" and no one was to claim individual credit. But what *was* strange was that suddenly she was being ostracized—as if she had actually done something wrong. Women were abrupt when they spoke to her, and groups fell into cold silence when she passed by.

She questioned Doreen who looked embarrassed, mumbled it was "nothing" and made an excuse to slip away. And then finally, one Saturday morning, Jean received a phone call from one of the coordinating committee requesting her to appear at the center. She arrived to find the other members already present, sitting rigidly as if in pews, gazing at her with religious severity . . . all of them there except Doreen.

The committee member who had phoned rose from the floor and faced Jean squarely, hands thrust defiantly in the pockets of her overalls. "It's our feeling that you've been appropriating this cooperative and the women's movement in general for your own self-glorification,'' she declared. There was a too-smooth tone to her voice as if she were delivering a rehearsed line.

"What do you mean my own glorification?" Jean demanded.

One by one, voices entered the fray.

"You're making yourself a media star on *our* backs . . ."

"And you've shown yourself for an opportunist. You're not interested in sharing and equality, you're a fucking elitist!"

". . . obviously you're into power . . ."

"I think you identify with *men*! You really want to be like one of *them*."

Jean's eyes swept the circle. There was Patsy, imperious and judgmental; there Delia with a look of dismal triumph. She understood what was happening: her sins were independence and the threat of leadership, her punishment to be purged from the ranks. In doing so, Jean realized, the Second Street Women's Cooperative had at last succeeded in a truly collective effort.

KATE COULDN'T BELIEVE HOW LUCKY SHE WAS. TO BE loved by someone as special as Stephen, as attractive and sharp and extraordinarily talented, at last fulfilled all her intimations that she had been marked for something wonderful. She floated giddily through her days, laughing out loud for no reason at all, skipping the bus in order to walk—or rather run—through the fall gold and icy brilliance of the air. The earth was changed: the words *he* and *she* took on mystical import; and one night she woke up in a cold dread because she suddenly understood what death meant—it was separation from Stephen.

They had the ideal relationship. Stephen himself declared this to be true. They were together strictly because they wanted to be, not because any official piece of paper or religious mumbo-jumbo deemed it okay. More important, neither one depended upon the other or leaned on the other in any way. They shared expenses equally, divided the chores, and maintained a separate life outside the relationship. Stephen sneered at what he called "Heckle and Jeckle" couples—the ones who were together to the point of suffocation. "We're not falling into that trap," he frequently boasted. "Once you do, you might as well be dead."

Stephen was an expert in maintaining his independence. He had his regular Tuesday-night squash game with his best friend Frank, after which they usually grabbed a bowl of chili together at O'Neal's. He went for drinks with other designers or clients and to professional awards dinners to which Kate was explicitly not invited. And he devoted long extra hours to his work, often over weekends. Kate began to dread the dismal Saturdays and Sundays when Stephen decided to go in to the studio and once again she found herself alone and drifting with nothing to do.

Money was becoming more of a problem than ever. After paying her half of the rent, electricity, and phone bill, she was left with less than sixty dollars to see her through each week. On that, she had to keep up with Stephen. He loved movies: they saw at least two a week. He frequently craved the Cuban roast pork at Victor's, and though it wasn't terribly expensive, it still cost more than eating at home. And when they took a cab—which Stephen always insisted upon after dark—it was understood that he paid the fare going and she was to pay it on the way back.

As a result, Kate was always running short. "Do me a huge favor and lend me ten dollars?" she asked Karen at work one morning.

"I'm out of cash. Wait till this afternoon after I go to the bank," Karen said.

"I can't. I'm meeting Stephen for lunch. Maybe Lynne's got it."

Karen was looking at her strangely. "You need it to have lunch with Stephen? Why doesn't he just pay?"

"We split everything," Kate said. "It's only fair that way."

"But doesn't he make a lot more money than you?"

"Oh, yeah, but there's no reason he should be forced to support me. I'm perfectly capable of supporting myself."

"I didn't say he's forced to," Karen persisted. "It's just that you'd think he'd *want* to do things for you."

"I think the reason he loves me is because I *am* independent," Kate said proudly. "Why should he want somebody weak and clinging that he has to prop up all the time?"

Karen shrugged, clearly not convinced. But Kate didn't care. She could hear what Stephen would say about Karen. "She's the kind of woman who wants to be liberated until it comes to her pocketbook," he would sneer. "Then suddenly she's just an old-fashioned girl."

Besides, Kate had always felt slightly sorry for Karen— the truth was she was just not very attractive to men. Not that women measured themselves that way anymore. . . . Still, Karen had spent last New Year's Eve home alone, peering through the blinds at a party across the street. And she was forever lamenting the miserable quality of the men she *did* meet. Kate felt a brief tug of satisfaction thinking about that. Clearly she had one of the very few desirable men around.

And so she continued happy. On cold mornings, she lay in bed, her leg pressing against Stephen's, feeling his warmth, his nearness, and thinking herself the luckiest creature alive.

On Thanksgiving she was to visit her parents in South Carolina; it would be the first time she would be sleeping apart from Stephen since they had moved in together, and the idea of it seemed bleak. But her parents were planning a cruise for Christmas, so this would be the only time during the holidays she could see them. The day before she left, she proposed to Stephen that they have their own special dinner together. "I can get out of the office early," she said. "So I'll cook—why don't you pick up some wine and dessert?"

"Sure," he said. "See you later, baby."

Kate left work with fervent expectation. She had a perfect image of how the evening would be. There was a recipe for chicken paprika she could make with fresh ingredients from the Hungarian specialty shops in their neighborhood. The little round table near the bay window would be set with candlelight. Pale wine and the food exquisitely presented on their best plates. She and Stephen lost in a romantic glow, absorbed in each other and in the perfect elegance of the meal.

By eight-thirty, the table was set, the candles lit, the chicken dish moist and done. But Stephen had not yet come home. Kate called his office; there was no answer. Perhaps it had taken him longer than usual to get the wine. Or he had stopped to find her some flowers . . . but no, Stephen was not the type for thoughtful little gestures and surprises.

She turned off the oven, blew out the candles to preserve their length, and waited. Nine o'clock passed, then nine-thirty. She began to worry. What if something had happened to him? A car accident, or a mugging . . . he could be in the hospital, he could be hurt or dead. Her heart constricted with fear. She tried to busy herself: she picked up the Edith Wharton she had been reading, turned on the radio—but she couldn't concentrate. Her ears strained for the sound of foot-steps on the stairs, a key turning in the lock. A car stopped below the window and gave her a burst of hope, but when she saw a stranger emerge from the idling taxi, she plunged into frantic despair. She picked up the phone and began to call his friends, panic eclipsing her voice so that she could hardly choke out the words. "Is Stephen there, Bill? Have you heard from him? I know, but he should have been back by now. . . ."

It was ten to ten when he walked in the door. Kate jumped up and ran to him. "Where have you been?" she cried.

"At Melanie's," he said. He carried an armload of records which he dumped on the couch.

"You were at Melanie's?" Kate repeated in a stupid voice. How could he have been with his old girlfriend on *their* last night together?

"Yeah. I ran into her on the way to the subway, and for once she wasn't acting like a supreme bitch. It seemed like a good time for us to air some things out. So we had a drink and it went pretty well. Then we went back to her place so I could pick up some records I left there. Look at some of this stuff!" He picked up an album from the pile, *The Who Sells Out.* "The British release with the original liner notes. You can't even *buy* this anymore."

"Why didn't you call?" Kate asked unsteadily.

Stephen glanced at her. "You mean check in?" he said in a dangerous tone.

"No, not to check in—to let me know where you were. I was worried, I thought something might've happened. I called up Frank and Billy and a couple of people looking for you. . . ."

"You called my friends?" he broke in.

"I was *worried.* I thought they might know where you were."

"Oh, that's fabulous. You know what they're gonna think now—that I'm tied to your apron strings like some little mama's boy."

She was terrified by the way he was looking at her, with the pale, flat eyes of an enemy. "I'm sorry, baby," she said frantically.

"Get one thing straight," he said. "I don't have to report my every move to you. I'm not your fucking dog on a leash—don't try to lay that trip on me."

"I'm not. Please, baby, listen to me. . . ."

"You listen to *me*. You've been overstepping your bounds a lot lately, baby. Just because we're living together, don't think you can take liberties. Because if this keeps on, we're through. Do you get that?"

"Stephen, don't say that!" She looked up at him beseechingly and burst into tears.

"Crying women! I'm sick to fucking death of crying women!" He started for the door and she grabbed his arm.

"Don't leave me alone,"she begged. He shook her off and continued out the door, slamming it behind him.

Kate sank onto the couch and cried until her breath came in painful gasps and her eyes were swollen and raw. He was gone and it was her own fault. He was absolutely right—she wasn't strong and independent at all. She really hated every single second they spent apart and hated the fact that he could enjoy himself without her. She had even been wildly jealous of his past, his good memories that didn't include her. And worst of all, she secretly envied the Heckle and Jeckle couples who spent so much time together—who seemed happy just drifting aimlessly through the park or browsing through silly Village shops, because they were with each other.

It was true: she was exactly the kind of clinging, possessive female Stephen most despised. And now that he knew it, he was gone for good.

But an hour later he returned. The fury had drained from his face; he sat beside her on the couch and regarded her for a suspenseful moment. "I guess I was being a little hard on you," he said at last. "But I think you know that I do love you, don't you?"

She fit gratefully into his arms, and a sweet sense of peace flooded through her, drowning out the pain. It was over now. She could feel lucky again—because from now on, everything was going to be all right.

*T*HOUGH IT WAS THE NIGHT BEFORE HER WEDDING, Andrea had refused all Jean's offers to help make up the couch Jean would be sleeping on. Instead she bustled about, tucking in the bottom sheet with tight corners, clucking a bit apologetically over the mismatched top sheet, smoothing down a bright Marimekko comforter and plumping a fat pillow just perfectly so against the arm of the couch. To Jean, it was a pure luxury to feel so completely taken care of—at least for the moment. Wonderful Andrea. She had forgotten how fond of her she was. How many times over the past few years could she have used the kind of unwavering approval she still saw in Andrea's eyes? It had been far too long since they had been together.

While Andrea busied herself, Jean told her the details of her disastrous employment at the Second Street Women's Cooperative.

"They must've been out of their minds!" Andrea burst out when she had finished. "You're the *real* liberated woman. What you've done, and who you are . . . I mean, you were out making it before any of us even *heard* of the movement. They should've made you their model!''

Jean shrugged. "They didn't see it that way. Who knows, maybe I came on too strong. But one thing's for sure—if I do make it, it won't be through either men or women. It'll have to be on my own."

"I think you're right," Andrea said. "You should go into business for yourself."

"Oh, I did. After I left the co-op, I had my own company for about four months. It was a service to lease artwork to corporations. I remembered how much money IMI spent on art for their halls and how tacky most of it was. Well, I found a German catalogue from which I could order some gorgeous posters for not too much money, and I cut a pretty good deal with a framer on Madison Avenue. And in less than a month I had orders from a few companies."

"And then what happened?"

Jean gave a wry smile. "The company that had given me the biggest order went belly up after three months and defaulted on their entire bill. I'd been counting on that money to pay the delivery man and to order new posters. I owed the framer, I owed the landlord, I owed the stationery store for my business cards. I just didn't have enough cash to cover the loss. So . . ." She shook her head angrily. "The thing is, it was working! If I had just had enough money to cover the loss, it could've really taken off. I had a lot of companies interested, it would have been no problem to get more clients . . ." She broke off with a short laugh. "Well, that's where I am now. I've got ideas, tons of them, and I know I've got the ability. All I need is the money to start."

Andrea gave intense attention to a corner of the sheet. Then with a breath she said, "Jean, I have some money."

Jean glanced up, then smiled indulgently. "I'm talking about a lot, Andy. Twenty or thirty thousand."

"I realize that. And . . ." She hesitated. "Well, I've got that much."

"You do?"

She nodded. "When my mother died, I inherited her trust. And then I sold our old house and furniture and things. My law-school tuition is using up a lot of that, but I've still got about thirty thousand left. So maybe if you did get something going, I could invest some of it. . . ." She began to flatten wrinkles on the makeshift bed with rapid motions, as if her own words had alarmed her. "The only thing is," she added, "it's all I've got. And I haven't even told Rick about it. It's like I still want there to be something that's all my own."

Jean sat up straight, her mind racing. Andrea's money would be a godsend, the very opportunity she was searching for. But how could she rightly expose Andrea's little inheritance to the kind of risk a new business would involve? Still, with the right idea and the money to back it up, the risk might not be so great. She was fully confident of her own ability—and if she did as well as she was certain she could, she'd be making Andrea's fortune as well as her own.

But she could already hear Andrea beginning to hesitate. "Now isn't a good time to be talking about all this," she said. "I'm going to be developing a few ideas over the next few weeks. By the time you and Rick get back from Wisconsin, I'll have something more concrete to show you. And then if you're still really serious . . ."

She stopped suddenly: Kate Auden, who was also staying here for the night, had just come into the room. Fresh from a bath, she wore a man's terrycloth robe, and her long hair was turbaned in a pink towel. How much had she heard? Jean wondered. Kate was one of the few at Hadley who had resisted all Jean's attempts to win her over—and now, after five years, Jean still sensed a coolness from her. What if Kate were to convince Andrea not to put up her money? Knowing how pliable Andrea was, Jean was sure it wouldn't be hard for Kate to do.

The thought pricked her with fear—for she was beginning to admit to herself how very much she wanted this money.

NO ONE GETS married anymore: that was Kate's first thought upon reading Andrea's letter announcing that she was engaged. None of Stephen's and her friends here in New York were married. Well, one couple were, Owen and Sally Fischer, but they had an "open" marriage—Owen was a freelance photographer and when he was off on assignment it was understood that both of them were free to do as they pleased. Everyone else Kate knew was either single and screwing around, or in a "relationship" but keeping separate apartments, or else simply living together. Marriage was fifties, suburbs, martinis, and nine to five. Marriage was domesticity.

And domesticity, according to Stephen, was the world's greatest trap. "That's one scene you'll never catch *me* stuck in," Stephen boasted frequently. And then he would explain to whomever he was with how he and Kate had the ideal relationship, with neither one dependent upon the other.

Yet it seemed to Kate that he was constantly watching her, as if waiting for her to prove that she really was like his mother, a clinging, dependent woman who had sprung upon his father the deadly trap of domesticity. And more and more frequently his suspicions were proving correct: he continually found her committing sins of dependency and possessive behavior. Her first offense had been the night he had come home late and discovered she had called his friends checking up on him. The second was right after she had returned from South Carolina. November had been particularly tough on her tiny funds. There had been the train ticket south, and back-to-back gynecologist visits—one for a new pill prescription, and the next for a case of trichomonas, one of those pesky vaginal infections that seemed to plague everyone these days and never quite went away. As a result, on the first of December she couldn't scrape up her half of the rent payment.

Timorously, she told Stephen. She watched his face close up like a fist. "So I have to shell out the whole thing?" he asked coldly.

"Just for now. I'll pay it back."

"How do I know that?"

"Can't you trust me that much?" she asked in a small voice.

"You tell me. All I see is that I'm working my butt off in a shitty job to earn a living, while you don't seem to give a damn about your responsibility."

"I thought you loved your job," she said in surprise.

He thrust his chin at her like a weapon. "I don't intend to spend the rest of my life doing commercial work. I've got more talent than that. And if you think I'm going to limit my scope to support you, you better think again, baby."

"I don't expect you to support me," she cried.

"Then where's your check for one hundred and sixty bucks?"

She apologized. She acknowledged it was her fault, swore it wouldn't happen again. The more abject she became, the more fury he unleashed upon her, a verbal pummeling from which she reeled as if from actual blows. He left her sobbing on the couch and went into the bedroom and shut the door. She heard him switch on the Watergate hearings which he was following avidly. She waited tensely, hoping against hope that he would come out again, that everything would be all right. But after a while she heard him turn off the television, go into the bathroom, and then get into bed. She crept into the dark bedroom, undressed as quietly as she could, and crawled humbly in beside him. He lay on his side with his back to her. Experimentally she brushed her leg against his; he jerked angrily away. She lay awake and suffering until morning, when he dressed in an icy silence that was even worse than his fury and left without saying goodbye. For two more days he continued to freeze her out. Then at last he relented: he came home from work and shot her the trace of a smile, and she flowed gratefully into his arms.

But it became a pattern: almost every week brought about a new crisis. Each time a fight ended with Stephen going out the door, Kate would be certain that he would never be back. And each time they made up, she felt the radiant return of peace that she thought would last forever—so that when the next blow came, it always took her completely by surprise.

They had had an exceptionally vicious blowup three days before Kate was to leave for Andrea's wedding. She could scarcely remember what touched it off. But at its fiercest point, Stephen began talking about other women. How there were many attracted to him—top-class women, for her information, women with money and high-powered careers. And don't think he hadn't been tempted by some of their overtures. It would be damned nice to be with someone *supportive*, for a change. Someone who wasn't depressed and clinging to him all the time. Someone who wasn't always dragging him down.

His words had made Kate crazy. She had always imagined that every woman was secretly yearning after Stephen, but the thought that he might actually respond to one was more than she could bear.

But this morning, as she packed the little red felt overnight case that had seen her through so many college weekends, Stephen was tender and cheerful. The idea of her going to Chicago on her own pleased him. "The break will be good for both of us," he told her. "It'll give us a breathing spell. I think that's what we've been needing."

He kissed her lovingly and promised that he'd miss her. Kate felt reassured and happy as she boarded the plane; she spent the flight dreamily listening to Carly Simon singing "You're So Vain" on her headset. But as the plane circled O'Hare, a new thought gripped her: What if Stephen discovered he liked his freedom too much? What if he found he really was happier without her? A knot of dread formed in her chest. She was so distracted that she nearly brushed past Jean Ferguson in the terminal.

"Kate!" Jean cried. "I thought I saw you get on, but I wasn't sure."

"Were we on the same flight?" Kate asked. "I didn't see you at all. Where were you sitting?"

"Up in first class. For an extra thirty-five dollars, what the hell."

Leave it to Jean to be up front, Kate thought. In the seat of privilege. After all this time, Jean still had the ability to make her feel klutzy. Even the way she looked—her sleek suit and sleek black frame of hair—made Kate in her jeans feel like a too-old love child. In Denny's last letter from Ecuador, he had mentioned Jean was working with some feminist group, something Kate found very difficult to imagine.

But before they could talk further, Andrea was swooping down on them, distributing hugs and kisses, pushing forward a slight young man with fuzzy red hair whom Kate gathered was Rick. She watched him squeeze Andrea's waist with fond pride and felt a flash of both envy and disdain: Stephen didn't believe in public display of affection. Stephen—her thoughts raced back to him. What was he doing? Who was he with?

She went through the rest of the day by rote, smiling at Rick's rather raucous pals, admiring the blue-banded stoneware sent by Andrea's old lawyer in St. Louis, laughing a bit too forcibly at Rick's third rendition of "My name is Jeffrey Spalding, the African explorer." What she was really doing was waiting—waiting for enough time to go by so that she could safely call Stephen without seeming too anxious.

It was ten-thirty when they finished dinner at Hong Lee's. Rick's buddies dragged him off for a final bachelor's tour of the Tenderloin, and Andrea, Jean, and Kate returned to Andrea's house. Even then, Kate forced herself to take a long bath instead of rushing to the phone. She let more minutes go by as she patted herself dry and wrapped her hair. As she walked back to the living room, she heard Jean saying something to Andrea, but she broke off suddenly as Kate approached. Kate felt a flush of uneasiness. Jean was staring at her so strangely: What in the world could she have been saying to Andrea that she didn't want Kate to hear?

But Kate couldn't worry about that now. "Do you mind if I use the phone?" she asked Andrea. "I'll call collect."

"Sure. Use the one in the bedroom, it's more private." Andrea added with a smile, "Give my love to Stephen."

It was eleven now which meant midnight in New York. We're having a fabulous time, she would say. I just wanted to say good night.

She let it ring twenty times before hanging up. The knot in her chest unraveled into a spreading web of panic. She was certain he was with one of the other women he had thrown at her; he was finding her fascinating, and this time he would see no reason to resist temptation. She crumpled onto Andrea's bed, nearly strangled by her own sense of desperation. But she couldn't cry. Not now: Andrea and

Jean were waiting for her. And somehow she was going to have to make it through the following day.

RICK AND ANDREA were married in Rick's cramped Scott Street apartment at the stroke of noon. The groom wore a cadmium yellow linen suit and pointy-toed English boots; the bride wore white and carried a bouquet of field daisies. It was a simple service performed by a nonsectarian clergyman who called himself "Skip"; there were readings from *The Little Prince* and the works of Richard Brautigan, and an exchange of the traditional vows in which the word *obey* had been changed to *treasure*. A younger cousin of the groom's sang Cat Stevens songs in a fluctuating falsetto, accompanying himself on the twelve-string guitar. Several of the guests tossed brown rice. And no one noticed the bride grimace when the groom, as he kissed her, goosed her playfully on the ass.

*T*HE IDEA HAD FIRST COME TO JEAN AT THE SECOND Street Women's Cooperative.

She had been working alone one afternoon when a woman had drifted in: a housewife from Linden, New Jersey, fiftyish, full-fleshed, and neatly dressed for business in a synthetic knit suit. She was looking for work, she explained, with a rueful smile that apologized in advance for the futility of the undertaking. She could type and she had taken a course in speed writing, one of those "if u cn rd ths" methods, but at the agencies she'd been to so far she'd been given the cold shoulder, meaning of course she was just plain too old. But she wasn't looking for much, you know, just to bring in a little money now that even the cost of a pound of chuck was enough to make your heart stop, and anyhow, since the kids were out of the house, it would be nice to feel, well, you know, sort of employed. And she had heard about the co-op on the television, the channel five news. . . . Here Mrs. Hyert had paused and again smiled her apologizing smile.

Jean told her regretfully that the co-op really didn't have the facilities to place people. All she could do was give Mrs. Hyert their pamphlet on reentering the work force and encourage her not to give up. Which was a shame, she had thought at the time. The executives at IMI were always lamenting the vast turnover of husband-hunting, lackadaisical girls, and meanwhile here was solid, dependable help going begging.

Why not put the two together, she had thought. An employment agency . . . no, better yet, a temp service, which would allow the women to work as much or as little as they wished. She would call it The Returning Worker.

Andrea and Rick had driven to Wisconsin for a two-week honeymoon on the Door Peninsula; while they were away, Jean worked furiously to develop the idea. The location was the first question. New York was out—too much here already. In tribute to Mrs. Hyert, she focused upon New Jersey, and after an afternoon's drive settled upon Paterson—it was near plenty of industry, office space was laughably cheap, and it was a quick commute from Manhattan.

She then began her homework. She interviewed at existing temp agencies to discover how they were structured and to compare their strengths and weaknesses. She buttonholed the corporate contacts she had made through the framing venture and sounded their views on the project. She spent hours on the phone collecting estimates on supplies and services. And finally, in one twenty-two-hour stint, she wrote a prospectus, detailing the business and projecting a profit by the end of the first year. This she sent special delivery to Chicago so that Andrea received it the day after she returned.

She called Andrea five days later.

"It does sound great the way you have it," Andrea acknowledged. "My problem is I just don't know much about this kind of business."

"But I *do*," Jean declared. "I've had experience from both sides, employed and employer. I absolutely know the demand is there. And the potential for profit is enormous. The expenses are minimal—no inventory. It could become a multimillion-dollar franchise, with offices across the country."

"You think so?"

"I'm certain of it. And what really makes it wonderful is that it's a feminist enterprise. Here are women who can't get hired anyplace else. . . . It's a chance for us to put into practice some of the lofty ideals about women and sisterhood we've been mouthing all these years."

The longer she spoke, the more her confidence and enthusiasm sparked Andrea's as well, and in a week, Andrea's hesitations had crumbled completely. By the end of the month, Jean had her check for twenty thousand dollars. She stared at it, hardly believing its existence. Twenty thousand dollars: the notation itself was satisfying—that broad stretch of zeros creating such a solid foundation on which to build.

Within a week she had rented a tiny second-floor office on the edge of Paterson's decrepit downtown and had hired as an assistant a recent graduate of the University of Tennessee. Her name was Chris; she was a small, skinny girl with broken skin and hair that hung like frayed, corncob-colored yarn to her shoulders—someone not likely to be distracted by a demanding social life. She seemed intelligent enough to handle chores of some complexity, but not so bright as to be soon imposing her own ideas on the running of the business. A loyal, rather plodding worker who wouldn't mind late hours: such was Jean's evaluation of her new assistant.

And there were plenty of late hours. The office was soon

flooded with women—women in cheap Sears housedresses, women in preciously coordinated Lord & Taylor outfits—all of them taking typing and dictation tests, filling in applications . . . the entire female population of northern New Jersey seemed to be looking for a job.

Jean spent her days making the rounds of personnel offices presenting her pitch over and over: "Our workers are motivated. They *want* to work, they need these jobs, they're not just marking time till marriage or something better comes along. They're more mature and more dependable. . . . They don't mind fetching coffee or doing errands younger women these days feel are beneath them. . . ."

And over and over she heard the same responses. Younger people have more energy. Women of that age are going through change of life and might be difficult to manage. And anyway, our execs *like* having young, fresh faces around.

Nearly five months slipped away with no contract landed. The twenty thousand dollars had dwindled at an alarming rate. It was, in fact, almost gone. Gone where? Jean wondered. She was living as frugally as possible and paid Chris a criminally meager salary. She *had* used part of the money to settle the last debts from her framing venture, but that had been only a few thousand. The rest had just dribbled away, into rent and electricity and postage and taxes. And now, with scarcely enough left in the account to cover dinner for two at Côte Basque, there was last month's phone bill still hanging, and rent due again, and another payment to make on the liability policy. . . .

The thought of another failure filled Jean with a fear more intense and purely unendurable than anything she had ever known. There had to be a way to make this business work. But she was getting nowhere with the personnel people, a breed singularly lacking in imagination and spine. She had to think of a way to get in higher.

Inspiration came while driving back to Manhattan in her rusting Volvo. A Hoboken news station was announcing that a company called Alcom Fasteners had been targeted by the Bergen County chapter of NOW for its alleged sexist treatment of female employees. The president, a Mr. Robert Carstairs, denied the charges and expressed his concern for reestablishing good will.

At precisely nine o'clock the following morning, Jean presented herself at Mr. Carstairs's office and informed his secretary that she had a suggestion to help counteract the NOW action. For twenty minutes she spoke to the at first skeptical, then increasingly receptive, president. By employing The Returning Worker, she explained, Alcom could effectively demonstrate its faith in the middle-aged woman—which of course it could then publicize to great advantage. Moreover, the predominance of older women in the company could effectively put to rest the implications of sexual harassment contained in the NOW charge.

By the time she had finished, Carstairs was nodding thoughtfully. "I'm going to send you down to my personnel man, Zack McConnelly," he told her. "I think you'll be able to work something out." He rose to shake Jean's hand, adding, "You know, the best damned secretary I ever had was a retired schoolteacher named Isabel Fine. When she cut out on me to retire down in Cocoa Beach, I was damned sorry to see her go."

An hour later, Jean was heading back to the Volvo in an ecstatic daze. This time the personnel director had been obsequious and accommodating. He had offered a contract: The Returning Worker would supply up to twenty temps a day for the next six months, with a guaranteed minimum business of thirty-five thousand dollars. Jean did some mental arithmetic: if they employed all twenty at thirty-five a day, it meant seven hundred a day total, or twenty-one thousand a month, which worked out to one hundred twenty-six thousand dollars for the six months. And if they renewed the contract, it was as much as a quarter million a year!

She raced triumphantly back to the office. "I did it!" she announced to Chris. "I got us a contract! For up to one hundred twenty-six thousand, maybe more."

She breathlessly described the details, while Chris listened stone-faced. "That's only if they take all twenty every day," was her response. "All we can count on right now is the thirty-five thousand. And eighty percent of that goes right out to pay the temps, so there's not much left for our expenses."

Jean made an impatient sound. Obviously, the important thing was to have the money coming in, the cash flow that now made them legitimate. And this was only the start. "I don't know why you're quibbling," she snapped. "An hour ago you were working for a company that earned *nothing*."

She insisted Chris immediately enter the guarantee in the assets column of the accounts. Chris, who had majored in business at Tennessee, had taken enough accounting to do the books for the present; Jean realized they'd eventually need a real accountant to refine their system of billing and payments, which admittedly was a bit slapdash . . . but all such things in time. The work at hand was to win more clients, build the business; the petty administrative details would fall into place sooner or later.

The Alcom contract served as a wedge which Jean used to force other doors. Within a month, she had signed a small contract with the Eastern Bank for Savings in Paterson and had deals pending with an Elizabeth insurance firm and three industrial corporations in the area. She was pushing herself to the limit: she ate on the run, slept less than six hours a night, and permitted herself no social life that didn't in some way relate to her business.

But often in bed at night, bone-weary but her system still racing on nervous energy, she would feel a sudden, brutally intense spasm of desire. She would touch her breast and imagine a man's lips there, the firm pull upon the nipple, the rough-bearded abrasion of his chin against the soft under-swell. She thought of his hand stroking her belly and thighs, the feel of his hardness forcing its way into her, the steady thrust between her legs, and she would whimper, her craving so strong that it seemed likely to make her mad.

Exhaustion finally overwhelmed her, and she would drop off to a heavy sleep. And in the morning she thought of nothing but the day's work ahead.

A MONTH BEFORE the first anniversary of Andrea's wedding, Jean called her at home. "Congratulations!" she said. "You now own forty percent of a five-hundred-thousand-dollar company."

It was 10:00 P.M. in Chicago, but Andrea sounded groggy. "You mean we've made that much?"

"Well, not *made* exactly. I haven't figured out exactly what our profit is yet, but we've got contracts that add up to a potential of even more than that."

"That's great. Really great. Because, God, Jean, I could really use a chunk of money right now."

"We can't take any money out *yet*," Jean said quickly. "We've got to throw every penny back into the business to make it grow. I've already been scouting locations in Westchester for a branch office there. And Paterson needs revamping, a switchboard for a start. . . . The only way we're really going to make money is by thinking on a large scale. You've got to trust me, Andrea."

"Oh, I do." Andrea gave a quick laugh. "I mean, God, if I can't trust *you*, then who else is there?"

"Are you all right? Is there anything the matter?"

"Well, it's just Rick and me. We're having some problems. It's nothing really. Stupid stuff everybody goes through."

"You sure?"

"Oh, yeah, I'm just working so hard right now, is most of the problem. But I really *am* excited about the news. . . ."

By the end of the following month, Jean had opened a branch of The Returning Worker in Chappaqua, expanded the staff to a total of seven, and moved Chris into a one-room central office in the West 40s of Manhattan. But she was becoming restless. The company was running on its own steam: the office staff was almost as effective at bringing in new work over the phone as she was in her canvassing; and the mundane business chores—hiring and firing, paying bills, ordering supplies, and supervising the staff—bored her immensely. She began plans to expand to Bridgeport, Connecticut, but even that failed to rekindle her interest. It was simply another heat of a race she had already run to her own satisfaction.

It was while she was in this restless mood that she received an envelope from her mother containing a note and a clipping from the *Washington Post*. The note, in her mother's exquisite handwriting, read, "If I'm not mistaken, dear, this is the man you used to work for?" Jean unfolded the clipping and read the obituary of John Dreiser.

It had been over four years since she had last seen him, weeks since she had even thought of him, but the news of his death filled her with a sudden, clenching anguish. She realized she had always expected to see him again—that at some indeterminate point he would recover and they would resume their relationship just as they'd left it. And now that fantasy was shattered forever—a brittle glass ball dropped from the slender chain that had held it.

She read the notice again. How strange that even this little summation of his life contained so many things about him she hadn't known: that his middle name was Reardon, that he had been born in Bermuda, that he had served on an economic advisory commission under Lyndon Johnson. . . . Had she even cared to know them? The thought added to her grief. All through these last years when she had been without any man at all, she had consoled herself with the fact that she at least had proven herself capable of intimacy. But now suddenly she was not so sure. What if she really wasn't capable of truly loving someone, of breaking the bonds of self-containment? Didn't that in some way make her less of a woman?

Sternly, she told herself she was being melodramatic, that it was necessary to make sacrifices now to achieve her goals, and that she'd have plenty of time to develop the other part of her life later.

Right now the best way to serve John Dreiser's memory was to put into action all he had taught her. *Synergy*: how many times had she heard him use that word? The acquisition of companies had been his passion. And Jean, his disciple, had learned her lesson well: diversify and grow—such was now her mandate.

She had an idea for a new venture. It would need a lot of capital to start, but she had an idea, too, where she might raise it. Through The Returning Worker's account with the Eastern Bank for Savings, she had developed a bantering friendship with one of the vice presidents: Ron Rogoff, a good family man, steady, just a shade dull, but at thirty-four still close enough to a "wild and crazy" fraternity career at Rutgers to be a little more flexible than his colleagues. Jean usually lunched with him every month or so at a Paterson pub that served overstuffed sandwiches and hefty steins of beer. She often pumped him casually for financial advice. But this time, she sprang a proposition on him. "Ron, I'd like to borrow two hundred thousand dollars to buy a funeral parlor."

She relished the goggle of surprise that distorted those solid-citizen features. "You're putting me on, right?" he sputtered.

"No, I'm serious! Listen." She rapidly outlined her plan to him: there was a family-owned mortuary in Newark; the patriarch and founder had recently died and the sons were eager to sell out quickly. They would take a price she believed was well below the value of the business.

"Yeah, but embalming and dead people and grieving loved ones . . ." Rogoff gave a fastidious grimace. "You want to get into all that?"

"Not in the least. I'm not finished yet. The business owns a fleet of eight stretch limousines. Now here's the deal: if I resold the rest of the business for what I think it's really worth, I'd gain the cars for practically nothing. And with the fleet, I'll start a limousine rental service in Manhattan."

"Seems to me that area's already pretty well covered. You've got Fugazy and Cary and a hell of a lot of smaller operations. . . ."

"I know, I know, but I've got a gimmick. Mine will all be driven by female chauffeurs. Now, don't laugh until you think about it," she added quickly. "Out-of-town businessmen adore stuff like that, especially the Japanese. And I've been sounding out a few restaurants about doing tie-ins, and the response has been good. The real beauty is that it will generate a ton of publicity. We'd hardly need to advertise—it would make a name for itself."

Rogoff bit his sandwich thoughtfully. "Even supposing the idea's feasible, you're talking about a substantial amount of money. How do you propose to secure the loan?''

''Well, in the first place there'd be the business itself and the property it's on. Presumably, its sale would cover most, if not all, of the loan. But if the bank needs additional collateral, I'm prepared to put up my assets in The Returning Worker.'' Jean leaned across the table toward him. ''The agency's been doing incredibly well, Ron. Better than I've let you know. I can produce contracts right now for nearly three-quarters of a million dollars.''

She watched his eyes widen with interest. ''Let's go back to my office when we're done,'' he said. ''I think we should talk about this further.''

JEAN WAS CONFIDENT of her success when she left Rogoff's office. By rights she should be dancing on air, but suddenly she was slapped by a feeling so unfamiliar it took her some moments to identify it.

It was a feeling of doubt. Hadn't she misrepresented the agency's prosperity? It was true they had substantial contracts, but after wages and expenses the net was still relatively small. The books showed a profit; but she was rapidly learning that books could be made to reflect just about any position you wished.

What if she couldn't make a go of this limo scheme? Risking the agency on it meant that if it collapsed, she'd lose everything. Bingo, back to square one.

For a moment she had the panicked impulse to back down. She was making great headway with the agency. Why jeopardize it?

But no—if there was one thing John Dreiser had taught her it was that only losers play it safe. The greater the risks, the greater the rewards.

He had believed in her. The least she could do for him now was to believe in herself.

ALL THE ENERGY and ingenuity Jean had expended to get The Returning Worker off the ground, she now poured into Dresden Limousines. With the same invigorating thrill she watched this enterprise, too, take off—at first ponderously, then with gathering speed and agility.

There had been an initial setback: the resale of the funeral home hadn't brought quite the price Jean had expected, and so the company was saddled with a fifty-two-thousand-dollar debt. But that was still cheap for eight limos in excellent condition. And she had been perfectly right in her supposition that the novelty of young women drivers would attract the media. There was a "Best Bets" in *New York* magazine, an item in the "Scenes" column of the *Voice*, articles in the neighborhood throwaways; a local newscast did a whimsical feature, the *Post* ran a photo of a cluster of the drivers saucily tipping their chauffeur's caps. And a popular German restaurant advertised: "Reserve for dinner and we'll send a Dresden Doll to pick you up," the copy framing a winking blond chauffeur.

And then an article appeared in a daily edition of the *Times* that was not about the company but about Jean herself. It was titled "A Feminist Entrepreneur" and detailed Jean's "astounding success" in creating businesses from scratch. "Money is power," the article quoted Jean. "A lot of women in the feminist movement seem to have forgotten this and confuse power with a certain way of dressing or a sexual orientation. But the bottom line for us is financial independence. My ventures break new ground in the employment of women, and that's the greatest contribution to feminism I think anyone can make."

She was thoroughly unprepared for the cannonade of calls

and mail that followed: from inventors, crackpots, Harvard students with bright ideas, from women's groups wanting her to speak or consult, loan officers, tax-shelter lawyers, investment capitalists.

She crammed her days with appointments. Never had she felt so sheerly alive—not even in the days as John Dreiser's assistant. Back then she had been merely an adjutant. Now she was the one around whom it all revolved—the lunches in cool, bright executive dining rooms, dinners in pastel-toned restaurants, the "quick drinks" that often stretched to hours at the Plaza, the Carlyle, the St. Regis. There was the constant swirl of introductions, each new handshake hinting at unlimited possibility, and the dazzling flirtation with new ideas. But most of all, it was the talk of deals, of leveraged buyouts, turn-arounds, start-ups. Such things had the power of an addiction for her. Creating and closing a deal: *this*, she realized, was where her talents were best put to use. Why squander them anywhere else? Once a business was underway, it was easy enough to find other people to do the day-to-day running of it.

One night, returning late to her apartment, she heard the phone ringing inside. She hurriedly fit the key to the lock. She had just come from a meeting involving the buyout of a modeling agency that had been founded by a former cover girl and mismanaged to the point of bankruptcy. Jean had put together a coalition of investors: after weeks of negotiations, the deal was finally ready to close. There were only a few minor details still to be ironed out. This could be one of the investors wanting to fine tune one point or another.

She raced for the receiver. But the voice on the line was a woman with the flat, nasal intonations of New Jersey.

"You wouldn't remember me, Miss Ferguson, but my name is Rosa Ephron, and you interviewed me last year for a temp position, at The Returning Worker, you know. Anyhow I hate to bother you so late and all, but I just thought you should know. Your place owes me for two weeks for way over a month now, and a couple of other girls are owed too. And nobody down there wants to tell us when we're gonna get our money. So I remember how you lived in Manhattan, and like I said, I hate to bother you . . ."

"There must be some mistake, Mrs. Ephron," Jean cut in. "I'll see that you get paid immediately." She took the woman's address and hung up, then dialed Chris's number. "I just received a call from a Mrs. Ephron," she snapped. "She claims that she's been owed money for over a month."

"There's a whole mess of them haven't been paid," Chris said. "All the ones we sent to Michaelson-Davis. What happened is when Michaelson-Davis paid *us* it mostly went for the overcost on the new switchboard system."

"Why wasn't I told about this?"

"I've been leavin' messages for you to call me for the last two weeks," Chris whined.

Jean realized it was true. But swept up in the glamour of her new deals, she had allotted very low priority to messages from Chris. "I have a company with billings of nearly a million a year," she said. "Do you mean you can't find *any* of that to pay a few women their thirty dollars a day?"

"Well, I could divert some funds from Chappaqua. But it'll look funny in the books and it might mess up the cash flow up there."

"Do it for now. I'll be in soon to straighten everything out." Jean hung up in irritation. Chris, stolid as she was, lacked initiative. Perhaps she should bring in someone with a bit more gumption. She would take care of all that when her life was not so wild. Right now, many more important things required her attention.

*A*NDREA'S MARRIED LIFE WAS, LIKE ANCIENT GAUL, DI-
vided into three parts: there was studying; there was Rick;
and there was housework.

She and Rick had originally intended to split the house-
keeping chores; they had even discussed a contract that
would specify in detail the division of labor: who would
cook on which days, who would change the sheets, who
would scrub the tub, who would haul the Navy duffel bag of
dirty clothes to the Same-Day Laundry Mart on Saturday
mornings. But Rick, after years of blissful, solitary sloth,
never quite got the hang of the routine. Having assembled
the Electrolux with all its various hoses and nozzles on the
living-room rug, he would get distracted by a Blackhawks
game and never manage to get around to the actual vacuuming.
Or, in the middle of cleaning out the refrigerator, he would
have the sudden urge for a melted cheese on an English; and
after fixing himself one, and washing it down with a beer or
two, he'd have forgotten totally about his original task. And

Andrea, who had no capacity for nagging or grandstanding insistence, simply began to do it all herself.

She soon took over all the cooking as well, for the sensible reason that she was the far better cook. She had at long last weaned Rick off junk food—the cheese dogs and Natchos and chocolate-covered grahams he habitually devoured when she'd first met him. Now she prepared him only natural foods—no preservatives, nothing processed or canned. But this of course prevented one-stop shopping at the giant Safeway. Instead she hiked eight blocks to the health-food store for brown rice and Jerusalem artichoke spaghetti and all-natural peanut butter, then crossed to the Korean fruit stand for fresh produce, tofu and sprouts, then a detour to Elsen's which had the freshest fish or the Kosher butcher for chicken, only then to double back to the Safeway to pick up bargains on detergent and paper products, Dannon yogurt and milk.

By the time she returned from these expeditions, Rick would be home, sprawled on the couch, his tie and suit jacket tossed on the nearest chair; he would be listening to the Watergate reports on John Chancellor while thumbing through *New Times* or *Rolling Stone* or the latest Bean catalogue from which he ordered his entire leisure wardrobe. Andrea would stop off for a kiss, then continue into the kitchen where she'd prop her evidence casebook on the windowsill over the sink; and while she chopped zucchini, soaked lentils, peeled eggplant and garlic and carrots, she would flounder in the oceanic ambiguities of evidence law.

After dinner, Rick would "volunteer" to do the dishes. "What a good, sweet Koala," Andrea would praise him. She would then heap her books on the dining-room table and study till midnight, while Rick twirled the TV dial or fiddled with the newest lens of his Nikon system.

And then it was time for bed.

If only she weren't so tired so much of the time, Andrea thought, she wouldn't mind Rick wanting to make love so much. After all, she was having orgasms now. Not every time—when they did it doggy-style or standing up, or in one of the pretzel-limbed positions Rick culled from *The Joy of Sex*, she was never able to come. Nor had she ever really learned to enjoy sixty-nine, which unhappily Rick seemed to favor more and more. But from time to time she managed to pull him on top of her the "right way"—or better yet, she would be the one on top. Then once she felt him rhythmically thrusting, she could squeeze the walls of her vagina tight around him till she had coaxed the delicately building sensations right to the edge; and then her entire body would stiffen as she concentrated deeply, concentrated on that brimming cupful of sensation, until at last it spilled over the rim. And then she would let herself go, throwing out her arms and making little humming sounds of pleasure in her throat.

Afterward she would have the urge to lick him all over, to nuzzle her head in the fuzzy warmth of his groin: he was so good to give her such lovely orgasms. But he would curl into himself and in a moment be sound asleep; and so she would content herself with simply nestling beside him.

But by the end of her final semester of law school, the frequency of their lovemaking had diminished, until Rick was approaching her only about twice a week instead of once or twice a night. Andrea supposed this was normal; familiarity cooled passion, that's what everybody said.

And secretly she was somewhat relieved. These last few months were the most difficult so far, with finals rushing up at her and anticipation of the bar exam creating a constant band of tension in her stomach. She was thankful that at least she had her job with Legal Aid sewed up. Other women in her class told her horror stories about interviewing with corporate firms: how the interviewers often cold-bloodedly grilled you on your private life—did you plan to get married, and if so did you want children? Some even demanded to know what kind of birth control you used! Thank God, thank God she didn't have to go through *that*, discussing her method of contraception with a perfect stranger.

She finished the semester with gratifyingly high grades. For several weeks she was immersed in the frenzy of reviewing for the bar exam; then the two-day ordeal of the exam itself. And then it was all over. To celebrate, Rick surprised her with a water bed; and though it made sex a bit slippery, their sweating bodies sliding out from under each other like fish on a slick deck, for several weeks the novelty of it resparked Rick's desire. But then, rather abruptly, it waned to even less than before.

They were certainly getting to be an old married couple, Andrea thought. And they hadn't even celebrated their first anniversary.

It was a Saturday, two weeks after Andrea had begun her six-week training period in Legal Aid. A good day, hot but dry with a teasing breeze off the lake. Andrea and Rick had spent it in a marathon movie session: a Woody Allen double-bill (*Play It Again Sam* and *Take the Money and Run*) and then the six o'clock show of *Airport*. She had indulged him in a bad Chinese dinner at one of those garish, plastic "palaces" on Division. Then they had strolled home beneath a glorious pink-and-crimson sky, Rick humming "Lydia the Tattooed Lady," Andrea belching a little from the cloying duck sauce, but feeling softly content. As they entered their little apartment, she felt a sudden burst of love for everything she saw: this cheery room with their combined possessions, and her funny, huggable, fuzzy-haired husband.

She followed him into the bedroom. "I've been thinking, Koala," she said. "We've never talked about having kids."

He shot her a look of alarm. "Kids?"

"Well, yeah. You know, it might not be the worst idea to have a baby right now instead of later. Then four or five years from now, I could go back and *really* start my career."

"I'm not ready to be a father," he howled. "Not right now. I couldn't hack the responsibility."

"You've got a lot of responsibility in your job, and you manage that pretty well."

"Hey, that's different. I could walk from my job tomorrow and nobody would be the loser but myself. But a kid, wow, that's a different thing altogether. That really ties you down." He had been steadily backing away from her as they spoke, and now he faced her from the opposite corner of the room. "We've got *plenty* of time to think about this," he said. "Christ, these days women can have kids till they're forty!"

"I guess you're right," Andrea said and watched his shoulders sag with relief. Of course he was right. How could Rick be a father when he still needed such taking care of himself? It was just that lately she'd been thinking about babies more and more. Probably just her anxiety about starting a job . . . her subconscious grasping at pregnancy as a way to get her out of it. Once she actually started working, these absurd longings would go away.

She watched Rick begin to undress, admired the smooth, taut muscles of his small back, the lean girth of his hips. They had not made love in over a week, and now that she was rested, she felt herself aroused. She wanted her husband—it was a luxurious feeling.

She wondered if, to entice him, she should put on the black crotchless panties he had stuffed in the toe of her

Christmas stocking. But that would make her feel too obvious. Instead she reached out and traced his shoulder blade with her fingers—a little timidly, for fear he wouldn't be in the mood. But he flexed and arched his back, then turned and helped her undress. He entered her almost immediately, which was new—he used to lavish time on foreplay, nibbling, and lapping with tireless energy. But Andrea was ready for him. She squeezed her muscles and concentrated, and with a little mewing cry lost herself in the delicious overflow.

Afterward, she nuzzled happily against him, drowsy, but wanting to savor this perfect contentment a while longer. It was some moments before she realized that Rick was still wide awake. She lifted her head. "Aren't you sleepy?" she asked.

He shook his head.

"What's the matter? Is something wrong?"

"Yeah." He reached up and flicked on the light. "I think we'd better talk."

She sat up, holding the sheets over her breasts. His face wore what she called his "no candy" look; her feeling of contentment was fast ebbing away.

"Now look, Herry," he said. "You know I've always thought we should say what we honestly feel and not hold back the things that are bothering us."

She nodded.

"Okay then. I feel I've got to tell you that I'm just not satisfied with our sex life."

"If you want to do it more often, that's okay," she said quickly. "I get a little tired sometimes, but if that's what you want . . ."

"It's not that," he cut in. "Its . . . Oh, shit, it's you. You're just not *good* enough."

Andrea's stomach contracted. "What do you mean 'good enough'?"

"Fuck, I don't know. You don't *do* anything. You don't move your hips or any of your body, and you don't pick up on anything I do. You're too passive. You just lie there waiting for *me* to do everything. And then when you come, it's like suddenly I'm not even around, you're a million miles away."

"But what am I supposed to do?" she cried.

"That's the thing, it's not something you can *explain*. It's supposed to come naturally. The whole problem is you just don't have enough experience. That one guy at college doesn't exactly make you a woman of the world."

It didn't make sense, Andrea thought wildly. For years people had been telling her how sexy she was when it was a fraud—she had been practically frigid. But now that she was finally having orgasms and really *did* feel sexy, suddenly it wasn't good enough. She needed more experience to learn. Which meant that all the time at school she had worried about being too promiscuous, it turned out she hadn't been promiscuous enough!

"What did you marry me for then?" she said in a breaking voice. "If it was so lousy and everything, why didn't you just find somebody else?"

"Because I loved you," he said.

"And you don't anymore."

"No, I still love you. But I thought after we got married it would get better. You'd feel freer and less inhibited."

"What am I supposed to *do*?" she burst out, tears pulsing in the corners of her eyes.

He put an arm around her shoulder and drew her toward him. "Hey, it's not the end of the world or anything. I think it's *good* we got it out in the open. Now we can start to work on it."

"We can?"

"Sure. Tomorrow night, okay? I'll show you everything I mean."

She nodded tearfully and rested her head against his chest. He really was her good, sweet Koala bear.

They went through the following day not speaking of it at all. After dinner, they watched "60 Minutes" and a rerun of "Hawaii Five-O." Then Rick turned off the set, and they exchanged self-conscious grins.

"Why don't you put on that black sheer nightgown and I'll get us some wine," he said.

"Okay." Andrea stood up and discovered there were butterflies in her stomach. It's only Rick, she recited to herself, he's your husband, you love each other. It's all going to work out. But in the bedroom, she undressed with jerky movements and her hands trembled as she slid on the nightgown. As an afterthought, she spritzed cologne down inside the neckline. The bottle of Wind Song Rick's sister Lynda had sent her for Christmas, it was still mostly full because she never remembered to put it on. . . . What a slob. A wonder Rick had put up with her this long.

He came in with a bottle of Soave Bolla and two glasses. He had put an Eric Satie on the stereo—one of only two or three classical records he owned and this one only because Blood Sweat & Tears or somebody had done a version of it too. He added to the romantic atmosphere by veiling the bedside lamp with a T-shirt. Then he undressed down to his briefs—pink-tinged, she noticed, no doubt from having been caught up with something red in the wash, damn that Same-Day Mart. Maybe the place down on Carlson would be better, though of course it was a much longer schlep . . .

"What are you thinking about?" Rick asked, pouring the wine.

She looked up with a start. "Oh, nothing. Just listening to

the music. This is such a gorgeous piece, I keep forgetting we even have it."

"Um." He handed her a glass and toasted her. "Here's to the partaking of a sensual feast!" They touched glasses and sipped in a rather foreboding silence. Should she say something to lighten the air? *Last night I shot an elephant in my pajamas. How it got in my pajamas, I'll never know.* But judging from Rick's expression, serious as a nun's, this wasn't the time for a Groucho routine.

At last he began to kiss her—deep French, with plenty of tongue, the way he had when they'd first started going out. But when his hands touched her breasts, she felt suddenly illicit. She flashed back to the New Haven motor court room with Douglas, then reminded herself again, It's Rick. Rick, your husband.

He drew the nylon gown up and over her head and eased her, naked, back on the undulating water bed. "Relax," he said as he continued to stroke her. "Close your eyes and get into the feel of it. Just let yourself go."

She tried. But the muscles of her arms and legs were pulled as tight as violin strings and obstinately refused to melt. As Rick's hands slid lower she became acutely aware of how bulky her hips were, how large and flabby were her thighs. Pockets of cellulite like some soft cheese . . . Revolting. And, oh God, she had forgotten to use the Feminique, please let the cologne make up for it . . .

She swallowed a yelp of pain as his fingers tweaked her clitoris too hard. He fondled her there for some moments and then stopped; she opened her eyes to find his face looming startlingly near hers.

"Are you ready for me?" he asked.

She lied with a nod.

"Okay then, this is what I want you to do. Rotate your hips up and down like this. . . ." He stretched out beside her and demonstrated, contracting and releasing his buttocks up and down in a gyrating motion. "See? It's a rhythm, you've just got to pick it up and go with it."

She tried. The movement bore a ludicrous similarity to a buttocks-reducing exercise she sometimes practiced. What's more she suddenly became aware of a sound, *squarsh, squarsh,* like someone washing clothes in a bucket. . . . Just the water sloshing in the bed as her ass slapped against it, she realized. God, if this was going to work at all, she'd have to get her mind off laundry.

"That's it," Rick was saying. "Now keep it up while I'm inside you." He shimmied out of his underpants and straddled her. But something was wrong, he was having trouble entering. She reached down to help and found that he was only half-erect.

"You're not ready," she said.

"It's okay. Just keep up with your hips."

"Don't you think we ought to wait a minute?"

"I said it's okay!" he snarled. He thrust against her, trying to mash the failing penis inside, while she dutifully kept pumping away with her hips, but this only made it wilt completely: she could feel it squashed up against her pubic bone like a fat and sluggish invertebrate. With a growl of frustration, he gripped her hips and tried to stuff himself in, flaccid or not, muttering "Damn, damn it" beneath his breath, until finally, with a choking sound, he pulled abruptly away, and sat in a sulk on the edge of the bed. "It's not something you can teach," he said in an accusing voice. "It's gotta come naturally, you've either got it or you don't."

Andrea lay huddled in a mounting wave of sickening shame. Oh, what was going to happen now?

THEY TRIED AGAIN on subsequent nights, but with little better results. Andrea also tried to improve on her own. She bought a copy of *The Sensuous Woman* and performed the Sylvan Swirl in secret on a peeled banana. She practiced her hip technique on the living-room floor with a pillow under her ass; and, summoning all her courage one afternoon, bought a pink, penis-shaped, battery operated "massager" from a drugstore in the Loop. But getting into bed with Rick now was like being pushed onto a stage without knowing her lines. No more orgasms, only this gripping, unshakable fear.

She came home one evening to find Rick with a friend of his, a bearish, sandy-haired young man named Bill Cooney. Of all Rick's friends, Andrea liked this one the least. He was a swaggering beer-guzzler who was perpetually on the brink of putting together the "bonzo" real-estate deal that would blow him over the top. In the meantime, he lived hand to mouth, never missing an opportunity to deputize someone else—Rick as likely as anyone—to pick up his bar tab. Life to Bill Cooney was a giant dirty joke. The word *fuck* was constantly on his lips, noun, verb, adjective, and expletive: he pronounced it with an obscene sucking sound, like a cork being pulled from a bottle: "fu-ouck." All his stories centered on "fu-oucking": the party in New Town where people took turns "fu-oucking" in the bathtub; the lady cab-driver in New York City who offered him a quick "fu-ouck" in the back seat. And his prescription for eternity: to have his brain preserved in a glass jar with the orgasmic nerve wired to a current—a never-ending "fu-ouck."

Andrea went straight into the bedroom and shut the door. After half an hour of listening to his braying laughter, she heard him leave and with relief came back out to the living room.

"What is it you like about that guy?" she asked Rick.

"Old Billy? I don't know. I guess he's a man's man."

Rick picked up his pipe—a habit he was currently working hard to acquire—and began stuffing it with loose tobacco. "You know, you ought to be nicer to Bill," he went on. "He really likes *you*."

"I've hardly said two words to him in my entire life."

"Yeah, but he thinks you're really attractive. He tells me so every time he sees you."

"He thinks every woman under the age of eighty-two is attractive," Andrea said.

Rick made a fitful gesture with his half-filled pipe. "Damn it, Andrea, why can't you just accept the fact that you're a very alluring woman? It seems to me that if you didn't always try so hard to deny your natural sensuality, it would solve quite a few of your problems."

Andrea didn't want to argue. Last week she had completed the training course and now, a full-fledged Public Defense lawyer, she had been thrown straight into arraignments. Each day was a grueling succession of faces, some of which would be burned forever in her memory: the teenaged car thief with the K-shaped scar on one eyelid; the rosary-clutching Haitian woman accused of murdering her sister's baby. But most were just the sad, burnt-out dregs of society, hookers and dealers, belligerent three-card monte players and spitting transvestites. One after another after another. And it was her job, after talking to each client for as little as five minutes, to advise him or her on what to plead and to negotiate the bail . . . one after another after another. . . . By the end of the day she was too exhausted to even think.

"Okay, okay," she said wearily. "Bill Cooney has the hots for me, and the next time I see him I'll be friendly as pie."

"Maybe you should take advantage of it," Rick said slowly.

"What do you mean?"

"Well, maybe he'd be a good person for you to . . . well, you know, work things out with."

"You mean you think I should go to bed with him?" Andrea asked incredulously.

"No. I mean . . . well, maybe it wouldn't be that bad an idea."

"It's a horrible idea!" she cried. "You're talking about— like wife swapping. Committing adultery! And I don't even like him. I think he's a creep!"

Rick pulled his innocent-wronged face, little boy misunderstood in his efforts to be good. "Do you really think it would be so bad?" he pouted. "Couldn't you look at it like the kind of sex therapy where they use surrogates?"

"I can't believe you're even saying this!"

"You don't have to if you don't want to."

"I don't want to," she said flatly.

He didn't bring up the idea again. But as several weeks went by and things remained as strained as ever, Andrea felt a growing sense of desperation. Her thoughts kept returning to Rick's accusation that first night: "You don't have enough experience." Maybe in order to save her marriage, she really should sleep with someone else. But who? The thought of either friends or strangers was equally disturbing. No, she decided, it was impossible. There had to be some other way to work things out.

One evening when Rick had left word he'd be working late, Andrea dropped into a market near her office to pick up some groceries for her own dinner. She wheeled her cart into a checkout line behind a stocky man thumbing through a copy of *Sports Illustrated*. He glanced around. With an embarrassed start she recognized Bill Cooney.

"Hey there," he said. "I didn't know you shopped here."

"I don't usually," she replied, "only it's so near my office . . ." Flustered, she dropped her eyes to his cart. There was a Gino's frozen pizza, a six-pack of Bud, the large-size bag of Natchos, and a Ring-Ding. His dinner, no doubt. Andrea found something rather touching about such a bald array of junk food.

"Just a few eats," Cooney chuckled awkwardly. "Thought I'd stay home tonight for a change, take in a ball game . . . you know. Sometimes ya just gotta relax."

Why, he's embarrassed too! Andrea realized. Of course—he comes on like such a swinger it must kill him to be detected in this bit of solo domesticity. The thought made her warm to him a little. He was a human being too. Even Bill Cooney had feelings.

He waited, clutching his sack of purchases, while she checked out. "You need a lift?" he asked. "I got my car right down the block."

"Yes," she said with some surprise. "That would be great."

He rather shyly led the way to a beat-up silver Corvette and held open the door with gauche gallantry. Andrea marveled at how different he seemed. Perhaps it was only around other men that he needed to bluster. Underneath, he was probably a very nice guy.

"Ricky tells me you're quite a cook," he remarked, starting the car. "Lucky guy."

"Well, I try. Though these days I don't get much chance to go all out. Like tonight. Rick won't be home, so I'll just fix some yogurt and fruit and stuff for myself and not even bother to cook."

Cooney shot her a glance. "You're on your own, huh? Say, I got an idea. Why not bring your food over my place and let's have a bite together?"

Frozen pizza and yogurt—what a combination. Still Andrea found herself nodding. "Fine with me," she said.

In the living room of his high-rise apartment, Cooney scurried about emptying ashtrays, then appeared before her with two sweating cans of Budweiser. "Funny us running into each other like this," he said, wiping the cans on his shirt sleeve. "You know something? Of all the chicks I know, I gotta tell you I think you've got the most on the ball."

"Oh," Andrea said modestly. "Well, thanks."

"Yeah. I mean, brains and a body. Wow! So when Rick said how you had this open marriage thing going I went apeshit. I've just been hoping we could sometime get together."

Andrea flushed, first with embarrassment, then with deep indignation. So Rick had already primed him for this! And to how many of his other friends had he suggested she might be available? Damn him, anyway! she thought, trembling with anger.

But then she took hold of herself. After all, Rick could only have been acting from the same motive that had brought her here herself—the wish to save their marriage. And it was just as well, wasn't it? She probably wouldn't have been able to go through with it unless the stage were already set.

"So what do you say?" Cooney pressed with a strained laugh. "You want to make it?"

She forced a smile. "Sure."

"Far out. Jesus! Look, just make yourself comfortable and I'll be right out."

He dashed excitedly into the bedroom, and in less than a minute burst out again. He was stark naked. Andrea gave a startled laugh. Good Lord, he was so hairy! Tufts and clumps of coarse black hair covered his chest, shoulders, and thighs. He was the most hirsute human being she had ever seen! And the thought of this great lumbering hearth rug, this *bear*skin of tufted fur, in contact with her own body was utterly repulsive.

She leaped to her feet and began backing to the door. "I just remembered I've got to get home," she babbled. "Thanks for the beer and everything, but I think Rick's expecting me back, and I don't want to be late. . . ."

Her hand groped for the doorknob and she shot out into the hall.

"Well, fu-ouck you!" she heard him call.

NEITHER RICK NOR Andrea knew who first mentioned separation: suddenly the word just seemed to be in the air. They were living together in a friendly but detached way—rather like strangers forced by inclement weather to share rooms in a lodge. They were politely, even strenuously, considerate of each other, yet they spoke little and made love not at all. For months something delayed the actual separation: a visit from his parents who were coming all the way from New Hampshire and would be broken-hearted to learn they were not getting along, Rick's birthday, a particularly demanding time for Andrea at work that left her no time to think about anything else.

And then at last there were no more excuses. One year, ten months, and four days after their wedding, Rick and Andrea sat in the little Scott Street apartment with a bottle of Beaujolais and several joints of Jamaican Red between them and divided their possessions. The wine and the drug made them giggly: they tossed things at each other with blithe abandon. "I think *you* should have this exquisite genuine Lucite fish platter since it was your Aunt Dottie who gave it to us." "Oh, no, I wouldn't dream of depriving you of such a priceless item. . . ." It was the most they had laughed together in months. There was a brief, nasty flare-up over the division of the stoneware that almost spoiled the mood. But then Rick suddenly insisted that Andrea have the Tiffany demitasse spoons that had belonged to his grandmother, a gesture of such complete and unexpected generosity that for a moment all Andrea's feelings for him came rushing back, a great, choking well of love.

It seemed natural at that moment that they go to bed; when they made love it was warmly, easily, with no judgments on either side.

But in the morning, the van arrived to pick up Rick's things and move them to his new one bedroom on Upper Lake Shore. Stripped of half its familiar items, the apartment suddenly seemed to Andrea cavernous. She sat and cried. She was never going to have a family, never be allowed to share her life. She dragged around the house the rest of the day feeling nothing quite mattered anymore.

By evening, she felt strong enough to at least go down and pick up the mail. There was only one envelope. It bore a logo design of a stylized woman, arms uplifted in the traditional gesture of victory, and a company name: Minervco.

A trickle of pleasure broke through Andrea's despondency. Her investment was successful. She was a woman of means, well able to stand on her own. And now, she realized, there was no one she had to pamper or cater to, no one to demand she shave her legs or cook a balanced meal or perform like the Happy Hooker in bed.

Suddenly she ran back upstairs and from her top bureau drawer took her circlet of Ortho-Novum pills. One by one she dropped them down the toilet. Goodbye fifteen extra pounds that would never come off. Goodbye migraines and excruciating cramps. Goodbye worrying about blood clots and cancer and increased risk of diabetes.

Goodbye, goodbye, goodbye.

*T*HE SQUARE RIGGER CANVAS CARRYALL LAY ON THE lower slope of the drawing board, where Stephen had flung it when he had come home. Now he had gone in to take a shower. Kate listened for the hiss of running water, the door's creak as he entered the stall; then cautiously she unzipped the case. It was crammed with work he had lugged home: layout sketches, contact sheets, odd pages from magazines and catalogues; she rifled through both sections before she found the appointment book she was after. This she withdrew, flipped it open to the present and began reading back through the entries. Most were familiar to her: names of clients he had mentioned, friends she knew, her own name here and there. And then her heart contracted: in the six o'clock slot for last Tuesday there was written simply "Marion." Her eyes raced back several pages more: lunchtime the previous Wednesday he had penciled in "Marion Sidarsky" and a phone number.

Marion Sidarsky. Kate knew there was someone. She could always tell. She knew that a week from now, or perhaps two, Steven would pick a fight and then fling this name at her, informing her that her drag-down behavior had *forced* him into sleeping with another woman.

She heard the shower trickle to a stop and quickly replaced the book and zipped the case shut. Depression, like a heavy black cloth, began to wrap itself around her, muffling all her senses. It would be a grievous mistake to let it show: Stephen was becoming increasingly less sympathetic to her "moods," accusing her of purposely using them to "get at him." But this cloth cocoon was smothering her: there was no way she could force herself to appear gay. Though maybe he was right. Sometimes it did seem to her that she was courting the pain—doing things purposely to bring about one of their blowups and with it the tears, the sleepless nights and long anxious waiting by the phone, and the sweet drowsy peace when it was all over. It was almost as if she had become *addicted* to it all.

Such a thought only deepened her depression. She sat slumped in a chair and looked up bleakly when Stephen emerged from the bedroom. He was wearing a black turtleneck and his dippy bellbottom jeans—hadn't anyone told him the sixties were over? she thought sourly.

"What do you feel like for dinner?" she asked in a listless voice. "There's some chicken in the fridge. I suppose we could do something with it."

He glanced at her sharply. "You sound so thrilled I can hardly stand it. Screw it, let's just go grab a burger at Dr. Generosity's."

She followed him without protest to the restaurant. As they waited for their food in silence, she searched for some topic of conversation that might interest him. Had it always been this difficult to come up with things to say to him?

Their order arrived. Stephen took a wolfish bite of his bacon cheeseburger, washed it down with a long sip of draft. Then he fixed his eyes on her, a look that meant he wanted to get down to business. "I've got something to say," he announced. "It's about our living situation. I've been feeling trapped by it lately. It's like all my options have been restricted by the fact that we're living together. I've given it a lot of thought, and I think it would be a good idea for both of us if we lived apart for a while."

A needle stabbed through the dull skin of Kate's depression. "You want to break up?"

"I didn't say break up, don't go twisting all my words around. I said live apart, temporarily at least."

"But why?"

"Well, for one thing, it's become clear to me over this past year that you're too far behind me in many ways. For instance, *I* see letting out my anger as a healthy, normal thing, while you see it as a total threat. You've got a lot of catching up to do, and the best way would be for you to stand on your own two feet for a while."

Kate breathed hard. "But you're saying . . . you mean you also want to start seeing other women."

"If we're living alone, naturally we'd be free to do whatever we chose. Which doesn't mean we wouldn't continue to see each other," he added quickly. "But if you felt like going out with another guy, or six of them, or even a hundred, I'd have nothing to say about it."

"I don't want to go out with anyone else," she said.

"Then that would also be your option."

"But I don't want *you* to see anyone else either!" she cried.

He picked up a french fry, doused it with ketchup, and popped the entire bloody wedge in his mouth. "That's another way we're unequal," he said primly. "You're so inflexible. Everything in this relationship's got to be on your terms. You've been trying to force me into conforming to this one-to-one thing because it's what you want.''

"I don't want to *force* you. I want you to want it too.''

"It's the same thing, for Christ's sake," he said. "Now, the kind of relationship I want is where we're both secure enough not to be joined at the fucking hip. For instance, if you wanted to go off to Wisconsin for six months to be a milkmaid, I'd say terrific, I'll miss you, but have a good time. And if I wanted to ship off to Katmandu or live with a belly dancer for a while, or simply lock my door and be alone for however long I wanted, you'd be able to say the same thing. It's the kind of relationship Sartre and Simone de Beauvoir have had for years.''

Sartre and Simone de Beauvoir . . . what in God's name did they have to do with her life? Stephen seemed to be talking complete gibberish. Kate stared down at her plate where her hamburger lay like a congealed slab of mud and fought back her tears, knowing that Stephen couldn't stand any show of friction when "people" were watching.

"Now, as I see it," he was going on, "you should be the one to look for a new pad, since obviously you wouldn't be able to afford our place on your own. . . .''

He seemed to go on for hours happily outlining his new plan. When at last they returned to the apartment, Kate let her tears burst freely. She was being banished from the place she loved: from the little bay window, and the table she had painted apple green, and the shelves they had assembled together. Banished from Stephen, which once she had equated with death.

Stephen was surprisingly tender. He held and rocked her and crooned to her soothingly. "Nothing's over yet, don't think that way. This is something I think we have to do. It will be good for both of us. But I hope to marry you someday, you know that, don't you?''

Kate peered up at him. He had never said that before. And now she had a burst of hope: Once she had finally proved to him how strong and independent she could be, everything might indeed turn out all right.''

STEPHEN THOUGHT IT would be best if they made the break right away, and so the following day Kate moved down to stay with Sissy Dreifus who lived on the ground floor of their building. Sissy had moved in a month after Kate and Stephen. She was flamboyant, auburn-haired, and worked as an associate producer of documentaries for one of the networks; her life seemed to be a glamorous tumult of ringing phones, late-night dates, and friends from out of town. The two sat up long into the night, sipping flat champagne and dissecting their relationships.

"You've got to give him rope," Sissy advised. "Let him have his precious freedom for a while. He'll find out how much he misses you."

"You think?"

"I know so. He just needs to get this stuff out of his system. But he really loves you, you can tell that. You've just got to hold out for a while."

Kate nodded bravely. But she kept imagining him with other women, touching them, fucking them, falling in love with them, until she thought she would go out of her mind. She took to hovering abjectly by Sissy's door, "accidentally" emerging when she heard Stephen's footsteps in the hall.

Finally he called. "I'm fucking fed up with having you spying on me. You're supposed to be getting a place of your own. When the hell are you going to start looking?"

"I *have* been looking," she lied frantically. "You wouldn't believe how bad the market is. There's absolutely nothing available."

"Don't give me that shit. If you'd get up off your ass, you'd come up with something."

"I have been looking, honestly I have."

"Well, you get this, baby. I've got a date coming by tonight and if I catch you lurking about spying and bothering us, you're going to be in big trouble."

There was hatred in his voice, a tangible desire to hurt her. "Don't you love me at all anymore, Stephen?" she asked in a small voice.

"I don't have time to play these fucking games," he snarled. He slammed down the phone. The message was clear—don't bother me until you've found a place of your own.

She began her search. It was the last week in May and a premature heat wave had clamped down upon the city. The asphalt bubbled beneath her feet, the subways were like moving tombs, the air was choked with a thick gray dust that stung the eyes and made breathing a miserable effort. Kate dragged herself in and out of the offices of agents who took one look at what rent she could afford and consigned her applications to stacks of neglect. She scoured the *Voice* classifieds, and when she discovered a rare listing in her price range, raced to it, only to find a dozen others already in line. At last she agreed to look at a listing with a rent of two-ten a month—thirty-five dollars higher than her maximum. It was a cigar box of a studio on a shabby block in the West 20s: one sunless room with decrepit plumbing and a dead roach reposing like a sacrifice on the ancient gas stove. But Kate could no longer bear the thought of looking further. "I'll take it," she told the agent.

Stephen helped her move in. "It's cute," he declared happily, stacking boxes against the one free wall. "You could fix it up with some paint and a lot of plants to look really great." He hauled up the last three plastic garbage bags full of odds and ends, then brushed his hands on the back of his brown cords. "I think you should have a night to yourself to get the feel of the place, so I'm gonna take off."

"Don't go," she begged.

"It's just for one night, for Christ's sake," he said testily. "Anyway, we wouldn't get much sleep in that little bed."

Why couldn't she go back with *him* then? Back home to their own queen-size bed? But she could see that Stephen was eager to be away from her—his entire body was straining toward the door. Desolately, she let him kiss her and leave.

She threw herself into unpacking, hoping the activity would alleviate her depression. But the sight of her clothes in this alien closet, her books stacked on this strange windowsill, her toiletries arranged neatly in the ugly little bathroom cabinet, stamped a sense of permanence onto her situation that left her feeling worse than ever.

But at least it had made her sleepy. She snapped off the light, hugging to herself the thought that perhaps tomorrow Stephen would want her to stay with him. But the street outside seemed a sudden cacophony of strange sounds: horns, cars thumping over potholes, trucks grinding into second gear. She tossed and turned for twenty minutes before drifting off. Then she was jolted by a piercing cry from the apartment above: it evolved loudly and rhythmically into the unmistakable sound of a woman in sexual ecstasy. "Oh, God, oh, my God, oh, oh!" she shrieked. "Fuck me, yes, Oh, God, fuck me!"

A window somewhere below flew open and another voice screamed out, "Put it in your mouth, why don't ya?"

But the woman's exhortations continued sharp and vocal until they peaked in a florid climactic surge, joined by the guttural moans of her partner.

For some minutes after that, the building was still. Then

Kate heard someone come home to the apartment next door. The door slammed, footsteps came toward her own wall, and music began—just loud enough for Kate to make out the voice and melody: Ringo Starr singing "Yellow Submarine." When the cut ended, footsteps pattered back toward the wall; there was the sound of the stereo arm being picked up and then "Yellow Submarine" began again. It was played a third time, a fourth, a fifth. . . . On the sixth, it continued on to "Only a Northern Song" and Kate held her breath—this time maybe the album would play through to the end. But no: there went the footsteps running to catch it, there went the arm, and there again "Yellow Submarine."

She sat up and turned on the light. It was horrible. This apartment was a cell to which she had been condemned and her neighbors were her torturers. She pounded her fist against the wall, but the damned song continued to gaily jingle through. It was absolutely horrible. She was independent, self-supporting, on her own—everything she was supposed to be. And she was more miserable than she had ever been in her life.

Hola, chica. ¿Qué tal?"

The phone had rung late in the evening some three weeks after Kate had moved, and she had answered it with the habitual burst of hope that it would be Stephen. In her groggy disappointment, she at first didn't recognize the voice. But then it came to her. "Denny?"

"That's right, it's me."

"Are you back? Where are you?"

"Alive and well and temporarily living in Maryland."

"That's fabulous! Hey, how did you get this number?"

"Called your old one and your guy gave it to me. Did you two break up?"

"No, no. We just decided to give each other some more

space for a while." She had the wild desire to ask Denny how Stephen had sounded. Had it seemed like he was alone? Had he said anything else about *her*? But she checked herself. This was Denny, whom she hadn't seen for three years. "You're at home right now?" she asked.

"Yeah, and it's death." His voice dropped. "My folks are splitting up. My old man's been running around with some local *chiquita*, the son-of-a-bitch, and Mom can't handle it at all. She's flipping out—yesterday I had to force a pair of scissors away from her, she was going around slicing up the curtains and upholstery. Anyway, she's going down to stay with my grandma for a while, so I don't have to stick around. I'll be in New York next week."

He showed up at her door with a white rose, a bottle of wine, and an intricately embroidered woolen shawl from the village he had lived in in Ecuador. He embraced her with a rambunctious swoop. "You look fantastic!" he said.

"Oh, God, no, I've lost a ton of weight. *You* look great though." It was true. He was lean and tanned. His hair was the same shaggy chin-length that it had been when she had last seen him, but he had grown a beard, a soft, dark shadow that emphasized his fine eyes. Kate had forgotten just how good-looking he was. In her mind, he was always just Denny.

They opened the wine, drank to each other; then he told her about the Peace Corps. "The bureaucracy was staggering. Anytime you tried to make a little headway, you were caught up short by red tape. Egos got in the way of practically everything. Not that it really made any difference though. You wouldn't believe the poverty, the lousy hygiene, the superstition. . . . Anything we *could* do was such a drop in the bucket you got to thinking it didn't even matter. Except that these were *people*, and even the least help you could give them was important."

He talked about how inadequately prepared the volunteers were and how it led to comic blunderings: the school hut they built that collapsed in the first heavy rain, the schoolchildren who ate the cakes of Ivory soap, a riot nearly touched off when Denny mistakenly used the word for *goat* instead of *shepherd* in reference to one of the village fathers.

And he had fallen in love, he told her. "It was supposed to be against the rules to get involved with someone else in the program, but everyone ignored that. There were all these torrid affairs going on all the time. It was like shipboard romances, though—they tended to disintegrate at the end of the cruise. Sarah went home last year and began an anthro doctorate at Ann Arbor. We wrote for a while, but it gradually petered out. I'm sure she's happily living with someone else by now."

Kate felt a momentary flash of jealousy. *Her* Denny interested in someone else—and someone whose pursuit of doctoral degrees in scholarly fields put her own drifting career to shame—was somehow intrinsically threatening. But that was selfish, she told herself. If she didn't want him "that way," she shouldn't be bothered by the fact someone else did.

"What now?" she asked him. "Are you going to stay in New York? Get a job?"

"Not nine to five, that's for sure. But I've got a skill now—one thing the old Peace Corps did was turn me into a pretty fair carpenter, and I think I can get by on it. In fact I've already got a job lined up. A kid I know's got a raw loft down in Soho—three thousand square feet—and he wants me to do the work on it. Plus he's gonna rent me a third of it to fix up for myself."

"You're going to be a carpenter?" Kate's voice sank with disappointment.

"Would you marry me anyway?" he teased. "Would

you have my baby?'' He grinned at the face of mock exasperation she shot him. ''Hey, you think you don't like it, you ought to hear my old man. 'Fourteen thousand bucks in college education and this is what he plans to do with it!' Christ, he's the one playing Leader of the Pack, and all he can do is total the educational investment I'm throwing down the drain.'' Denny took a long swallow of wine. ''Anyway,'' he said cheerfully, ''this carpentry thing's not my only gig. I came back from the jungle with a few things to say, and I want to write a few plays.''

Kate brightened. ''Oh, good. I remember that one-act you did for Alsing's theater seminar—about the kid who shaved his little brother's head. I thought that was great.''

''Oh, Christ, fifth-rate Ionesco with a few direct steals from Sam Beckett. I'm out of my absurdist period, the world will be happy to know. I think I'll try a little modest realism. But I don't want to talk about me anymore. What about you? How are things with this man of yours?''

''Oh, fine,'' Kate said vaguely. ''You can meet him next Friday night, if you want. We're having a sort of cocktail party if you can come.''

''Sure, I'd love to come. And hey, speaking of invitations,'' Denny added, ''I'm having lunch with Jean next week. It's the earliest she could make it—it seems she's so busy these days you've got to book way in advance. Anyway, it would be fun if you came along.''

Kate's heart sank. She hadn't seen Jean since Andrea's wedding over a year ago. But she remembered vividly Jean's coolly superior air punctuated by her ironic smile. And the blank silence that had greeted Kate when she walked back into Andrea's living room the night before the ceremony still disturbed her. No, she didn't want to see Jean—not like this, becalmed in a nowhere job and living in this dingy little hole. ''Our office is so crazy I usually don't have much chance to get out for lunch,'' she said. "We can all get together some other time.''

"Sure. Hey, I'm here to stay." Denny shook the last drops of wine from the bottle into their glasses, then again raised his to her. "By the way, did I mention yet how absolutely terrific it is to see you?''

KATE HAD BEEN strongly looking forward to the party she was giving with Stephen, as she did to anything that involved them as a couple. Living apart had so far made their relationship no more tranquil; if anything, they fought more than ever and with slighter provocation. Almost once a week, Kate would call Sissy and blurt out the details of their latest eruption, tearfully declaring that this time Stephen really meant it when he said he was through with her. "It's not going to change," Sissy insisted. "If you go on with Stephen, you're just going to make yourself miserable.''

At times, Kate would reluctantly agree and start thinking, with a certain amount of relief, about being on her own. But then Stephen would call: he would want to talk, there would be remorse or tenderness in his voice or he would dangle some bright promise for the future. And Kate would dance swiftly back into his arms. After all, she reasoned, every relationship had its problems. All the couples she knew were continually on rocky ground—you never knew from one day to the next who would still be together.

Kate arrived at the Eighty-fourth Street apartment early the next evening to help him prepare for the party. Usually this was when she was happiest—when she and Stephen were engaged in some task together, side by side, joking and giggling or—as Stephen loved to do—endlessly analyzing the people they knew. But now, as she unwrapped cheeses, smoothed cushions, and straightened chairs, helped him arrange the plastic cups and utensils beside the array of liquor bottles, she felt a flutter in her chest, as if she were about to face some terrible ordeal.

The guests began to arrive. Most were Stephen's friends. Of the people Kate had known before she met him, she had let most drift away—largely because Stephen had expressed so little interest in ever seeing them. Sissy was here of course. And then, late to arrive, Denny.

Kate's anxiety increased as she watched him shake hands with Stephen. And then suddenly it seemed she was seeing Stephen through Denny's eyes—she noticed that his face was rather flat, his legs too stubby in proportion to his long body, and the last haircut he'd gotten (from a cheap local barber) had lopped off too much from the sides leaving a kind of comical Woody Woodpecker thatch on top. She cringed, noticing, too, that he was wearing his corny bell-bottom jeans and using antiquated sixties expressions like "man" and "far out." God, Denny was going to think he was a hopeless nerd. Right this moment she was actually ashamed of Stephen, something she had never felt before.

The party had taken swing, and Kate was busy greeting new arrivals, replenishing the ice bucket, selecting new music for the stereo. But she remained acutely aware of Stephen and her new perception of him. At one point, she listened to him boast of how he had outwitted a cabdriver who tried to take advantage of him. She heard his braggart's laugh ring out as he described flipping a nickel tip into the front seat, and she saw Denny glance quickly away. Everyone must be silently mocking him, she thought. Thinking him a fool.

Then she realized something else: she simply didn't like this man. She didn't like his looks, his voice, his hustling, scrappy attitude. Suddenly she couldn't care if she never saw him again!

She shuddered and poured herself a tall vodka and tonic.

The drink took hold, the party swelled around her: she was soon caught up in eddies of conversation, laughing and gossiping with people she was after all glad to see. In the process of having a good time, her sudden feeling of revulsion toward Stephen faded. By the time the last couple left at well after 2:00 A.M., she was in soaring spirits; she hummed "Crocodile Rock" and began to empty ashtrays into a paper bag.

But then she glanced at Stephen and froze: he was gathering the used glasses in a silent and deliberate manner, and his face wore an expression of aggrieved fury.

"What's the matter?" Kate gasped.

He said nothing, only continued to stack glasses.

"Stephen, what is it?" she demanded. "What's wrong?"

"You know what's wrong," he said hoarsely.

"No, I don't. Tell me." Only a few hours before she had been convinced she hated him, but now just the hint of his withdrawal sent her into a deep panic. Frantically she reviewed her behavior at the party to try to detect what she had done wrong. Had she talked too long and too intimately with Charlie McGowan? Had she hugged Denny goodbye a bit too warmly? Or could Stephen have somehow sensed her brief moment of disloyalty, seen her stare at him with momentary distaste?

She reached out to him, but he brushed by and marched rigidly into the kitchen. She followed him meekly, terrified by his sealed face, his black slitted eyes. "You've got to say something," she begged. "You're driving me crazy. I don't know what's wrong."

He stuffed the glasses in the big red pail under the sink, then straightened and gave a stony smile. "You're not going to sucker me into playing your little games, baby. I happen to be much too tired. So just fuck off."

"But what am I supposed to do?" she pleaded.

"I don't give a fuck what you do. *I'm* going to bed."

He turned and began to head to the bedroom. She stared at his rigid, retreating back. No, she couldn't stand this limbo of no response, she wouldn't let him freeze her out. There was a broom leaning in a corner of the kitchen. She grabbed it and lunged with it at his back. He whirled, wrenched it out of her hand, then slapped her violently across the cheek with his half-closed hand. She let out a yell; he grabbed her shoulder and began slamming her against the wall. "You bitch!" he screamed. "You've been asking for this a long time. You think you can get away with all your shit, but I'll show you, I'll fucking show you, you bitch!"

Kate went limp. She was aware that some part of her welcomed the violence—she had forced him to acknowledge her, he was no longer shutting her out. But there was the stronger fear that he could really hurt her, and so she offered no struggle as he pounded her and screamed at her, knowing if she did it would provoke him further.

And then it was over. Still shaking, she walked to the bathroom, wrung a washrag in cold water, and applied it to the ugly purple bruise that was deepening on her cheek.

"Do you think you should see a doctor?" Stephen asked from the doorway.

"No, it'll be all right." She covered her whole face with the cool cloth. And then she felt Stephen's arms around her waist. "Why do I hurt you like this?" he crooned. "I'll make it up to you, I swear I will. You know I love you, baby."

Slowly, Kate let her hands fall to cover his. Inside of her pirouetted a tiny figure of hope. Maybe—oh, just maybe—he had finally gone far enough to be truly sorry. And if so—if it would make things really change—she was willing to endure a bruise ten times as great as this.

*N*ERVOUS VERSUS POPCORN. THAT'S THE DIFFERENCE BE-
tween the East and West Coast.''

The young woman at the Geary Street roommate service
made this enigmatic statement as she took Andrea's completed
application form. Her name was Ms. Geller, and she was herself an amalgam of East and West, her faint Bronx accent at
geographic odds with a freckled and seemingly permanent tan.

"I don't get it," Andrea said. "Nervous and popcorn?"

"Well, ya know how in New York you dial N-E-R-
V-O-U-S when you wanna get the time? Well, here it's P-O-P-
C-O-R-N. And like I'm telling you, that's the whole difference
between living here and back there.''

Andrea smiled. She had never lived in New York, but she
was now a resident of San Francisco, and she rather liked
the idea of its being popcorn, buoyant and crisp with no dis-
cernible significance beyond a good time. God only knew
she was sick to death of being NERVOUS. It had been two
months since she and Rick had filed separation papers, two

months since they had stood on the steps of the courthouse and pecked each other on the cheek goodbye. It had been early November; winter had just begun to lock into Chicago, and she had had the feeling that if she were still in that city when the December winds howled off the lake she would certainly freeze to death. And so, astonished by her own daring, she had quit her job, sold what furniture she had left, and set off for San Francisco, the golden city of the sixties.

So far she had been lucky. She had found a job with a small firm of private practitioners that specialized in civil rights and criminal defense work. It paid more than her Legal Aid job and the work, while still giving her the opportunity to help people in need, promised to be not quite so grim. She would have to take the California bar, of course, but she had already enrolled in an evening prep course and expected to have no trouble passing it.

"Lucky thing you don't mind sharing," Ms. Geller was saying, scanning her application. "You'll be able to get a good neighborhood without paying through the nose."

"I'd actually prefer to have a roommate," Andrea said. "I just moved here and don't know anybody. It would be nice to have somebody to come home to."

"Really," said Ms. Geller.

Andrea took the third apartment—or "flat" as it seemed to be called here—that she was sent to. It was located on a sunny side street of North Beach. From the window of her bedroom she could spy upon a broad swatch of the city: pastel rooftops plunging down the nearby incline of Vallejo Street, eucalyptus trees muted by dust to the same silver-gray as the fog, and beyond Telegraph Hill, a bright blue spangle of bay. It was the view that sold her: a positive declaration that she was in San Francisco.

Her new roommate was named Michelle, a small, thin,

crabby girl who was an account-officer trainee at Wells Fargo. One night, about a week after Andrea had moved in, Michelle tapped on her bedroom door. She came in holding up an empty jar—an incrustation of ashes and dried tomato sauce hinted at a provenance of the bottom of the garbage.

"Did you eat my applesauce?" she demanded.

Andrea stared at her. "I don't know. Maybe I did when I came home so late the other night. I didn't know you were saving it."

"I've noticed you've eaten my stuff a couple of times before. I just haven't said anything till now."

"I'm sorry. I'll replace it if you want."

"It's Mott's, the sixteen-ounce size. I'll leave it on the counter so you'll remember."

The following evening, Andrea came home to find all the food in the refrigerator and cupboards that Michelle had bought labeled with bits of masking tape marked with an *M*. Andrea was perplexed. Whenever she had lived with roommates in the past it had been taken for granted that the supplies were communal. What's more, though it was true Michelle made a scant salary from Wells Fargo, her father owned some sort of snowmobile distributorship in Minnesota and each month sent her a hefty supplemental allowance. Why was she going nuts over thirty-five cents' worth of applesauce?

But Michelle's parsimony didn't stop at food. She placed a pad by the telephone to record all local calls so that they would be able to divide up the message units as well as long distance. She left large notes taped to the kitchen counter listing her petty household expenses: "lightbulb for living room lamp—49¢." "New bottle of Joy Liquid—$1.05." And once Andrea caught her slinking out of the bathroom with a roll of toilet paper—her *own* roll, Andrea realized, which she was evidently hoarding in her bedroom rather than take the chance that Andrea might use more sheets of it than she.

All Andrea's hopes of finding a confidante in her roommate—another Kate, another Barb—were quickly banished. Still, she had no trouble making friends among the single women with whom the city seemed to abound. Young, educated, free-spirited, most had been drawn to the city by a promise of an easy "lifestyle." But, as Andrea rapidly discovered, what they had also found was a lack of available men—or rather, available heterosexual men. San Francisco was well on its way to becoming the gay capital of the world—and many of Andrea's new friends reacted to the fact with unabashed hostility.

"Damned faggots!" they would hiss quite audibly, passing a male couple linked arm and arm in the street. "I can't stand the way they've taken over this city. I wish they'd all go back into the fucking closet!"

At first Andrea was shocked. She liked gay men: they seemed just the sort of "gentle people" San Francisco was supposed to be filled with. She liked their sense of style, the marvelous physical shape most kept themselves in. Even the most effeminate among them had an endearing fussiness that appealed to her.

But as the months passed, she found herself increasingly sympathetic to her women friends' grumblings. It really was depressing to have to assume every man was gay unless conclusively proven otherwise. She felt flashes of resentment when she encountered mafias of them in the chicest boutiques and restaurants. And when she ventured into Polk Gulch or the Castro, where not one pair of masculine eyes registered her existence, she found herself almost missing the suggestive remarks and kissy catcalls of the Chicago laborers.

The shortage of straight men was undeniably oppressive.

Andrea had had a few dates, but none with men who really interested her. There was a six-foot-seven-inch accountant who was as bone thin as he was tall; a latter-day hippie who worked as a packer at the Safeway and had been nice about helping her locate black olives; a prematurely bald young man who lived next door and lectured her on the effects of dairy products on one's mucous levels. Andrea spent each date dreading the moment the man would make a move to touch her.

It was really more pleasant just to spend her time with other women. She began to go out almost every evening—after all, what was there to go home to?—in groups of three, four, a half-dozen women. They went to plays and dance concerts and French and Italian movies; they spent long hours talking over Mexican dinners and late cappuccinos. They all spent money freely, and Andrea was no exception: it trickled through her fingers like sifted sand. She had never before paid particular attention to her clothes, but now suddenly she was fascinated by them—she indulged herself with Frye boots, voluminous wool skirts, a hound's-tooth hacking jacket. She joined a Union Street health club, took yoga and ballet, and swam on weekends; she enrolled in a class in printmaking at the School of Design. Self-improvement became almost an obsession.

But for what? Sometimes the answer mocked her: if only she firmed her thighs, learned to speak French, dressed like Diane Keaton in *Annie Hall*, then she would be worthy of someone's love.

BURTON PROUSE WAS the editor of a computer industry trade magazine: forty-four years old, with a pleasantly round face, crinkly eyes, and a taste for designer jeans, old flannel shirts, and Adidas. He had recently separated from his wife and as such was the prize of a post-Christmas cocktail party given by one of the legal secretaries in Andrea's office. By the end of the evening, he had clearly singled Andrea out from a knot of single women that included the flatly disconsolate hostess.

The following weekend he took Andrea to dinner at the Café Sport and poured out his soul to her. Most of the nineteen years of his marriage had been a sheer torture, but he had hung in out of guilt and a misplaced sense of duty. Then some months back, he had enrolled in an est seminar. "It made me realize I have to take full responsibility for my life," he declared. "I can be happy or I can be miserable. My choice, just so long as I accept the consequences." Thus enlightened, he remained home long enough to pack his son Miles off to Oregon State, them moved out to bachelor's quarters in Sausalito. The sense of relief when he finally left was like shedding a pair of trousers four sizes too small: that marriage, he chuckled, had had him by the balls. And now he was trying to reconstruct his life according to the mandates of his new gospel, attending divorce therapy with his wife twice a week so that she wouldn't take him "completely to the cleaners" in the settlement.

He invited her to dinner the following night in his Sausalito condominium. The living room had a just-moved-in look, cartons and crates still stacked in corners. The kitchen, however, was dazzling, with butcher-block counters and brushed stainless-steel sinks. Rows of red and yellow enameled Le Creuset skillets hung from iron racks above a five-burner Wolf range. There was an electric pasta machine, a Pavani espresso maker, and Burton's pride and joy: a Cuisinart—the first food processor Andrea had ever seen.

Burton reigned supreme in this culinary paradise. He prepared his specialty, salmon Mirabeau, with rather fussy ceremony, delegating to Andrea only the menial tasks of spinning the salad and setting the table.

"Why is it," she said, laying out the silverware, "that when women prepare a meal it's cooking, but when men do it, it's cuisine?"

Burton frowned thoughtfully. "All the great chefs *are* men," he declared. "It could be because women are so enmeshed in the basic life function of childbearing that the more subtle senses are less developed."

Andrea said nothing. The thing she found least attractive about Burton was his propensity to take her every joking remark seriously. Oh, damn, she did sometimes miss Rick's sense of humor.

After dinner and demitasse, Burton rolled a fat joint in E-Z Wider papers. They smoked, listened to the first half of *Heart Like a Wheel*, and then Burton began to kiss her passionately. "Let's go upstairs," he muttered hoarsely, his hand inside the neckline of her dress, plucking at her bra strap.

"I'm not protected," she blurted out.

He plumped himself away from her with a look of fussy irritation. "Well, I wish you had told me this sooner."

Why? she wondered. Wouldn't he have bothered to make her dinner? Did this now constitute a total waste of a Saturday night?

Burton picked up the half-smoked joint from the ashtray. "I suppose we might as well do the rest of this," he said.

ON MONDAY, ANDREA made an appointment with a Dr. Land who had fitted a friend of hers with an IUD. Pruey Marshall raved about it, said that after the first day she had totally forgotten it was there. It seemed to Andrea the only alternative: she would not go back on the pill, and as for the diaphragm, the thought of using it with a man she hardly knew was far too inhibiting.

Dr. Land was in his fifties, slightly stooped, with a mild, scholarly countenance that Andrea found reassuring. "I think you've made a very wise decision, Andrea," he said. "I've been recommending IUDs to all my patients who can't tolerate the pill. Sex is a splendid thing. I'm a firm believer in making it as hassle-free as possible."

He explained to her that with women who hadn't had a child there were often problems retaining the coil or the Lippes Loop. But a new device had recently been developed called the Dalkon Shield, which had a much lower incidence of expulsion. He showed it to her, a paramecium-shaped bit of plastic surrounded by prongs. The look of the prongs worried her; but Dr. Land had already risen to lead her to the examination room, and she hated to make a nuisance of herself with ignorant questions.

The insertion was intensely painful, a deep, hot spurt that made her cry out in spite of herself. If sex was so damned wonderful, she thought, why did there always seem to be so much pain involved with it?

The nova subsided into a nasty, crampy ache in the lower right side of her groin. Dr. Land gave her a paper envelope of Darvon and a paternal pat on the shoulder. "In a week I promise you won't even remember it's there. And then enjoy, enjoy!"

Now she was fixed, she thought wryly. There were no more obstacles to going to bed with Burton. He called that evening to see how it had all gone, and they made a date for the weekend. This time he prepared chicken risotto and they were listening to Paul Simon when he leaned over to kiss her. Then he led her up the little spiral staircase to his loft bedroom.

Once inside her, he seemed to go on forever—but not with

the religious exuberance Rick had brought to their marathon sessions in bed; rather Burton seemed to be performing some sort of grim and monotonous duty, like an assembly-line worker striking the same lever arm over and over and over. Her vagina was beginning to feel bruised and sore; she wished he would finish. Maybe he was holding himself back, waiting for her to come. She began to breathe heavily and let out little moans, building them to a nicely timed crescendo, until with a great gasp of intolerable ecstasy, she shuddered and clutched at him tightly. One thing was sure— she could still fake a damned creditable orgasm.

And it worked. Burton immediately pulled out and flopped over onto his side of the bed. In her relief, it was several moments before she realized that he hadn't climaxed, at least as far as she could tell. Oh, God, she was so inept at sex he wasn't even interested in finishing. Any minute now he'd let her know what a lousy lover she was.

But when Burton began to speak, it was in a quavering, desolate voice. He was worried sick about his son, he told her. Miles had begun to address him as "Bertie" and talk to him only in a very sarcastic tone of voice. "I can't reach him anymore!" Burton cried. "I've lost his respect, his love, everything. And there's nothing I can do about it."

Andrea listened, held him, soothed him with comforting reassurances, and at last he fell asleep. It was an hour before she, too, was able to drop into a fitful doze. She was jerked awake at six by the sound of Burton pulling on a pair of White Stag jogging shorts. "I always run at dawn," he told her. Forty-five minutes later, he returned, drenched in sweat; he stretched back on the bed and within seconds was once more unconscious. But now Andrea was fully awake. She wrapped herself in one of his shirts and stumbled down to the kitchen.

Love, she thought, is never getting enough sleep.

* * *

IT WAS A nice relationship: that was the way Andrea began to think about it. It was nice to feel needed, not in the importunate, desperate way of her clients, before which she often felt a glacial helplessness, but needed in the uncomplicated manner of a scraped knee needing a bandage. It was nice, too, the way Burton delighted in the "old-fashioned" attentions. "Would it be completely sexist if I opened the door for you?" he would inquire in all earnestness as they approached a restaurant, and afterward: "Would you think I was a total chauvinist if I paid for this dinner?"

He did have his faults. He was not completely reliable. He didn't always call when he said he would. He was sometimes late for dates for the haziest of reasons or canceled at the last minute with no explanation at all. And their sex life remained erratic. Sometimes Burton would come the instant he entered her, other times he would labor for long minutes, then simply quit. But since he didn't seem to find it lacking, Andrea was certainly not about to complain.

Her Dalkon Shield, which she was supposed to forget all about, was still, after a month, painful. There was always a tenderness in the lower right of her groin which at times flashed into a hot sharp ache. She made a follow-up appointment with Dr. Land. Again she lay on his metal table and stared up at his white particle-board ceiling, while he poked and prodded in his dignified, thoughtful way. She remembered reading—in *Ms*?—that the examination robe allowed the doctor to forget that the vagina was an extension of the entire woman and that a feminist should strip it off and fling it to the floor. She imagined the expression on Dr. Land's pastoral face if she were to do that—just fling it to the floor—and she almost giggled. Oh, well, it was too chilly in here anyway to do without the paper robe. Her cunt would have to remain—at least for this time—a disenfranchised entity to Dr. Land's view.

Dr. Land withdrew the speculum. "Well, it's still in place. I didn't feel any slippage. But it's impossible to judge how any one person is going to react to these things. It could be you're just having a mite more trouble adjusting to it than most." He edged back on his stool and peeled off his gloves. "Now, I *could* take it out. But I'm going to play a hunch."

Andrea looked up, uncomfortably aware that her vagina still winked at him. But as he hadn't yet told her to remove her feet from the stirrups, she kept them in place.

"The pains you're experiencing," he said. "You wouldn't call them excruciating, would you?"

"No, not excruciating," Andrea said hesitantly.

"I've got some patients who can't tolerate any kind of pain. The slightest twinge and they start hollering. You, Andrea, don't strike me as that kind of girl. I suspect you're made of sturdier stuff."

She felt an irrationally strong glow of pride.

"So here's my thinking. Rather than fool around with this thing, I suggest we just let it alone for a while. What do you say? Can you put up with it?"

"I guess so," she said meekly.

"Atta girl." He walked around the side of the table and rumpled her hair. "What's a few aches and pains anyway, compared to a terrific sex life?"

Andrea supposed he was right. But as weeks went by, it seemed to her she never felt completely well anymore. All through the day she fought a throbbing malaise. And when she stood up suddenly or moved her legs in a certain way, the pain shot out like a vicious snake, its fangs extending the length of her leg.

On one of the worst days, she received a call from Rick to

tell her that their divorce was finalized. His voice on the phone was so immediately familiar, it was hard to believe it was almost a year since she had last spoken to him.

"There's another thing I gotta tell you," he said. "I've met this girl. We've been going together for a couple of months now, and we're kind of talking about getting married. It's nothing definite yet. But I wanted you to hear it from me first, rather than secondhand."

"Yeah, thanks," Andrea said. She felt suddenly hollow, as if his words had scooped out the vital center of her being.

"That's the one good thing about us," Rick went on. "We were always able to be straight with each other. It's weird how things turn out, huh? Christ, Herry, do you realize that in three months I'm gonna be thirty? The big three-o."

She let him indulge in a little self-pity, then told him she had a client waiting on another line. "Let's keep in touch, okay?" he said.

"Sure, let's." Andrea hung up and stood for a moment, still clutching the receiver and absently rubbing the tender area of her groin. The call had left her feeling dismally alone. She needed company, someone to talk to. Burton had talked about going to see *Amarcord* tonight . . . she dialed him at his office.

He sounded flustered. "I know I should've called you, honey, but I've had a bitch of a day. What I'd really like to do is just go home and hit the sack early."

She assured him she understood and hung up. It didn't really matter—she could always round up one of her women friends to go out with. Her first call was successful: Rachel had to work late but agreed to meet Andrea at Henry Afrika's at eight-thirty.

Andrea as a rule avoided singles bars. She hated the feeling of being on display—meat on a rack, her friends called it. Even in a group, it made her feel trampy, what her mother used to call a pickup girl. But tonight, the garish hubbub of Henry Afrika's seemed exactly what she needed. She arrived several minutes early and waited for Rachel by the front of the bar near the door. Two lawyerly-looking men in three-piece suits stood drinking near her and vaguely she tuned in on their conversation. "This girl is the ultimate dog, honest to God," one was saying. "I mean, on a scale of one to ten, she owes *me* points. But the thing is, if I buy her a couple of drinks, I can plow her for maybe a week without having to put out another cent. . . ."

What a pig! Andrea thought with disgust. The trouble with most straight men in this town was that they were spoiled rotten by their advantage. She moved away to be out of earshot of their offensive conversation and nearly bumped into Burton Prouse who had just come in the door.

His face turned pale as he recognized her. He opened his mouth as if to say something, but instead he gave a tight little nod and walked quickly to the back of the bar. Andrea stood in stunned confusion for a moment. Then she turned and raced out, catching Rachel who was coming up the street. "Let's not go there," she cried wildly. "That place is full of creeps."

Burton called the next day. They had a grim little lunch at Perry's, at which he did most of the talking. "It's too soon since I left Margaret," he told her. "I'm still too confused. I'm not sure yet how I really feel toward her or to all women in general. There's a lot of antagonism I've still got to work out. I just can't make any commitments right now."

"I understand," Andrea said bleakly.

"No, you don't," he said. "You see, you're just the kind of woman I feel I *could* commit to if my head was in a better place. That's what's been tearing me up. It's not fair to keep you dangling while I'm getting myself straight."

Slowly Andrea realized what he was saying. They weren't going to see each other anymore—despite the fact that he liked her, maybe even loved her. Or maybe *because* of those feelings. She kept nodding, murmuring that she understood, but really she felt like running to the bathroom and throwing up. And all the while he was pronouncing this sentence, he still kept soliciting her sympathy. Poor Burton, what a terrible time he's going through, what a difficult decision he's had to make.

"Take care of yourself," he said sadly as he left her on Union Street.

"I will," she nodded, thankful that at least he didn't propose they stay in touch.

But now that she was no longer sleeping with Burton, she could have Dr. Land remove the Thing that was tearing up her insides. She had spent the past few days in court hardly able to keep her mind on the proceedings, almost missing the calendar call one morning because she had felt so unwell. Yet as she made an appointment, she dreaded that Dr. Land would think her one of those silly, bellyaching women who complained at the least bit of discomfort.

This time when he did the internal, she gasped with pain. His probing brought tears to her eyes. He pressed firmly on various spots on her lower abdomen, asking each time, "Does this hurt," and each time she answered emphatically, "Yes."

His face, when he finished, was somber. "You should have come in long before this, Andrea. No one told you to be such a stoic. This much pain should have alerted you that something was wrong."

"What is it?" she asked, frightened.

"You've got a darned good case of pelvic inflammatory disease. I'm afraid that it's gone to the tubes. What I want is to check you into Children's for a few days to make sure we knock the infection out completely.''

Andrea entered the hospital that afternoon and stayed for four days. The IUD was removed, she was given great doses of antibiotics and subjected to an unpleasant routine of tests. But mostly she slept. It was a luxury—it seemed she had been tired for years.

A week later she sat again in Dr. Land's walnut-paneled consultation office. The pain had completely vanished: she was rested and revitalized, felt better than she had in months. Yet the doctor looked glum.

"The infection was extremely severe," he told her. "It left your tubes badly scarred. You have to understand that this can result in infertility.''

It took a moment for his words to acquire meaning. "You mean I can't have children?'' Andrea breathed.

"Now, nothing's written in stone, Andrea. I like to be optimistic about these things. There's no use prophesying doom before it's certain. However, I think you should be aware of the realities. . . .''

Andrea left the office numbly. She wandered down California Street, hardly knowing where she was going, replaying their conversation in her mind. Never to have children. Never, ever to have a child of her own.

At last the sight of a superette drew her attention. She walked in and began filling a cart with junk food: with mint-chocolate-chip ice cream and Entenmann's sour cream coffee cake, Gino's frozen pizzas, cream cheese and date nut bread, and Reese's peanut-butter cups. She was suddenly ravenously hungry. All she wanted to do was go home and eat.

DENNY FERGUSON WAITED AT THE SIXTY-FIRST STREET heliport for the chopper that was to bring his sister back from a meeting in Philadelphia. A March wind sweeping up from the East River slapped his face and forced tears from the corners of his eyes. Christ, it was cold! But the tiny ticket house was jammed with waiting commuters and stifling with cigar smoke—he preferred the quick sting of the wind to that sort of choking slow death he'd find in there. He shoved his hands into the pockets of his Windbreaker and danced from foot to foot to stir up some circulation.

Why the hell had he agreed to meet Jean here anyway? Stupid question. Because it was so pissing difficult to get hold of her at all these days, now that she had become a bona fide mogul. The last time she'd squeezed him in, he'd had to share his time with two unctuous creeps from Delaware, sleazy hustlers looking to bankroll a country-western magazine. They'd spent the whole time purring on about direct market surveys and demographics while Jean popped up every two minutes to answer the fucking telephone. He had sworn the next time he saw her it would be on his own terms: let her come downtown to his loft or go to hell. Yet here he was, freezing his ass, while Jean the baby tycoon pursued her meteoric career.

He gave a little chuckle, remembering something from years ago—he and Kate sitting around his crazy room at Hadley talking about some rock group that had blazed in glory briefly, then plunged totally out of sight. The Turtles maybe? Anyway, Kate had said, "That's what I call a *real* meteoric career: straight down." Well, maybe they had been stoned was why it had seemed so hilarious at the time. Still, that was Kate, her way of looking at something from a slightly ajar angle, her special irony. That was why he had flipped over her. Oh, sure, there was also her bright scarf of hair and long-lidded eyes and that lanky body that could fold so fetchingly into odd corners of a room. The package was damned attractive. But it was brilliant little twists of mind that had really done it for him.

But she had made it plain as day she wasn't interested and he was never one to go bleating after something hopeless. Kate went for the cool bastards. Like this Stephen: lots of glib charm but something surly there all the same, defensive, daring you to come at him just so he could prove to you he wouldn't take your shit. A bully for all his "I like women" boasts and protestations. And Kate, no matter how much he stomped with storm trooper's boots on her ego, would keep on defending him and blaming herself for whatever went wrong.

Christ knows though, it wasn't just Kate. Most of the women you ran into these days were somewhat schizzy. They claimed they wanted men to be sensitive, in touch with their feelings, and all that rag, but down under it all they were still pretty damned hung up on the Marlboro Man. He'd never had much trouble attracting them, thank God;

but just let him try to act anything less than macho for two seconds and most of these liberated women took to high ground. Like Christine the other night . . . Christ, she was a psychologist, two years older than himself, making an easy forty grand a year and living in splendor on 11th Street . . . but when he'd casually suggested they split the check, she'd nearly spat in his eye. And last week in bed with that crazy Helen—a mistake to begin with, but what the hell—he had asked her what it was she'd like, trying to be, you know, sensitive to her needs, and she'd snapped at him like a worried dog. What a turnoff it was to have to *list* it, she'd said.

And then there was the thing about his prospects. He could spend an hour talking to some woman about why he loved carpentry . . . how he loved the feel, the smell, the sight of new wood; how building something precise and beautiful from this fragrant material gave him a satisfying joy. And then the minute he was through, she would start quizzing him on his writing—about the Off-Off Broadway thing he'd had mounted last month, and did he think he'd ever have anything that could make it to Broadway or, even better, a screenplay, break into the movies. . . . It was the same old thing—liberated or not, they still wanted to know what kind of breadwinner he'd turn out to be.

And Christ, the thing is, it wasn't as if he were trying to be some jerk-off textbook example of the Liberated Man. It was just that it would be a fucking relief not to have to always be King Kong.

The *thwack, thwack, thwack* of the helicopter blade broke into his thoughts. He watched the craft approach, then hover, gusting blasts of bitter wind about him; then it slowly sank onto the twin white pads. Jean waved gaily at him as she emerged. She looked fucking terrific, he'd grant her that. She wore a suit, but not of the tailored, uniformlike kind: this was of a soft mauve material, with a long, full skirt and a short jacket prettily fitted at the waist.

She hurried toward him, hugged him vigorously. "God, you must be frozen!" she said. "Why didn't you wait in the car?"

He turned and saw the black stretch limousine with a young blond woman at the wheel. "I didn't know it was yours," he said.

"It's a Dresden, you should've known that by the lady driver. Anyway, she should've known *you*. I notified them you'd be here." Jean hustled him toward the car. The young woman leaped out and swung open the back door. "Why didn't you identify yourself to my brother?" Jean demanded. "He was standing there freezing to death."

"I'm sorry, Miss Ferguson. The dispatcher said the second party would be with you."

Jean let out a sigh. "Why is it that you can never delegate without something going haywire? All right, now we're going to Three-o-six East Fifty-sixth and please hurry." She settled back in the seat and turned to Denny. "I hope you don't mind if I dash home first. We've got reservations at the Four Seasons for seven-thirty so there's a bit of time. I feel like I've been in this damned suit for a week."

"I'm not exactly dressed for the Four Seasons," Denny said with a wry smile.

Jean glanced at her brother and for the first time seemed to really focus on him. "I'll say you're not. Where in the world did you get those shoes?"

"These? They're Earth Shoes. Specially designed to prevent problems in the lower back."

"They're hideously ugly. We'd better just go to Melon's instead."

"Suits me," Denny said. "At any rate, I'll get to see your new place."

"It's nothing much, believe me. A stopgap measure—I'm actually looking around for a building to buy. Something farther uptown, I think, the Seventies, around there. My plan is to purchase it through Minervco, lease the lower floors to several of my other operations and keep the top floor for myself." The car had pulled up to a curb; a doorman opened their door. Jean greeted him and hurried inside the building with Denny tagging somewhat awkwardly behind.

She whisked him up to an eighth-floor apartment and deposited him in a silver-gray living room. "I'll be just a second," she called as she disappeared down a hall. "Do you want a drink? I know there's some Chivas back in the pantry."

"I'd rather a beer," he answered. When there was no response, he perched on an arm of a plush gray couch and looked around. Not a bad place, sleek, expensively furnished in that penthousey ultramodern style. But there was something rather sterile about it. What it was struck him suddenly: the room contained absolutely nothing of a personal nature—no dog-eared books or old magazines, no tchotchkas on the mantel. Not even a picture on the wall.

Jean floated back dressed in a simple red silk shirt and black pants.

"I guess you don't spend much time here," he said.

"Hardly any. My schedule is so jammed, I use this place just to sleep and change."

"I'm surprised you got the time to furnish it at all."

"Oh, I didn't. I rented it already furnished. Through Minervco, of course."

"What the hell is this Minervco?" Denny burst out.

"God, haven't I told you about this? It's my consulting company. The way it works is that I donate all the assets I own in other ventures to Minervco, which then gives me one large total net worth to borrow against. It's an ingenious plan, really. And I need substantial leverage right now because I'm putting together something really big. Did you hear me on WPVR Tuesday night?''

''Uh-uh. What was it, some kind of radio show?''

'' 'The Financial Woman.' I was the guest speaker on it and that's where I unveiled the idea.'' She paused for a dramatic beat and Denny found himself leaning forward, pricked by suspense. ''It's a credit card for women!'' she revealed. ''You know, who've had traditionally a hard time obtaining them in their own names, not their husbands' or fathers'. I'm going to call it Womancard. And so far the response has been phenomenal. I'm turning away interview requests, there's just too many of them.''

''A credit card?'' Denny repeated. ''That's amazing. But don't you need a hell of a lot of money to pull off something like that?''

''Of course. But Denny, over the last few years I've learned a tremendous amount about financing. This concept of leveraging is brilliant. With even small assets, you can end up controlling the use of far, far larger amounts of capital. It just takes ingenuity and brains.''

Her lovely wide-spaced eyes were lit with an exhilarated glow that was instantly familiar to Denny. As children, he had seen that same expression in her eyes whenever their father had pitted them in a new competition: *Who can climb to the top of the beech tree the fastest? Let's see who can shell the most peanuts before I count a hundred.* . . . To his sister, then, this was just another race—one that she would fling herself into winning with her entire heart, mind, and soul. She was simply incapable of doing otherwise.

Thinking about their childhood startled Denny into recalling that Jean was only two years older than himself. Only twenty-eight, and here she was commanding fleets of limousines, jockeying millions, while he was living hand to mouth without even a savings account to his name. He felt a momentary tug of inadequacy, but he shook it off sharply. Christ, he was even beginning to do it to himself: *What are your prospects?*

"Let's go get something to eat," he said.

AT J. G. MELON'S THEY sat at a back table. Sipping a pale Lillet, Jean leveled her "let's get down to business" eye at her brother. "On the phone you said there was something you wanted to talk to me about."

"There is," he said, sipping the cool foam of his beer. "Mom and Dad. Particularly Mom."

Jean's lips set in a wary line. "What about her?"

"She's not taking this divorce thing very well. Dad's been flaunting this new chick of his all over town, and his lawyers are giving her a hard time about the alimony settlement. They want her to sell the house and give up the club and practically everything else she's come to rely on. I think she's starting to drink a lot—she's been acting really crazy. I'm worried as hell about her."

"I asked her if she needed any money. She said no."

"It isn't money she needs. It's a bit of support."

"But it's her own damned fault Dad dumped her," Jean burst out. "What did she expect after the way she kowtowed to him all those years? Never making anything of herself, being a perfect lady instead of a person—can you blame Dad for not wanting to live with some cardboard Emily Post cutout?"

"Come on, Jean, you know the way she was brought up. She couldn't've possibly been any other way. She was programmed right from the start."

"And if it had been up to her, she would've programmed *me* in exactly the same way," Jean said bitterly. She shook the ice in her glass, then angrily drank down the last drops. Denny gazed at her and said nothing. "Okay, okay," she said, setting down the glass. "I'll be going down to Washington a lot over the next month for this deal. I'll try to get up and spend some time with her."

"Good." He smiled. "That really would be great, Jean." He watched her push her thick bangs back from her brow. He knew that gesture by heart, had seen it a thousand times while they were growing up and knew it prefaced something serious.

"You know, Denny," she said, "when you said you wanted to talk, I didn't think it would be about Mother. I thought it would be about you."

"Yeah?" he said warily. "Why?"

"I thought you might be looking for a job."

Denny's face darkened. "I've got a job. In fact, I've got almost more work than I can handle right now. They're converting lofts like crazy downtown . . ."

"I mean a *real* job," Jean broke in. "Now don't get that look on your mouth, I know what you're going to say. But I could use you, Den, I really could. Things are happening like mad for me now; I've got a tremendous number of irons in the fire. You could have a hand in any one of them."

"Forget it, Jeanie. I'm not a businessman."

"Neither were a lot of the people I've hired. I don't think experience is anything—in fact I like people who haven't found out yet that they can't move the world. I've got a guy your age running Dresden Limos and you know how I found him? I put an ad in the *Times* looking for someone with no other qualifications except initiative and being a self-starter. And I hired Dale simply because he impressed me as having the right attitude." Jean leaned avidly forward. "I could really make it happen for you, Denny."

"I'm telling you, I'm not interested," he said. "I've got

my cabinetmaking, and I've got my writing, and if you don't think either of those is really work, then the hell with you.'' He stared obdurately into his sister's wide-set eyes, so like his own, but containing now an expression that chilled him. It had the same shadings of pity, bewilderment, and contempt that he had often read in his father's face; and the meaning was the same—they both considered him a failure. He had the sudden urge to lash out at her. ''Is all this wheeling and dealing of yours really so goddamned fulfilling? Do you have a lover, any real friends, anything at all outside your fucking work? You're a woman too, you know. Or did you somehow manage to leverage that as well?''

As soon as the words were out, he regretted them. Jean's face was hard and remote. He shook his head slowly. ''For Christ's sake, don't listen to me. I didn't mean a word of that. I'm proud as hell of everything you've done and you know it.'' He placed his hand on her wrist. ''I'm sorry, okay?''

She relented with a smile. But there was still a brittleness in the air between them, treacherously thin ice upon which one of them had to take the first step. ''Hey,'' Denny said quickly, ''do you remember that kid Russell Meltzer who lived on the end of our block?''

''The fat red-headed kid?'' Jean said.

''Yeah, who'd never let anyone play with that crazy geiger counter he had? Well, would you believe I *saw* him lately, in a bar in the Village, and he hasn't changed a bit.''

THE REST OF the dinner passed in gleeful reminiscing, and when Jean parted from her brother it was with an affectionate hug. But as she returned alone to her apartment, she felt intensely agitated. Denny's words cut her far deeper than he could have guessed: his accusations were the very fears that had nagged her since she had learned of John Dreiser's death.

She poured herself a Courvoisier—an evening ritual to which Dreiser had accustomed her—and wondered if it was true: Was she somehow deficient as a woman? Certainly, in her business dealings, she conducted herself like a man. But that was a matter of survival—one of the first lessons she had absorbed was to circumvent any situation in which her femininity would make her conspicuous. If she sensed a man edging up to greet her with a kiss, she warded it off by thrusting a businesslike hand toward him. She tried to be the first to arrive at meetings, so that no man would leap to his feet when she entered the room. And though she had softened her style of dressing from the strictly tailored suits she had worn at IMI, she allowed herself no provocative necklines (nothing scooped below the collarbone), no body-clinging cuts or fabrics, no flashy or distracting jewelry. Not even perfume—not since the time a vital presentation had been completely undermined by a cagey old banker who had interrupted her at regular intervals to inform her how "perfectly ravishing" she smelled.

And yet men still looked at her, that she knew. Even without the frills, her jaunty small figure, sleek hair, and dark, wide-set eyes had their own appeal.

It wasn't for lack of attracting men that she hadn't found one to love. Rather it was that since John Dreiser she had met very few men she considered her equal. There were, she decided, three basic types. The hostile, he-man types who resented or felt threatened by her power. The ones so intimidated by her they fairly quaked when she approached them. And, finally, the brash bastards, the ones who thought they could get something from her, whose advances were blatantly opportunistic.

From time to time during the past year she had actually

dated a few of this last category. She had even gone to bed with one or two of them, simply to ease the violent physical cravings that continued to claw at her before she went to sleep. But afterward her feelings would always be the same—boredom mixed with impatience, the conviction that she had just been wasting her time.

And yet she would like to fall in love. To experience all those sensations she imagined would go with it—the swirling, dizzying, heady rush of completely letting go. But the man who could make her feel this way would have to be extraordinary. A modern-day knight on a white charger.

She curled on the couch, drew her feet up under her, and smiled slightly. It was just possible that she knew him already. Dick Milani . . . the name trickled lazily into her thoughts. He was a lawyer, one of the main participants in the Womancard venture. From the moment she met him, she had approved of what she'd seen: thatchy brown hair, handsome features lit by intelligence and urbane humor, a body hardened by squash and tennis and summer sailing. She approved, too, of his vaulting ambition: at thirty-four, already a full partner in his firm and giving no indication of stopping there.

Yet so far their relationship had been scrupulously businesslike. If it was to change, she would have to be the one to initiate it. Dick was in Atlanta on another deal at the moment but scheduled to return tomorrow. She resolved to call him at his office and propose they get together: the thought gave her a flush of nervous excitement.

But when the time came to call him, she found herself actually shivering with nervousness. Her palm clutching the receiver was damp; she caught her breath as she heard him pick up. "Jean!" he said heartily. "Glad you called. I think I've finally got all the papers on line for the Womancard deal."

He related the details, and she filled him in on what news she had since he'd been away. And then, after a moment's pause, she plunged ahead. "Listen, Dick? I was wondering . . . could you come by my place for a drink tonight?"

"Excellent idea. Look, my phone's going berserk, I've got about a dozen people hanging. Let's say about seven, okay?"

"Perfect." She gave him the address and hung up, melting with relief. It had been so easy after all. But why had she been so skittish, she who had tackled bank presidents and chairmen of the board in the course of business without any such fear? What in God's name was so alarming about simply asking a man for a date?

Nevertheless, she was feverishly excited as she prepared for him. She inspected the munificent tray of cheeses and crudités her Jamaican housekeeper had prepared on her instructions; then she put two bottles of Veuve Cliquot in the refrigerator to chill and laid out two crystal champagne glasses. For twenty minutes, she soaked in a hot tub, dusted herself with L'Interdit powder, then slipped into a filmy Stephen Burrows dress the color of cyclamen and fastened elegant gold hoops at her ears. She came out into the living room, lit the soft lamps by the couch, selected a Schubert quintet, and set the stereo volume low.

What else? She had only invited him for drinks, but the rest of the evening was entirely open. Perhaps she should make a reservation somewhere for dinner? Or they could order something sent up from the steakhouse across the street. . . . She wondered if he would stay the night and shivered with anticipation.

She gave a start as the intercom buzzed. She answered it, told the doorman to send her visitor up.

Dick strode in briskly carrying a large attaché. She caught a ghost of surprise in his face as he looked at her, but he masked it quickly with a smile. "You look marvelous," he said. "And this is a great place. Where do you want to work, over here on the couch? Don't you think we'll need more light?"

Jean felt a momentary confusion that settled quickly into deep dismay. Dick had interpreted her invitation to mean she wanted to work. And now she felt intensely foolish with her siren's red gown and seductive lighting.

Dick had made his way to the couch and was bending over the laden silver tray. "Great, you've got some munchies. I was running so hard today I never got in lunch." He selected a floweret of broccoli and, nibbling, began to pull papers from the briefcase. "You know what else I'd like," he called. "A good stiff scotch. Black Label, if you've got it, otherwise anything. A double, on the rocks."

Jean flicked on the overhead lighting and turned off the Schubert. She filled two rocks glasses with ice, went to the liquor sideboard, and numbly poured from the first bottle she laid her hand upon. She brought the glasses and sat beside him on the couch.

Dick handed her a brimming folder. "If we can just get through the assignment of shares, then I think we'll be well ahead of the game," he said.

Jean tried to concentrate on the pages in front of her, but her mind still dwelled on what had gone wrong. How could he have totally misread her intent? Didn't he see her as a *woman* at all? She clung to one hope—that when they were done with the work and could relax, the tenor of the evening might yet turn around. She could offer a glass of champagne, guide the conversation toward lighter, more personal matters . . . and then who could say where it might lead?

But after about an hour, Dick began to glance at his watch. "Do you mind if I make a call?" he asked finally.

"No, of course not. There's a phone right behind you. Or you could use the one in the bedroom. . . ."

"This one's fine." He dialed from memory and lowered his voice to a domestic murmur. "Hi, it's me. Look, I'm still tied up here, what time did you say this thing is?" There was a pause; then he covered the mouthpiece with his palm and glanced back up at Jean. "Mind if I told someone to meet me here? It would give us more time to keep pounding this stuff out."

She struggled to keep her expression placid. "No, go right ahead. I don't mind."

Twenty minutes later, she opened the door to a tall, skinny girl: her hurricane of blond hair whipped around a face that was as broad and blank as a dinner plate.

"Hi, I'm Deanna!" she cried. "What a neat place you've got here! My girlfriend Harriet lives right down the block, so I knew just what avenue to come by. Hi, Dickie!" She pursed her lips and made kissy sounds in his direction. Then to Jean: "You guys work so hard it's like reform school or something. I know if I had to think all the time I'd just about go out of my mind."

The girl was a fool! How could this brilliant and vital man be attracted to such a wooden-headed puppet? It was monstrously, abhorrently unfair!

Dick was stuffing papers back in his briefcase with a strangely flustered speed. "Sorry to cut out on you like this, Jean, but we've got a curtain to make. This new thing of Joe Papp's at the Public . . ." He pulled on his Burberry. "I think we've made a lot of headway, though. Thanks for the drink. We'll speak tomorrow, okay?"

He whisked away the giant Deanna, leaving Jean alone among the remnants of the debacle. How it all must have looked to him—the silver tray stocked with Leydens, bries, Neufchâtels, and the gorgeous fan of vegetables . . . the

purely mated crystal glasses . . . her too-obvious dress.
. . . With what scoffing pity he must be thinking of her
now!

She poured herself another stiff scotch and continued
drinking till long past midnight when, still in the red dress,
she curled into sleep on the couch. She woke after nine the
next morning and for the first time ever was late getting to
work. She waved away the brace of assistants who tried to
waylay her in the hall and marched directly to her own office. To her irritation, there was a man seated in the chair
opposite her desk.

"Who are you?" she asked curtly.

He swiveled and smiled with calm deference. "I'm Paul
Coulter, ma'am." When she continued to stare at him he
elaborated: "We spoke on the phone last week? I'm the
accountant—the friend of Simon Drucker, who told me you
were looking for someone. You suggested I come in today."

Jean remembered it now grudgingly—she was in no mood
to conduct an interview. As she took her seat facing him, it
struck her that he resembled somebody else . . . yes, Keir
Dullea who played the astronaut in *2001*. The same sort of
tabula rasa all-American looks that could mean almost anything: an astronaut, a second baseman, a psychotic killer.

"You're from California, aren't you?" she asked.

"California all the way. Born in Palo Alto, Stanford B.A.
and M.B.A. And for the past four years I've been working
with a venture capitalist outfit in San Diego. But you can get
all that in my résumé."

He pushed a black folder across the desk. Neatly bound,
impeccably typed . . . and an original, not a copy.

"Why have you come to New York?" Jean asked.

"Change of pace, broaden my horizons, all that. This
outfit I was with had become pretty conservative, only bet-

ting on sure things. I'm looking for something with more vision—the kind of risks that can ultimately pay off big. So when Simon mentioned you, I jumped, believe me.''

''You knew about me then?''

''Sure. I read that piece in *Barron's* about how you turned around Birgitta Modeling. Brilliant! As you can see there, I've had some experience in the area of saving failing businesses. I think I could be very helpful to you in future ventures, Miss Ferguson, although . . .'' He paused as if suddenly embarrassed by what he had been about to say.

''Although what?'' Jean prompted.

''Well, this is going to sound mighty presumptuous. But I didn't expect you to be so young, and . . . well, to be frank, you're an incredibly attractive woman. I just am wondering if that might make it kind of hard to work closely with you.''

Jean stared into the pale blue eyes: she could read nothing there but straightforward admiration. ''I haven't had any breakfast yet,'' she said. ''Why don't we go over to the Brasserie and talk about all this further?''

''That would be a real pleasure,'' he said.

Part 3

*I*F SHE WALKED THE TWENTY BLOCKS TO HER THERAPIST'S office instead of taking the bus, she could save thirty-five cents. And while up on 96th Street, she could stop in that little bodega and pick up a quart of milk for a dime less a quart than the A & P. . . .

Of such mean economies did Kate's life now consist. She wore eighty-nine-cent panties from Lamston's until the elastic sagged and holes dotted through. She filled each empty Prell tube with water to soak out the final bit of shampoo before throwing it away. And she agonized over each purchase: did she really need that emery board, the extra pair of pantyhose, the tea with her grilled-cheese sandwich for lunch? But though she scrimped on everything she possibly could, she was still barely getting by. It was this damned inflation—prices had zoomed, but her salary had only risen to one hundred eighty-five dollars a week; out of which she had her own apartment to support, and now these therapy sessions as well. It was true that, at twenty-five dollars a session, Dr. Greenfrier was practically seeing her as a charity patient, but it still drained the last of her spare cash.

Stephen had suggested she see him. For several weeks following the night he had bruised her cheek, Stephen had wallowed in guilt, and Kate had luxuriated in a false sense of security. And then one night when he had left her waiting in his apartment, she fell into a sulk, expecting him to react with the kind of abject contrition he had been showing lately. Instead he went off like a land mine. "You can leave me out of your rancid little guilt games, baby," he had exploded. He threw her purse and coat into the hall, shoved her out after them, and locked the door. For three days he refused to take her phone calls; on the fourth he informed her they could go on only if she agreed to "see a shrink." He even had a name for her—someone who had "cured" the wife of a friend of his several years before. "Maybe *he* can find out why you're so driven to be so destructively manipulative," he had declared.

And so Dr. Greenfrier.

He was a bland old Freudian with a smoker's cough and a habit of thoughtfully massaging one earlobe. A vague stench of coffee rose from the old wool of his jackets and shawl-collared cardigans whenever he shifted position or reached out to turn the red desk clock more fully to his view. He made only the most infrequent and noncommittal comments, and Kate, after the first few months, had simply run out of things to say. She had come to dread the horrible passages in which Dr. Greenfrier sat blankly, neither encouraging nor disparaging the silence, while she frantically scoured her mind for something significant enough to relate.

Today, at least, she had come prepared. She had been having two recurring dreams. In one, she was trying to call Stephen. He was expecting her call, he would be furious if he didn't hear from her, but her fingers kept misdialing—

over and over she began his number, and each time it came out wrong.

In the second, she would touch her teeth with her tongue and discover they were jiggling and loose. She would realize with horror they were about to fall out. She always had this last dream just before waking in the morning, which gave it a vivid and particularly terrifying reality.

She presented the dreams to Dr. Greenfrier and waited for his comment, a bit nervously, like a hostess anticipating a guest's reaction to some specially prepared dish.

"Loss," he intoned. "You've lost the ability to dial, the ability to communicate. You're losing your teeth."

"Does it mean I'm afraid that I'm losing Stephen?" she asked.

"Is that how you see it?"

"Well, I don't know. We've actually been getting along pretty well lately. I told you he's got a share in a summer house in East Hampton and we've been going out every weekend. It seems to've taken some of the pressure off our relationship. I guess we've just been too bottled up always being in the city."

Dr. Greenfrier nodded, which Kate knew did not so much signify agreement as simply acknowledgment of her response. "What would the loss of this man mean to you?" he asked.

"Oh, God, everything! I love him."

"I don't mean in the abstract sense. I mean concretely. Describe exactly how your life would change if you were to lose Stephen."

Kate rested her head against the leather of the dilapidated Morris chair. "Well, for one thing, I wouldn't be able to spend any more time at his apartment. Which means I'd be stuck in my own place which I hate. I couldn't borrow his car anymore, and of course I wouldn't be able to go out to the beach. And he has a lot of friends I really like. If we broke up, I probably wouldn't see much of them anymore."

"And why can't you have a nice apartment and a summer house and interesting friends of your own?"

"Oh, God, I can't afford it. I'm barely scraping by on the money I'm making. And if you want to know interesting people you've got to keep up with them. Stephen's friends all make far more money than I do."

Dr. Greenfrier gave his nod of information received and lapsed into silence—it had already been an uncharacteristically long exchange. Kate squirmed in her chair while she grasped about for some new topic. She hit upon a letter from her sister Ginny, pregnant with her third child and living in Wichita Falls. She spent the rest of the hour discussing how difficult she found it to relate to any of her sisters, who had all opted for the kind of suburban domesticity she had fled from. At last the time was up. She handed Dr. Greenfrier a twenty-five-dollar check which, as always, he folded precisely in two. "One more thing," he said. "Beginning with your next session, I would like to raise the fee to thirty-five dollars."

She stared at him aghast. How could he ask this when she had just told him how desperately strapped for cash she was. "That will be very hard for me, Dr. Greenfrier," she said.

His head bobbed. "As you know, Kate, one of the first principles of successful therapy is the patient's full commitment. The responsibility of payment is a necessary way of reinforcing such a commitment. I'm afraid I must remain firm in this particular."

KATE WANDERED FROM the office in frantic confusion. How the bloody hell was she going to scrape up an extra ten dollars a week? She had already eliminated every superfluous expense and whittled down all the necessary ones. Except for one extravagance—the East Hampton weekends with Stephen. On these, she was forced to spend money. They drove out in Stephen's Fiat, so she paid gas and tolls—only fair, after all. And with the three other couples who shared the house, they all chipped in equally for food—again only fair; she could hardly expect to be the sole exception. Inevitably the group voted for lobster or prime rib, and of course they laid in substantial supplies of wine and beer and Jamaican dark rum, so the food shares always seemed to mount up pretty high.

Yet she didn't dare scrimp on any of this.

The only solution was that she make more money. And God knew, Haber and Switt owed it to her. For four years she had toiled faithfully for them, meekly accepting her tiny raises without a squeak of complaint. She was now the senior assistant. The three who had been there when she started had at last drifted away, to go back to school, to try a hand at writing sitcoms in L.A. . . . Kate had trained their replacements; she knew the job intimately, could do it comatose if she had to—and such expertise must be worth *something*, even to a miserly stiff like Harold Switt.

She shrank from the thought of confronting Harold. He had a way of directing overtly sexist comments at her that never failed to fluster her. If she brought him a list of morning radio talk shows in the Denver area, she would feel his eyes on her chest, and he would say: "I've been trying to decide all week whether or not you wore a bra." Or as she was leaving, he would roar out: "What lucky pole is gonna stick you tonight, Kate?" She had learned to say, "Fuck off, Harold," or, "Don't be more of a chauvinist pig than you can help," but always in a jocular tone—he was, after all, her boss. And afterward she would hate herself for wishy-washily tolerating such slime. It was easier just to avoid him as much as possible.

But now there was no alternative. In the morning she marched resolutely into his office.

Harold was hollering into the phone, his mouth smack up against the mouthpiece. He waved her to sit down, proffered a pack of Juicy Fruit which she declined, popped a stick in his own mouth, then slammed down the receiver and crooned, "Kate, Kate, your tits look great."

"I have to talk to you a minute, Harold," she said firmly.

"What's up, honeybun?"

"It's about my salary. I'm not happy with it. I think I deserve more. After all, I've been here a long time, and I think I've done a pretty good job. And what with inflation and everything, I'm just not making it on what you're paying me."

Harold grinned, chewing with his front teeth. "I'll be up front with you, babe. You've got a real problem, which is the fact that, at any given moment, I can go out there and get a hundred other kids to take your place."

Kate was prepared for this argument. "No one can do it as well as I can," she stated. "I know all the clients, I know how the office works . . ."

"Hey, face it, honeybun, it's not a very hard job. A new kid could pick it up in a jiffy. And Bob and me're used to a certain amount of turnover around here."

"What about a promotion, then? I could handle a lot more responsibility."

"Promote ya to what? Look, kiddo, if I needed another press agent, I could pick up the phone and in two seconds flat get some guy with all his own contacts and twenty years hard experience. And for peanuts. They're going begging out there."

Kate looked at him with loathing. Here was a man still wearing Beatle bangs ten years after the last self-respecting fifteen-year-old had shunned them. If only she could wipe that sassy grin off his face and force him to take her seriously. "I'm afraid I'll have to start looking for something else then," she said bitterly.

"Be sorry to see you go, babe. But ya gotta do what ya gotta do." He crossed his arms on his chest and tilted back his chair. "But look, I got an idea for you."

"You know of another job?"

"A situation. I've got a pal in San Francisco, a hell of a nice guy, around fifty-six, fifty-seven. In the importing business, big bucks. His wife's got the crab—ya know, the Big C. Bad scene. So Andy comes to New York maybe once or twice a month, and what he wants is to set up a young chick in an apartment. There'd be an allowance, everything you need, and all you'd have to do is give him a little TLC when he was in town."

"You want to set me up as your friend's mistress?" Kate said incredulously.

"It's a dream situation. He's a good-looking guy, you'd like him."

"No thanks, Harold. That's not the kind of job I had in mind."

"Suit yourself, babe. But let's face it—girls with B.A.'s in New York are a dime a dozen."

Kate rose to her feet. "I am not just a 'girl with a B.A.,' Harold. I happen to be a *woman* and a graduate of one of the best colleges in America. And if you think I can't do any better than being a call girl for your friends, then screw you, Harold, and screw your job too!"

She marched back to her desk. As the rest of the staff watched curiously, she threw her personal things into a large manila envelope and walked out. Harold could mail her the money he owed her, the bastard. She was trembling with anger, but it was a good anger: for the first time in a long time she had stood up for herself.

But outside, in the blank glare of the New York July, her noble surge of spirits gave way to starker realities. She had quit her job—the full fact hit her with sudden force. She had forty-three dollars in her wallet, no savings, and no immediate prospects . . . and this when she needed more money than ever.

There was one thing she could do immediately. Waitressing—she had plenty of experience from all those summer jobs on the Cape and in Boston. The money was good; and in New York every waitress was an aspiring something else—dancer, model, photographer, singer—so there was really no stigma attached to the work.

She spent the afternoon walking into the trendier bars and cafés up and down Second and Third avenues: Daly's Dandelion, Mike Malone's, J.P.'s. She finally had success at a tiny café called Parasol. It was both popular and pricey, which meant tips would be good, and her schedule—Monday through Thursday nights and Friday lunch—left her weekends blessedly free.

She was nervous about how Stephen would react to what she had done. But when she told him, he seemed amazingly to approve. "You were on that job too long anyway," he said mildly. "Now you can take your time looking around for something with a real future."

They were in his apartment. She watched him remove his Prince Graphite racquet from its press and do a few experimental lobs in the air. Stephen had taken to tennis with a fury this summer; just the feel of the racquet stem in his hand seemed to ease him into a benevolent mood. "By the way," he said, "for your birthday next Friday, how would you like to have dinner at Elaine's?"

"I'd love it," Kate said. She was delighted that he was making plans this far in advance. Last year he had simply asked the morning of her birthday, "Anything special you want to do tonight?'' and they had ended up at one of the schlumpy neighborhood places they always went to. What was more remarkable was that he should suggest Elaine's. Stephen was fond of mocking the ''sheep'' who would subject themselves to the kind of abuse anyone except the distinctly famous was guaranteed there; he placed them in the same pitiable category as people who waited docilely on movie lines and those who paid double in rent to live in flimsy doorman buildings.

''We can leave for the beach directly from there, then,'' Stephen said, replacing the racquet in the press. ''Oh, and Benno and Lynn would like to come along too.''

Kate's delight disappeared. The mystery was explained. Benno Geiss and his live-in girlfriend Lynn Schmidt were video artists who Stephen had met last Christmas and become immediately infatuated with. They were attractive, vivacious people with a certain hard-edged, androgynous style that got them easily into Studio 54. Kate liked them well enough—or at least Benno; Lynn tended to treat her in a manner iced faintly with condescension. But it was of course they who had proposed going to Elaine's; and it was because of them that Stephen was so enthusiastic.

Still, when the evening came, and the four of them entered the restaurant, Kate found herself having fun. She felt pretty dressed in a black halter top and slim black jeans; as they stood at the bar, she was gratified to notice several men glance at her admiringly. There was a twenty-minute wait for their reservation, and when they were seated it was in the back room, but Lynn and Benno were greeted loudly by several people at the prestigious tables in front, so they seemed satisfied. They had brought Kate a present—a little green plastic monster that, when wound up, waddled forward on flipperlike feet and breathed sparks of fire. Benno, declaring that it was a momentous celebration, insisted they order champagne. Kate began to succumb to their charm; she was sorry now she had resented their coming along.

Stephen was ecstatic. He sipped his champagne with rapture and laughed heartily as the green monster tried to walk into the wall, its little flippers plodding with useless might. Then he set down his glass and turned to Benno and Lynn. "Well, I had a very interesting experience last week," he announced.

"What was it?" Benno prompted.

"I was in Philadelphia for a few days, staying at a downtown hotel. And while I was there, I took the advantage to do something I've always been curious about. I experimented with a prostitute."

Kate felt a numbing cold streak down to the tips of her toes and fingers. She glanced at the other couple: their eyes were glistening with expectancy. Lynn's diamond-shaped face thrust forward, a snake beckoned by a charmer. "That's wild!" she said. "What was it like?"

Stephen glowed in the dazzle of their captured attention. "I was propositioned by two hookers in the lobby—I think they asked if I wanted a date. Needless to say, I selected the better-looking of the two. We went directly up to my room and she undressed—a bit too matter-of-factly, I thought. I guess I expected more of a provocative, striptease thing. But anyway, then I undressed and naturally she gave me the standard stuff about how well-endowed I was."

It seemed to Kate that he was speaking at tremendous volume, that his words must be carrying to all the surrounding tables. On the other hand, she seemed to be shrinking, to be becoming tinier with every word he spoke.

"And then we got down to business, as it were," Stephen was saying. "And what really impressed me was the way this lady made me feel *she* was getting the greatest fuck of her life. I don't know, maybe it was sheer professionalism, but from the way she was carrying on, I was convinced the earth was moving for her."

Kate got up and bolted from the table. She ran blindly through the restaurant, out onto Second Avenue where she wildly flagged down a cab. She began to cry in the taxi, not caring that the Korean driver kept glancing back at her with bewildered alarm; by the time she reached her apartment she was heaving with uncontrollable sobs. She threw herself on the bed, conscious only of the phone, both dreading and longing for Stephen's call.

It came less than an hour later. Oh, please let him realize how much he hurt her. She whispered a hoarse hello.

"You've really done it this time, baby." Stephen's voice crackled with fury. "Your little trick made me look like a royal asshole. Lynn and Benno couldn't fucking believe it. And when the waiter came up and asked if you were coming back, what the fuck was I supposed to say? I had to sit there with egg on my face. Well, you've hung yourself with this one, baby. You can forget about coming out to East Hampton, because I don't want to see your fucking face."

He hung up. Kate felt the familiar black misery slam into her once again. She huddled into herself on the bed and cried herself to sleep.

SHE WOKE EARLY. The day was going to be a scorcher, she could tell that right away. Her little air conditioner was cranking away on high, but still a muggy thickness hung in the apartment; and outside, under a white sky, the sun's stare was brutal, merciless, constant.

Kate spent the morning reading *Sense and Sensibility*, trying to lose herself in Regency glades. But it was so quiet. The street outside, save for an occasional truck clattering by, was eerily empty. There was no sound from the screaming sex lady upstairs. Even the stereo next door was suddenly still.

By afternoon, the silence had begun to oppress her. The thought kept haunting her that she was the only person left in the city—everyone else had fled the heat wave, escaped to places as cool and green as Jane Austen's world. She laid the book aside, turned on the radio, and began to pace the apartment. What a squalid little place it was, so dark and ratty. She never had gotten around to fixing it up—to do so would have been an admission that she wouldn't be moving back with Stephen. As long as it was so makeshift, she had been able to reassure herself that it was really just temporary.

But here she was, incontestably stuck in this horror of an apartment. And she was twenty-six years old; oh, God, how far she was from the glittering future she had imagined for herself back in college. How easy it had seemed then, how smugly confident she had been that she could just waltz out into the world and effortlessly make it all happen.

What a flimsy house of cards she had built her self-esteem upon. One kick from Stephen and it had all come tumbling down.

The monotonous disco beat pounding from the radio began to press on her nerves. She snapped it off. But the silence . . . it was going to drive her crazy. She had to hear a voice of some kind. Any kind.

She snatched up the phone. If only she could talk to Sissy—but Sissy, she knew, was out at her own summer share on Fire Island. Denny, that's who she could talk to! She was always meaning to see more of Denny. But no, she remembered now that he had gone to Colorado for the month. She picked up her address book. It was sparsely filled—funny how she had let her own life slip when she became engulfed in Stephen's. She went through the few listings: but one by one the phones shrilled endlessly in empty apartments.

There must be someone she could talk to. She thought briefly of calling her parents. But she had always put on the most upbeat face for her family. She wrote home about the exciting parties she had been to, celebrities and interesting new people she had met through her job. When she and Stephen had driven to New Mexico last February, she had sent her mother a glowing report, neglecting to describe how often they had fought along the way or how in Taos Stephen had left her stranded an entire day in the motel while he went to look up an old girlfriend. She couldn't stand to let her parents know she was leading anything but a fascinating and glamorous life.

What about Andrea then? People in San Francisco didn't clear out for the weekend the way they did in New York. Kate hunted for the letter in which Andrea had written her new number. She found it on the windowsill, dialed, and breathed relief at the sound of Andrea's gentle hi.

"Andrea, I'm so glad you're home!" Kate burst out. But then she stopped. Andrea had gone on talking—no, it wasn't Andrea but some sort of recording: . . . *I'm not home right now, but please don't hang up. You can leave your name and a message right after you hear the beep, and I promise to get back to you as soon as I can.* . . .

Kate let the receiver drop. She stood numbly a moment, the silence screaming at her. Then her eyes fell upon a tennis racquet leaning against a chair. Her birthday present—Stephen had promised to teach her to play out at the beach. She picked it up, examined it—then suddenly she began to smash it against the wall. Again and again she brought it down. Now it was Dr. Greenfrier with his coffee stench and his fucking higher fees. Now it was smirking, sexist, gum-chewing Harold Switt. But mostly it was Stephen. Damn Stephen. Damn his rules for relationships, damn his traps and his temper. Damn him and his cheap, money-grubbing ways. Damn him to hell! She hated him, hated him, she was shrieking as she splintered the racquet head harder and harder against the cracking plaster wall. Oh, God, she was going out of her mind!

And then the phone rang.

She stopped, stared at it a moment. Then she answered in a trembling voice.

"It's Donny, down at Parasol, darling. I didn't wake you, did I? You sound a little foggy. Listen love, one of my girls punked out on me tonight, could you possibly work dinner? Oh, you're an angel, you've absolutely saved my life! Big kiss . . ."

Kate stared down at the ruined racquet in her hand. Her tantrum suddenly seemed ludicrous. She really wasn't the last person left on earth.

The café was soothingly cool and dim. There were few patrons, largely tourists bedraggled by the heat, more interested in iced drinks than food. Kate, having little to do, loitered by the bar, sipping a Pepsi and trading wisecracks with the bloated Welsh bartender. It was like another world here, a sanctuary in which she could almost forget her shattering loneliness.

At around nine o'clock, the door opened and a couple came in. They were far too striking to be tourists. The woman was particularly stunning in a cool dress of red-and-white polished cotton and a broad-brimmed red straw hat. Looking at her, Kate felt a pang of envy. Why wasn't she the one wearing clothes like that, sashaying elegantly into expensive restaurants?

The couple selected a small table in the direct stream of the air conditioning. Kate roused herself, picked up two menus, and took them to their table. "Good evening," she said brightly. "Could I bring you something cold from the bar?"

The red hat brim tilted up toward her, and a pair of wide-set gray eyes lit with recognition. "Kate, what a surprise! How are you?"

Kate stared down in horror. She could conceive of nothing more intensely mortifying than the fact that she was waiting on Jean Ferguson.

Her fingers bent the corners of the linen menus. She was paralyzed, unable to speak, or even to turn and run.

"Kate, it's me," Jean pursued, with a trilling laugh. "Don't tell me I've changed that much!"

"No, of course not," she managed. "Hi, Jean."

"That's better. But what is this? Are you actually working here?"

"Well, yes . . ."

"But what happened to your job at that talent agency you were doing so well at?"

"Publicity," Kate amended stiffly. "I just quit a few weeks ago. I'd gone as far as I could there, and now I've got a couple of things on line, but . . . well, it's summer, you know. I just wanted something nontaxing for a while, a kind of mental vacation." She could see that Jean hadn't swallowed a syllable of this pathetic rationale. If only lightning would strike, the floor collapse, a black hole rip down from the reaches of space and suck one of them into its illimitable void—preferably Jean.

"Why don't you sit down with us a few minutes," Jean said. "By the way, this is Paul Coulter, an associate of mine."

The young man bobbed to his feet, shot out a hand and pumped Kate's smartly. "Good to meet you," he said in a tone just a calculated shade warmer than polite.

Kate assessed him briefly. Fresh-faced, super-straight Colgate smile. Probably completely under Jean's thumb.

"Come on, Kate, grab a chair," Jean repeated. "I'm dying to hear everything you've been up to. And I want to tell you about some interesting things I've been doing.''

''I can't, I'm too busy.'' She saw quizzical amusement pass over Jean's face and realized the last other table had departed, and Jean and Paul were now the only diners left in the café. ''Besides it's not allowed,'' she added quickly. ''No fraternization.''

''Well, I certainly don't want to jeopardize your job,'' Jean said.

Damn that condescending smile! ''What do you want to order?'' Kate snapped.

''Just drinks. A margarita for me, and Paul will have a Dewar's, rocks.''

''Right,'' said Paul.

Kate fetched the drinks from the bar and fled quickly, before Jean could trap her in any further conversation. She retreated to a back table and pretended to be engrossed in sorting out the evening's checks. But her eyes seemed compelled to travel back to the couple in front. She was right, she decided, in her assessment of the man, Paul. An adoring slave. While Jean did most of the talking, he listened raptly, nodding where appropriate, his eyes dancing lively attendance on her face. Jean however . . . Jean was lustrous, *radiant* with success. The very sight of her seemed a reproach to the miserable mess Kate had made of her own life.

Of course, she knew about Jean's success. Impossible not to—over the past year, the media had practically canonized her as some sort of First Saint of Feminism. A woman who had Made It: a prototype held up for the struggling ranks of the oppressed sex to revere and follow. The launching of Womancard had splashed her name and face through every publication in the country, and, when that furor had died down, it still seemed impossible to pick up a magazine or newspaper without stumbling across some reference to her.

Jean featured as one of *Cosmo*'s "Ten Most Important Women in Finance." Jean quoted in a *Daily News* article on "business dressing with impact." Jean Ferguson, a contributor to the *Times*'s "Neediest Cases Fund," her thousand-dollar check earmarked for destitute women raising families on their own.

Each time Kate had encountered her name she had recoiled as if from a spurting acid and turned the page rapidly. She had never wanted to encounter Jean's success. She had even found herself lately avoiding Denny, just because he might refer to his sister. And yet here she was in the utterly demeaning position of having to serve her. It was, she thought melodramatically, the worst moment of her life. Oh, if only she hadn't walked out on Stephen, she'd be safe and happy at the beach right now instead of in this hideous mess.

Jean was motioning to her, scribbling into her raised palm to signal for the check. Kate dragged herself back to their table and waved away the Womancard Jean had poised. No way would she accept a tip from Jean Ferguson. "This is on me," she declared.

"Don't be silly . . ."

"No, I mean it. I'll take care of it."

"Okay," Jean said with a smile. "I'll let you buy me a drink. But on one condition—you'll come to see me on Monday."

Kate glanced at her. "Come to see you?"

"At my office. Look, Kate, I'll tell you frankly, I'm appalled to see you wasting your time like this. I can help you do better." Jean picked up the cocktail napkin from under her glass and jotted an address on it. "Here's where I am. I'll expect you at ten o'clock Monday morning. Paul, you'll remember that?"

"I'll put it in the book."

"I can't possibly make it," Kate said. "I've already got an appointment. And anyway, I don't think . . ."

"It's up to you of course," Jean cut in. "But as far as I'm concerned, we've got a date. See you, Kate."

She glided out, Paul at her heels. Kate crumpled the damp napkin in her hand. She was damned if she'd go crawling to Jean Ferguson for any favors. Yet instead of tossing the wadded napkin into the trash, some second thought made her put it in the pocket of her blouse.

Still she didn't intend to keep the appointment. Not through the long Sunday, another scorcher that condemned her to the B movies on TV. Not through the endless Sunday night in which her hope Stephen might call finally dwindled to nothing. Not even when she popped awake at six-fifteen Monday morning facing another aimless day. But when, at nine-thirty, she headed toward the uptown IRT, she told herself it was just curiosity—she would listen to what Jean had to say, and of course proudly refuse any offer.

The address proved to be a narrow sandstone townhouse in the middle of a charming residential block in the East Eighties. There was no answer to Kate's repeated ring. Finally two men in delivery uniforms emerged, and when one held open the door, Kate, with a shrug, let herself in.

There was no one in the small foyer, just a couch with a UPS parcel sitting on it, an empty umbrella stand, and in the center of the floor a magnificent grandfather clock that seemed startled to be there. As she wandered down the hall, a stocky, frazzled girl in aviator glasses bore down on her frantically. "Are you from the catering? Say yes and save my life!"

"Sorry, I'm looking for Jean. I've got an appointment."

"Shit on a stick! Look, when you go up, tell her the clock's come, but I'm still waiting for the typewriter repairman and I don't have a *clue* about the caterers."

She vanished. Kate, taking the word *up* as a clue, mounted the stairs off the foyer. Hearing Jean's voice, she followed it into a large front room. Jean sat presiding behind a huge Victorian oak desk, talking into a red phone. Beyond her sat Paul on a pale green couch, with a white phone pressed to his ear.

Jean waved her into a chair, then covered the mouthpiece with one palm. "Paul, field this for me, will you? It's the Houston gang with the tax arrangements on the Forrester deal. Oh, and take it in another office, will you?"

Paul made the "okay" sign with his fingers, punched a button on his phone, then hurried out of the room.

Kate sat down, took somewhat disgruntled stock of Jean's dress (an elegant fawn-colored silk with long tapered sleeves), then said, "I'm supposed to tell you the clock is here, but not the repairman or the caterer. There was a rather distraught girl in Gloria Steinem glasses . . ."

"Sandy. She subsists on crises." Jean laughed. "I guess we are something of a proper madhouse here, but we're still just settling in. Actually I bought the property seven months ago, but there were some drastic structural problems. The whole façade needed repointing for a start."

"It's a lovely house," Kate acknowledged.

"Thanks. It has a rather notorious pedigree. J. P. Morgan lodged one of his less presentable mistresses here—or so I'm told."

"But what do you actually do here?"

"Everything! This company"—she waved a hand to indicate the surrounding office—"Minervco, is a company I formed to consolidate my holdings in a portfolio of some fifteen other ventures. These are very diversified—everything from limousine rental to a science-textbook house. Now, some of these were existing companies I salvaged from bankruptcy or acquired in one deal or another. Others I started from scratch on just an idea, a little seed money, and a lot of chutzpah.''

"Very impressive," Kate said grudgingly.

Jean leaned toward her. "You know, I'd have given fifty-fifty you wouldn't show up for this meeting. You've always resisted my overtures in the past. Why not now?''

"Just curiosity. I've been hearing so much about you, I thought I'd like to see for myself just what you were up to."

Jean's smile was a trifle condescending. But she changed the subject. "So you saw my clock?" she said. "Isn't it a beauty? Sheraton style, circa 1810. With only some minor restoration work, I can have it brought up to museum quality."

Kate murmured politely.

"I've become passionate about acquiring art and antiques," Jean went on. "I'm limiting my collection to American, but all periods, Colonial through modern. It's not only fascinating, but an excellent investment. Those Warhol Marilyns''—she gestured to the silkscreen series on the opposite wall—"have nearly doubled in value since I bought them. The reason this office is so barren is that I'm taking my time selecting the right pieces. I want only the best." She jumped to her feet. "Come on—I want to really show you the rest of the house."

Kate followed her, puzzled. What was the meaning of this sudden show-and-tell?

Jean led her to a small room next door in which a young woman in Jordache jeans sat entering a message on a Telex machine. "This is the communications room," Jean said to Kate. "The Telex hooks me in to a worldwide network— any city in the world at my fingertips. This''—she tapped an Intell desktop computer—"is brand new. We're about to enter all our files into it. Eventually I'll have a few word pro-

cessors in here as well.'' She stepped back into the hall.
''Now, next door is Paul's office. . . .''

They entered a room slightly smaller than Jean's office
and more completely furnished. Paul was on the phone at a
rosewood desk. He covered the mouthpiece: ''Drew La-
Motta from Chase Manhattan . . . ?''

''Tell him I'll call him back. I'm busy right now.'' Jean
pointed Kate to a small console with a TV screen. ''Ever see
one of these? It's a Quotetron. It keeps us in constant touch
with Wall Street—stock quotes, price of gold, the latest interest rates . . .''

''Nice,'' Kate murmured.

''Indispensable. Now downstairs . . .''

On the first floor they poked into several small offices in
which various employees—mostly young and female—were
occupied at various tasks. They ended in a vast and seemingly unused kitchen—about the size, Kate noted with a
pang, of her entire apartment. Jean inspected several un-
opened cases of Moët & Chandon; then she opened a double
door into a pretty, fenced-in garden. ''We're throwing a
little cocktail out here Wednesday night for Roy Goodman,
our congressman, you know. . . . You should see that dog-
wood in May. Heaven.''

''It's all very nice, Jean,'' Kate said.

''We're not done yet. We'll skip the basement—nothing
much down there yet, though I'm thinking of turning it into
a workout room. . . .'' She led the way back upstairs then
up another narrow flight to the roof. The two women
stepped out into the sunlight. They stood gazing across a
vista of rooftops to the rise of the midtown skyline.

''I love it up here,'' Jean said quietly. ''Anytime I need a
lift, I come here. It gives me an instant sense of renewal—
knowing that this piece of sky, this *reach*, belongs to me.''
She swung her eyes to Kate and said with sudden fierceness,

"This, Kate, is the way the world *should* look. Not viewed from a crummy waitressing job in some stale café, but from the top of your own townhouse."

Kate recoiled, but at the same time her heart began beating faster.

"Listen," Jean went on. "A hundred years ago—even ten years ago, the only way women like us could get this was by being the wife or the whore of some fat cat like J. P. Morgan. But now . . . now it's all there for the taking. The best things, the most powerful people . . . whatever you want, it can be yours. But you have to *think* like this—not in terms of tips, a buck here, a buck there. But in terms of the sky!"

Kate felt something lift in her chest. Jean's words were infectious . . . or was it Jean herself causing her to believe at this moment that anything was indeed possible? "Why are you telling me all this?" she asked.

"Why? Because I need people, I can't run my operations without them, and I prefer them to be women. But frankly there aren't too many women who have the kind of vision I'm talking about. But I think you do." Jean stepped closer, her eyes shining. "I can open this door for you, Kate. And once you walk through it, you'll never walk back."

"Are you offering me a job?" Kate asked eagerly.

"Not so much a job as an opportunity. I've been talking to Paul about it, and I think we've come up with something . . ."

The door opened behind them and the girl in aviator glasses popped her head out. "Jean, I've been looking everywhere for you, you've got lunch at J. Walter in exactly forty-five."

"Shit, I didn't know it was so late. Kate, we've got a lot to iron out. Let's have breakfast tomorrow, seven-thirty at the Carlyle. . . ." With that, she fled with Sandy, leaving Kate to make her own dazed way out.

Something about it all didn't seem quite real. This whirlwind meeting, Jean's exhortations and dramatic hints of things to come. . . . And yet she had instilled in Kate a feeling of unquenchable expectation. It was ironic that after all these years she should be putting her faith in Jean Ferguson.

In this mood, she treated herself to a cab home. The phone was ringing when she opened the door: she knew without a doubt it was Stephen. She ran to catch it. But then she stopped: she could suddenly hear what he would say—the self-satisfied voice rubbing in what a wonderful weekend he'd had without her . . . then his tone switching to include just the right amount of conciliatory regret. "I did miss you, you know, baby." That deft flick of a finger drawing the yo-yo skimming back up.

No, she thought. She wouldn't answer it after all.

AT TEN MINUTES TO TEN, ANDREA SLIPPED FURTIVELY into her office, hoping that Carl or Berger, the two partners at her end of the hall, hadn't seen her sneak by. She knew it had escaped no one's attention that she was consistently the last of the associates to arrive in the morning; but even for her, fifty minutes constituted grave tardiness.

But she was late because she was having trouble getting up when her alarm went off at eight. And the reason was that almost every night she found herself jolted wide awake at 3:00 A.M. by a vague sense of dread. Her skin would feel clammy and loose, and if she sat up, a wave of nausea would almost overcome her. Sometimes she was able to get up and go into the kitchen, where she would read cookbooks: the mild but authoritative tone of the recipes—particularly those calling for long lists of savory ingredients—had the subtle power to soothe her. But more often she would simply lie in bed. As the minutes of the night stretched on, the problems of her life would suddenly seem insurmountable. A letter she had forgotten to answer would take on scarily profound significance; a sweater shrunken by careless dry cleaners would seem a loss of tragic dimension. Only with the first glow of dawn would she at last be able to drift back into a fitful sleep.

"It's an anxiety attack," a friend told her. "I get them. My God, I live my *life* with them!"

"What do I do?" Andrea asked.

"You'll have to get to the root of what's making you anxious. But before you can even start to do that, you've got to alleviate the symptoms. Valium, my dear. In twenty minutes flat, your entire world will change." She gave Andrea the name of a "sympathetic" doctor on Geary who wrote the magic prescription: thirty two-milligram pills, twice refillable. They had worked at first: she washed one down before going to bed and slept soundly through the night. But lately—several nights in a row—the old pattern was reasserting itself: she was waking at three, and even swallowing another pill wasn't putting her back to sleep.

Now she flung her trenchcoat over her chair, fetched coffee from the Mr. Coffee in the hall, came back to her desk, and lit a cigarette. So weird to think of herself as a smoker. Sinful. But she weighed one hundred thirty-eight now, a good twenty-five pounds too heavy for her five-foot-five-inch frame. She had ballooned from size eight to tens and twelves: she felt enormous, hideous, with saddlebag bulges on her thighs, tits like an Italian mama's, a voluminous ass like a shelf jutting out behind. Sticking to a diet seemed hopeless, and so last month in desperation she had turned to cigarettes: Krakatoa Kreteks, an Indonesian brand which, because they contained cloves, seemed somehow a bit more healthy than the standard American kind.

She puffed, sipped the more-bitter-than-usual brew and, thus fortified, considered the morning's possible tasks. She could catch up on the back issues of *U.S. Law Week* mounting reproachfully on the filing cabinet. She could call some of the clients she'd been avoiding all week or the deputy district attorney on the Balletti case who had already left two messages this morning. Then again, she could proof the draft of the pleading her secretary had finished typing up yesterday afternoon.

But she felt a vast reluctance to do any of these things. She skimmed through the *Law Journal*, blinking back grainy waves of fatigue that kept rolling up behind her eyebrows. After some minutes, she tossed the issue aside and simply stared into space.

What was she doing here? she wondered. She had become a lawyer to help people . . . but whom was she really helping? In her civil cases, she was usually little more than a middleman; her "success" was winning a five-thousand-dollar sweetener to a personal-injury settlement or, in a matrimonial, if she simply kept the husband and wife from slaughtering each other before the divorce was finalized. As for her criminal clients . . . the fact was that most of them were plainly guilty. Yes, they were entitled under the Constitution to the best possible defense. . . . But who, who was it helping to put armed robbers, junk dealers, even murderers back on the streets instead of locked away where they could do no further harm?

She thought of the case Berger had just assigned to her. A young prostitute charged with assault with a deadly weapon. She had stabbed a john in the hip with a steak knife, in self-defense, she claimed—and indeed she had bruises on her face to support her statement. Marita, her name was. Andrea kept seeing her sullen face, the expression that flickered between wary submissiveness and aggrieved self-pity. She was lying of course. It was her pimp who had smacked her. But when Andrea pressed her, her eyes became opaque and she clung dully to her ridiculous story.

Perry Mason hadn't had to spend the greater part of his time trying to get his clients not to lie to him. Nor had he invested long hours browbeating his clients into paying him. And he never, never had to put up with the grinding tedium of wills and incorporations and real-estate closings. Damn Perry Mason!

"Knock, knock."

Meryl Kirkrider stuck her head in the door. She was an associate who had been hired about the same time as Andrea; she had just returned from a two-week vacation visiting her family in Pennsylvania.

Andrea was grateful for the distraction. "How was your trip?" she asked.

"Good. Aggravating. You know, family—it's great for the first ten minutes, then you're ready to climb the walls. But listen, I don't want to tie you up, I just wanted to tell you I ran into someone you know."

"Who?"

"Well, my brother Will, you know, is teaching at Lehigh, and it turns out his big pal in the English department there is an old flame of yours. Doug somebody?"

Andrea's heart began inexplicably to race. "Douglas Carroll?"

"That's it. You went out with him, right?"

"Yes, God, practically all through college. But how did my name ever come up?"

"I don't know . . . Oh, right, one of Will's students just transferred to Hadley, and they were talking about her and I said I knew someone who went there, and when I mentioned your name, Doug went apeshit. He practically tackled me to find out more about you. For some reason, he could hardly believe you'd become a lawyer."

Andrea struggled to keep her voice casual. "What about him, what's he doing? Is he married?"

"Married, two-point-five kids, domestic as the day is long. Oh, and this'll really make you laugh—his wife looks exactly like you! She's not as cute, but she's got your color hair and similar features and she even *talks* a little like you. Isn't that a stitch?"

"Yes," Andrea said tonelessly.

Meryl glanced at her watch. "I've got to run. Meet you for a drink tonight and I'll give you all the dirt."

Andrea felt a shiver, as if she had just been exposed to a frigid gust of air. Douglas. It was funny, she could clearly picture how he must look: a little fat—he'd always had that porky kind of face that prophesized early middle-aged spread. Stodgy professorial tweeds with soiled suede patches at the elbows. A pedantic but kindly air. A good father, a steady husband.

She should have married him. *She* should have been the one with the faculty apartment in Lehigh and the 2.5 babies and the settled life, instead of here dodging calls from accused drug pushers and deputy district attorneys.

As this thought passed through her mind, she was struck by a realization of such sudden and disquieting force that the paper she held in her hands began to shake. She could be doing this the rest of her life! Slapping the alarm off at seven forty-five, catching the bus down Columbus, sweating out ten-hour days, if not with this firm then with another indistinguishable from it. But so what? she tried to tell herself. Haven't men always had to work all their lives? But men had been conditioned since childhood to expect to be permanent breadwinners, whereas she . . . well, she supposed she always expected to be rescued in some way. That at some misty and indeterminate point in time, another Douglas, a more secure Rick would come along and take her away from all this.

What were the prospects? Since her short-lived relationship with Burton Prouse, her lovelife had been frankly lousy.She seemed to attract nothing but even sorrier replicas of Burton—wounded-deer types, freshly divorced, still licking their guilt, their anger, their ambivalence toward women. Sooner or later each of them had smugly announced that he couldn't possibly make any commitments. Andrea began parroting what all her friends had long been saying: *There are no men . . . all the good ones have either been taken or they're gay.*

Her skin suddenly felt as tight and sweating as it did when she woke in the middle of the night. The phone rang and she grabbed at it, for once welcoming whatever it might bring.

By forcing herself not to think too much, she got through the rest of the day. At seven, Meryl collected her; they each had two grasshoppers at a "fern bar" called Carson's, then, at Andrea's suggestion, moved on to North Beach for pasta with red clam sauce and cheap wine. It wasn't until nearly ten that Andrea had to go home.

She lived alone now—less by choice than by attrition. Michelle had moved down to the Peninsula last year after having been transferred to a Wells Fargo branch there. Her place had been taken by a ditzy photographer named Sally who disappeared after five months owing two months rent and taking with her the best items of Andrea's wardrobe. For some weeks after that, Andrea had shared with Tisha, a marginally anorectic social-studies teacher who was into Primal Scream and who would emit ear-piercing shrieks at odd and unpredictable hours of the day and night. When Tisha moved out to live with some people she had met through her therapy group, Andrea hadn't the energy to look for someone else.

She wasn't crazy about living alone. The worst part was coming home still pumped up from the outside world and cruising into this terrible stillness. Usually, no matter what hour she got in, she would run to turn on the television just to hear other sounds, some other voices that weren't her own.

But tonight she was greeted by a flashing light on her Phone Mate answering machine: a pulse of human contact beaming welcome through the deserted flat. She knelt and rewound the tape the one notch it had advanced, sending a silent prayer for it not to be a hangup. But there was a message: "Hi, Andrea, this is Randy O'Keefe, we met at Alison's last Sunday if you remember. It's now, uh, eight-twenty, Tuesday, I'll try to catch you later tonight."

She could hardly believe it. Randy O'Keefe! She had met him at a cookout in Bernal Heights. He was a lawyer—practically everyone there had been a lawyer. They had talked for some time, the usual topics—Camp David, Billy Carter, the best restaurants in North Beach—but though he had taken her number, Andrea had never expected him to call. He was simply too attractive. Tall, well-built, preppy in the best, not the stuffiest, sense of the word—in fact, with his short sandy hair and cute features, he reminded her of the boys who had liked her back in high school. Before she had become such a cow, of course.

Just as she thought this, the phone rang again. She answered with a sharp intake of breath, her hands suddenly icy.

"Hi, Randy O'Keefe here. Remember me?"

How could she forget? "Sure," she managed lightly. "How are you?"

They talked about the party a few minutes—how much longer he had stayed after she'd gone, and what she had missed. Then he gave his reason for calling—he remembered she had said she was interested in dance. Alvin Ailey was in town—would she like to go on Saturday?

She would. Oh, yes, she would.

Andrea starved herself for the rest of the week, subsisting on bouillon, Kavli Norwegian flatbread wafers, herb tea, and Pepsi Light, so that by Saturday she had managed to shed four and a half pounds. She put on her most slimming black peg-legged pants and her most bosom-minimalizing striped silk blouse, swearing as she sucked in her stomach that she would never eat again.

Randy arrived looking gorgeous in a blue blazer and red-and-blue rep tie. Here in Casual-land it was an event as rare as heavy snow for a man to put on a jacket. To Andrea there was a romantic formality in the gesture, an implication that this was important to him. She had the agreeable sensation of being courted.

"You look fabulous," he told her. "I love your trousers. You know what would go wonderfully with them? A man's vest—say in drab green or khaki. There's an antique-clothing place on Filbert that carries them for a couple of bucks."

Andrea was charmed. With the exception of Rick who had complained she wasn't sexy enough, no man had ever expressed real interest in the way she dressed.

Their seats at the dance concert were tenth-row aisle—Randy confessed modestly that he knew someone connected to the company and had used some pull. And afterward he took her to a recent "discovery"—the perfect nontouristy café tucked away on a back street of Telegraph Hill. They shared scampi and scallops and talked easily. Over cappuccinos, Andrea found herself telling him about her anxiety attacks. "I sometimes feel this terrible panic. It's as if I'm in a bottle of some kind and running out of air—I can't breathe, but the cap, the bottlecap, can only be screwed off from the outside. It makes me feel so helpless and scared as hell."

"I know what you mean," he said gently. "I've felt that way. But what I've learned is you've got to forget about the cap and just break the bottle. It's hard because you risk getting cut—and of course we all try to avoid getting hurt.''

"Yes," Andrea said, nodding rapidly. "I'm a *real* coward that way."

"So's anyone with any feelings. Did you ever do any therapy? I was seeing a wonderful woman who helped me through a lot of craziness I was going through. I'd recommend her to anyone."

Most men, Andrea thought, would have brushed her off with a joke, have another drink. . . . But Randy miraculously wasn't afraid to respond to his own feelings as well as hers. She could talk to him the way she could to her closest women friends.

He brought her home and at her door kissed her lightly on the lips. "I had a very good time. See you soon," he said.

No pressure to jump into bed. She liked that—he seemed to recognize her need to go slow. Again she had the pleasant feeling she was being courted. A thought crept gently into her mind: perhaps Randy O'Keefe was the one. But then she reprimanded herself sharply. There you go again, fantasizing love and marriage and happily ever after, after just one date. Wait to see if he even *calls* you again.

FOR THE NEXT two months, she saw Randy about once a week. He always proposed something special: the circus, a new and offbeat restaurant, Finocchio's once because Andrea had never actually been to it. He continued to be attentive to her clothing—complimented new purchases, lent her items from his own wardrobe to pull together particular outfits; his taste was, to her mind, flawless. And he was the easiest man to talk to she had ever met—he was interested in practically all the things she was. Best of all, he continued not to pressure her about sex. He would come up to her flat and they would neck, sometimes for hours; but he made no move to go further. She knew how sensitive he was to her feelings: it was not surprising that he would wait until he was sure she was ready.

There was only one troubling thing: at the end of every date, Randy would thank her for a great evening and leave, but without ever making another date to see her again. She would never know whether it would be the next day or the next week or never that she would hear from him again.

But that was a trivial thing, hardly worth dwelling upon, particularly when the rest of it was so amazingly good. The demands of her job seemed suddenly less onerous: she hummed as she entered the offices in the morning, and she was once more able to listen to her clients with the impartial receptivity they deserved. "Uh-oh, Herry's in love," Meryl Kirkrider teased, coming across her practically prancing down the hall. But it was her friend Rachel who really put it into words: "My God, Andrea, it actually sounds like you've got a good one!"

It was true. And suddenly she felt a hot full sweep of desire for him. She wanted to sleep with Randy O'Keefe—the sooner the better. She couldn't wait to let him know.

They had a date that Friday: dinner in Chinatown and then the lastest Eric Rohmer film. They came back to Andrea's place, consumed a bottle of Pinot noir, then snuggled into each other's arms. After a while Andrea whispered, "Want to stay over tonight?"

"I'd love to," he replied.

"Let's go to my room then."

He undressed with his back toward her and left his shorts on. How funny, Andrea thought—he was so sophisticated in most respects she'd never have imagined he'd be shy this way. But she left her underwear on as well as she climbed in beside him.

He lay on his back. She settled snug against him.

"Comfortable?" he asked. He gave a wide yawn. "I'm exhausted. I've had a grueling day."

He groped for her hand, and they lay quietly for some moments. Delicious to prolong the anticipation. But Andrea was ready—more so than she had ever been in her life. She signaled with an importunate little tug of his hand. With a strangely awkward motion, he heaved himself squarely on top of her. "Oomph!" she said.

He shifted some of his weight to his forearms. "Is that better?"

"Perfect." She smiled and he began to kiss her. She shuddered with pleasure. Randy always kissed wonderfully, but now the proximity of his nakedness added a thrilling dimension. She accepted his tongue deeply into her mouth, let it intertwine with her own, returned the pressure of his dry lips with passionate greed. She strained her hips against his and felt the bulk of his erection against the cotton of his silly red briefs. Exciting, oh, hurry . . . Instinctively she reached inside the elastic waistband and curled her fingers around his penis. As she did, he ejaculated in her hand.

It was a second before she realized what that warm gush meant. Then frustration rose in a wave that left her quivering with rage. Furiously she pushed him away from her and retreated to the far side of the bed.

"I'm sorry," he said in an anguished voice.

She made an irritated sound in the back of her throat. But hearing him sigh she repented. He must be suffering even more than she . . . feeling inadequate, a failure. . . . She supposed he had been simply overexcited. They had prolonged things a little *too* long. The thing to do now was to reassure him, restore his ego, help him relax. No doubt he'd be fine on a second go-around.

She turned back to him. "It's all right," she said soothingly. "It happens to everyone at some time or other."

"I really let you down, didn't I?"

"It's okay. There'll be plenty of other times."

"Christ, I feel awful," he said.

"Don't. You shouldn't. Really, it happens to everyone. You said you had a rotten day, that's bound to take a toll. Don't blame yourself."

"It was a hard day," he said eagerly.

"So you see? Hey, would you like me to rub your back? I'm good at it."

"You must be too tired."

"No, I'd like to. And I think it's just what you need." She pushed at him. "Come on, turn over and I'll give you a good long massage."

With a grunt he flopped over onto his stomach. She caressed the long, flat planes of his shoulders, then adeptly began to knead and soothe the muscles—if there was one thing she had learned from Rick, it was how to administer a first-class backrub.

"That is nice," Randy murmured.

"You see? Just let it go." She continued slowly working down the damp declivity of his back. That beautiful symmetry . . . the sight of it, and the feel of his springy skin, his strong muscles beneath her fingers were beginning to make her excited again.

But then suddenly she noticed his breathing had become regular and deep. Damn it, he had fallen asleep. Her body buckled again with frustration. She was beginning to feel sympathy for all the men who had wanted to touch her when she wouldn't allow it. At last she was discovering what pure torture it could be.

But asleep didn't mean dead. She could still arouse him, couldn't she?

She began to stroke and fondle his buttocks; but that only seemed to put him deeper to sleep—his breathing came heavier and acquired a stentorian rasp. Undaunted, she bent over and teasingly nibbled his neck, then nuzzled her entire body against his back. But with a querulous little toss, he shifted onto his side. Andrea paused a moment to survey his position. Those ridiculous underpants. She'd have to take a bolder tack. Again she reached inside the waistband, cresting the ridge of his hip—but just then he drew a leg up blocking the progress to his genitals.

Damnation. He was impregnable.

Suddenly Andrea had an eerie sense of familiarity about all this. It struck her with ludicrous force—these were exactly the kind of maneuvers she had once used to evade Douglas's assaults . . . way back in New Haven, when she would pretend to be asleep.

She sat up and snapped on the bedside light. "Randy," she said. "Randy, you're not really sleeping, are you?"

He stirred, then he lifted his head with a rather sheepish look.

"Don't worry," she said, "I'm not going to bother you anymore." She reached for a pack of cigarettes from the bed table drawer.

"Could I have one?" he asked.

"You won't like them. They're that Indonesian brand."

"I don't care."

She handed him one and balanced a clam-shell ashtray on the sheet between them. They puffed wordlessly for some moments. Then Andrea said, "I don't get it. If you didn't want to make love, why did you stay over?"

"But I did want to," he said, glancing at her. "Really. It's just that . . . well, you know, I've never done it before."

She lowered her cigarette and stared at him. " 'Done it before'?"

"With a girl, I mean."

She continued to stare, but now fully anticipating what he would say next.

"You've always known I was gay, didn't you? I didn't try to keep it a secret or anything. I just presumed you knew."

And of course she had. A hundred signals. . . . She had known without wanting to really know, was all.

"Randy," she said slowly. "I don't really understand what you want from me. What you're *doing* here."

He fixed his eyes on the opposite wall and smudged out his cigarette. For a long time he'd been conflicted, he told her. Not about his sexuality, but about his life's goals. The gay lifestyle was one of transience, instability; but he wanted more roots, a family some day. He knew he'd always prefer men, but if he could train himself to become bisexual . . . many of his friends were . . . "And Andrea, you looked so experienced and, well, sensual, I thought you might make a good teacher."

The irony of this was so acute that she let out a quick, caustic laugh.

"I suppose I'd better go," he said.

"I guess so," she said hollowly.

"I'll call you. We can still be friends, can't we?"

She made no reply. He picked up his clothes and modestly retreated to the living room. Andrea sat smoking one cigarette after another until she heard him leave, the door click shut behind him.

Sex, she thought. That's what caused all the trouble. Do it, do it, do it. Well she had done it, and it had brought her precious little besides pain, humiliation, and grief.

But no more. From now on, she was through with sex. No more being pawed at and poked and exposed to disease and left stranded in grotesque situations.

From now on her body would be completely her own.

KATE ARRIVED AT A GLOOMY, BLANK-FACED WINDOW ON lower Broadway, clutching the key to the studio that now belonged to her—or rather to Vidstar Productions, of which she was officially president and chief operating officer. A directory in a bedraggled, if once-elegant lobby indicated it was in the basement—not, she thought, an auspicious sign. She rode a laboring elevator down and unlocked a battered steel door.

She groped for a light and surveyed the looming space. The high ceiling was a waffle of metal pipes dotted with lights; heavy cords hung down like jungle vines. She counted three cameras on dollies, some hulking equipment that was totally unfamiliar, and toward the rear huge sheets of paper pulled down from suspended rods. She wandered behind these and found a graveyard of discarded props: plastic clocks, moldering clothing, plastic potted plants, the bottom half of an enormous stuffed penguin.

She walked up into the small glassed-in control booth, examined the two video decks with their myriad switches, then sank into a chair. Panic seeped through her. What was she doing here? Electrical equipment and switches, gadgets and machines—it was the kind of stuff men knew about. What insanity had possessed her to think she could just waltz in and take over?

It was now three months almost to the day since her first meeting with Jean. In the weeks following, Jean had given her an exhilarating rush. There were breakfasts, lunches, dinners, meetings of every sort, with sedate corporate types, with brash rich kids who had money to burn, and once she had driven with Jean and Paul in a chauffeured limousine to New Jersey to survey a house on a lake Jean was thinking of purchasing. There seemed to be no horizons in Jean's world: and the longer Kate was with her, the more she, too, learned to acquire this unlimited vision.

And then at last Jean detailed the "opportunity" she had fashioned for Kate. It seemed that in the course of a "leveraged buyout" of an audio-visual company, Minervco had also acquired an unused video studio. Jean was anxious to put it into production. "There's a tremendous upside potential," she raved. "Wall Street is extremely high on cable right now— there's going to be a huge demand for video product. And we could throw enough work through Minervco alone to get you off the ground. Commercials, and oh, meetings could be taped. . . . It's perfect for you, Kate. I remember how you used to make movies back in college."

Kate had assented uneasily. It was true that for several months sophomore year she had dashed around with a Super-8 borrowed from the theater department and shot a few home movies with the lofty earnestness of an Antonioni. But then she had grown bored and moved on to something else: pottery, tie-dying . . . who could remember?

Yet Jean's utter confidence had convinced her. Why

shouldn't she be able to run a production company? She was bright enough, and creative, and certainly hungry—and she'd have Jean behind her to show her the ropes of business. And it was indeed an extraordinary opportunity. She'd be crazy to pass it by.

Two weeks ago, Jean announced she had closed the deal. Paul had chartered a Delaware corporation called Vidstar Productions. There were three stockholders: Kate held forty-five percent of the shares, Minervco forty percent, and something called the First Charter Holding Company was assigned the remaining fifteen. There was funding of eighty-five thousand dollars—Jean apologized for this being less than expected, but to Kate it was a dazzling sum, more money than there seemed possible to be in the world. Jean had gone on to explain the terms of the deal, but Kate had understood little of leveraged assets and structured payments. She had simply signed the contract Paul put in front of her. Then Jean had broken open a bottle of Dom Perignon and they had toasted and hugged each other in a mist of euphoria. "We're partners now!" Jean exclaimed. "And we'll be right there working together. Here's to making a million!"

But since that afternoon, Kate had found it strangely impossible to get hold of Jean. First she had been in Boston, then Washington, but even since she'd been back, she had returned none of the daily messages Kate left for her.

More than ever Kate now realized she needed Jean. In five weeks she was scheduled to shoot a television commercial for the Dresden Limousine Service and she hadn't an inkling where to begin. As she gazed out over this yawning cave of equipment, she felt nothing but a desperate urge to run away.

She locked up, took a bus home, and put in another call to Jean. This time Paul Coulter picked up. "I can't pull her out of a meeting," he said testily.

"But I've *got* to speak to her. I feel like I'm totally at sea," Kate wailed.

"Everyone does at first. But you're a bright gal, you'll pick it up fast."

"But how am I going to learn to operate cameras and things in five weeks?"

"Hey, hire yourself some people—cameraman, technician, what have you. Listen, Kate, I've got to hop, I'll catch you later, okay?"

The phone clicked dead. But Kate felt far less panicked now. Of course she could hire people, she had all that money at her disposal. . . . Just a question of finding someone good.

Denny could help her, she thought. He always knew everybody.

It had been months since she had been to his loft. She was amazed at how finished it now was—cabinets and closets all built, the wood floors scraped and burnished, the walls freshly painted.

"It's beautiful, Denny!" she gasped. "You've really made it into a home."

"It is a nice space, isn't it? A guy offered me a fortune for it the other day."

"You wouldn't think of selling it after you've done all this work?"

"It was fun." He shrugged. "Nobody believes me, but I really like to build. And anyway, I might need the money."

"What for?"

"For school. I'm thinking of going for architecture."

She stared at him in surprise. "Since when?"

"Since I came to the conclusion that I'd be a better architect than a playwright. A hell of a lot better." He gave a laugh. "What do you think of the idea?"

"If it's really what you want to do, I think it's great."

"Yeah. The only problem is it's a long haul. By the time I got out of school I'd be almost thirty." He laughed again but more sharply. "Dropping out sure took up a fuck of a lot of time."

"Well, look at me," Kate put in. "I didn't even have to drop out to waste time."

"You're doing okay." Denny reached for a half-smoked joint lying in a saucer on top of the smoke. He lit it, took a drag, and passed it to Kate. "So this thing with Jean is really happening," he said as she exhaled.

She nodded. "It really is. And I still can't figure out why she's doing it for me."

"That's easy." He accepted the joint back from her but didn't put it to his lips. "Jean's into control. This Lady Bountiful thing, distributing the wealth—it's just another way of hers to get more. Especially from someone like you."

"That's totally unfair!" Kate countered. "If anything, she's given me too much control over this deal. I've got the most stock, I'm running the whole show . . . I mean, I was in a complete panic today."

"I still think you should be careful, Kate."

She met his eyes. "I trust Jean. And I'm really beginning to wonder why you're trying so hard to get me not to."

"Meaning?"

"Meaning maybe it's a little sour grapes."

He started to deny it with an angry flush, but then he stopped. "Fuck it, maybe you're right. I've been competing with Jean all my life, even if I never wanted to admit it. But just don't forget, Kate, that I know her pretty damned well."

"I'll take my chances," she said stiffly.

Denny tilted his chair back on two legs and swung his feet onto the table. "Hey," he said, with a complete change of expression. "I've got a guy for you. His name's Ross Campbell; he knows everything there is to know about video. I've told him about your gig and he's really interested."

Kate melted. She couldn't blame Denny for having complicated feelings toward his sister. Family relationships were always a bitch—the oblique way in which she preferred to deal with her own sisters wouldn't bear such close scrutiny either. And no matter what Denny felt about Jean, Kate was certain he'd always come through for *her*.

Ross Campbell turned out to be a soft-spoken young giant, all stalklike limbs and the graceless, loping walk of a whooping crane. He seemed a knowledgeable technician, but best of all he had an unassuming "can-do" sort of attitude that made Kate want to pour everything into his oversized hands.

Under his gentle direction, they got to work. With their first job scheduled so soon, there was an incredible amount to do: the entire studio needed cleaning and restocking and all the equipment overhauling; there were phones, lights, plumbing to be installed; stationery and other supplies to be ordered; a press release to be sent out, and a listing to be entered in the *Producers' Blue Book*. Kate had to devote almost an entire week to organizing a system for record-keeping and billing and another day just to pay the bills that had already begun to come streaming in. And then the pace grew even more frantic as they began to prepare for the taping itself.

Kate arrived at the studio before eight each morning and rarely left before midnight. Her life had effectively reduced itself to work. She purchased several weeks' supply of cheap underwear to eliminate the need to do laundry. Housework was completely out of the question: great gobs of dust had settled like unearthly tumbleweed under the bed and a slick film was hardening to a crust in the bathtub. It was fear that drove her on—the fear that she'd blow it, this one chance she had to really make it—that she'd be back pushing quiche and margaritas at Parasol. She drove herself until her knees were watery with exhaustion and still there was more, more to do.

The taping of the Dresden Limousine commercial was a disaster. The studio was in chaos; the engineer was an hour late; one of the young women drivers being used in the spot had a cold, the other couldn't be persuaded to take her eyes off the Teleprompter. There were endless equipment failures. At six o'clock they ran out of tape, and the grip had to be dispatched across town with two hundred dollars in cash to pick up some more. Kate, faking her way as floor director, came several times to the edge of hysterical tears, and even Ross's implacable calm seemed in grave danger of splintering.

A week later, Kate watched the edited sixty-second result. It was ghastly! It had an amateurish, made-on-a-dime look, even though they had gone drastically over budget. Oh, it was grotesque, it would expose her for what she was—a total fraud.

And yet . . .

And yet, when Ross ran it for her again, she saw that, stilted and naïve though it was, it still got the message over with a hint of wit and charm. And compared to other late-night cheapo ads—guys in baggy suits shrieking, "I sell cars like pizzas!"—she had to admit it was infinitely better.

Most of all it was real. An actual creation that had come into existence largely through her own efforts. And with this realization, all the frustration and pain of the preceding weeks ceased to matter. Suddenly she couldn't wait to do it again.

* * *

THROUGH THE REST of the autumn and into the holidays—the season in which New York is at its most brilliant
and enticingly alive—Kate was aware only of Vidstar Productions. She spent a restless Christmas day in Groton,
Connecticut, with her sister Pammy who had four hyperac-
tive children and a husband who worked on submarines; but
she took a train home that night, and the next day plunged
right back to work.

They groped along using trial and error as a textbook.
There were plenty of errors—the major ones, such as the
deposition in which everyone ended up sounding like Daffy
Duck; but also a myriad of little ones which, being more in-
sidious, ended up the more disheartening.

The eighty-five thousand dollars that at first seemed like
such a ransom melted like spring snow. The cost of running
the studio was staggering: it was a constant scramble to pay
the current bills while waiting to collect payment for past
work. Their largest job had so far been with Minervco companies, and these, surprisingly, were the worst in paying on
time.

But the greatest shock to Kate was the discovery of how
much she owed to Minervco, according to the contract she
had signed. Fifteen percent of gross receipts went to Jean's
company, as well as another twenty-five hundred dollars a
month for "consulting fees." This more than anything else
drained their resources and made their existence continually
tenuous.

If she could only talk to Jean for more than two minutes at
a time, Kate reasoned, she was certain she could convince
her to make the terms easier.

At last she succeeded in obtaining a lunch date. Jean arrived at the Brasserie nearly twenty minutes late. She wore
the exquisite fawn-colored silk dress she'd had on the first
time Kate had gone to Minervco, yet remarkably there was

the slightest tinge of soil on the cuffs; and Kate noticed as well faint half-moons of shadow under Jean's wide-spaced eyes.

"Sorry I'm late," she remarked. "There's something of a cash crisis at one of our companies, so I'm a bit over-loaded. Mind if we order right away? I'm going to have to get back pretty soon."

They both opted for Niçoise salads and Perrier rather than wine.

"So tell me how it's all going," Jean began, sipping the sparkling water rather greedily.

"Well, we're working incredibly hard . . ."

"That goes with the territory, kid. You work twenty-six hours a day, eight days a week for at least the first year. After that, if you're lucky, you're allowed a few hours a week off for some sleep. But isn't it great?" she added eagerly. "Doesn't it give you a tremendous satisfaction to be able to immerse yourself in work?"

"I love the work," Kate assured her. "Though it's been tough having to sacrifice my entire personal life. I haven't had a date since I broke up with Stephen, and that was months ago."

"Yes, you do have to give up a good part of that side of life. But don't you think it's worth it? In the long run, I mean—isn't it worth a little loneliness now, when you think how far you might eventually be able to go?"

Kate looked at her intently. There had been something in Jean's voice that had sounded almost like pleading—as if Jean was beginning to doubt her own convictions and was now looking to Kate to reaffirm them. The thought was frightening—if Jean faltered, where in God's name did that leave *her*?

"It must be worthwhile, otherwise I'd have folded up my tents the first two weeks," she said with deliberate lightness. "I wasn't exaggerating when I said how tough it's been. Which brings me to something I want to talk to you about. The percentage and consulting fee we pay to Minervco—it's a huge drain on us. You know I was utterly naïve when I signed that contract . . ."

She hesitated. The shade of vulnerability had vanished from Jean's face, and she was once more the complete businesswoman—cordial, but firm. "How much would you say that equipment in your studio's worth, Kate?" she said. "A hundred grand, give or take? Add to that the eighty-five thousand seed money, and the value of the jobs I've thrown your way . . . Would you grant that I've contributed at least a quarter million to getting you started? Do you know what the monthly interest payments on a quarter million dollars would be? Somewhat more I think than the fees you are talking about."

Kate nervously picked up her glass. "I hadn't thought of it that way. I know I owe you a lot, Jean, but . . ."

"I'm taking a huge risk on you, Kate. If you fail, I stand to lose far, far more than you."

"I understand that, and really I'm very grateful for everything you've done."

"Are you?"

"Of course I am, Jean. You know that."

"Well, then maybe you could do something for me," she said. "The cash crisis I told you about is with my temporary agency, The Returning Worker. If your company could take on two or three temps for the next six months . . ."

"I don't have enough work for them to do," Kate said quickly.

"They wouldn't actually have to show up. I'm asking the heads of all my ventures to do the same thing. Really, Kate, I wouldn't ask unless it was absolutely necessary. And if you mean it about being grateful . . ."

Kate looked down at her plate. After all her protestations, it didn't seem she had much choice. "Sure," she said slowly, "I guess we could do that."

SHE RETURNED TO the studio in a despondent mood. Not only hadn't she gotten her obligations lightened, she had actually taken on even greater ones.

She noticed Ross had finished editing the job they taped the day before—a corporate annual meeting—and she thought it might cheer her up to view the final result. But as she ran it, she saw with horror they had somehow neglected to color balance the cameras: the dais switched from royal purple to aquamarine; the faces went from pink to ruddy red to a sickly pale orange.

They would never get it right. Never, never, never! Who was she trying to kid? She'd never be anything more than the Brown Person, a second-rater, a fraud. Why the hell was she even trying?

The door to the studio opened.

"Ross?" she called out.

There was no reply. She felt a tug of alarm. It really was isolated down here—she should never keep the door unlocked when she was alone.

She peered cautiously through the dim light. Then her heart started to pound. It was Stephen picking his way across the floor. God, his radar was terrific—he seemed to know the very instant she was at an ebb. Nevertheless, at the sight of him, all the old yearning came flooding back. She wanted only to flow into his familiar arms.

"How've you been?" he smiled.

"Oh, not bad," she managed to reply. "And you?"

"All right. Well, actually I've been kind of sick lately. I've been getting headaches—super migraines. Fucking doctors, man, they don't know a thing. All they tell you is take two Tylenol and stay in bed.''

"That's too bad,'' she said solicitously. It was the old bait, dangling for her sympathy, and she still couldn't help going for it.

"Hey,'' he said, ''I've tried calling you a few times, no luck.''

"I'm not home that much these days.''

"I guess not. I finally found out about your thing here from Sissy. Sounds like you landed yourself a terrific gig.''

"Well, it's been hard. I'm still not sure I can pull it off.''

"Come on, baby, have a little faith. You've always been too quick to put yourself down.'' He moved a little closer. "You know, I've been doing a lot of thinking about us lately. I think this separation's been a good thing. It's obviously made you pick yourself up and stand on your own two feet. The biggest problem between us was your always having to be dependent on me.''

"Stephen . . .''

He held up a hand. "Wait a minute. I know I'm to blame, too. I kept fighting how much I really cared for you. But I think now we could really make it. We've logged a lot of years together. We'd be stupid to piss it all away without giving it at least one more try.''

She looked at him with confusion. She knew all she had to do was nod, or step toward him, and he would gather her in his arms—and a part of her urged her to do just that. But then her eye suddenly fell upon a shooting script lying on a table. It was for a small commercial they were scheduled to shoot next week. Ross had asked her this morning to finish going over it so he could time it out tonight. . . .

Real people depended on her in this job, she realized. They needed her for who she was and what she did—not in the way Stephen needed her, to feed off her emotions like some monstrous, sucking child. Suddenly she really saw him—how thin he seemed and somehow smaller. And there was a pinched pallor to his face, a miserliness of expression she had never noticed before. A shudder of revulsion rose from the pit of her stomach.

"It's over, Stephen," she said flatly. "Those years we were together were the worst of my life, and I've been far, far happier since they've ended. I don't want to go back with you. I don't even want to *see* you anymore." She expected him to lash out at her, the way he always did when things didn't go his way—always having to make someone else suffer for his own failures or disappointments.

But he simply stood there, hunching a little into himself and nodding. "Well, I guess I waited a little too long. If you change your mind . . ."

"I'm *not* going to change my mind."

"Well, that's cool, I guess."

He just kept standing there. At last she said, "Stephen, I'm really busy right now."

"Yeah. Well, I guess I'll see you around."

She watched him walk to the door. Poor Stephen. How strange that after all the violence of emotion—the breakups and reunions, the storms and pacifics—that it should come to this sad whimper of a parting. And that all she should feel for him was vague pity.

Thank God, she thought, that she had work to do.

IT WAS UNLIKE JEAN TO LET HER MIND WANDER FROM A point of business; but now, as she sat in her dusky office listening to Paul brief her on a current deal, her eyes kept drifting to the window—to the darkening street beyond, with the ginkgo trees powdered in spring buds and long shadows beginning to creep out of doorways. Some feeling that she couldn't quite shake gripped her strongly: a yearning or a regret. It was just the advent of spring, she told herself. Everyone found it difficult to work in April.

With an effort, she wrenched her attention away from the smoky pane and back to Paul's neat Brooks Brothers cuff as he flipped a page. "I figure I'll do a real numbers crunch on it this evening so we know exactly what we're dealing with when we meet with Hanaway tomorrow," he said. "Then hopefully he'll be able to take it to credit policy by the end of the week."

"Good," Jean said guiltily—she really hadn't assimilated a word of what he'd said.

Paul closed his black binder, then handed her a typed

sheet. "Here's the list of calls while you were out this afternoon."

The usual. People looking for funding for new businesses, most of which would prove flaky. A recent graduate of Sarah Lawrence looking for a job. A Wall Street acquaintance with a tip on a new venture, the producer of a women's issues talk show wanting her for some sort of panel . . .

"Don't forget you've got dinner with Wallace Harvey," Paul went on. "Seven-thirty . . ."

"At Doubles, I know. I'd better get rolling."

"Do you want to hear these numbers when I'm done with them?"

"Yeah, I'd better. Why don't you work at my place tonight? I won't be too long at this thing, and we can go over them when I get back."

"Sure."

The grateful tone in his voice made her want to snap at him. "Did you see that IBM rep today?"

"No, he had a conflict . . ."

"Damn it, Paul, I want those word processors installed and I want them soon, not sometime next year!"

"Sure, Jean. I'll get on it first thing in the morning," he said quickly. "Anything else?"

"No, I'll see you later."

Why, she wondered as he left the office, did she sometimes feel the need to hurt him? Perhaps because of the way he so persistently stood for it—the same impulse that made some people kick a cringing dog. But she could never quite figure him out. He displayed the kind of devotion that came from being in love—yet he had never said anything, never touched her nor made any kind of move to declare himself. He seemed curiously content with the intimacy she accorded him as her . . . She stopped herself: the word that had come into her mind was *slave*.

Yes, there was something slavish about Paul. But wasn't it true that lately she had become as fettered to him as he was to her? The thought made her shudder; but she couldn't dismiss it. In that ever-amiable way of his, he had made himself thoroughly indispensable to Minervco—his hand was in the systems, the books, every facet of operations. She had begun to depend on him far too much. And that, she knew, was dangerous.

There was more: in the past few months it seemed that whenever a man was attracted to her, something always happened to prevent anything coming of it—phone messages would be distorted, a series of crises would arise causing her to break dates . . . Nothing she could attribute directly to Paul's intervention. And yet . . .

She roused herself. Time was getting short. She would have to resolve these questions later.

The dinner party she was about to attend was in honor of a German banker with "great access" to Arab money. The host, Wally Harvey, was with Morgan Guarantee, and from time to time escorted Jean to some of the more prominent social functions around town. He was attractive, of good family, and a sexual neuter—the type of man who simply preferred not to muss his Turnbull and Asser "shirtings." There seemed to be a lot of these around lately, Jean thought with disgruntlement.

The dinner promised to be a bore, but the guest of honor could prove a valuable contact. She prepared herself to be scintillating.

She decided the gray cashmere dress she had on would do with just a change of accessories. She exchanged her pumps for gold sandals and fetched her second-best strand of pearls from the locked bottom drawer of her desk. As she fastened the clasp and threw her new Russian tanuki over her shoulders, another thought crept over her. She had bought herself pearls, furs, property, each purchase another brushstroke in the portrait of success . . . yet the portrait remained unfinished. She still didn't have that feeling of wholeness, of knowing she had really attained what she had set after . . . that feeling she had the day she mastered a back flip her junior year in high school.

She suddenly had a strong impulse to clear a space on the floor and see if she could still perform the stunt. Her heart leaped: she bet she could!

But no, now was not the time. She'd have to strip down to her underwear . . . and what if someone came in and caught her?

Anyway, her limousine was waiting.

SHE WAS THE last of the party of about a dozen to arrive at the private club. Wally kissed her primly on both cheeks and performed the introductions with the social fluidity he had been born to perpetuate.

She was seated beside a slender, dark man of about thirty. His black hair, slicked back Gatsby style, dramatized high cheekbones, narrow long-lashed eyes, a broad mouth. He offered a pack of Gitanes, and when Jean shook her head, lit one for himself with a gold, monogrammed Dunhill.

"I'm sorry but I didn't catch your name," she said.

"Robert Silenieu."

She noted briefly that his initials did not match those on his lighter. "I'm Jean Ferguson," she offered.

He let out an indolent stream of smoke. "I made a special point of catching yours."

The trace of an accent in his speech made it difficult for Jean to determine if he was being sardonic or truly complimenting. She decided to accept it as the latter. She decided, too, that she found him exceptionally good-looking.

"Do you work with Wally?" she asked.

"No, but he and I go back quite a long way. At a very tender age, we were both imprisoned in the same boarding school in Switzerland."

"Are you Swiss?"

"Thank God, no. My name, Silenieu, is Rumanian, but I was born in France and my mother is White Russian. Which makes me, I suppose, a true mongrel. And which is why I can never decide where I want to live. When I'm in New York, I begin to miss the Avenue Foch. When I'm in Paris, I start thinking about Beverly Hills. And when I'm there, my God, all I want to do is be any other place in the world!"

Jean smiled. "What do you do?"

"Ah, well, at the moment I'm involved in quite an exciting little venture. Some partners and myself have discovered a way to move frozen funds from Italy through the distribution of American films in northern Europe. We've secured upfront guarantees for fifty pictures to date, and if all goes the way it should—well this could be the biggest deal in the history of the American film business." He brought his cigarette elegantly to his lips. "And you, Jean? Are you also a member of the financial community?"

"Venture capital," she said. "I finance start-ups, revitalize failing companies . . . that kind of thing."

"Then you must be the one Wally was talking about. You're a very high-powered woman, aren't you?" His eyes with their feminine curtains of lashes narrowed intently on her face. "I like that," he murmured.

Jean felt a rush of blood to her temples. Not only was this man glamorous and exciting to look at, he seemed neither threatened nor intimidated by the fact that she, too, commanded a certain amount of power.

Throughout dinner they discussed deals, people they knew in common, whether the taking of the hostages in Iran was likely to effect further fluctuations in the price of gold.

They shared a common language—the patois of dynamic business—that seemed to draw them into a pleasant conspiracy. And Jean couldn't take her eyes off his face. That overdrawn mouth, those languorous eyes . . .

But then during dessert, Wallace drew her to the other end of the table to give her "a better crack" at the guest of honor. She recognized instantly that Klaus Hiller was someone who could be of considerable use to her, yet she was scarcely able to speak even politely to him. From the corner of her eye she watched Robert: he had turned his attention to the young woman on his other side, a brunette who looked like a college student but was actually a lawyer for Coudert Brothers.

The dinner was breaking up; Jean despaired of another chance to talk to him. But then as Wally went to fetch her coat, Robert was suddenly standing behind her. "I want to see you," he said softly. "I'll wait for you outside the Pierre."

Her heart beat wildly. When Wally came back, she babbled something about being exhausted, no need to see her home; and then she fled on trembling legs down Central Park South to the Hotel Pierre. He was there. With a bright laugh she wrapped herself into his arm. He guided her down the block, past a doorman, and into an elevator that opened into a vast apartment. Beyond a huge sweep of glass, the lights of Central Park shone with a diffuse radiance.

"This is magnificent!" Jean breathed. "Is this where you live?"

"Unfortunately, no. It belongs to a very old and dear friend of mine who lets me stay here while she's in Palm Beach." He gestured to a portrait on the wall of a smiling middle-aged woman in a pale pink suit.

Jean went to the wall of glass and gazed at the view. It seemed to her that everything that anyone strived for in New

York was epitomized in this gorgeous panorama: that to own such a vista was the final declaration of success.

Robert touched her shoulder and she gave a start. "What would you like?" he asked.

"Oh, anything. A cognac." She felt a chill. Here she was with this exciting man, and her mind was on a view. Could she really be so detached from her emotions?

He leaned toward her and murmured, "I wanted to kiss you the moment I saw you." He brought his lips to hers, and at their touch such fervent desire ran through her body that she knew her misgivings were groundless. She was capable of feeling so very, very much.

"Do you really want that drink?" he asked.

"Not now," she whispered. "Not now."

THEY HAD MADE love three times on the satin-spreaded canopy bed. Every inch of her flesh had responded with electric joy: how she had needed, craved this for so long. Now as she dressed in the dim morning light, the sensation of the night still lingered upon her like a sumptuous garment. Robert was unlike any of her previous lovers. His endurance delighted her. He had spoken continuously to her as he caressed her, praising her breasts, her ass, her cunt— frankness that had at first shocked her, then heightened her own excitement. Once though he had made her cry out in sharp pain as he bit her deeply on the shoulder—so deeply he had drawn blood. But she was willing to endure a little pain if that was what pleased him.

SHE CALLED FOR her car from a phone in the living room. As she waited, Robert padded in dressed in a long black robe.

"You were leaving without saying goodbye?" he said.

"I didn't want to wake you. I took the number here—I was going to call you later."

"I'm leaving for Boston shortly."

"When?" she asked in a thin voice.

"This afternoon. There are some very important people I have to see. I'm afraid I can't put it off."

"Will you be back soon?"

"Not in the foreseeable future."

Jean glanced away. She was in love with him. For the first time in her life she was really in love. And to be stripped of him so soon . . .

He came over and took her shoulders. "Darling, I'd like it very much if you came to meet me somewhere. Someplace warm. I'd love to show you Ibiza. Or St. Tropez. Would you do that?"

She lifted a glowing face to him. "Of course," she said.

It was not until she was in her car, the places he had named still shimmering in her imagination, that she remembered: Paul! She had told him to come to her apartment last night.

She saw at once he had been there: a glass on the coffee table, cigarette stubs, yesterday's *Times* laid neatly on the stack of papers by the fireplace. But whether he had left at midnight or five minutes ago was impossible to tell.

What would she tell him? she thought frantically. But then she checked herself. Why must she let Paul Coulter dictate her life? It was he who worked for *her*, not the other way around. She wouldn't tell him anything at all.

He was waiting for her when she reached the office. "I'm sorry I didn't make it last night," she said crisply. "This thing went on later than I expected."

"No sweat."

She looked at him. Those round blue eyes could at times

be maddeningly opaque. "Did you finish those numbers for Hanaway?"

"They're on your desk. But something's come up, Jean. Kittredge called—there are major problems at Womancard. Retailers are reporting they're three months overdue on re-imbursements and some of them are refusing to take the card."

"Why aren't they getting their money?"

"According to Kittredge, the cash isn't coming in to them." Paul pulled a sheet from a sheaf in his hand. "Last quarterly report showed a fourteen percent default rate on the part of cardholders. It's bad, Jean. The main problem is the card was issued to too many women with no established credit."

"But that was the *point*!" she exploded. "If they'd had credit, they'd have gone to Master Charge or American Express. We were after that untapped market. It's just a ques-tion of weeding out the deadbeats and establishing a base of good subscribers. It's a question of time. You've got to buy us some time, Paul."

"That could be tough. We're almost overextended now—every one of our ventures is leveraged to the hilt. And if Womancard folds, a lot of other things could come down with it."

Jean sank into her chair. Why was Paul talking about being overextended? She had always borrowed heavily, using one company to raise capital for the next—but it was a basic rule of business that growth required capital. It was worth going out on a limb on the chance that one of the ven-tures would suddenly take off—become the next McDon-ald's, the next Data General—the cash cow that would then feed the rest of the system. But until she really hit, she couldn't put all her eggs in one basket—she had to continue to take risks, to find more and more deals.

The phone rang, and reflexively she grabbed it. It was Dale Comisky, the twenty-nine-year-old president of Dresden Limousines.

"What is it?" she said wearily.

"Problem, Jean. We signed a contract last month with a company called Westex to provide our entire fleet for their annual meeting at the Hilton tomorrow. Trouble is we've only got five cars on the road. Two are in the shop, you've got one, and I'm afraid one got totaled the other day."

"Totaled! How did that happen?"

"New chick was driving out to Jersey for a pickup and nodded off at the wheel. Turned out to be a junkie. Lucky thing she was loose—she got out with hardly a scratch. Car's shot to hell, though."

"You hired a junkie?" Jean said, her voice barely in her control.

"Well, nobody knew she was, of course. We don't get time to screen all that carefully, there's such a heavy turnover. And anybody can get a chauffeur's license these days. The insurance on this one's gonna be real sticky. We'll be lucky if we collect at all."

Jean let out a breath. "And the two in the shop, what's holding them up?"

"Nothing. They're ready to roll. It's just that we've got no money to bail them out."

"Goddamn it, Dale, I put you in there to manage that company, not run it into a hole and come begging for help."

"I'm not begging, Jean," he said stiffly. "I'm calling because Minervco owes us thirty-two hundred dollars in rentals and I want to know when the fuck we're gonna collect."

Jean was furious. Before she had given him this opportunity, Dale Comisky was nothing but a University of Arizona dropout driving a cab for a living.

"If you need bail-out money, you can sort it out with

Paul," she snapped. "I'll send the car I have back this afternoon. Get Fugazy to supply you with the rest if necessary." She slapped the hold button and motioned to Paul to pick up. She felt perilously close to tears. Time. Why wouldn't they give her time?

She picked up the phone and dialed the number of Robert's apartment, breathing with relief when he picked up. "I have to know when I'm going to see you again," she said recklessly.

"I don't know where I'm going to be, darling," he said.

"It doesn't matter. I'll come meet you anywhere."

"All right, then, the weekend after next—would that suit you?"

"Yes."

"I'll call you then, darling."

SHE THREW HERSELF back to work with a fervor that surpassed even that of her earliest days building Minervco. It was the thought of Robert that supplied the extra fuel. Robert. Before him she had been an emotional virgin: her pale conception of passion had in no way prepared her for the gale that shook her now.

He called from St. Thomas. Exploring some interesting possibilities, he told her. There was a Friday noon flight from New York to Charlotte Amalie; she promised to be on it.

There was again the problem of Paul. She debated telling him a lie—concocting a phantom business trip to Washington or Denver—but of course, such a story could be easily exposed. In the end, she simply told him she was going away for the weekend.

"Righty," he said, with that opaque blue glance. He was no fool—he must suspect she was meeting someone. But he would have to know sooner or later: why not now?

Robert met her at the island's tiny airport. She shivered when she saw him, lean and elegant in a beige linen shirt and white trousers. He ushered her into a silver BMW and drove quickly and casually to a villa perched in the cliffs above the port. It belonged, as did the car, to friends of his mother, an elderly homosexual couple who summered, April through September, in Deauville.

"You must have a lot of friends," Jean said, smiling.

"No," he remarked seriously. "Just a few very good and very dear ones."

She knew he would elaborate no further. She had already become accustomed to his elusiveness and she found this quality exciting. It was like a present with many wrappings—undoing each one only extended the pleasure of anticipation.

She crowed with surprise at his preparations: great, fragrant masses of flowers in glass vases; a tempting pyramid of the ripest tropical fruits; Taittinger cooling in a silver bucket. But she was permitted to taste neither the champagne nor the papaya: he swept her immediately into a sun-splashed bedroom, and there, beneath a clattering, long-bladed fan, they made love. She gripped his body to her, reveling in the lean girth of his hips, feeling herself to be ravished one moment, the ravisher the next. And if again he hurt her a bit, gripping and twisting her wrists until she cried out, she didn't mind: it was little enough to give him in return for all that he was giving her.

Afterward, they bundled into identical terrycloth robes and, on a lanai overlooking the vast sweep of harbor, indulged in the treats he had denied her before. She asked him about the film distribution deal he had been working on, and he shrugged. "There's been a slight hitch," he explained. "Nothing to worry about, but we've put it on the back burner for now. Happily we've become involved in something even more exciting, a way to hedge international currencies with agricultural futures. I can't give up the details yet, but we're tremendously excited about the prospects.''

Jean reached for an icy green slice of kiwi. "Who's we?"

"Myself and my partner, a man named James Brilling. You'll have the opportunity to meet him tomorrow. He's hopping over from St. Croix.''

Jean felt a murmur of disappointment—she had expected to have Robert entirely to herself. Yet she was pleased that he wanted her to meet his partner.

The hours slipped pleasurably by. They bathed at a secluded beach, explored the cobblestoned back streets of Charlotte Amalie, and dined at a restaurant by a starlit cove. Robert diverted her with stories of backgammon tournaments in Milan, the Cannes film festival, Christmas week in Dorset. It thrilled Jean to think of him as a citizen of the world, at home on several continents, proficient in many languages.

But the following day was marred by the appearance of James Brilling. He was a sloppy, pudgy American, as gross as Robert was elegant: he had lewd humor and a slimy, insinuating personality. The three had lunch in a café situated in a palm grove. Brilling dominated the conversation, punctuating his monologues with gross snorts of laughter, and when the waiter refused to accept his personal check he created an ugly scene, braying threats and insults, until Robert resolved the situation by settling the bill with cash.

"Don't mind Jimmy," he told Jean later. "He likes to come on strong, particularly when he has a new audience. But he's really a very clever man. And anyway, he'll be leaving tonight.''

"And I've only got till tomorrow," she reminded him.

"I know, darling. But there's something I plan to show you tomorrow that might make your leaving a little easier.''

He refused to explain further, just smiled and insisted that she trust him.

In the morning he drove her to the harbor. She followed him mystified over the piers, past large boats and small, until at last he stopped before an enormous white cruiser. "The *Gillian*," he announced. "It's a Cheoy Lee long-range motoryacht. Fifty-eight feet, only three years old, and in mint condition."

"Does it belong to someone you know?" Jean asked.

"Not yet, darling." He called: "Marcel!" and a young man with sun-streaked hair and wearing nothing but khaki shorts appeared on deck. He waved to Robert, then helped them on board. He and Robert conferred for a moment, then burst out in hearty laughter. Robert rumpled the boy's hair, then beckoned to Jean. "Come on, I'll show you around." He led her through the boat, reciting details: three staterooms, each with private shower; crew accommodations for three; full galley; twenty-four-mile Koden radar; Wagner autopilot. . . .

"Do you like it?" he asked as they emerged back on deck.

"It's gorgeous. But I still don't understand."

"Let's go get a drink, and I'll tell you everything."

They ordered gin and tonics in the same palm-shaded café where they had lunched the day before, and Robert explained. The boat was for sale: the asking price of three hundred sixty-five thousand, based on a hundred-grand cash down payment, was a steal. James had discovered it on St. Croix the week before, and he had conceived of a plan: to time-share the boat, in the same way vacation condominiums were time-shared. A subscriber would invest, say, eleven thousand dollars and pay a yearly maintenance of perhaps three hundred fifty dollars. This would give him the use of the boat one week every year for perpetuity.

"And so James is going to buy it?" Jean put in.

"No, such small numbers don't interest him. It was just a mental exercise, but I picked up on it, thinking the crazy idea that it might be something for *us*." She looked at him, and he grinned, reaching for his cigarettes and Dunhill lighter. "Think of it, darling. Assuming the figures I mentioned, we could clear a profit of a couple hundred thousand and still have the boat for ourselves a month each year. But what I like most of all"—his eyes lingered on hers as he lit a cigarette—"is that it's something we could have together. We could think of it as our child. Yours and mine."

Jean caught her breath. She had never had a strong maternal instinct: she liked children but only in small doses, and from an early age she had assumed she would never have any herself. But last night, watching Robert sleep, with a glint of moonlight on his back, she had been seized with a sudden desire to have his baby—a feeling so intense it had entered her dreams. He must have sensed it too.

"Are you certain we could get enough subscribers to cover the costs?" she asked eagerly.

"I have absolutely no doubt. Before you came, I casually shopped the idea around among some people in Miami and Palm Beach. I've already received half a dozen verbal guarantees—more than enough to cover the down payment. The only problem is one of time—other buyers are already sniffing around. Now, I'd write a check immediately except that my assets are all tied up with that little deal of Jimmy's. But here's my suggestion." His eyes captured hers again. "If *you* can deliver the hundred thousand within the week, I could be in New York no later than two weeks from now with the first of the subscriber payments and reimburse you."

She hesitated. He reached out and took her hand. "If I didn't know you were used to making decisions under pressure, I'd never put this before you. I'll leave it to you to trust your business instincts. And your instincts about us.''

Their fingers intertwined. A thousand thoughts flew through her head, but foremost among them was the prospect of this connection between them: the creation of an indelible link between herself and Robert. "You say the boat's in good shape?" she asked.

"It has very low hours. And I've had it gone over by the best nautical engineer in the Virgin Islands."

"Then let's do it!" she declared. "I can send a check as soon as I get back to New York."

"Wonderful, darling. I'm thrilled to death." He lifted his glass. "Here's to a very long and very happy partnership."

Her plane left at four. As she packed, they discussed details. Robert owned a shell corporation he thought they could use—it would just require writing her in as a director. And then they were speeding back to the airport: the weekend was over.

It was nine when the plane touched down at Kennedy. She decided to stop in at the office before going home. She was amazed to find Paul there. At this time, Sunday night . . . something must be wrong.

"You're back," he said flatly.

"I said I'd be getting in tonight, didn't I? Why are you here? Is something the matter?"

"There's a lot the matter. I had to sell out Airex Charter. We had contracted to come up with an additional investment of three hundred thousand by the fourteenth. Which, as you might remember, was yesterday."

"We took a loss?"

"A quarter of a million. And there's more: unless we can come up with the seven hundred we've pledged to Worth Holding, we're going to lose our control."

"Oh, Jesus. Well, we can scramble it up from somewhere, can't we? There must be something we can put up to get the cash."

"I've been combing the books. Everything's pretty much played out. The bottom line, Jean, is that this company's out of money."

"Let me go over it with you," she said wearily. The glow of the weekend was already fading. She pulled a chair next to him and picked up a ledger.

Three hours later, she slammed down her pencil in disgust. It was completely exasperating: no matter what solution she proposed, Paul came up with some roadblock, some surly reason why it wouldn't work. "This is getting us nowhere," she said. "You might as well go home."

He made no protest, just put on his jacket rather stiffly and told her he'd be in at seven.

Jean remained sitting in her office. There was a dry taste in her mouth and her head ached. Damn Paul and his conservative thinking. He had always lacked creativity—that had always been his biggest fault. And now he was showing signs of also losing faith. But she hadn't lost hers: this was just a temporary crisis . . . she had weathered them before and she would now.

But there was one thing for certain—she was not going to let this affect her deal with Robert. She *couldn't*. She knew that what attracted her to him was her strength, her success—the fact that she was his equal. If she were to admit she couldn't go through with the deal, that she was strapped for cash and would have to back out, some vital part of his interest in her would begin to wane.

A hundred thousand dollars—it really wasn't all that much. She had engaged often enough in dealings of three and four times as much. And it needed only a float of two weeks—that shouldn't be so bloody impossible to arrange.

Especially since she had spent years cultivating bankers, acquiring good faith—just for such occasions as this.

There was Frank Hokosawa at First Pacific Seamen's in San Francisco, for instance. An aggressive young guy, on the way up, always looking for action. She had done a few small deals with him, made his bank some money, and he was eager for more.

So then here's what she could do: she would send Robert a check from First Pacific. Then she'd call Hokosawa and ask him to release the funds right away even though her account there was almost depleted. He'd do it of course—he was very anxious to retain her business. Then she'd send *him* a check from her New York account—which by the time it made the round trip back from San Francisco to be cleared in New York would be covered by the deposit of the first time-sharing payments.

It would be close, but it would work.

To hell with Paul, she thought. Let him wallow in his defeatism. She'd show him what a bit of initiative could do.

*A*NOTHER DAY, ANOTHER DINNER, KATE THOUGHT WEArily, stepping into the shower.

It was her third dinner date of the week. Tonight's was with a man named Ron Halcomb, head of investor relations for a medium-large corporation: tall, sparse dark hair, not exactly her type but on first meeting pleasant enough and worth a try. She wondered as she soaped herself how he would really turn out to be. Nice, but a droner, boring her to tears by the end of the first course? A cocky bastard? A total jerk? Or worst of all, an attractive, interesting, perfectly acceptable man with whom she felt no chemistry at all?

And at the end of the evening would there be that dreadful game of trying to avoid his advances without seeming to reject him? Or if she did succumb and went to bed with him, how would it be? Would he snore loudly and keep her up all night? Or call out the name of some other woman, making her feel like a sudden intruder? Would he be a premature ejaculator . . . or worse, the type who thinks unless he keeps banging away for anything less than an hour his virility will be in question?

Such thoughts were so discouraging that, by the time Kate emerged from the shower she was wondering why she kept putting herself on the dating treadmill.

After fourteen months in business, Vidstar Productions was finally beginning to turn the corner. In the past few weeks, they'd had several breakthroughs: a lucrative contract to tape a series of sermons by a visiting bishop of the Church of England; and their first industrial, on making zippers, for a Brooklyn manufacturer. Each little triumph gave Kate a sense of elation that lasted for days. She was growing steadily in confidence and professionalism: never in her life had she felt the Brown Person so thoroughly vanquished.

And yet it wasn't enough. Work was important—maybe the *most* important slice of the pie—but there was still something missing. The warmth and touching that went with intimacy, the sharing and companionship of a relationship—that was what was lacking. That was what kept her plodding on the treadmill—the hope that maybe just this once it could be The One.

As she slipped on her ''dating dress''—a black print rayon from the forties—she reflected that at least her situation wasn't unique: almost every woman she knew was going through the same thing. And she had met hordes of women since she had started in production. How they had flocked to creative jobs, these bright, ambitious daughters of liberation: they were in advertising, in public relations; they had swamped the publishing industry and were making headway in broadcasting and journalism. Kate could spot them everywhere, in Bloomingdale's, on Madison Avenue—they had style, the sheen, even, of glamour that went with success. You could tell many of them were now, in their late twenties and early thirties, more attractive than they'd been in college. They walked with quick confidence, dressed in the best, their own money to spend.

But the one thing they particularly had in common was that almost none of them could find a comparable man.

They joked about it, of course. Constantly. How many times, Kate wondered, had she sat doubled over with laughter while one friend or another described in uproarious detail another disastrous brush with a man?

Yet often the humor was underscored by bitterness and desperation. And why not? Kate thought. After too many years of unproductive dating and failed relationships, too many emotionless fucks and solitary New Year's Eves . . . why the hell shouldn't they become bitter?

And yet it chilled Kate. She didn't want to become like them. She wouldn't let herself. She would go out on this date not with reluctance but with every expectation of having a good time.

As dates went, Ron Halcomb turned out to be not bad: neither a prince nor a frog; a bit of a show-off, but at least an entertaining one, and if he talked too much about himself, well, that was only typical of how radically spoiled men were these days. They had dinner at the Russian Tea Room, then dashed up to the Carlyle to catch a set of Bobby Short —to his credit, he certainly wasn't cheap. And later, after he had invited himself up to her place for a nightcap, she let herself be drawn to bed—partly because he *was* a nice guy, and partly because she was just too tired to resist.

The sex, too, was nice. It was strange though—these days when she was alone she had become almost obsessed with sex, as distracted by thoughts of it as an eleventh-grade boy. Yet as soon as she got into bed with a man, her desire seemed instantly to vanish. And tonight was no exception— try as she would, she just couldn't find the right spark. But Ron at least neither snored nor hogged the bed, and she

managed to sleep afterward. And in the morning he was
considerably quick in the bathroom and left without in-
sisting on breakfast. Thank God, Kate thought. She hated
those ghastly morning-after breakfasts, instant coffee and
stale raisin bread and avoiding each other's eyes.

She hauled herself out of bed and into the bathroom.
There she stopped, aghast: the sink basin was littered with
tiny black hairs, the fallout from his shave with her electric razor. The sight filled her with a sudden and deep
revulsion—not for the hairs themselves, though they were
disgusting enough, but for what they made her realize. She
had slept with a man. She had traced with her fingers the
crack of his ass and been penetrated by him; her sheets were
rumpled with the contours of his body and her sink was
filled with the residue of his beard. And yet there had been
no true intimacy at all between them. None, none at all.

SHE WAS PUNCTUAL getting to the studio, but once
there she felt so listless that she wondered if she should even
have come. At lunch she asked Ross if he could carry on by
himself a few days next week.

"What's up?" he asked.

"I think I'd like to get away for a while. I might go down
to see my parents."

"No problem on my end. You sure you want to see your
folks?"

"You got a better suggestion?"

"Maybe. I been meaning to talk to you about this anyway. You know those promo video clips record companies
are starting to do? Groups doing their latest singles and
stuff?"

Kate nodded. "Peter Wells ran me a tape of one on
Blondie."

"It would be good stuff for us to do. You get to be innovative as hell and play around with technique a lot, and the budgets are pretty good too. I've got a friend at Majestic Records out in L.A.—a guy named Mitch Winkler, head of A & R. I already half sold him on using us. Instead of waiting for him to get out here, you could go out to L.A. with our presentation tape and show it to him there."

"A business trip?" Kate said. She had to admit the idea appealed to her.

"Why not? It's tax deductible, isn't it?"

"In that case," she said dryly, "what have I got to lose?"

She flew, not first class, but Supersaver, and booked at the rather blowsy Sunset Marquee, rather than one of the luxury hotels in Beverly Hills. More than once she got hopelessly lost on the Laocoonian tangle of freeways and boulevards. She discovered she had packed far too formal a wardrobe for the laid-back music industry, and she came perilously close to exceeding the twelve-hundred-dollar credit ceiling on her Master Charge.

Nevertheless, she hit it off splendidly with Mitch Winkler, a long-haired hippy-at-heart, thirty-seven going on eighteen and vocally unsuppressible. He admired the work she showed him, praised her ideas, and passing a soggy joint, agreed that yes, he could definitely toss something her way. Soon, in fact. The label had just signed a New Wave group called The Fed . . . they'd need a promo clip to match the release of their first single . . . and since they'd be playing club dates in New York next month . . .

An hour later, Kate, feeling somewhat stunned, walked down Sunset Strip to the lipstick-red Mustang she had rented from Budget. The transaction with Mitch Winkler had been so effortless, she suspected it couldn't possibly be legitimate— and yet she had in her possession a letter of agreement with his signature on it.

Since her Supersaver fare stipulated that she stay in California for at least a week, she had another five days to kill. She called PSA: a shuttle flight to San Francisco cost only twenty-seven dollars. She called Andrea and told her she was coming.

IT WAS ALMOST six years since they had last seen each other at Andrea's wedding. Six years: it seemed to Kate both only half as long and an eternity. She remembered how miserable she'd been spending a night apart from Stephen, how she had envied Andrea her "security" with Rick, and how she had resented and rebuffed Jean. Such feelings seemed so alien to her now they could have occurred in another lifetime.

Andrea was not among the crowd collected beyond the security check to meet the plane. Kate continued to the baggage claim, retrieved her bags, and waited. Her eyes idly took in an attractive woman wearing a sober beige suit and glasses—an executive of some sort, judging from her briefcase and demeanor. It was not until the woman started waving gaily at her that she realized it was Andrea.

They fell into a bear squeeze. "You look fabulous!" Andrea cried. "How do you stay so thin—I hate you for it! And your hair!" She grabbed a handful of the light brown strands that curved at Kate's shoulders. "When did you cut it?"

"God, about a year ago. I forgot you've never seen me with it this short. Last time I saw you I could still sit on it."

"It was gorgeous. But I like it this way too, you and your great bone structure."

"You look wonderful too," Kate told her. "So professional. And when did you start wearing glasses."

"Back in law school. Rick hated them though. He said seeing me in them made him feel old, so I naturally developed a complex against wearing them. Now I need them all the time instead of just for reading." She gave a deprecating little laugh. "The things we do for men, isn't it lunacy? But come on, let's get out of this place!"

They piled into Andrea's Toyota and drove into San Francisco, talking breathlessly, laughing freely. Andrea took pride in seeing Kate's excitement as the city came into view. "We'll do the grand tour tomorrow," she promised. "Tonight we'll just unwind. You've got a lot to tell me about, lady."

Kate found Andrea's second-floor flat vast by Manhattan standards, as tidy as Andrea's rooms always had been, but somewhat ramshackle in its furnishings. An enormous smoke-colored cat padded up to nuzzle Andrea's ankle; she scooped him up and planted a kiss between his orange eyes. "This is Waylon. My baby," she laughed.

She settled Kate's bags into a small room which, judging from its stacked clutter, doubled as a sort of urban attic. Then Kate followed her into the kitchen, the most well-fitted room in the house. "It's so great having company—I can cook all the fattening foods I don't dare make for myself," Andrea said. "Tonight I'm going to do a cioppino. That's not so fattening, but no one should leave San Francisco without having it at least once." She dexterously opened a Sonoma Chardonnay and poured it into pale green-tinged tulip glasses. There was, Kate realized, a manner of self-sufficiency about her—in the way she handled the wine, in her zippy driving—that Kate had never seen before.

They toasted each other with an exuberant clink of glasses.

"Isn't it amazing?" Kate said. "Can you believe that both of us are almost thirty years old?"

"And that we're both still single?" Andrea put in. "If anyone had predicted this when we were back in school, I probably would've jumped off Schenner Hall."

"Not me. I'd have just said marriage is an irrelevant and

archaic institution. Or something equally pretentious. Besides, back then I didn't really believe I'd ever *be* thirty."

Andrea giggled. "And to think you're working now with Jean when all that time you practically despised her."

"Oh, I've had to eat every word I've ever said about her. With salt and pepper."

"Well, I always knew that if the two of you ever really got to know each other, you'd hit it off like fireworks." She extended her pack of cigarettes.

Kate shook her head. (Andrea smoking! That would take some getting used to.) "I quit years back when I was so poor," she said. "Couldn't afford the habit."

"It's a filthy habit," Andrea said with a face. "I started it to lose weight, and you can just see how well *that* worked. But I've really got to quit and get into shape. Everyone here's so healthy and body-beautiful conscious, I feel like a degenerate."

"Do you like San Francisco?"

"Pretty much. It's a beautiful place. And I always did hate cold weather. But there's this flaky element here. There really is. For instance, you'll be invited to a dinner party and every course will be asparagus. Or you'll meet someone and it'll turn out they've just joined a religion that worships eucalyptus trees. Or whatever. And of course," she added with a small sigh, "it's the gay capital of the world."

"That's what I've heard. That there are even fewer men to go around out here than in New York."

"Believe it. I wasn't having much luck, that's for sure. But I finally solved that problem by taking myself out of the market."

Kate glanced at her. "What do you mean?"

"I stopped dating. *Finito.*"

"Are you serious? You don't go out at all anymore?"

"Oh, sure, with friends. Women mostly, but also a few

guys from work. And I've got a few gay friends I hang out with.''

"But . . . well, what about sex?''

Andrea shrugged a "what about it?'' "I've been pretty much completely celibate for over a year and a half now.''

"Don't you get incredibly horny?''

"Not really. I mean, sure, there are times I'd love to be hugged. It's the touching I miss. But the fucking, pardon my language, no, I don't miss that. For the first time in a long time, I feel my body belongs to *me*. I've started to know myself again, what *I* want and what *I* need. It's a feeling of being—well, centered. Does that make any sense?''

Kate opened her mouth to speak, but Andrea continued. "You know, being celibate has made me see a lot of things I never did before. The way the sexual revolution was sold to us, just like detergent or candy bars. Stuffed down our throats whether we liked it or not. Do it, do it, do it. The only thing was nobody told us what would happen when we *did* do it. I mean, my God, it wasn't even *san*itary, there were all sorts of diseases and funguses and now herpes. And they never got around to telling us we'd be guinea pigs either. That they were going to experiment on us like so many white rats with their pills and coils and prongs. And *we* were the ones that had to suffer of course, not the men. God forbid it should be the men. They got to fuck like bunnies and have a gay old time, while we took all the risks. And for what, I'd like to know? I can count the number of orgasms I've had on my fingers.''

Kate stared at her in amazement. She had always considered Andrea to be so—well, sexy. "I know how you feel,'' she said. "I've felt the same kind of resentments. But Andrea, don't you think it was still better than the old way of having to protect your virginity at all costs?''

"As far as I'm concerned, the pressure to do it, do it was

just as great a thrall," she replied. "And the consequences were a hell of a lot worse. You know what? I was one of the Dalkon Shield guinea pigs. And the result was that I came down with a massive case of PID that has probably left me sterile."

Kate reached out and touched her wrist. "That's terrible, Andrea. I know how you always wanted kids."

"The only thing I've ever *really* wanted," she said softly.

"That's not true, is it? What about your career?"

She glanced bitterly up. "That's another thing. Careers. Our generation was forced to go out and get one whether we wanted one or not. We weren't *allowed* to just get married and stay home and be housewives and mothers."

"Come on," Kate countered, "you've got to admit that being a lawyer is a lot more fulfilling than just being a housewife. Do you think you could really be satisfied for very long with furniture polish and diapers?"

"That's the way they always put it, waxing furniture and changing smelly diapers. Well, I've come to realize that raising children is as difficult and creative a career as any other. If not even more. You're shaping *lives,* for God's sake! What could be more meaningful than that?"

Kate was silent. Then Andrea suddenly shook her head and grinned. "God, listen to me bitch! I'm sorry, Kate. I really didn't mean to lay all this on you the first minute I saw you."

"That's okay. I know how it is when you're really unhappy about something. . . ."

"But the thing is I'm really happy right now." Andrea hesitated, then said quickly, "If I tell you something, will you promise not to tell anyone else?"

"Of course."

"I'm going to try to get a baby."

Kate gave a startled laugh. "What do you mean?"

"I mean I'm going to adopt one. I really think I can do it. I've met another lawyer through a friend of a friend. He has connections with pregnant girls in places like Florida. I'd have to pay for the girl to come here and live until she has the baby, then pay a fee to both her and this other attorney. The adoption itself can be done in one day in Juarez."

Kate stared at her. "But, God, Andrea, isn't that like buying a child?"

"I know it sounds totally reprehensible. But if I don't put up the money someone else will—or else the mother will have an abortion. And there's no other way I'm going to get one. No regular agency will approve me as a single woman."

"No, I guess not. But it would cost a lot of money, wouldn't it?"

"About fourteen thousand cash. And then I'll want to take at least a year off after I've got the baby, so I'll need a lot more. But I don't care about that."

"You've got all that saved up?"

"No, not saved. Invested. With Jean." Andrea grinned at Kate's look of surprise. "You didn't know, did you? I was the one who financed Jean's first company, The Returning Worker. She first told me the idea the night before the wedding when the three of us were staying in my apartment. I put in twenty thousand dollars to get it going."

Kate had a sudden memory of the vivid silence that had greeted her that night when she had walked into the living room. Of course—Jean had been doing a deal. It all made perfect sense now.

"Jean was out before Christmas," Andrea went on. "She was swamped with appointments. The only time I managed to see her was at breakfast at the Fairmont with a banker friend of hers, so it was a little difficult to discuss figures. But from what she's indicated, my shares are worth about three or four times my original investment. Which makes it anywhere from seventy-five to a hundred thousand dollars.'' She gave a little laugh. ''I think I can live on that for a while.''

Kate hesitated. What Andrea was saying was in direct contradiction to what she understood—that The Returning Worker was deep in debt and in danger of folding altogether. Should she tell Andrea this? She owed loyalty to Jean as well. It was just possible that Jean had plans to revitalize the company—had probably already come up with new infusions of capital, fat new contracts. . . . No, she shouldn't say anything to Andrea yet.

Andrea jumped up from the table. ''We're going to starve to death if I don't get this dinner rolling.'' She began to pull out food from the refrigerator, fish fillets wrapped in butcher's paper, carrots, potatoes, celery stalks. ''I'll put you in charge of the potatoes, okay?''

''Will do. Hey, remember crazy Mary Ellen Gruber who only ate the skins of baked potatoes and left disgusting mounds of scraped-out insides on her plate?''

''God, yes! No one on squad ever wanted to get her table.''

''Or Jamie Mitchell's either, because she was always picking up stoned-out townies and dragging them back for dinner. Remember the one that chucked all over the buffet?''

''Oh, God, yes, that was gross!''

THE FIVE DAYS KATE HAD SPENT WITH ANDREA HAD
passed far too quickly. Andrea had conducted her promised
tour, leading Kate through the standard tourist attractions—
Fisherman's Wharf, Lombard Street, a cable-car ride from
Nob Hill to Chinatown—but also sharing with her her own
favorite places: little cul-de-sacs, twisty alleyways that rose
to sudden, smiling views of the bay, shy places that captured
the subtler and more truly persuasive charm of this pastel
city.

And when it was time for Kate to leave, she parted from Andrea with sincere regret. Both of them vowed not to let another
six years slip away before they saw each other again.

Kate took the shuttle back to Los Angeles to catch her return flight. It had been overbooked in coach, and she was
bumped up to first class, a welcome luxury. Directly after
takeoff, her seatmate introduced himself. His name was Edward Dunn; he was about forty, Kate guessed, good-looking
with just the hint of an executive paunch on an otherwise fit

body. He explained that he was a securities analyst who specialized in chemical companies, and Kate braced herself for a bore. But his conversation proved surprisingly interesting: Off-Broadway, nouvelle cuisine, Reagan versus Carter. A phrase popped into her mind: a good catch. It was an outdated and possibly sexist concept; but still Kate couldn't help thinking that Edward Dunn fit whatever was meant by it.

He asked her rather bluntly if she were married.

"No and never have been," she replied.

"I'm divorced with two kids," he volunteered. "Which makes me either a cliché or a classic." It was a line Kate suspected he had used previously to advantage—nevertheless she gave the appropriate smile.

"Perhaps we could have a drink sometime," he added.

"That would be nice," she said, as noncommittal as had been the suggestion.

At Kennedy, he offered to share a cab into Manhattan. But there was a problem at the baggage claim—Kate's bags apparently hadn't made it onto the flight. Despite her protests, Dunn gallantly waited for her to go through the tortuous process of filing a lost baggage form. It was well after ten by the time they finally fell into a cab.

"What about having that drink now?" Dunn proposed as their cab approached the Midtown Tunnel.

"I'm pretty tired," Kate said.

"I'll bet you are, but if you're anything like me, you could use a bit of unwinding. After a flight like this, I'm still going like sixty. What do you say, a quick nightcap?"

"Well, all right."

"That's the spirit. My place is in the Forties, about ten blocks out of the tunnel."

Kate glanced up—his apartment was not what she'd had in mind. But then why not? She had just spent six hours with the man, enough to be reasonably certain he wasn't the mad slasher or anything.

The cab pulled into the circular drive of a featureless new high-rise. Dunn insisted upon paying the entire fare. But he had nothing smaller than a fifty, and when the driver balked, Kate drew out her wallet.

"I've got some cash upstairs. I'll pay you back," Dunn promised.

He had the standard affluent bachelor's apartment, all white walls, Betamax, and oatmeal Haitian cotton. He poured scotch, put something low and jazzy on the stereo, and they chatted, somewhat more self-consciously than on the plane. Dunn flipped the record, refilled their glasses, summoned her to the window to admire his unobstructed view of the Chrysler Building—at which point it was only natural that his arm should slip around her shoulders, that he should begin to knead her upper arm and tell her how beautiful she was and how he could hardly believe it when she had sat next to him on the plane—and that he should then kiss her.

Kate kissed him vigorously back. Maybe it was alcohol, maybe the effects of travel, maybe the man himself, but she suddenly found herself intensely excited. It was she who led him toward the oatmeal-colored sofa. They tumbled down still locked in a deep kiss, bodies pressing eagerly. She assisted him in removing her clothes and his own, loving it when they were finally naked together. For once her desire had not waned at all; she was fully, almost explosively ready.

But after five minutes it became obvious that Edward Dunn couldn't maintain an erection.

"Brewer's droop," he giggled.

The edge of Kate's desire began to blur, then fade. A grit of resentment took its place, and then that began to lapse into boredom, as—out of etiquette more than anything else—she did her best to help him. At last he managed a forty-second performance and a tepid climax for himself.

They stickily untangled from each other and, averting their eyes, pulled on enough clothes to cover themselves. Dunn broke the strained silence with another nervous chuckle. "I want you to know I'm not usually so perfunctory," he said.

"That's all right," Kate said dutifully. "It happens to everyone."

"Not to me it doesn't. This is a very unusual occurrence." There was a hint of something accusatory in his voice that put her on guard, as if he was implying it was somehow her fault.

"You probably run into a lot of men though that are having this problem," he pursued.

Kate began to bristle. How promiscuous did he think she was anyway? "I wouldn't really know," she said coldly.

"Well, you couldn't blame 'em, could you? Not the way you women come on these days."

"What do you mean the way we come on?" she demanded.

"I mean the way you come on so damned strong you've taken away all the thrill of the chase. It used to be women made men feel like *men*, but now they've got to call all the shots. They want to be on top, and take over the whole frigging thing. Christ Almighty, there's no satisfying any of you anymore. You women won't stop until you've made us all a pack of pussy-whipped faggots."

The consummate hostility in his voice sent a freeze up Kate's spine. What was she doing here? she wondered. Why was she still settling for sex that was devoid of kindness, friendship, God knows of love—of any kind of emotion at all? She began hurriedly to put on the rest of her clothes, stuffing her pantyhose in her bag and hunting under the couch for the mate to her red pump.

"What are you doing?" he asked gruffly.

"I think I'd better leave," she said.

He made no reply, just lit a cigarette and stared sullenly at the ceiling. Kate found the missing shoe, grabbed her purse and coat, and left.

Outside the temperature had dropped a good ten degrees and a sleeting rain had begun to fall. Kate wrapped her trenchcoat tightly about her, but the wet cold crept down her collar and flayed her bare legs. She stumbled toward Lexington Avenue and searched for a cab. But then she remembered—she had only two dollars and change left. Dunn never had reimbursed her for the cab ride in. Oh, God, she thought, what now? She didn't dare take a subway at one-fifteen in the morning—not in this neighborhood. She'd have to wait for a bus. She trudged miserably to the stop, trying hard to repress the feeling that this was a punishment, that she was only getting what she deserved.

SHE FELL INTO A DEPRESSION. Not the desperate bottomed-out kind she had often plummeted into with Stephen, but rather a blurred, unshakable sensation that something was wrong. The studio was very busy, and, as always, throwing herself into work helped. It kept her thoroughly engaged from nine in the morning to whatever time she dismissed herself at night. But when she got home, there it would be, waiting like a repulsive pet at the door—the feeling that something, somehow had gone wrong.

It was on one of these discontented evenings that she received a call from Denny. She had heard little from him since he had started at Columbia architecture, and now she realized how much she had missed him.

"I thought you'd forgotten me," she teased.

"No way, my dear. It's just that here you've got just slightly less time off than in the army. Why don't you come up and let me show you the barracks?"

"I'd love to. Tomorrow night?"

"Perfect. I've got a jury tomorrow—that's when you submit a drawing to a panel of your fellow students who proceed to savagely tear it apart. I'll probably need some consolation."

"I'll bring Band-Aids. Where do I find you?"

"The studio's in Avery Hall. Come in through the main gate, go diagonally across the library steps. You'll see it."

The studio was a large, open, brightly lit room containing some fifty cubicles. At seven in the evening, fifteen or twenty students were here at work at their drawing boards or chatting casually as they drifted to inspect each other's work. There was a faint odor of food—a number of students munched absently on sandwiches or picked from cardboard takeout containers; and reggae music beat softly from an unseen radio.

Kate found Denny before he had noticed her. He sat hunched over the drawing board concentrating on a drawing. *He looks so different,* was her first thought. Not physically—there was the same lanky body in T-shirt and jeans, the same shaggy, soft hair. It was his expression that was new, the total absorption in his task. She recognized that intensity from somewhere else. Where? Yes, of course: the few times she had been with Jean while she was closing a deal, Kate had seen that identical expression on her face.

Some sixth sense informed Denny he was being watched. He whirled and his face lit with a grin. "Hey, you made it."

" 'Course I did. So this is the salt mines."

"This is it. I've been here so long it feels like home to me."

"Can I see what you're working on?"

"Sure. It won't look like much. I'm working on the concept of the path." She shot him an inquiring look, and he laughed. "A lot of what we do the first year has to do with understanding the abstracts—basic things like corridors and columns. It's a lot of experimentation, just to learn how you feel about space, color, texture, emptiness as opposed to activity, volume—that kind of thing."

"You're liking it, aren't you?"

"Loving it. Here, let me show you my new tools." He pointed out the parallel rule and triangle, lead holder and templates, handling each instrument with reverence and delight. Denny had always been able to convey infectious enthusiasm for whatever he was involved in. But now this enthusiasm was tempered by an incipient professionalism. It occurred to Kate that if she were meeting Denny for the first time now, she would find him extremely attractive indeed.

"From what I've seen of eating habits around here you could probably use a real meal," she said. "I'll treat, as long as it's not Lutece."

"There's a great Korean place a few blocks from here. And it's so cheap that I'm going to pay the bill."

The restaurant was scarcely more than a luncheonette, neon-lit and no tablecloths, but the food was generous and good, and the prices could only reflect the discount labor of second and third cousins in the kitchen. Denny was still eager to talk about his classes and Kate more than willing to indulge him. "What really excites me," he said, winding noodles with a plastic chopstick, "is the prospect of taking an idea—an abstract concept—and putting it into a form that can be universally understood, discussed, eventually translated into brick and steel and stone. Creating order from chaos, the tangible from the intangible. I guess that was part of the romance I had with carpentry—this feeling of being able to alter reality. This was such a logical step though, I can't believe it took me so long to make the move."

"You mean you had thought about it before?"

"On and off. Shit, I read *The Fountainhead* back in college and wanted to be Howard Roark, just like everybody else. The thing is that for the longest time I had no conception of anything past the next five minutes. I had all these great-sounding ideals, but when it got down to it, life was nothing more than a couple of well-rolled joints of Hawaiian and the Dead on the stereo."

"Isn't it funny how as you get older the creature comforts start to be a little more appealing," Kate said wryly.

"Fuck if they don't. But it's more than that, too. I just couldn't go the rest of my life kidding myself that I wasn't competitive at all, that having a little influence and prestige didn't mean anything to me. Because they do. I don't want to sell my soul to get them, but I'd still like a taste. And if I'm ever going to think about a family, kids and all that"—he shrugged—"that comes into it too."

Lucky kids who'd have Denny as a father, Kate thought. "How does *your* dad feel about all this?" she asked him.

A shade of resentment passed in his eyes. "When I was accepted at Columbia, he wrote me a letter saying that the average starting salary for architects is around thirteen thousand dollars, compared to thirty-eight for a corporate lawyer. And then he made it pretty clear he wasn't going to pay for the school. Which he couldn't even if he wanted to—not with two alimonies to cough up and a new live-in tootsie to support. And I'd never have asked him to pay for it anyway. The bastard." Denny gave a sharp laugh. "You know, for the longest time I think I was really scared that no matter what I did I'd still wind up just like him. Like it was in the genes or something. It's only slowly dawning on me that's not necessarily true."

He twisted off a can of Miller's from the six-pack they had brought with them and refilled his glass. Watching him, Kate had a strangely troubling thought: what if these resolutions of Denny's had a more specific motivation? "You going out with anyone in particular these days?" she inquired in a casual voice.

"As a matter of fact I am," he replied. "A woman named Nancy Koska. She's a photographers' rep, I met her through one of the kids in my Structures course. You'll have to meet her sometime."

He hasn't been too busy to see *her*, Kate thought peevishly. But then she instantly reprimanded herself: she really had to relinquish this proprietary attitude toward Denny. She should take pleasure in the fact that he was happy. "Is it anything serious?" she asked.

"Well, we've only been going out about a month. But it's been a nice month. The only problem is that she's what you'd call a visual person. Very bright, but she tends to express herself through what she sees. Which means I can't always talk to her the way I can talk to you, for instance. Still"—Denny gave an enigmatic smile—"she's got a lot of compensating qualities."

Kate felt a strange pull in her chest. She didn't want to meet this Nancy, she decided—nor did she want to meet any other woman Denny smiled like that about. She didn't want there to *be* any other one. Not because she didn't want Denny to be happy, but because . . .

Because she wanted Denny for herself.

The thought so unnerved her that for a moment she couldn't swallow the bit of cellophane noodles in her mouth. She tried telling herself it was just her old habit of being greedy—of not wanting to share Denny's attention. But some deeper sense assured her this wasn't so. She had an almost unconquerable urge to reach out to him, to touch the high curve of his cheekbone with her fingertips and trace the long upper line of his lip.

By why now, after all this time? Perhaps because it had taken her twelve—or was it thirteen?—years of dating and disillusionment simply to be able to separate fantasy from fact, to be able to recognize that there was really nothing better than this good-looking, good-humored, intelligent man who had always been her friend.

What if it were too late, and he were already madly in love with this Nancy? No, she told herself, somehow she'd know if that were true. But that still didn't mean he felt anything for *her* beyond the brotherly bonds of friendship. Back in college he probably did, but that was a lifetime ago and passions, God knows, have a way of cooling—she could scarcely recall what it had been about Keith that had caused her so much anguish. How could she make her change in feelings known without risking what she had of Denny now?

God, it was crazy, this turning of tables . . . after all these years, to be suddenly plotting ways to pursue Denny. . . .

Somehow she managed to get through dinner without betraying the turmoil inside her. But afterward, when Denny had flagged a cab for her on Broadway and bent as usual to kiss her on the cheek, she turned her face suddenly, impulsively, almost as an accident, and let his lips brush just so gently against her own.

*H*E WAS HERE.

Jean, gazing from her office window, watched Robert emerge from a Checker cab. He was as immaculate as ever in a blazer, gray trousers, a Burberry thrown over his shoulders in the Italian manner; his hair was sleek and perfect, his narrow eyes hidden behind the familiar Porsche sunglasses. In just the moments it took him to reach her, she felt a stirring of impatience. And then he was breezing into her office, grinning broadly and waving a check.

"Darling, we're a success!" he exclaimed.

"The money came through?" she asked breathlessly.

"Indeed it did. We've sold five shares, and I predict the rest will be gone by the end of the month. And in the meantime, I've deposited fifty-five thousand dollars to our corporate account. And I have here a check on that account for fifty thousand made out to you."

She hugged him, feeling, along with her delight, not a little measure of relief. It wasn't that she hadn't trusted Robert: it was just that she felt so much better having the money actually in her hands. "But where are your suitcases?" she asked, drawing back a bit.

"I've just a small satchel. I left it downstairs with the little redhead who let me in."

"Aren't you staying long?"

"One night only, I'm afraid." He laughed at her fallen expression. "I'm such a bastard to tease you. I've got a surprise for you, darling. You're coming with me."

"Coming where?"

"To the *Gillian*. You and I have the boat entirely to ourselves for the next two weeks. I've hired a cook and crew—everything's set. We're leaving from Charlotte Amalie on Thursday."

"But, Robert, it's impossible," she said. "I can't leave now."

"That's exactly what I expected you to say." He mimicked in falsetto: "Oh, darling, I can't leave now." He continued in his natural voice, "We are so much alike. Business always first, there's forever something of drastic importance hanging over our heads. Just tell me this—when was the last real vacation you had?"

"I don't know, I . . ."

"I believe you've never taken one." He caressed the short silk sleeve of her dress, almost as if petting a sleek animal. "Darling Jean, we owe ourselves some time together. I think we have something very special between us. But I'm warning you—unless we nurture it, we run the risk of having it die."

She looked at him with alarm. "Robert, I'd love to go with you. I'd give anything to be able to. But it's really impossible. Maybe in a month . . ."

"The boat will be already committed. And anyway," he added acidly, "who knows what new emergencies might spring up to prevent you then. No, it's now or never. I'll tell you that I have rather crushing demands on my time right now too, yet I was willing to put things off to be with you. It's a pity you can't do the same for me."

She hated the cold accusation she suddenly heard in his voice. She hesitated, and he went on. "One way or the other, I'm going to be on that boat. It's up to you whether or not I go alone. And if I do . . . I can't make any promises for the future of our relationship."

"All right," she burst out. "I'll go with you. Just give me the rest of the day to get things straightened out." She looked at his face and felt immediately she had made the right decision. For years she had fought hard to succeed in a man's sphere: in doing so she had too often had to give up being a woman. But she wanted both . . . she *would* have both. She placed her hands around the nape of his neck, drew his face toward hers. As she kissed him, she heard Paul walk into the room.

She turned quickly. He stood staring at them with an unreadable expression, turning a folder in his fingers.

"Paul . . ." she faltered. Then she gathered her composure. "Paul, I want you to meet someone. This is my good friend, Robert Silenieu. Robert, this is Paul Coulter."

Robert stepped smoothly forward and extended his hand. "Jean's told me a lot about you, Paul."

Paul perfunctorily gripped his hand. "Has she?" he said coldly.

"Definitely. She boasts that you're her right-hand man."

"Uh-huh. Well, your name's got a familiar ring to it too. Ever spend much time in California?"

"A fair amount. I have friends in Bel-Air, Beverly Hills. And business takes me to the Coast from time to time. Is that where you're from, Paul?"

"San Diego. Did you ever work with a guy named James Brilling?"

Robert smiled. "We've had some dealings."

"Yeah. And wasn't it just about two years ago that the two of you were sued by the L.A. County D.A.? Some shady scheme to sell paper offshore banks for tax dodges, wasn't it?"

Jean glanced nervously at Robert, but he still stood relaxed, smiling. "It's funny you should even remember that, Paul," he said. "The suit was just a quibble over our advertising. Nothing ever came of it."

"They slapped you with a pretty hefty fine, didn't they? I don't call that nothing. I call that being a crook."

"Paul!" Jean cried out.

"It's all right, Jean," Robert said easily. He leaned to a silver bowl of cigarettes on a low table and selected a pack of Camels. "The reason we settled that fine, Paul," he said, cracking the pack, "was that we didn't want to be forced to disclose the names of our clients. That's simply good business. And as for what you call a 'shady scheme' . . ." He lit a cigarette with deliberate motions and exhaled languorously. "Let's face it, Paul—all the easy deals have already been done. For a venture to be profitable these days, it's got to take place in that very slender gray area between legality and illegality. Sometimes it's just a question of semantics— whether you choose to interpret a certain regulation one way or another. Every major corporation employs an army of Wall Street lawyers just for this very purpose—to search out that thin, thin gray line."

Before Paul could reply, Robert glanced back at Jean. "Darling, you've got work to do, and I'm in the way. I'm lunching with a very old friend at the Box Tree. I'll ring you afterward." He kissed her on the cheek, then directed his sly smile back to Paul. "It's been a very great pleasure to meet you, Paul," he said.

Jean waited until he was gone before turning in a fury to

Paul. "Why did you do that?" she exploded. "Barging in here and insulting my guest with below-the-belt accusations . . ."

"Whatever I said was true," Paul cut in. "I don't know much about that guy, but his friend Brilling's a real sleaze. Oil, currency, securities, you name the hustle, he's been in it. And I've got to believe your friend's right in there with him."

"You're so quick to jump to conclusions. If you were half that quick in the performance of your job, you might have proved a bit more valuable around here."

"And just what do you mean by that?" he demanded.

"I mean you think like an accountant," she flung out. "You always have and you always will. You'll never understand people like Robert—or like me either, for that matter. We've got some creativity, imagination. We take risks, we make leaps of faith. We don't always go by the books, books, books!" She stopped, seeing a look on Paul's face she had never seen before. She knew she was on the brink of pushing him too far. And phones were ringing, she realized, four or five at once, a shrill, importunate choir of phones. Why wasn't anyone picking up? Damn it, what did she pay anyone around here for?

"Paul, I'm sorry," she said. "I didn't mean that. You know how important you are to me. To Minervco. I don't want our relationship to sour over some little spate of jealousy." She looked at him, saw his mouth tighten, but she thought it best to be frank. "I know my being interested in Robert has colored your opinion of him. And I'm willing to admit I may be making a mistake. He might be all wrong for me. But the only way I'll find out is by spending some time with him. He wants me to go away with him tomorrow. I've decided to go."

"With him?" Paul repeated. "You can't do that."

"I can, and I'm going to."

"No," he said. "I won't let you."

Her temper rose. "I'm still head of this company. I do what *I* want, and not what you or anyone else tells me to."

"But now, with everything coming down around our heads . . ."

"For God's sake, if I can't rely on you to keep things going for two weeks, what can I rely on you for!" The phones were still singing shrilly. She slapped the button of the Speakerphone. "Yes?"

"A Mr. Weller on one, says it's very important. And a Susan, I think it's Slaker, from Dean, Witter's been holding for about five minutes on three. And . . ."

"Be right there." Jean turned off the speaker and glanced coldly back at Paul. "I'm leaving tomorrow whether you like it or not. Until then there's a lot of work to do. For both of us."

He seemed about to say something but changed his mind. "If that's the way you want it." He shrugged and walked stiffly out.

Jean was somewhat relieved. She had expected him to make more of a scene. But she wasn't too worried about his injured feelings. He'd sulk and steam, but in the end Paul always came around.

*A*NDREA RIPPED THE TOP STRIP OFF A PACKET OF TENDER Vittles cat food. With Waylon curling impatiently about her ankles, she shook the food into his bowl, added hot water, then mushed it with a fork into a sort of stew—the only way, she had discovered, the big cat condescended to regard it as food.

"Here, puss-puss," she crooned, setting the bowl down for him. "You eat that up, you big fat old pussy cat." She watched him attack it with dainty greed; then, humming "Silly Love Songs," she began to prepare her own dinner. A kind of daffy, babbling happiness overtook her while she assembled the ingredients for a meatloaf, causing her to bob up and down on her toes: a feeling that stemmed from her last communication from the attorney in West Palm Beach. He had located a young woman in the beginning of her second trimester, and in a month she would be ready to relocate to San Francisco. The fees had been established: all that remained now was for Andrea to make payment. She had immediately written to Jean detailing her wish to convert her

shares in The Returning Worker. She assumed that Jean
would purchase them herself. At any rate, Jean had always
led her to believe there wouldn't be any problem.

As she began kneading the meatloaf, the phone rang. Oh,
hell, she thought. It was probably that dreadful friend of
Louise Haymen's who'd been pestering her to go out with
him. She was about to switch on the answering machine—
sooner or later she was going to have to learn to say no
instead of always resorting to this sophomoric dodging business.

She wiped her hands on a paper towel and picked up.

"Is this Andrea Maysell?"

Who could be calling her by her married name? She had,
in a gesture of feminism, taken back her maiden name,
Herry, when she had moved to San Francisco.

"Yes," she said warily.

"This is Paul Coulter. We've never spoken before, but
I'm an associate of Jean Ferguson's."

Andrea brightened. "Oh, hi. Jean must've received my
letter, then."

"Yes, or rather I've gotten it. Jean's out of the country at
the moment."

"Will she be back soon? I'm very anxious to convert my
shares. You see, I'm dealing with something of a time fac-
tor . . ."

"Yes, well, I'm sorry to inform you that your shares in
The Returning Worker are effectively worthless."

Andrea gave a little laugh. "What?"

"The company has been operating deeply in the red for
years. It's been artificially maintained with funds diverted
from other sources, but those sources, too, have dried up.
There's no alternative but to fold the company."

"You mean my money's gone?" she breathed.

"I'm afraid so. You might salvage a penny or so on the

dollar from whatever assets remain. But I advise you to file a claim early. There'll be a lot of creditors.''

"But I just saw Jean a couple of months ago. She didn't say anything about any of this. I thought everything was fine.''

He gave a harsh-sounding laugh. "There's going to be a lot of people sorry they trusted Jean Ferguson.''

"But wait!'' Andrea cried, but he had already hung up.

It couldn't be true, she thought. This man, whoever he was, must be a phony—someone playing a practical joke. Jean would never do this to her—Jean, whom she had loved, idolized, trusted completely. There had to be some mistake.

She dialed Jean's number and received an answering service which confirmed the fact that Jean was out of the country. Andrea's heart began to beat wildly. Where could she get more information? Kate—chances were she would know. She wildly looked up Kate's number in her book and dialed, breathing relief when Kate answered a sleepy hello.

"Kate, it's Andrea, did I wake you?''

"No, no. I just got in from a long day, and I'm beat. What's the matter? You sound upset.''

"Oh, it's nothing probably. It's just that I got a very weird phone call from someone named Paul . . . well, I've forgotten his last name, but he said he works with Jean. Anyway, he told me The Returning Worker was about to go out of business. That can't be right, but I thought I'd check with you.'' She waited for Kate's quick reassurance, but instead an ominous silence issued from the other end of the line.

"Oh, God, Andrea, it might be true,'' Kate said at last. "I know the company's been in trouble for a while. About a year ago, I had to help Jean bail it out—and there've been a lot of rumors since then.''

''You mean you knew this when you were here, and you let me go on thinking everything was fine and dandy?''

''You were so happy, I couldn't stand to spoil it. And there was always the chance that Jean would still make it work. She's pulled it off before.''

''You were supposed to be my friend.''

''Oh, Andrea, I am your friend. But I had a responsibility to Jean, too. I felt I owed her at least the benefit of the doubt. You can understand, can't you?''

''I don't know,'' Andrea said wearily. ''I can't tell what to think about anything anymore.'' As she hung up though, she was conscious that she wasn't really mad at Kate. Kate had just been another one of Jean's dupes, charmed out of any sense.

Her entire body seemed to contract with the bitter rancor she felt for Jean. She had always been good old Andrea, taking whatever was dished out, forgiving and forgetting. But not this time. She was a professional with influence and contacts, and she was determined to use whatever she could to get back at Jean.

She spent a sleepless night. For the first time in her career, she arrived at her firm before eight. There remained in her desk, she remembered, the card Jean's banker friend had given her. She could recall him clearly at that breakfast: a trim Oriental in banker's blue with a name like some strange clash of cultures. Yes, here it was: François Hokosawa, First Pacific Seamen's Bank. She had a hunch he'd be interested in what she had to say.

She placed the call at nine. The banker cordially pretended to remember her well. But his polite tone faltered when she related her information.

''I'm certain her assets are quite sound,'' he said. ''However, I am a bit concerned—I've just authorized the release of rather a large sum on the strength of a check from a New York account. I tell you what: I'll make a call to New York and check out the account picture on that end. I'll get back to you.''

"I'd appreciate that," Andrea said.

JEAN DROPPED HER VALISES ON THE FLOOR OF HER APARTment and poured herself a large Courvoisier. She had returned a day later than she'd intended. The boat had needed repairs—exactly what had never been made clear—stranding them an extra day in St. Eustatius. She had tried to hire a sea plane to jump back to St. Croix in time for her original flight, but bad weather had grounded all small planes until it was too late.

Paul must be frantic, she thought. She had tried to reach him several times in the past few days, but there was always some difficulty in the connection. God save us from banana republics! She supposed she should call him now, but she hadn't the energy. Time enough to talk in the morning.

The voyage had not been a success. Robert's behavior had been disturbingly strange. He had brought with him a powder box full of cocaine—several thousand dollars worth at least—and the moment they were on board, he had begun to do it up. Which had been his prerogative, she supposed—after all, it was a vacation, and she had no grounds other than middle-class puritanism to disapprove. Still, the sheer amount he was doing made her uneasy; moreover, she had sensed a brittleness to his mood that she could only attribute to the drug. There was an edge to his charm she had never noticed before: the barest shade of sarcasm beneath his praises, the hint of something about to snap—yet so subtle, she could never be quite sure it was actually there.

And in bed, the little tendency he had to hurt her suddenly increased to an alarming degree. Several times his biting and slapping had caused her to recoil and plead with him to be more gentle—and then one night he took a folded belt and began to flay her thighs. She had screamed and curled into herself to protect herself from the blows, and he had thrown the belt down in disgust. "You prudish American bitches bore me to tears!" he spat out and stormed naked out onto the deck. She had lain in shock—no man had ever spoken to her like that before. But then he had returned almost immediately, apologizing profusely, swearing he had never meant it, it was just the tension of business manifesting itself in strange ways. . . . He continued with such tender endearments that Jean allowed her forgiveness. It was the drug, she thought again. She would try to persuade him to ease up on it for the rest of the trip.

The following day they were joined on the boat by the revolting James Brilling who had flown up from Bogota, bringing with him a skeletal, pinch-mouthed young German man of some indeterminate connection. The three had spent much of the time in huddled consultation from which Jean was pointedly excluded. It was an emergency, Robert told her: "A bitch, I know, darling, but it can't be helped." Jean had sprawled restlessly on a deck chair on the prow, thumbing through old issues of *Forbes*, thinking resentfully of all she had left behind to be with him. Why had he dragged her down here just to ignore her like this? It was obvious that he didn't care for her at all. But just as she had resolved to jump ship at Aruba and catch a flight back to New York, the intruders departed. And for the last four days, Robert had again been tender, spinning tantalizing plans for their future. And yet . . . that hardness, that almost smirking edge had become even more pronounced. Or was she just completely paranoid now, suspicious of every little thing he did?

She didn't know. She should, but she didn't. All these years she had been living for her work while other women were experimenting in love. She simply didn't have the experience to interpret Robert's behavior. Oh, God, she thought wearily. I'm thirty-two years old and cannot even tell if the man I'm in love with has any feelings for me at all.

Maybe her thoughts would be clearer in the morning. She had energy now only for a steaming shower before collapsing into bed.

It was her custom to rise at six forty-five and be at the office some forty minutes later, but this morning, utter exhaustion made her oversleep. She arrived at the Minervco brownstone after nine. To her irritation, she found the door still locked. She must be the first to arrive. Damn it, she had only been gone two weeks, and already they had begun to slack off. Everyone seemed to be taking advantage of her lately: her staff, Robert, Dale Comisky, and all the others she'd given a head start to. . . . Good old Jean, let her slave and sacrifice while everyone else gets a free ride. Well, there were going to be some changes made, beginning right here at the office. Tighter discipline for a start. No more of this first-name basis, no more coming and going as everyone pleased. From now on, Minervco would be run like a real business.

She let herself in with her own key. The foyer seemed strangely empty. Yes, the clock was missing—the Sheraton grandfather clock that had blocked up the entrance. Perhaps Paul had found a less unwieldy place for it. . . . But something else was different . . . the Steichen prints that marched down the wall of the corridor were gone as well. A burglary! was her first thought. Someone had broken in.

She hurried upstairs to her office. The Rauschenberg, the Warhols, the Stella were gone from the walls, but the two new Hockney lithos that were on approval and unpaid for yet were still leaning against the desk. Several antiques and the stereo equipment were missing from the shelves. But the typewriter that was leased was still here, as was all the leased furniture.

What in God's name was going on? She picked up the phone to call Paul, but no dial tone came through. She clicked the phone several times, then tried the other lines: all were dead. Nor did any of the phones work in Paul's office, nor at the deserted reception desk downstairs.

A bewildered fear clenched at the pit of her stomach. She ran outside to the pay phone at the corner of Third Avenue and dialed Paul's home number. A mechanical voice responded: *The number you have dialed has been disconnected.*

The fear surged upward. She had the dizzying sensation that she had been gone not two weeks but two years and that everything had disintegrated in the interval. Don't panic, she ordered herself. There must be a perfectly good explanation to all of this. Some harebrained economy move on Paul's part, maybe. As soon as she reached him, it would all be sorted out.

And in fact there he was now, in his tan suit, at the door to the office. She hurried back down the block, waving with relief. But as she came closer, she realized it wasn't Paul at all, but someone shorter, darker—a stranger. And he was accompanied by a woman also wearing a light brown suit.

"Miss Ferguson?" the man said, stepping toward her.

He displayed a set of credentials in a folded leather wallet. "My name is George Schindler. I'm a special agent for the FBI. I have a warrant for your arrest on federal charges of bank theft and fraud by wire. You will kindly not put your hands anywhere near your sides and give your pocketbook to this female agent."

The ground gave a sickening lurch beneath her feet. "I don't understand," she blurted. But the woman had already plucked the purse from her hand, and now she began patting her down to search for weapons. The touch of strange hands was shocking, a hideous violation of her private self; her entire body recoiled. The man, Schindler, was reciting the list of rights made familiar by a hundred television shows. The woman stepped back and nodded. Schindler rather sharply grabbed Jean's arm and fastened handcuffs over her wrists.

"What's this all about?" she cried. "I don't understand what I've done."

"This isn't the time to go into that," he said. His voice was polite but chillingly firm. "When we go downtown you'll get a chance to talk to the prosecutor, who'll explain the charges."

"Can't I call my lawyer?"

"Downtown." He gripped her roughly by the upper arm and led her into the back seat of a black LTD idling at the curb. Another man, red-haired, dark-suited, sat behind the wheel. The woman slid in beside him, and they pulled away.

This can't be happening, Jean thought. They were dragging her away on some insane charge of robbing a bank, with no warrant, no chance to call an attorney. They must think she was someone else, Patty Hearst, Bonnie and Clyde, whoever. Couldn't they tell just by looking at her they were making a hideous mistake?

She wasn't panicking. In fact she was proud of just how calm she appeared to be. Her thoughts were coming with even greater clarity than usual. Coolly she surveyed the man beside her. Too young, too short, too light-eyed to be what he claimed. His suit, a tan European-cut poly-blend—didn't that have too much style? And look—on his feet, tan socks and penny loafers. It was a known fact, wasn't it, that FBI men wore black shoes and white socks? Jean seized upon this last thought with wild hope. A dead giveaway: this had to be a hoax, a practical joke of some sort. . . .

But the car cruised up to Federal Plaza, and now Schindler was taking her into a sterile, imposingly modern building marked FEDERAL BUREAU OF INVESTIGATION. Abruptly her calm gave way to a consummate terror. The bones in her legs were replaced by something soft, liquifying, making it difficult to walk. It was actually happening: she was under arrest!

And she didn't even know what she had done.

Inside the building, she was hustled from room to room. In a numb dream she heard her rights barked at her again and again; she was fingerprinted and photographed under harsh and demeaning lights, just like a common criminal.

And then, after hours or an eternity, Agent Schindler at last brought her to his office and placed her in front of a phone. She grabbed at the receiver as if a lifeline: but with her fingers on the dial she stopped short. Who could she call? She knew lawyers—scores of them. But they were contract lawyers and investment lawyers . . . they dealt in money, in deals, not people. Many of them had never even seen the inside of a courtroom, wouldn't know an arrest warrant from a parking summons.

Andrea, she thought. Andrea was the kind of lawyer who helped people in trouble. But futile thought: Andrea was three thousand miles away; and even if she were to come, she wasn't licensed to practice in New York State.

Schindler noticed her hesitation. "If you don't have an attorney, the court will appoint you one," he said.

"No!" she cried, shaking her head in alarm. And then suddenly a name did come to her. Warren Head—someone she frequently ran into on the social circuit. He had one of the most prestigious private practices in the city—had defended Gerard Blackstone when he'd been indicted for trading on inside information and gotten him off clean. . . .

Thank God her name was sufficiently known to summon Warren himself instead of having her be shuffled off to one of his associates. His voice was low, well-bred, indicating neither surprise nor judgment. "Have you been told your rights?" he asked.

"Over and over," she choked. "They must think I'm some sort of cretin not understanding the first time."

"All right. Now they have the right to obtain pedigree information from you, which is simply biographical information and facts about your financial status. But other than that, you're to say absolutely nothing."

She felt a little better as she hung up—or at least she no longer felt so brutally alone. But now Schindler was handcuffing her again.

"Now what?" she asked faintly.

"We're going across the road. You'll have your interview with the assistant U.S. attorney."

The brief walk across the plaza seemed endless. Through her entire life, Jean had placed herself in the center of attention, but never had she felt as utterly conspicuous as she did now. She seemed encased in a glaring beam of light: passers-by turned and stared, craning their necks for a better look, until such shame consumed her she wondered that she even continued to exist.

The prosecutor, a Miss Kinney, was a tall, freckled black woman with reddish hair clipped almost to her scalp and a broad, sympathetic face. Something about her office seemed instantly familiar to Jean. . . . Yes, it reminded her of the office of that Macmillan editor who had been discussing a book with her on women in finance. Here was the same cubiclelike space, papers and books scattered about, notes and clippings tacked chattily to the wall. But that editor's office was part of the real world, while this existed in the looking-glass hell Jean had suddenly plunged into.

"Do you understand the charges against you?" Miss Kinney asked.

"No," Jean said vehemently. "I don't understand them at all."

"You've been arrested for perpetrating a check-kiting scheme involving two banks, First Pacific Seamen's of San Francisco and Chelsea Trust of New York. There is also a charge of wire fraud, indicating that you used interstate phone lines for this purpose."

Jean's fingers turned to ice. She felt suddenly as if she had been sucked into a great vacuum, a pull of such strength and dimension that for a moment she could neither see nor breathe. The check for the *Gillian* . . . Hokosawa, calling him to release the funds. . . . But that was nothing, just a means of obtaining a few days' float, a trivial bending of the rules. Whole businesses operated on such maneuvers, it was done all the time. . . . And she had covered the checks finally, she hadn't stolen anything. Why were they terrorizing her with handcuffs and fingerprints and baby-faced agents in penny loafers?

She looked into Miss Kinney's rather pleasant face, glanced around her homey, cluttered office. She felt a desperate desire to blurt everything out: about Robert and the boat and Paul's tiresome economies, about how lonely she had been and how she had thought this simple little manipulation would make everything work out without hurting anyone. But Warren had forbidden her to say anything: she forced herself to stay quiet.

After Miss Kinney was finished with her, she was marched in to see a chunky, severe-faced probation officer who compiled information that—the woman informed Jean—would be used in determining her bail. And then finally, finally, she was taken to the magistrate's courtroom where Warren was waiting for her.

He was so well dressed! The rich brown stuff of his suit jacket, the subtle silk of his tie, the white smooth crease of his collar—she wanted to burrow into it and let its wealth counteract the sordidness of the past few hours. *This* was her world; and Warren, with his beaky features and top-rising crest of brown hair, seemed like some great rescuing bird who would lift her in his manicured talons and fly her back to it.

"Holding up okay?" he asked.

"I think so," she said weakly. "My stomach feels a bit seasick though."

"That's a natural reaction. Being arrested is always a great shock. Now, I've read the complaint, but I want you to tell me very briefly what happened."

She managed to keep her voice steady as she related the story until she reached the events of this morning; then it began to crack. "Oh, God, Warren, they're calling me a thief when all I did was try to get a float of a couple of days, and you know people do that all the time, it's not that terrible a thing, and I wasn't going to steal anything . . ."

"All right, now calm down," he said, gripping her shoulder. "I'm here now, so don't worry."

She caught hold of herself and nodded wanly.

"Now then," he went on, "our main objective is to get

you out of here, so I'll need some information to negotiate your bail.''

Jean was beginning to feel that the details of her life were like items in a rummage sale, available to be picked over, bought, or rejected by anyone who pleased. And by now, having been so handled, even the simplest facts had a soiled quality: she half expected to see an expression of finicky disgust on Warren's face as he made notes on his fresh legal pad.

She held on to Warren's well-tailored sleeve as the hearing began. The magistrate was a middle-aged woman with dyed raven-black hair pulled slickly back from a heavy forehead; she spoke with the flat, inflectionless voice of an auctioneer. And now Miss Kinney, who had seemed so sympathetic in her office, suddenly revealed herself as Jean's deadliest enemy. ''Your honor, this is a typical crime for personal gain,'' she declared. ''Moreover, the defendant was recently out of the country in the company of a man named Robert Silenieu who has twice been indicted in this country on counts of currency fraud. His whereabouts are currently unknown. Given the nature of their relationship there is good reason to believe she will flee to join him.''

Jean saw Warren frown and a shiver ran up her spine. Why were they dragging Robert into this? And how did they know about the ''nature of their relationship''? She felt stripped bare—no part of her life or her person left unviolated.

Warren rose and made a strong plea to have her released on her own recognizance. But the magistrate remained unmoved: she set bail at a twenty-thousand-dollars cash assurity.

A marshal came forward and Jean shrank toward Warren in a fresh wave of panic. ''You mean I've got to go to jail?'' she asked wildly.

"You'll be held in the Metropolitan Correctional Center until the cash is delivered to the bailiff. Presumably it won't be too long." He spoke calmly, as if such a thing were an everyday occasion, an annoyance on the level of being detained by bad weather in an airport.

A wave of nausea overtook Jean so strongly that she placed her hands on her midriff and bent forward. Warren placed a supporting hand on the small of her back. "It's a good facility," he assured her. "Very clean and modern, a model of its kind. And we'll have you out as soon as possible."

She opened her mouth, but the words stuck dryly in her throat. This can't happen to me, was what she meant to say. I'm the girl who did everything right. The girl who got all A's, who ran for office and made all the teams. The good girl whose hair was always combed and whose clothes were clean and who was never once sent to the principal's office.

And then without knowing why, she reached into Warren's breast pocket and removed his silver Mark Cross pen. "Would you lend me this?" she whispered.

"Of course," he said with puzzled solicitude. "If you want it, take it."

She clutched the pen fervently while the marshal handcuffed her again and took her away.

A long series of connecting tunnels led directly into the detention center. It was an empty, modern building, preternaturally quiet and sealed so that the air though not hot was stifling. There was a *1984* sense about it, the feeling that electric eyes scanned every movement and hidden machine guns were trained on your every step. Jean felt a mounting terror as the building swallowed her up.

She was taken to a small room and placed in the hands of an unsmiling corrections officer who ordered her to strip.

"Everything?" Jean faltered.

"Everything."

With trembling, icy hands, she fumbled out of her clothes. The officer brusquely searched her nakedness, ran fingers through her hair, under her arms, through her crotch and made her spread her buttocks, while Jean's entire body shrieked with indignation. The search concluded, the officer rather grudgingly told her to keep her underwear and shoes, then issued her a uniform—a faded, light-blue pajamalike outfit that reminded Jean of a hairdresser's outfit. Everything else the officer confiscated—her sapphire ring, her hoop earrings, the thin gold chain around her neck. It was terrible to give them up. How used we are to identifying ourselves with our choices, Jean thought. It's just such trifles as a ring or a pin that mark us as individuals.

"And that pen," the woman ordered.

Jean realized she was still clutching Warren's pen. And now she understood why she had taken it. It was a precious link to Warren, to beauty and comfort, to the suddenly inaccessible outside world. Her sense of self and dignity had been entirely stripped away from her: she couldn't let them take this too. "I need this," she said desperately. "I'll have to write things down, take notes, please, it's very important."

For some reason, the officer accepted this babbled plea. "All right, you can bring it along," she said. "Let's go."

They ascended to the fifth floor and into a large, brightly lit common room. It contained some twenty-five women all in their pastel beautician's suits. Most were young, black or Hispanic; they played cards, watched television, crocheted, or simply sat and smoked. There was raucous laughter, and a whiff of marijuana in the motionless air.

Jean huddled into a seat against a wall. She felt an overwhelming desire to burst into tears. But she sensed that both inmates and guards were watching her, testing her, measur-

ing her vulnerability. Her survival instinct warned her that
she had to stay under control. For the first time in her life
she wished that she smoked. Instead, she squeezed the silver
pen between her fingers and kept her eyes and mind fixed on
the badly focused TV screen.

For some time she stared rotely at a series of soap operas
and game shows. Then the local news flickered by: a fire in
Far Rockaway, two dead; Mayor Koch slinging back insults
at a teenaged heckler outside an entrance to the BMT . . .
And then with the searing shock of a hot iron, her own name
flashed out at her: *"Jean Ferguson, feminist entrepreneur
and one of the first women to break many of the barriers of
venture capitalism, was arrested today in Manhattan on
charges of check-kiting . . ."*

Oh, God, no!

A picture of her appeared on screen behind the face of the
newspaper: her eyes were shining and she was smiling with
almost insolent confidence. She recognized the photograph
immediately—it was one that had appeared with a *Redbook*
article entitled "Ten Women with Real Clout."

There was a stir in the room, and a dozen pair of eyes
swung in her direction. "Hey, is that you?" said a black
woman sitting near her. "That's *you*, ain't it?"

Jean ducked her head. My God, she thought, they were
acting as if she were some sort of celebrity. Their excitement only mocked her own horror at learning her disgrace
was now public. Family, friends, colleagues, all of them
now knew. How could she ever face any of them again?

Suddenly she was glad she was shut away.

SHE SPENT THE night on the upper bunk of a narrow
metal bunkbed, staring into the dark. The lower was occupied by a nineteen-year-old Colombian named Teresa who
had been busted along with an American boyfriend in a

rather inept attempt to smuggle cocaine. Teresa had been here over two weeks; she offered coffee, chocolate, cigarettes, from her considerable private stash. Jean responded as politely as she could to her kindness and huddled from her curiosity. It occurred to her that she had not slept in the same room with another woman since her freshman year in college.

In the morning she tried unsuccessfully to swallow a few bites of molten, microwaved scrambled eggs. Then she crept back to her same chair, clutched her pen, and fought back the terror of not knowing what was going on in the outside world. Hours leaked into each other. Time had collapsed into a formless void in which she drifted endlessly.

And then a guard snapped "Ferguson, W.A.B." She knew this meant "with all belongings," and yet, at the sound of her name, she still felt an irrational dread. What more were they going to accuse her of? What else were they going to say she did?

But the guard told her, "You're getting out. Your bail's been paid."

She was given back her possessions. She dressed and was escorted to the front entrance. Someone was standing by the guard's desk, a woman with light brown hair. It was a moment before she realized it was Kate.

But Kate stepped forward immediately, her arms stretched solicitously before her. "Jean," she said, "what a terrible ordeal!"

Jean stared at her. "What are you doing here?"

"I thought it would be better if someone came to meet you. I've been trying frantically to reach Denny but he's camping in the Adirondacks and won't be home till tonight. Your lawyer agreed that I should come, and as soon as we had the bail paid, I came straight here."

Confusion swept over Jean. In her shaken state, nothing Kate was saying seemed to make much sense.

Kate put an arm around her. "Let's get the hell out of this creepy place. Mr. Head's waiting for you in his office. We'll get a cab, okay?"

They emerged onto Park Row in daylight that seemed blinding. Kate waved down a cab and gave the driver Warren Head's Park Avenue office address.

As if mesmerized, Jean watched the blocks whiz by. She realized Kate had said something to her and turned to her with a start.

"Are you all right?" Kate repeated.

"Yes, fine," she replied somewhat sharply. "It's just that I'm having trouble putting some things together. What do *you* have to do with my bail?"

"God, Jean, I thought you knew. I paid it."

"*You* did?"

"Yes. I took out a bank loan based on the studio's assets. I guess you weren't able to have much contact . . ."

"But why you?"

Kate hesitated. "Mr. Head said there was no one else."

"I don't understand. What does he mean, no one else?" Jean ran an agitated hand through her dark fringe of hair. "I sit on the board of eighteen companies. I own stock in all of them and property in three states. And Paul—why didn't Warren get hold of Paul?"

Kate bit her lower lip. "Jean, I'm afraid you're going to have to prepare yourself for more bad news. Paul has left town. Before going he dissolved as many of Minervco's companies as he could. Warren can tell you much more about it. All I know is that my company is one of the few solvent ventures you've got left."

"That's impossible!" Jean cried. "Paul's not in charge

of Minervco. He doesn't have the power to do that kind of thing on his own.''

''Maybe he had a lot more power than you realized,'' Kate said. ''Oh, God, Jean, don't you see? You got so removed from the running of your own companies that you gave up a lot of control. We've all been running things on our own for a long time now.''

Jean was on a seesaw and Kate, on the opposite end, seemed to be flying high in the air. ''Are you saying there's some sort of conspiracy to force me out of my own company?'' she demanded.

''No, of course not.''

''Then why are you in cahoots with my lawyer, trying to get an advantage over me by paying my bail and pushing in where it's none of your business?''

''Jean, believe me, I'm just trying to help you.''

''You help *me*? Aren't you forgetting that I'm the one responsible for everything you've got today? You'd still be pushing martinis if it wasn't for me. I've made the sacrifices and all the rest of you have just come along for the ride. And now you're all ganging up on me behind my back. But I can still fight back, you know. And I fully intend to.''

The cab had reached their destination. She got out, slammed the door, and strode quickly into the building. An elevator took her to Warren's suite where a receptionist buzzed her immediately into his private office.

''Something's very wrong here,'' she burst out to him. ''Why did you go to the officer of one of my least significant holdings to make bail?''

''Sit down, Jean,'' Warren said somberly.

She looked at his face and felt a sharp recurrence of dread. She sank into a chair. ''Is it true then about Paul?'' she asked faintly.

Warren nodded. ''Mr. Coulter has apparently left town,

taking with him whatever of Minervco's tangible assets he could. We could hire an investigator to locate him. But at the moment I don't think it would be wise for you to incur any additional expense."

"What's happened to my company, Warren?"

"Minervco still exists. But from what I gather, Mr. Coulter has dissolved most of its holdings, and the remaining assets—what there are of them—are being held in receivership by creditors."

She looked at him, stunned. "But I'd only been gone two weeks."

"Apparently Mr. Coulter began initiating bankruptcy proceedings sometime before you left. And it was a domino effect—your companies were so leveraged upon each other that when one went, they all began to collapse."

"So you're saying I have nothing left?"

"No. Vidstar Productions is solvent, as is your textbook operation. However neither at present is generating substantial income for its stockholders."

Jean noticed that her hands were beginning to tremble uncontrollably. She buried them in her lap. "Warren," she said. "Those checks—the money they say I stole . . . I had covered them with a deposit of a hundred thousand dollars. Why didn't they clear?"

Warren nodded gravely. "That was mentioned in the complaint. The check you deposited was drawn upon an account that had already been closed out."

"That's impossible!" she cried.

"Nevertheless . . ."

"But I still have half the boat, don't I? The *Gillian* . . . the contract that was in my office file . . ."

"I've looked it over. And I've made a call to St. Thomas. The boat has left its moorings and has left no forwarding destination. And as far as your shares in it are concerned—

well, Mr. Silenieu had set up the deal as an offshore corporation in the Cayman Islands, to which we simply have no recourse.''

''And so I've lost that, too?'' she whispered.

He made a mouth of regret. ''I'm afraid that when you got mixed up with this man you took on someone of fairly professional experience.''

It was beginning to sink in. Robert had used her: had gotten what he could from her and disappeared. She could sense Warren's bewilderment at how she could have been so incredibly naïve. But how could Warren know she had been blinded by love—or rather a storybook phantasm of love she had concocted for herself. Suddenly she saw it so clearly that she almost laughed. She had constructed an ideal, a knight on a white charger, something to which most men didn't—couldn't—live up. And then Robert came along. With his looks and charm and savvy, and the way he seemed to respond to her own power, he seemed to perfectly embody that ideal. And she had wanted so desperately to believe it that she refused to recognize what had been staring her in the face.

She gulped air into her lungs to stifle a horrible urge to scream.

''I think we should discuss your options in regard to the charges against you,'' Warren was saying.

''Yes,'' she said quickly. ''What are my options?''

His expression became grave. He folded his hands in a ''this is the church'' on the desk in front of him. ''I unfortunately believe the government has a very strong case against you. They can present as evidence the checks with your fingerprints on them. They will have a handwriting analysis done to verify your signature, and they'll have the testimony of the bank officers. And the fact that most of your holdings are in bankruptcy will go badly against you. It's my opinion that if we fight the charges we will lose."

"But what else can I do?" she asked.

"I suggest we see what kind of a deal we can get through plea bargaining. The government is apparently very interested in Mr. Silenieu. Whatever information we could provide them would be a great bargaining tool."

Jean raised her hands; then, dropping them, she shook her head and gave a harsh laugh.

"You're certainly not going to try to protect him? This man has used you very badly."

"It isn't that," she whispered. "It isn't that at all. The truth is I really don't know anything about him."

Warren was silent a moment. "I see. Then we'll have to look for other means of reducing the charges."

"But I can't plead guilty," she said. "It would be admitting I'm a thief, and I'm not."

Warren gazed at her solemnly. "Jean, you're looking at a hundred-and-fifty-thousand-dollar defense, one which you have only a faint chance of winning. I'll be frank with you: I've only come this far because you're a friend. But if you decide to plead not guilty, I'll have to advise you to seek free legal counsel."

Her eyes widened in alarm. Don't desert me! she wanted to cry. But then suddenly she slumped into her chair. She felt both dead and battered, a rag doll whacked repeatedly against a wall by a petulant child. "All right," she said tonelessly. "Whatever you think is best."

He stood up and came around to her. "You've been through an incredible ordeal. Go on home and get some rest. The government has ten days to get an indictment, at which time you'll be formally arraigned. Till then, try not to think too much about it."

She nodded mutely.

He patted her shoulder. "Don't worry. You'll be all right."

SHE WAS SURPRISED to find her apartment just as she had left it—as if the entire world hadn't been devastated in the time she had been away. There was the same disposition of furniture, same half-drawn Levolor blinds; her still-packed valises remained propped at the foot of the bed. She touched one of the suitcases experimentally, as if testing its corporeal existence. Could it really be only forty-eight hours since she had been on the *Gillian* with Robert?

Oh, God, Robert!

The phone started ringing. Woodenly, she picked it up.

"Hello, this is Howard Kaffler of the *Post*. I'd like a statement from you as to . . ."

She slammed it down. She yanked the jack from the wall, then unplugged the other three phones in the apartment. Then she shut the blinds in all the rooms and double-bolted the door.

Her hands were shaking again. "Stop that!" she ordered, but they refused to obey.

Suddenly she began ripping off her clothes: the striped taupe blouse, slim black skirt, her bra, panties, shoes, stockings, all of it. They had been part of the nightmare and so were contaminated. She rolled them in a bundle and stuffed them in the kitchen trash. Then, naked, she ran into a steaming shower, hot almost to the scalding point, and scrubbed until her skin was a raw puckered red and her face had the tight grinning feel of a mask.

She pulled on a clean robe and, so cocooned, walked into the living room where she began to pace in an agitated circle around the couch. What had she really done wrong? She had not set out to steal that money—she had always intended to make it good. They were persecuting her for nothing. And as for her ventures—all businesses needed time to get out of the red. With just a little more time, she would have stopped the debilitating drainage of cash and made them begin paying themselves.

With just a little more time.

Into her thoughts broke the voice of the television newscaster: *"Jean Ferguson, the feminist entrepreneur, was arrested today . . ."* She imagined her father listening to it and turning away in anger and disgust. She could see her old coworkers at IMI chortling with satisfaction, and the women of the Second Street Cooperative congratulating each other for having purged her from their ranks.

And then she had the image of John Dreiser listening to it from a hospital bed. The thought began to seize her that she was responsible for his death. That was crazy, she told herself. He had died years ago. And yet she couldn't shake this ghastly feeling that she was somehow to blame.

You've got to stop this.

She detoured from her circle to the bar and poured a large tumbler of bonded bourbon. She drank it down, refilled it, and continued to drink until she fell at last into a deadened sleep.

She awoke from a dream: she had been flying a biplane from the roof of Minervco into a sky as vast and green as a sea. A boundless feeling of freedom remained with her a moment; then the black weight of reality came crushing back down. With a groan, she tried to bury back into the dream, but it was no use. She was awake.

Breakfast, she thought. She wasn't hungry: her head was pounding, her intestines were on fire. You have to keep up your strength. Make the effort.

She pulled herself into the kitchen, flung open the refrigerator. Nothing much to choose from—just a few porterhouses in the freezer. She unwrapped one of the solid chunks of meat and dropped it in a pan under the broiler. Steak and eggs made a very acceptable breakfast. She had no eggs, of course; but no matter, she'd compromise. Now, what to go with it? A bloody mary. Yes, that would be like a real brunch, very civilized. She was doing quite well. There was no celery though . . . no tomato juice either for that matter. Which called for another compromise . . .

She went out to the bar and poured a glass of straight vodka.

Sipping, she began again to pace the living room. Thoughts like bats kept winging into her brain: she fought them off by walking faster. And then a loud piercing tone sounded just behind her. She jumped, her heart pounding with terror. It came again and she whimpered, feeling concerned. But then at the third tone she gave a wild laugh of relief. It was just the smoke detector by the kitchen door. Yes, now she could see white wisps of smoke curling in the air. It was just a fire.

She went back to the kitchen and pulled out the incinerated remains of the steak. "I must have lost track of the time," she declared aloud. No matter, she hadn't really wanted it anyway. There must be plenty of nourishment in vodka. Made from potatoes. Vitamin C.

Now what?

There was still business to be done, wasn't there? She had to get back in the thick of things, start pulling it all back together. She really had no time to waste.

She plugged in the desk phone, opened her Rolodex, and began calling.

"I'm sorry, Mr. Sintellek's just stepped out . . ."

"Oh, Jean, listen, I've, uh, got some people in my office, can I get back to you?"

"I'm terribly sorry, but I can't seem to locate her right now. Can I take a message?"

One by one, the response was the same. She was through, they were telling her. Finished. She had stumbled off the high wire and there would be no Old Boy net to catch her. They were just going to let her fall.

And wouldn't they be gloating as she hit bottom!

She pulled the phone out again and stared numbly around her apartment. What was she doing cooping herself up like this? She wasn't a prisoner. She could go anywhere she damned pleased.

She dressed hurriedly. She who had always taken such meticulous care in her wardrobe now pulled things at random from closet and drawers, a rumpled blouse, an outdated skirt. Then she bolted out of her apartment and rode the elevator down. Outside she began to walk blindly, not noticing the direction. The world had changed: what used to be a familiar, unthreatening landscape now seemed menacing and alien. She jumped at the sound of a horn, skittered from a boy hoisting a blaring radio. The throngs of midtown shoppers alarmed her: she was certain that everyone knew of her disgrace, that they were staring and pointing her out. She walked faster, keeping her eyes fixed rigidly in front of her.

And now suddenly she found herself on a warehouse street empty of other pedestrians. Idling trucks backed rudely onto the sidewalk and workmen hollered to each other as they tossed gauzily colored bolts of cloth. Where am I? she wondered. How did I get here? She was lost, and she had the terrible sense that she would never find her way home.

And then her attention was caught by a woman. She was large and gaunt and filthy. She wore an orange T-shirt that read ALL THIS AND BRAINS TOO over a mud-encrusted skirt which in turn fell over a derelict's rust-green trousers. Her frizzled gray hair was bound in a rag, her neck was caked with grime, her bare calves and ankles were scabrous above ragged, flopping tennis shoes from which deformed black toes poked out. She was picking through a wire trash basket, scrutinizing each item with a watchmaker's exactitude. She rejected the newspapers, the crumpled coffee cups, a mutilated umbrella. She fished the remainder of a bagel from a Blimpie's bag and crammed it into her mouth. And from the bottom of the basket she drew a treasure—a red-white-and-blue plastic souvenir baseball bat. This she stowed carefully with a cackle of satisfaction in the Lord & Taylor shopping bag at her feet.

Jean couldn't take her eyes off her. She had seen hundreds of such shopping-bag ladies, seen them without really seeing, as if they were a form of life that had no intersection with her own. She had given them no more notice than the cardboard boxes that gusted around corners on windy days or the scruffy cats that skulked beneath parked cars. But now as she watched this woman, she felt a dreadful kinship. That could be me, she thought. My future. Wandering the streets, sleeping in doorways, subsisting on the dregs, the garbage of society.

A convulsive panic seized her. She stumbled to the corner of Tenth Avenue and wildly hailed a cab. "Take me home!" she gasped to the driver.

He turned and grinned. "You'll have to be a little more specific."

This wasn't a Dresden limousine, she reminded herself. "I'm sorry," she said. "It's two-forty East Seventy-fourth."

"You've got it." He stepped on the gas and they sped away.

He was an actor: posted on the Plexiglas divide was his résumé and an eight-by-ten black-and-white "composite" photo. Loudon Mills. Twenty-five, sandy blond, with crinkling, mirthful eyes and a feminine curl to his upper lip. His credits consisted mostly of workshop productions and summer stock with one spot in a Mountain Dew commercial given prominent display on the top of the list.

"Check it out," he said happily, noticing her studying it. "I need all the exposure I can get. I'll follow up any leads, I don't care how crazy, so if you know of anything, let me know."

"I don't, I'm sorry," she said.

"Never hurts to ask." He glanced at her again through the rearview mirror. "What line of work are you in?"

"Me? Oh, business," she said vaguely.

"When you waved me down, I thought you might be an actress. You've got the face for it. You know who you look like a little? Patricia Neal. Remember her? She was in *The Fountainhead* with Gary Cooper. You into old movies? It's around the eyes you kind of remind me of her. Except you're much better looking."

"Thank you," she said. Something inside her responded strongly to his silly praise. She raised her eyes to meet his in the mirror and he winked. He was flirting with her: this realization made the terror subside from her blood. No longer did she see herself akin to that repulsive old crone. She was young, desirable: she still had connection to life.

She leaned forward. "Do you get a lot of response to your résumé?" she asked.

"So-so. I've had a few cards laid on me, a few promises. So far nothing's panned out. 'Course I've only been driving a month."

"Wouldn't you be better off out in Hollywood?"

"Hey, I *come* from there. La-La Land. Throw a stone on Sunset Strip and you hit twenty guys my type. I figured here in New York where everyone's doing Al Pacino I might stand out from the crowd. And also out here you get a shot at the big ad money. I'm reading for a Certs commercial next week." He affected a mincing falsetto: "Oh, Stanley, your breath just killed the canary, and now it's taking the shine off our double-wax floor."

Jean laughed—the first time she had done so in days.

"What d'you think? Do I get the job?"

"Absolutely."

They pulled into the circular drive of her high-rise. He turned around and said in a Clark Gable accent: "That'll be five-sixty, my dear."

Jean looked at her empty hands. "This is embarrassing, but I seem to have come out without my purse," she said. She saw his pretty upper lip pull down and added hastily, "If you'll just come up to my apartment, I'll give you the money and make up for the inconvenience."

"And what do I do with my cab?" he said petulantly.

"It'll be all right. The doorman will keep an eye on it."

"Well, okay."

He followed her inside. She had left the door of her apartment ajar—just as well, she thought, since she had also left her key behind.

"You shouldn't keep your door open like this," her companion observed. "You don't know what kind of maniacs might be running around." His sunny humor seemed to have completely returned. "Hey-o, what a view! Where I live you gotta have a permit to see the sky."

Jean retrieved her purse from the mantel and drew out a twenty-dollar bill. "Here you are," she said.

"A twenty, fan-tastic. Hey, I feel like the guy in the Harry Chapin song. 'Har-ry, keep the change.' " He folded the bill and slid it into his jacket pocket. "So, I'll be seeing you I guess."

"Would you like a drink?" Jean said suddenly.

"You mean right now?"

"Yes. If you've got the time."

His eyes crinkled in an easy grin. "I guess it beats hauling my ass through rush-hour traffic. As long as my car's okay."

"It'll be fine." She moved to the bar and poured two double scotches. She handed him one and took a long swallow of her own. Immediately she felt so nauseated and dizzy that she had to hold on to the bar cart for support. It occurred to her that she hadn't really eaten in two days.

"Are you okay?" The young cabdriver appeared solicitously behind her. She nodded. The dizziness subsided; suddenly she turned and took his handsome face in her hands. "Hey, there," he smiled and bent to her lips. She kissed him back hungrily, with parted mouth. "I knew this was going to happen," he exulted in her ear. "Soon as I saw you in the back seat, I could feel the chemistry."

She didn't reply, but took his lips again and began urgently undoing the buttons of his shirt. She wanted him, his beauty, his strong smiling life. In the past, her desire for a man had always centered upon his position, his abilities and success, but now all she cared about was the feel of muscular flesh against her fingers, the hard pressure of his mouth; she could think of nothing but what he would feel like inside her. She led him into the bedroom, tore at his clothes, helped him with her own, then pulled his broad nakedness against her. He smelled of sweat and soap: she rooted in the hollows of his shoulders and beneath the smooth arc of his rib cage, inhaling with sharp pleasure. She was the aggressor, straddling him, filling herself with him, taking his vigorous life into herself. And then all consciousness caved in. There was only sensation: she was falling, and he was filling her, and all else ceased to matter.

SHE MUST HAVE slept for several hours afterward, for when she opened her eyes it was dark, and she was alone.

She put on her robe and padded out to the living room, but that, too, was deserted. Her visitor was gone.

It occurred to her there was something different about the room. Something was missing. She realized with a start that the coffee table had been picked clean. He had taken everything: the Steuben ashtray, the little Delft posnet pot, the painted ivory fan.

For a moment she was simply numb. And then she felt a shattering, total despair. Of course—he had simply used her because she was available, nothing more. She could have been anyone. . . . And now she had forfeited her last shred of dignity and self-respect.

The feeling of worthlessness that suddenly swept over her was more terrifying than anything else that had happened to her in the last two days. It was a feeling she had never had before in her life. It made her want to run, to hide away where no one would ever see her or get to her again.

She went to the window, drew up the blinds, and gazed down. She had never been the sort of person who brooded about death. Now she thought of it as something safe, a nothingness that was also freedom. The street was fifteen floors below: she looked down as if into a long cool well and thought of falling—of dropping into it as she had into her orgasm, a blissful letting go. It would be fast and thorough. And the empty horror of what she was feeling would be over.

She placed her palms against the pane. And then suddenly she spun around in a panic as someone began pounding at her door.

"Jean? Are you in there? Jean, let me in."

It was Denny. Her whole body contracted. Go away, she willed him. Go away, please, and leave me alone.

"Jean, goddamn it, open the door or I'll fucking kick it in." He began to kick at it with such a violence that she imagined he really would come crashing through. Scarcely breathing, she walked to the door and turned the bolt.

He flung it open. "Thank God you're okay," he said.

"How did you get past the doorman?" she asked rigidly.

"I walked. Christ, Jean, we've all been worried sick. I've been calling every ten minutes. Mom's on the edge of a complete nervous breakdown. Even your lawyer's been frantic."

"So they all know then. Mother, Dad, everyone . . ."

"All we know is that you've been arrested for some bad-check thing, and all the lines at Minervco are down . . ." He seemed to really look at her for the first time and caught his breath. "Jesus, Jean," he whispered. "Just what the hell has been going on?"

She turned stiffly away. "What's been going on is that my company is bankrupt and Paul has absconded with everything that was left and the entire world is suing me, and I've spent a night in jail and I'm very likely going to go back. I'm finished, my future is shot. I've failed at every single thing I've set out to do, and I wish to God I was dead." She walked to the bar. She could scarcely hold a bottle her hands were shaking so much. "And I imagine all of this gives you a pretty great satisfaction," she added.

He looked at her, aghast. "Why do you say that?"

"You've always accused me of selling out, haven't you? Weren't you just waiting all this time for me to fall on my face and prove you right?"

"You really think that?"

She shrugged coldly. "There you are all safe and snug in architecture school with a brilliant career no doubt all laid out in front of you. And here I am back to nothing. It seems pretty cut and dried to me. You were right, I was wrong."

She put the glass to her lips. Denny grabbed it away and slammed it on the table. Then he yanked her by the arm and sat her on the couch. "I want you to listen to me for a minute," he said. "I admit I acted pretty smug at one time about what I was doing as opposed to you. But you've got to understand where it was coming from. Remember all those fucking races when we were kids and you'd complain I wasn't even trying? Well, you were right, for Christ's sake. I wasn't. Because as long as I didn't try, I couldn't really lose. And if I didn't really lose, I couldn't really be the failure Dad thought I was."

"I didn't think you ever cared what Dad thought."

"Didn't you? Christ, I cared so much I was willing to ruin my life just to prove a point to him. I actually managed to convince myself for a while that I had finally gotten out of the old man's control. But the fact was I was so busy doing the opposite of everything I thought he wanted, I was really giving him more control than ever. He was still running my life, just as he's been running yours."

"Mine?" she said numbly.

"Yeah, yours. Haven't you been knocking yourself out long enough just to drag back trophies for his approval? He's not fucking worth it, Jean. Look at him buying toys, running around with girls half his age, trying desperately to pretend he's still twenty-five. Do you really want to go on making all your efforts for some bastard who's so royally fucked up his own life? And who's never going to appreciate what you do anyway?"

Jean was silent.

"The truth is," Denny went on, "I've always been amazed, awed, a bit scared, and most of all damned proud of who you are and what you've done. The only thing I really didn't like was that some of the pieces didn't fit—they seemed to be only there to please someone else. From now on whatever you do has got to be entirely for yourself."

She was trembling now throughout her entire body. "It

doesn't matter," she said. "I can't go on anymore. I just want to die."

"Don't talk shit. You've touched bottom—use it to push off. You can start making your way back up now."

"I can't live with no future. I've got nothing left."

"You've got yourself. Your talent, your looks, your intelligence . . ."

"Oh, Christ, Denny, don't patronize me."

"I'm not. You're the strongest person I know. And to see you giving in to this whining, defeatist self-pity makes me so fucking sick I almost feel like pushing you out that window myself."

The fierceness of his tone startled her for a moment. Then she said, "How did you know?"

"Know what?"

"It was the window?"

He looked confused a moment. "Did I say that?"

"Yes. And I really had been standing there thinking about jumping out. Just before you came."

He shrugged. "Maybe we've been closer than we've wanted to admit these past few years. We're both kind of stubborn, you know."

"God, don't I know." She closed her eyes and leaned her head back against the couch. "I've really fucked things up, haven't I?"

"Don't you think maybe it's because you were playing a fucked-up role to begin with?"

She tried to answer him and couldn't. Instead her mind was filled with a vivid image of herself running on a limitless rolling highway. She was pursuing an enormous flatbed truck which for some reason she knew she was supposed to be onboard. It had a high, powerful engine and the gears shrieked when they were engaged. She couldn't quite tell who was the driver. Perhaps her father, perhaps John

Dreiser. Or it could even be some stranger who didn't even know she was in pursuit. But the faster she ran, the more the truck accelerated until the distance between them had become untraversable. And now as it spurted toward the horizon she suddenly sensed that once it was finally gone she would be free. She could stop running if she pleased; or she could go on taking this turn or that: whichever, the decision would be hers alone.

The image remained with her a moment as vivid as a dream. Then it dispersed and she opened her eyes. And then she felt a slight rumbling in her stomach, a vital drawing feeling that she recognized with some joy. "Hey, Denny," she said. "You know what? I'm *hun*gry."

WHAT DO YOU wear to a sentencing? Particularly if it's your own?

Jean had stood before her closet for close to an hour this morning feeling almost overwhelmed by this simple question. Warren had advised something modest but not dowdy. *Ladylike* was his word. She had tried on and discarded half a dozen outfits, coming close to tears in a panic of indecision. Her mother had finally stepped in, choosing the perfect gray linen suit and plucking from the back of the rack a demure mauve cotton blouse to go with it.

Jean hadn't wanted her mother to come. "The last thing I need is Mother weeping and going to pieces all over the place," she had declared to Denny. But Dorothy Ferguson had whisked in dry-eyed and determined. The woman who had never seemed quite capable of taking charge of her own life now suddenly mustered enormous reserves of fortitude. She took efficient charge of the details that had lately overwhelmed Jean, and she sternly disallowed her daughter to wallow in self-recriminations. Jean had at first hesitantly, then with great relief, let herself lean on her mother's shoulder. In the past few weeks they had become closer than they had ever been before.

And now as she sat in the dim, dark-paneled courtroom, Jean was grateful that her mother was sitting behind her. Denny was there too, of course. And Kate. Jean was still ashamed of the abominable way she had treated Kate when Kate had come to pick her up from the detention center. She had been literally out of her mind that day. Fortunately Kate seemed to understand—and she had remained one of the few people to stick by her through all this. Jean smiled slightly. She had a feeling some of Kate's staunch loyalty had something to do with Denny. How funny if after all these years they were to finally get together. . . .

Jean's thoughts were pulled by a more repulsive thought: there would be reporters sitting back there too. She had never gotten used to the public trumpeting of her arrest and arraignment. She had stopped reading newspapers and sank into a depression whenever she inadvertently heard a mention of herself on radio or television. Now they would be back there x-raying her with their eyes, taking down everything she said and did. . . .

But she would not allow herself to think about that. She sat up straighter on the bench and glanced at Warren beside her. He gave her an encouraging nod. He had plea bargained to get the charge of wire fraud and one charge of bank theft dropped in return for a plea of guilty to the "B" part of the statute covering the remaining charge. "It's still bank theft," he had cautioned her, "but it carries a lesser charge. And since this is your first offense and you've agreed to make total restitution of the funds, I think we're in a good position." They had drawn a Judge Carmine Cappola. "He's fair," Warren had pronounced. "We've got a chance."

And now Judge Cappola was entering the courtroom. He was small, dark, barrel-chested; his high forehead and recessed black eyes suggested intelligence. Jean felt a surge of hope. She clasped her hands tightly together in her lap.

The government attorney declined to make a statement. Then Warren rose and delivered his plea for leniency. Jean hardly heard his words. Her hands were cold in her lap; there was a tightness in her stomach and the inside of her mouth felt dry as sand.

And then it was her turn: the judge was asking if she wished to make a statement. She rose and faced him, feeling suddenly in complete control. This after all was where she excelled: she had always had the ability to handle herself well under fire.

"Your honor," she said. "You and every man in this courtroom have one singular advantage over me: you were brought up with the expectation that you would become something—that you would make a mark in life. As such, you were encouraged to understand the workings of the world right from the start. By the age of twenty—the age I finally decided I would have to find what was out there for myself—most of you had already been at it twenty years.

"I was a complete pioneer. Not only did I have to countermand my entire upbringing, I also chose to enter a field that was particularly unreceptive to women. Few women had ever achieved any sort of success in venture capital. I had no guides, no allies. I was met with prejudice and resentment all along the way. I had to kick down door after door, and fight every step, to take greater risks, be more adventurous, creative, and aggressive than most of my male colleagues.

"And in doing so I had to make a lot of sacrifices. My success was, I'll admit, gratifying. But I had almost no personal life at all. The lack of love—of sharing and intimacy— left me feeling horribly incomplete. I had always believed I could get everything I wanted by hard work and determination. To find out that this wasn't true—that I was still lacking this one most important part of my life—made me desperate. I lost perspective. I made a bad alliance, convinced myself that it was all right to bend the rules. And as a result, rather than getting everything I wanted, I lost it all instead.

"I know that what I did was wrong. When I wrote the checks on empty accounts, I was fully aware that I hadn't the funds to cover them. But theft had never been my intention—I always intended to make the money good. I have suffered severely as a result of my mistakes, and I've also learned from them. What I ask now is a chance to start again—and this time to do it right."

She finished with a deep breath and looked at Warren who gave another nod. She must have been all right.

And now Judge Cappola was addressing her. She dug her fingernails into the palms of her hands.

"The court is not unmindful that you were undergoing emotional stress, and that you've agreed to restitution," he said. "However, white-collar crime must be treated as seriously as blue. There is a growing perception by the public that we've become too lenient in dealing with white-collar offenders, and this may have some justification. I'm compelled to add that it is unfortunately rare that banks are willing to press charges—therefore, when they do, it is especially necessary to give a sentence that will deter others from engaging in similar activity.

"The eyes of the community are watching. I hereby sentence you to a period of imprisonment of three years, imposition of sentence suspended on the condition you serve three months and the remainder on probation."

Jean heard nothing after that, just the pounding of her own heart, the rasp of her breathing and the one incredulous thought—that she, the golden girl, was about to go to jail.

*A*NDREA HERRY BROLENSKY PAUSED BEFORE THE FADED wooden door and nervously adjusted the waistband of her gabardine skirt. She was stalling for time. It had taken every scrap of her courage to call Jean this morning and tell her she was in New York; and though Jean had responded immediately, Andrea still dreaded the possible awkwardness—even hostility—of the meeting. Nearly a year had passed since they had last spoken; ten months since Andrea had placed the call to François Hokosawa. She had no idea how Jean felt toward her now—nor for that matter what her own feelings for Jean actually were.

Her own life had changed dramatically in the past year. She still kept in her wallet the folded clipping from the *Bay Guardian* personals which by now she knew by heart:

  Widower w/2 chldrn, 27, 5'11", 155 lbs. Warm, sincere, affectionate and attractive. Into long walks in city and country, camping, bluegrass, good health in body and

> *spirit. Seeks sincere, open, family-oriented woman for*
> *loving and committed relationship.*

It had been the mention of children she supposed that had prompted her to respond, even though she was almost four years older than twenty-seven and had never answered a personal before. He had called within a week. His name was Gordon Brolensky, and he had a gentle, kidding voice that she found appealing. They made a date to meet for a walk in Golden Gate Park the following Sunday.

She had recognized him immediately. He was balding and bearded with mild brown eyes that matched his voice; and he was dressed in a rather musty corduroy suit that would be shed (Andrea was certain) for baggy pants and an ancient sweater the instant he got home. A black Labrador puppy frisked at his feet, and he held the hands of two little girls. One was blond, the other a curly brunette, but their identical moon faces declared them sisters. They were dressed in matching pink smocked dresses with puffy sleeves. Andrea took one look at them and fell hopelessly in love.

Their names were Laura and Maggie. They bounded on ahead with the Lab, Ayatollah, while their father strolled more sedately with Andrea. He was shy at first: but once the ice was broken, he talked eagerly about himself—not in a self-centered manner but in a way that suggested he sincerely wanted her to know. He worked as an administrator for the city's labor resource department. Not a great job; "I'm not hugely ambitious," he admitted. But the generous vacations allowed him more time for the kids and to do the things he really liked—camping and photography and noodling on the banjo. He grew up in Lafayette, Indiana, had gone to college in the Bay Area and fallen in love with it— now couldn't imagine living anywhere else, except maybe the Canadian Rockies near Vancouver. He had married his wife Kiki in his senior, her junior, year. She had been a social worker before she'd had the kids, and she had drowned three years before while sailing Lazers in Puget Sound.

"How hard for you," Andrea had said softly. "Especially with the girls so tiny."

"It was rough," he acknowledged. "And I was pretty bitter for awhile. But her death did have some positive effects for me. It made me closer and more spiritually bound to my kids than I think I could ever have been otherwise. And it also renewed my faith in God." He explained that he hadn't been brought up in a very religious household. His parents were only nominal Catholics, and like everyone else at college, he had regarded the whole idea of organized religion as pretty ludicrous. "But when Kiki died, I needed I guess you could say *meaning*. For lack of any better way, I started going to mass. And then suddenly it hit me—you had no choice. You either had faith, or you had nothing. The void." He paused and then fixed upon her his mild smile. "I don't want to sound fanatical or anything. But it was the thing that got me through."

And then abruptly, as if a little embarrassed by his confidences, he invited Andrea back for lunch.

They lived in the Haight, a neighborhood which had swung from hippie haven to drug-infested slum, and now, as young middle-class families reclaimed the old Victorians, was becoming "gentrified." Andrea volunteered to change the children. She helped them out of their dresses, inhaling their fragrant hair and happily answering their relentless questions while she buttoned up their "dungies." Then she led them into the kitchen where Gordon (having indeed exchanged his suit for comfortable old clothes) was slapping mayonnaise on slices of sprouted-wheat.

After lunch, it had been pleasant to sit with him in the

scruffy little back garden, watching the girls dig in the dry dirt while the dog sunned lethargically at their feet. Gordon brought her Emperor's Choice tea in a handleless Smurf mug, then peppered her with questions about her childhood, her career, the things she liked to do. She remembered that he had asked her if she was happy being a lawyer, and she had replied that she would be if she thought she were doing more good. "My wife used to complain about the same thing in her job," he said, and added, "You remind me a little of her."

The following Saturday they had gone for a picnic on the Bear Peninsula—a huge success until Ayatollah picked up a tick in one shoulder, prompting an early return. And that evening it had been Andrea who had tucked the girls into bed, heard their prayers, kissed their rosy, damp foreheads good night.

She began going to the Haight in the evenings as soon as she could escape from work. And on Sundays she began going with them to church. She had forgotten the sensation of sitting in a hard-backed pew while the peace and solemn stillness of liturgy washed over her. The diffuse light, the wording of the prayers, the sonority of a fading organ chord—such things carried to her a sense of continuation, a bridge to the distant years of her childhood; and, rather than distressing her, this seemed comforting and right. The mass was very different from the simple service she had grown up with. She was bewildered by the number of times the congregation, on some invisible cue, suddenly rose or sat down again, or swung to their knees; and the celebrant's ritual was equally mysterious to her. Yet when the congregation began to recite the familiar words "Our Father, Who art in Heaven," she closed her eyes and loudly recited the prayer with them. She no longer knew quite to whom she was praying. Certainly not to the florid-faced man in the square black glasses. But the radiant peace that had then flooded over her must have had to descend from somewhere—and it was to that source then that she had directed her prayers.

One drowsy Sunday night, while Andrea sat skimming the draft of a pleading she would need for the following week, she had sensed Gordon's eyes upon her. She glanced at him over the top of her glasses and smiled.

"Hey, Andy?" he had said. "Do you want to get married?"

"Hmmm?"

"Do you want to get married?"

She had let the pages drop into her lap while she stared at him speechlessly.

"I love you," he had said. "I'd be terribly, ecstatically happy if you married me."

"But we've only known each other a few months," she had replied.

"So? Are we on some kind of time schedule?"

"No, but don't you think we should get to know each other better first?"

His smile implied he'd already anticipated this objection. "You really think that what we don't know by now we ever will?"

He was right; she saw that immediately. She was thirty-one years old, had been dating for fifteen years—she ought to have a pretty good idea by now of what she wanted.

And as for Gordon. . . . Well, he knew she was four years older than he was, that she was divorced and might be sterile, that she was twenty pounds overweight and didn't seem likely ever to be much thinner. If none of these things had deterred him, probably nothing else about her was likely to either.

And one thing was for certain: she wanted his children. She thought of the moon faces flushed in sleep, the tiny

hands curled in hers when they went walking. She was fond
of Gordon, felt comfortable and happy in his company. But
she was desperately, passionately in love with his children.

"Okay," she had replied. "Let's get married."

"Laura and Maggie're gonna go wild," he had said.

That night for the first time they made love. Gordon was
tender and patient, and Andrea tried very hard to take the
pleasure he was so anxious to give. But they had not been
alone in the bed. No, Douglas had been there with them,
with his bullying hands forcing things from her she wasn't
ready to give. And Rick, he was there too, making her feel
she was too fat and too hairy, that her body odors were
repellant, and that anyway she would never learn to Do It
right. And Burton pulling out in the middle of things, and
Randy, shrinking from her touch—they had been with them
too. And continued to be ever since, preventing Andrea
from ever really letting go.

But afterward that first night, Gordon had stroked her
hair, and the dog on the floor murmured and stretched, and
one of the children had coughed softly beyond the door.
Nothing else mattered, Andrea had realized. She could live
her life without orgasms, despite what she had once been
made to believe. But she couldn't live her life without love.

QUIT STALLING, ANDREA told herself sharply. You
can't stand outside this door all day. Resolutely she turned
the dented brass knob and pushed it open. Inside was an
office—small, unluxurious, one might say shabby—but emi-
nently functional for all of that. And behind a green metal
desk sat Jean looking as elegant and composed as Andrea
had last seen her.

She rose and smiled. "Hey," she said. "I'm glad you
made it." She came around her desk, then hesitated; and
Andrea realized with a slight shock that Jean was as nervous

about this meeting as she was. She decided to make the first move: she took a step forward, arms warily opened; and then both rushed to meet in a tentative, rather clumsy, embrace. They separated and smiled at each other a shade too broadly.

"Well," Jean said. "Sit down." She indicated a homely green corduroy couch. "God, it's been a long time, hasn't it?"

"Almost a year," Andrea said. "It seems like ages."

"You look terrific. And you said on the phone you've gotten married again. Who, when, and where?"

"His name's Gordon Brolensky. He's a widower with two children and he works for labor resources," Andrea recited. "We were married four months ago, a very small wedding in a vineyard a friend of his owns up in Sonoma County. Just a dozen people and the girls as our attendants. This is sort of a delayed honeymoon for us. We're visiting Gordon's brother, who's an oculist out in Morristown, New Jersey. Tomorrow we're taking Jerry's four kids along with our own and going camping in the Poconos." She wondered if she was rattling on too much and stopped, a bit flustered.

"How old are your husband's children?" Jean asked.

"One's going on five, the other's six. Gordon's got them up at the Natural History Museum, scaring the pants off them I'll bet with the dinosaurs." Andrea gave a little laugh. "I miss them already."

"It sounds like you do," Jean said. An awkward silence fell between them. Then Jean added abruptly, "You know, Andrea, I've wanted to call you for a long time. But frankly I was afraid you wouldn't want to hear from me. I thought you might hate me."

Andrea glanced down at her hands. She compared the scraggly, bitten fingernails with Jean's, which were short but smoothly shaped and gleaming with clear polish; and for

a moment she felt a tug of her old desire to be more like Jean
Ferguson. "I guess I did hate you for a while," she said
slowly. "Or at least I thought I did. It took me till now to
realize that what I was really angry at you for was not being
the perfect, infallible idol I'd built you into. You were supposed to be everything I ever wanted to be and couldn't."

Jean gave a dry laugh. "Talk about feet of clay."

"No, not clay, just flesh and blood like everyone else,"
Andrea said quickly. "But you know, I was petrified of calling you, too. I felt so guilty about what I'd done to you. After I found out I had lost all my money, I should have waited
to talk to you and see if we could work it out. I shouldn't
have gone vindictively behind your back and called that
bank."

"No, you had every reason to do what you did. I had
acted completely irresponsibly. And sooner or later it was
all going to come tumbling down anyway." She smiled.
"You know, Andrea, when I was first arrested and they
gave me a phone to call a lawyer, the only thing I could
think of was calling you."

"Oh, God, Jean, and there I was sabotaging you! How
could I be so rotten?"

"You don't have a rotten bone in your body," Jean declared softly. "And anyway I ended up with a damned good
lawyer."

"You did have to serve a few months, didn't you?" Andrea said delicately.

"Three. Luckily I was allowed to do them here in the detention center. It's a pretty decent facility."

"Still, I know enough of prisons to know it's never any
fun."

"No, it certainly isn't. There's such excruciating boredom, for one thing. And you feel totally disgraced, of
course. But worst of all is just the sensation of not being

free.'' A shudder went through Jean's thin shoulders. ''You can't possibly imagine what it's like until it happens. Every day, I'd sit there thinking about little things—kicking up snow in a freshly fallen bank, or running down a beach, the way the sand at the surf-line feels crispy under your feet. Or simply walking down the street on a fall day and throwing your head back to look at the sky. I'd realize that this—this exuberance of life—is ninety percent of everything. And I'd wonder why I'd spent so much effort chasing that ephemeral little ten percent. The money and power and all that.''

Andrea looked so stricken that Jean laughed. ''I'd think that lawyers would be immune to this kind of talk.''

''Oh, you get used to hard stories. But somehow, hearing it from *you* . . .''

''But there were some good things about the experience too,'' Jean cut in quickly. ''The other women—some of them were extraordinary. You know I'd always given lip service to the concept of women helping each other, but now I was actually seeing it happen. Instances of amazing generosity and courage . . . It made me thoroughly ashamed of all my empty talk before.''

Andrea nodded sympathetically. ''And what are your plans now?''

''Well, I've got no assets, a lousy reputation, and roughly a quarter million worth of debts and legal fees. But crazy or not, I'm starting all over again.''

''A new company?''

''Several things actually. I've got a corporate barter service that's starting to get off the ground, and I'm looking into a few small real-estate deals. And I've been working on nonprofit funding to put together an employment reference service for women with criminal records.'' She caught Andrea's wary glance and added, ''Don't worry, I'm not slipping back into my old ways. I'm starting small—just me and a phone, basically, until the business can really support expansion. And this time I'm not letting it take control of my life. One of the conditions of my parole is ten hours a week community service. I'm doing it at a Methadone clinic—and it's a hell of a good way to keep your perspective. I've also been getting up each morning and running two miles in the park. And I'm seeing a man—someone older, someone I respect a lot. . . ." She seemed suddenly abashed by her own outpouring; gazing down, she pushed a sweep of dark hair back from her chin. But she added firmly, "In five years, I'm determined to make it again. But this time I want to do it right—in a way that really gives *me* a sense of achievement and self-respect."

"I know you will," Andrea burst in. "I've still got a supreme amount of confidence in you."

Jean accepted this with a simple smile. "Hey, how about some coffee? I've only got instant, unfortunately, and no milk . . ."

"That sounds fine."

Jean rose and set an enameled red kettle on a hot plate on her desk. She plugged in the plate, then heaped teaspoons of Yuban into plastic mugs. Andrea, watching her, wondered why this little labor seemed so incongruous—until it struck her that she had never seen Jean perform any domestic task before—not even one as simple as this.

Jean turned back to her. "I want you to know, Andrea," she said, "that I intend to pay back every cent of the money you lost."

"You're not obligated to," Andrea said quickly.

"God, I couldn't live with myself if I didn't."

"Well—if you ever do strike it rich, I won't pretend we couldn't use the money. Gordon makes no great fortune working for a city agency, you know. And I make nothing at all as a housewife."

Jean stared at her. "Do you mean you've quit law?"

"For the time being. Now I take care of my children, and I help Gordon in his career when he needs it. I tend the garden, bake sunflower-seed bread, crochet bedspreads, and do volunteer work for the local Democratic Club. I also wash the dog, write letters to the paper, and for the first time in twelve years I've read a novel in French." She steeled herself. "Are you shocked?"

"I'm surprised, yes."

"Do you think I'm a complete fool for wasting all my education and hard-earned expertise?"

"No," Jean said. "It's your choice to make. If what you're doing makes you happy, who am I to say it's not valuable?"

"Thanks. Some of the women I know have made me feel like a traitor for dropping out."

"Do you think you'll ever go back?"

"I don't know. Part of me is really made for the domestic role. But I miss the influence and authority I used to have. And I still have a bit of my old hankering to save the world. This political stuff I've been getting into is pretty intriguing. Who knows, maybe I'll run for assemblyman one of these days." She gave a ripple of laughter, but some note behind it made Jean look at her in a new way.

"Damn it, Andrea," she said. "You just might end up amazing us all yet." She filled the two mugs with boiling water and carried them with several packets of Sugar In The Raw back to the sofa.

This is nice, Andrea thought, dissolving the light brown crystals into her steaming mug. Here we are, two women sitting on a couch sharing our thoughts over coffee—just as women have done for years and years before us, and will probably go on doing for years and years to come. Despite changes and upheavals and God knows what triumphs and reverses, this no doubt will endure.

"You know, Jean," she said suddenly. "Maybe if we can just keep from judging each other—as women I mean—well, maybe *that* will finally be our biggest step."

*I*T HAD BEEN SIX MONTHS NOW SINCE KATE HAD MOVED IN with Denny. In many ways it had been Jean's arrest that had been responsible for the change in their relationship. It was that crisis that had thrown them steadily together. It had given Kate endless opportunity to respond physically to Denny; and his gratitude to her for putting up Jean's bail had—Kate suspected —been the first step to rekindling warmer feelings.

She would, of course, have helped Jean in any case—her own debt to Jean was enormous. But her feelings for Denny had simply made it that much easier to give his sister her fullest support.

And yet even for some time afterward, Kate couldn't decide if she had made any progress. There were times when she thought she caught him looking at her in the old way, and some quick bright bird of hope would flutter inside her. But then, if he caught her eye, the fleeting tenderness would broaden into a grin of uncomplicated good humor, and Kate would wonder if she had seen what she had hoped at all. She

409

often found herself plucking an invisible daisy petal: he doesn't care, he does. He doesn't.

The irony of it had not escaped her. A decade spent tripping into bed with strangers whose names you barely caught, strangers of a day's acquaintance, an hour's—and here she was at a total loss for a way to turn a friend of that decade's duration into a lover. Crazy, mixed-up decade. She remembered how back in college she had been overwhelmed by what she had thought were new rules. But she had been wrong—there had been *no* rules. No role models, no signposts, no guides of any sort to help them out of the virgin savanna they had suddenly found themselves stranded in. They were the first—and it had been up to them to hack their own paths through.

One evening she had called Denny and suggested they go out for a drink. A year before she would have simply told him she felt like coming up to see him, but now she found herself elaborating a long story about having to be in the neighborhood anyway. And as she picked him up at his apartment, she had felt suddenly as if she were fourteen again and he were the most popular boy in the class. For every baby step forward it seemed she was also taking two whacking giant umbrella steps back.

They had walked over to the West End bar, where Denny ran into several people he knew. He'd always had a lot of acquaintances—no matter where he went, invariably someone would be pushing forward to greet him. Watching him, Kate recalled how intensely she used to monitor Stephen with other people—how, if they had seemed to admire him, she would swell with pride, but if she had sensed the least mockery or disdain she would immediately want to withdraw. She realized now that she didn't care in the least what other people thought of Denny. The whole world could ridicule or praise him, but her feelings would remain the same.

Afterward they had strolled out into the soft night, heading west toward Riverside Park. For several blocks they were silent. When Denny began to speak, it was about Jean. It was several weeks since her sentencing and he still hadn't recovered from the shock of it.

"I can't help thinking that if I'd gone to work with her, the whole thing never would've happened," he said. "When she suggested it, I acted as if she wanted me to drop napalm on Vietnamese babies. All the time congratulating myself for being so nobly noncompetitive. Never facing the fact that I was just scared shitless of competing with her. Better to drop out of the game completely than risk getting licked by my big sister."

"Even if you had though, what good would it have done?" Kate countered. "You said yourself Jean never really relinquishes control."

"Not without a fight. But don't forget, we come from the same stock. When it comes down to it, I can be as persistent and mulishly stubborn in my own way as she is in hers."

"And how long do you think you'd have been happy going head to toe with Jean every day?"

He shrugged. "I could've stuck it out. And who knows, we both could've been filthy rich by now." Kate shot him a skeptical glance and he grinned. "Okay, maybe you're right. I'm not cut out to be an empire builder."

"Just a builder."

"Yeah, one of these days. But Christ, sometimes it seems like it's going to take forever." He slapped the pockets of his long leather jacket. "Damn, I left my cigarettes in the bar."

"Want to go back toward Broadway?"

"No, skip it. I'll give my lungs a rest."

They continued wandering down Riverside, skirting the park. "Where are we going?" Denny asked.

"I don't know. I guess we're just walking."

"Why do I get the feeling there's something I should be saying?"

She glanced at him.

"Lately whenever we're talking," he said, "I get the feeling you're listening for something. And whatever it is, I don't seem to be coming up with it."

His perception flustered her. "It must be some hangover from work," she said. "You know, when you look and listen to as much stuff as I do every day, you're bound to start editing every conversation." She added quickly, "By the way, whatever happened to that woman Nancy you were seeing?"

"Nancy Koska? She's around. I haven't called her in a while."

"I guess you've been pretty distracted."

"Yeah. But it wasn't going anywhere anyway."

Kate brightened. "You seemed so enthusiastic about her for a while."

"There was a hell of a physical attraction. But the thing was she had no conversation. I got tired of bouncing the old ball and having it just drop dead at her feet." His hands hunted his empty pockets again, a smoker's reflex. "How about you?" he said. "You seeing anybody special?"

"Me? No."

"That advertising guy at Walt Link's party ever call you up? The one who kept deluging you with vodka gimlets?"

"I gave him a phony number. You seriously didn't think I'd be interested in a jerk like that?"

"Seriously, no. But I've given up trying to figure who goes for anyone anymore."

Kate gave him a quick look. "You're thinking of me and Stephen, aren't you? I know you couldn't stand him."

"I wasn't crazy about the guy, that's for sure."

"You must have thought I was completely out of my mind staying with him all that time."

"Well, I always thought you were selling yourself short. But I guess I could see what attracted you to him."

"God." Kate shuddered. "I can't anymore."

"Oh, I think whatever it is you once loved about someone you're always going to love. Even if the rest of what they are seems totally revolting now."

Kate again felt that swift flutter of hope. She turned her eyes to the park. Through the ragged black patches of trees she caught a glimpse of the river and the sheer wall of the palisades beyond. To the south, the silhouettes of tall towers seemed fabulous and remote, the shadow of a city built upon the most fragile of aspirations. "Denny," she said suddenly, "were you ever in love with me?"

He gave a startled laugh. "You mean you couldn't tell? Back in school, I thought it was public record."

"Back in school," she echoed. "I suppose it must be pretty hard for you to imagine now."

"Are you fishing for a little flattery? Well, I don't mind telling you I still get a little click of something whenever I see you. It's what I said before—if it was there once, it's always going to be there in one form or another."

She kept her eyes turned away. "You want to know what's funny? I've kind of fallen in love with you."

There was no reply. Her heart sank. Stupid, stupid, to expose herself like an idiot! Denny must be horribly embarrassed, probably pitying her, wondering how to let her down tactfully without totally blowing their friendship. "I told you it was crazy," she said with a strained laugh. "I guess I've just been in the mood for incest lately. Forget I even said that."

She turned from him and began to walk back along the highway.

"The hell I will," she heard him say, and then in the next moment she was safely, perfectly, in his arms.

SHE HAD AWAKENED that next morning in Denny's bed, with Denny breathing gently beside her. Her eyes had opened upon objects that were at once familiar and new. There was his old Gibson guitar leaning against the bureau; there was the garish orange clay owl he had dragged back from Guadalajara and the curling photograph of his mother as a girl in Georgia. She had seen these things a thousand times, yet now they were transformed, visitations from some more hallowed and shimmering dimension.

And riding the subway home (the same graffiti-splashed IRT local that had hauled her back and forth from Dr. Greenfrier's) she had hugged moments of the night before to herself. Their bodies had been shy with each other at first. But then emotion had taken over and they had spilled into long, laughing, cuddling love, filled with discovery and surprise.

After all the years of thinking it *had* to be hard—that pain was inevitable, that men and women were somehow different species that never could be reconciled—it had made her dizzy to think that it could actually be so easy. That it was possible to make love with someone and wake up the next morning fully confident of still being wanted—of not suddenly finding some snarling or icily aloof monster beside you. It was all so breathtakingly easy. . . .

And it had continued easy, Kate had moved into Denny's apartment, and they had begun living happily together. Sunday, the day she used to dread, the day of endless afternoon bleeding into forlorn night, now became a time to treasure. A lazy browsing through the *Times*, an aromatic sluice of coffee beans into a grinder. The quiet shared, not suffered.

And Kate loved the way they could talk. Not just "how

was your day" kind of rote conversation, but often really sharing their thoughts, informing each other and making each other laugh. Kate shuddered to remember how once before going to meet Stephen for dinner she had actually sat down and written out a list of Things to Talk About. How completely warped and unnatural! This *flow*, this easy give and take was the way it was supposed to be.

They had of course had a fight or two. Over some silly thing or another, hurling words like *insensitive* and *utterly selfish* at each other. But even at their most heated points, Kate had never worried that it signaled the end of their relationship. Denny had made it perfectly clear that he was committed to her. He gave her the security in love that Stephen had made her feel somehow deficient for wanting. Which was all wonderful.

Except . . .

Well, lately she had a strange restlessness. Not that she had stopped loving Denny. It was just that the little requisites of sharing sometimes made her feel restricted. For instance this morning, Maxine Bludhorn who had been in her class at Hadley had called to invite her to dinner. "Laurie Haas's going to be there," Maxine said. "Remember her? She was in Decker House. Now she's doing research on recombinant DNA up in Boston. You guys think you can make it?"

Kate had given her standard reply: "Sounds good. I'll check with Denny and get back to you." But the moment she hung up, she felt some small cinder of resentment smolder within her. Why should she have to check with anyone before making plans? For years she had been a free agent, coming and going exactly as she pleased. Why should she be so restrained now?

The catch phrases of her generation began to whisper at her. No one person can supply all your needs. Why give up your options? Who knows what romance you might be missing out there?

It was true that lately she had caught herself looking at other men with a certain wistfulness. A lean, blond man emerging from a taxi in front of the Plaza. Warren Beatty on a talk show. A kid in the subway, he couldn't have been more than twenty-two, but with one of the most truly beautiful faces she had ever seen. . . .

What was she missing?

This evening her restlessness was at a peak. Everything about Denny tonight seemed to trigger in her some irritation. His chipped front tooth that marred his wide smile. The way he absently gulped his dinner at his drawing board.

And when they finally went to bed, he kissed her and fell quickly asleep. Although they had made love just the night before, even this annoyed her. We're getting bogged in a domestic rut, she thought testily.

The phone rang sometime after two, jerking her awake with a foggy dread. Dad . . . or Mother . . . She lifted the receiver fearfully.

"Kate?" It was a woman's voice, tearful and desperate. "It's Sissy. Can I talk to you a minute?"

"Sissy?" Kate swam through an odd displacement in time. She was once again camping on Sissy Dreifus's couch plotting ways to get Stephen to take her back. But then her thoughts cleared, dispersing that dreadful notion. This was four years later. Stephen was long over, and though she and Sissy kept in touch, they had drifted into different circles, different neighborhoods, different habits of life. "Sissy, what's wrong?" she asked. "Has something happened?"

"Oh, God, Kate! I'm going out of my mind. It's Ben—I don't know what to believe and what not to anymore. He keeps telling me the divorce is going through and then I learn from his best friend that he hasn't even filed separation papers yet. He lies about everything, how much money he's got, his father being in the State Department, and about other women, and when I confront him, he tells me *I'm* the one who's sick and suspicious, and I'm the one who needs help. Tonight we had a terrific fight, and he accused me of using sex as a weapon to get at him, and so I threw my diaphragm out the window, really launched it like a flying saucer, so then he called me crazy and a real sicko and walked out. And oh, God, I just had to talk to someone!''

"Listen, Sissy," Kate broke in. "Why don't I come down there, okay?"

"Could you?"

"Sure. I'll be there in about half an hour, okay?"

Kate pulled on jeans and a sweater, and, after assuring Denny she'd be all right, went down and hailed a cruising cab on Broadway. Twenty minutes later she rang Sissy's bell.

Sissy's broad face was swollen to grotesque distortion from the violence of her crying. She attempted a feeble gesture of welcome; then, like a child, burrowed against Kate's shoulder. Kate held her and patted her back. How strange to recall that she had once envied Sissy her flamboyant style and ostensibly glamorous life! Then into her mind flashed a picture of herself crawling to Sissy's door with bruised red eyes and sniveling nose, and a muscle contracted in her stomach.

"I feel terrible dragging you all this way down," Sissy said weakly. "I didn't even think what time it was."

"Don't worry about that. Just tell me what happened."

She lifted her hands in baffled helplessness. "It's the same old thing. He says one thing and does another until I'm just completely traumatized. He keeps swearing he really loves me, but if he does, why does he keep treating me this way? I've been *living* on Valium, but it doesn't even do any good anymore, I'm such a total wreck.'' Her face crumpled and her shoulders began to heave. "Oh, God, I can't stand it anymore. I really can't.''

Kate pressed her hand. "Sissy, look, if it's this bad and you don't think it's going to change, maybe you should break it off.''

"Oh, fuck, Kate! I just turned thirty-six. I want to have kids before it's all over, and there just isn't that much more time. And anyway, I don't know if I even *could* do the whole thing again. I've had so many relationships, and each time they've gone nowhere. Just nowhere. And when I think about going back and starting with dating again, I want to lie down and die.'' She looked beseechingly at Kate. "Don't you remember how it was? There's just not all that much out there.''

"Yes, I remember,'' Kate said. And suddenly she did. The dating treadmill. Another day, another dinner. . . . The hollow despair of being with yet another man you didn't love, could never love. . . .

"You're so lucky, Kate,'' Sissy was saying. "I guess that's why I called you. You're the one person I know who's really got it made. Your work's going well, and you live with someone who loves you and makes you happy. It's all happened for you just the way it was supposed to.''

Don't envy me, Kate was about to object. My life isn't so perfect. I've suffered disillusionments.

But then suddenly she thought of her little studio: of how she was looking forward to doing the final editing tomorrow on the Heart Association ad and of how proud she had been of winning an art directors' award for their last industrial. And she thought of Denny waiting warmly for her home in bed.

What Sissy had said was true: it *had* happened for her. Not in the way she had once envisioned it: those grandiose castles of fame and Heathcliffian romance had remained firmly suspended in the sky. But it had happened nevertheless. And all her misgivings of the past few days seemed suddenly inconsequential.

But it was as she looked into Sissy's devastated face that she realized what made her truly lucky. I'll never look like that again, she vowed. Even if it should all disappear tomorrow—if Denny should leave me or I leave him or the company goes under—even then, I'll still have myself. Not the Brown Person. Not someone else's conception of who I should be.

But myself.

And that might not be enough. But, thank God, it would be something.

ABOUT THE AUTHOR

LINDSAY MARACOTTA is the author of *Hide and Seek*, *Angel Dust*, and *The Sad-Eyed Ladies* and has contributed articles to *Harper's*, *Working Woman*, *Playboy*, *Viva*, and *Rolling Stone*. She has lived in San Francisco, Paris, London, and Chicago and currently lives in New York City.

Tomorrow the Glory

by Shannon Drake

✯✯✯✯✯✯✯✯✯✯✯✯✯✯✯✯✯✯✯

Written by an author of
stunning talent comes
a thundering saga of an
epic love forged by the war
that shattered a nation.

✯✯✯✯✯✯✯✯✯✯✯✯✯✯✯✯✯✯✯

☐ 42354-3   TOMORROW THE GLORY $5.95

BESTSELLING AUTHORS
FROM PINNACLE BOOKS

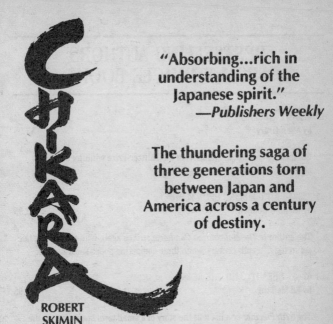